Praise for
Gin, Turpentine, Pennyroyal, Rue

"In her latest book, *Gin, Turpenti*
winning author Christine Higdon
achingly beautiful story of sisterho
and those bound by their shared predicament of living and loving in the absence of agency. Ever a consummate wordsmith, Higdon's elegant dispatch from the front lines of the battle for gender equality tells a tale as relevant and essential today as it was a century ago. Endlessly evocative and gorgeously rendered, an exquisite novel destined to be called a classic."

— BOBBI FRENCH, author of *The Good Women of Safe Harbour*

"Christine Higdon is a brilliant storyteller. *Gin, Turpentine, Pennyroyal, Rue* is a joy and a privilege to read; undoubtedly one of the best books I've read in years."

— DONNA MORRISSEY, author of *Pluck*

"I would read anything Christine Higdon writes, but *Gin, Turpentine, Pennyroyal, Rue* is a particular gem. Set in Vancouver in the 1920s during prohibition, this gripping novel implicates the reader in the lives of four very different sisters, each with their secrets and passions. It is impossible not to root for the McKenzie sisters as they fight for justice and forge their own identities, demanding the right to love and learn freely, despite the subjugation under which they live. It's also impossible not to appreciate the craft and beauty with which Higdon conjures Vancouver of a century ago, a city and a natural landscape both eerily familiar and utterly different than that of Vancouver today. And finally, it's impossible not to be struck by the parallels with our own time, where women are once again (and still, and relentlessly) grappling with laws that limit choice and human agency."

— RACHEL ROSE, author of *The Octopus Has Three Hearts*

"'Why are women so angry?' asks the unloved husband of one of the remarkable McKenzie sisters. Christine Higdon answers this essential question with a tale both brutal and beautiful, delving deep into the mysteries of sisterhood, loneliness, and love. This novel had me, heart and mind, from the opening line to the last."

— ALISSA YORK, author of *Far Cry*

Gin, Turpentine, Pennyroyal, Rue

A NOVEL

Christine Higdon

Published by ECW Press
665 Gerrard Street East
Toronto, Ontario, Canada M4M 1Y2
416-694-3348 / info@ecwpress.com

Editor for the press: Michael Holmes / a misFit Book
Copy editor: Rachel Ironstone
Cover design: David A. Gee

LIBRARY AND ARCHIVES CANADA CATALOGUING IN PUBLICATION

Title: Gin, turpentine, pennyroyal, rue : a novel / Christine Higdon.

Names: Higdon, Christine, author.

Identifiers: Canadiana (print) 20230438679 | Canadiana (ebook) 20230438709

ISBN 978-1-77041-706-9 (softcover)
ISBN 978-1-77852-194-2 (ePub)
ISBN 978-1-77852-195-9 (PDF)
ISBN 978-1-77852-196-6 (Kindle)

Classification: LCC PS8615.I368 G56 2023 | DDC C813/.6—dc23

This book is funded in part by the Government of Canada. Ce livre est financé en partie par le gouvernement du Canada. We acknowledge the support of the Canada Council for the Arts. Nous remercions le Conseil des arts du Canada de son soutien. We acknowledge the funding support of the Ontario Arts Council (OAC), an agency of the Government of Ontario. We also acknowledge the support of the Government of Ontario through the Ontario Book Publishing Tax Credit, and through Ontario Creates.

Canada Council for the Arts Conseil des arts du Canada

Canada

PRINTED AND BOUND IN CANADA

PRINTING: MARQUIS 5 4 3 2 1

In memory of
Joanna Chrystal and John Tanasychuk,
people even more beautiful than most.

stepping over a viper
a burning hot bath
a controlled tumble down the stairs
quinine
ergot of rye
tea of tansy
hot brick on the navel
blue cohosh
juniper
cotton root
oil of cedar
black draught
myrrh
hot footbath
feverfew
motherwort
savin or thyme
crochet hook
bicycle spoke
rubber catheter
knitting needle
corset stay
straw from a broom
pickle fork
hat pin
coat hanger
gin
turpentine
a cup of pennyroyal tea
rue

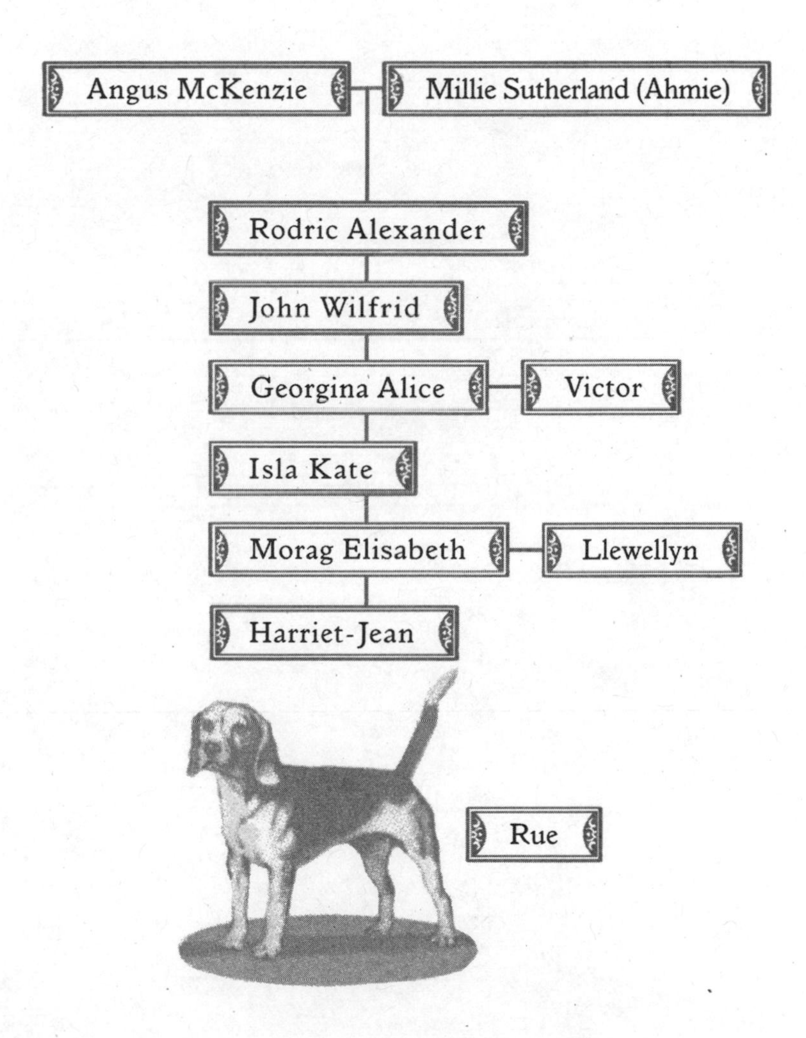
Angus McKenzie
Millie Sutherland (Ahmie)
Rodric Alexander
John Wilfrid
Georgina Alice
Victor
Isla Kate
Morag Elisabeth
Llewellyn
Harriet-Jean
Rue

In my chest, the sound of an
exhausted swallow
falling gently to earth.

—*Tin Man* by SARAH WINMAN

THREE YEARS LATER—MAY 1925

Here are two women. One of them has loosened the dirt beside the grave with the tines of a kitchen fork. Onto the dark-brown earth she tips a handful of seeds. Earlier, at home, two nails were hammered into a cedar stake, one at the top, one near the bottom, and between them, tied a length of garden twine. Now, using a rock, she pounds the stake into the ground, two inches from the headstone. There's an image in her mind: those sweet-pea flowers, a month from now, twining up, their green tendrils reaching out for the little granite angel, smothering it with fragrant pinks and purples.

She traces the engraved names—a woman's, a man's.

'Such lovers there never were,' she says.

On the grass, the other woman, shoes off, stretched out on her back as though ready for the dark earth herself, laughs and slides her hands over the round hillock under her maternity smock. She does not open her eyes. 'What a silly romantic you are.'

Hip against the headstone, the sweet-pea woman frowns, whether against the sun or the other woman's words cannot be known. She is flooded with an ache so familiar, so formless, it is like dust: these two loved ones dead, their child taken away. The King's courts concurring with the child's grandparents, those high-and-mighties: they are the only ones with the "*financial* and *moral* wherewithal" to raise an orphaned two-year-old. *Wherewithal.* Oh, sorrow: the little boy's face the day they took him, his mouth an open maw, no sound coming out of it, tears rising but not falling, his eyes wet blue.

She wipes the dirt off the tarnished fork and puts it in her jeans' back pocket. 'It's easier that way,' she says and, searching the graveyard with an unhurried gaze, kneels to glide her own hands under the smock and onto that taut belly. There's a kick, and she lifts her hands briefly, as she always does, then places them back on the warm skin. 'Hello, beauty.'

The squint of an eye opened, a smile. 'Are you talking to me or the baby?'

She lies beside her. Not close. Not too far. Fingers touching, then locking. The sky is cloudless, birds are singing, the breeze is gentle. The old dog is just over there, snuffling a dead person's roses. For reasons that are the animal's alone, it barks, just once, the sound a herald of this beautiful day. Somewhere nearby, a cow is lowing, deep and dissatisfied.

'You or the baby . . .' she says, closing her eyes. She inhales spring. Does it matter? She touches the thin gold circle on the other woman's ring finger. 'I would have married you.'

'A woman marry a woman?' The pregnant one rolls heavily to her non-heart side and smiles. 'When pigs fly.'

ISLA

We blamed up.

Some families blame down: The younger siblings are held responsible for every broken teacup. For the dirt trod into the house the day the floors have been washed, waxed, and polished. For the missing belt, cardigan, garter, stocking, shoe, skate, pencil, ink bottle, hair ribbon, knitting needle, darning egg, spool of blue thread, biscuit, mint humbug, five-cent piece, brooch, book. For the stolen friend. (Especially the stolen friend.) In families with a multitude of children, there is always someone else to point the finger at—up, down, this way, that.

We blamed up.

Our eldest, Rodric, lies in Mountain View Cemetery, six feet under, so I can't ask poor Roddy how he managed the shameless accusations of his four little sisters for so long. I suspect it never bothered him much. Roddy was a forgiving soul. And he loved us. Our second eldest, the one we call Baby John, who none of us but Roddy spent any living time with (and that was when he was just a baby himself), escaped all that. Baby John the Blameless, left behind, poor wee bugger, buried thousands of miles away, over the Atlantic Ocean in Scotland. Harriet-Jean, the youngest, was free to blame us all, all the way up the ladder—Morag, me, Georgina, Roddy. I'm the middle child. Up or down. You do the math.

We are grown now, and still.

I think that's my own pointer finger tapping at my chest.

And you? Is that your finger too: tap, tap, tap?

Whose destiny did I change by loving my sister's husband? His? Mine? Hers? Some girl's, fifty years from now?

Call it what you will; I'm going to call it a love story.

Maybe you will forgive me. Maybe I will forgive myself. Perhaps there is nothing to forgive.

But carve these words on my headstone when I am gone: *If only.*

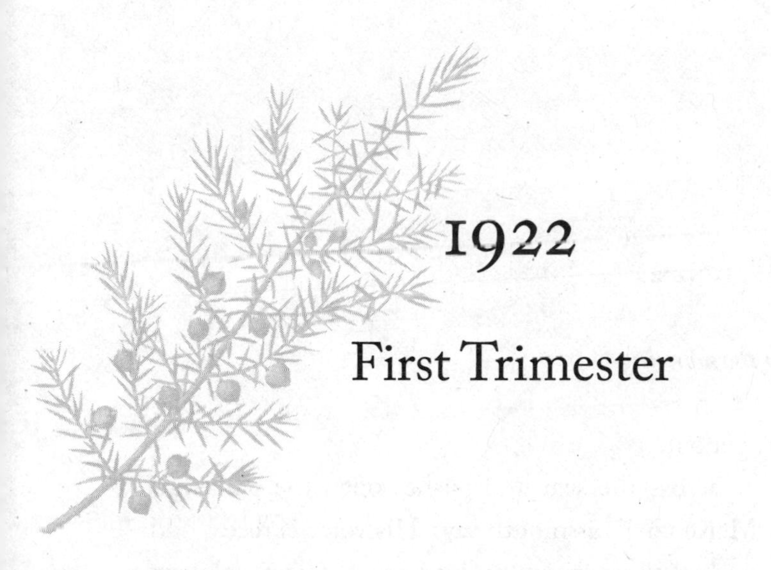

1922

First Trimester

SATURDAY, JUNE 24

8:30 in the morning

He doesn't get out.

He leans across the seat and pushes open the passenger door. 'Isla McKenzie?' his mouth says. His voice is reedy, odd. He wears no hat; there it sits, on his knee, a cream-coloured fedora with a bright blue band. His hair, as blond as his hat, is slicked back with pomade. A single curl has fallen forward on his brow. What does it tell her? Later, she'll know: you cannot trust strange men in cars. He lifts his chin at her, a small jerk.

She gets in.

He cannot know that she is thinking of her sisters. That she wishes them here (however ironic that would be), Georgina, Morag, and Harriet, crowded into this automobile that is now ferrying her east, along Cordova.

She'll get out, she thinks. When next the car stops, she'll fling open the door and get out. It is not too late. She owes him nothing yet, this man whose name she does not know.

He does stop. He pulls up to the curb. 'Close your eyes,' he says, and, meekly, she does. Then, that is his hat being placed on her head, being pushed down over her eyes. She cannot see. She will not know where he has taken her.

They drive on.

He will take her sixty-five dollars. He will nearly take her life.

5:30 in the evening

"Well, look what the cat dragged in." Morag looks at the clock. "A whole two hours early."

"Shall I ask the cat to drag him back out?" This dark-haired man—they call him Llewellyn—takes two steps backwards, his hands behind his back.

"You shall not." Morag leaps up from the armchair, dropping her book—she is reading Edith Wharton's *Summer*; she was crying earlier—and puts her arms around his neck. He doesn't return her embrace, and she peers over his shoulder. "What've you got there?"

"Nothing you'd be interested in." He rocks left then right, half smiling, only half-heartedly teasing, avoiding her pawing hands. They have performed this dance countless times before.

"Give," she says.

He produces a bottle. It's gin.

"A man after mine own heart." She kisses him, gently at first, then in her hungry way.

He draws his wife tightly into his arms, his hands on her shoulder blades, more to still her than to hold her. He kisses her neck, a peck, then rests his chin on her shoulder. He wants to think. The blinds are half-closed. The apartment smells musty, like last night's bed. The breakfast dishes are still where they were when he left this morning, on the kitchenette counter, not done. There are cookie or cake crumbs and coffee cup rings on the table. Morag has done nothing all day but read. He allows himself a second or two of thinking his irritation (it may be envy) is justifiable. But he doesn't really care. Or at the very least, he knows he shouldn't. She has quit her job as, he believes, women with husbands should. What else is she to do all day?

"Did you see your sister today?"

"Which one?" she asks. "Isla?"

Llewellyn nods. His wife, this eager woman, smiles at him. Her face, her eyes, her hands, even her eyebrows, arched and dark, are eager. There are moments—this is one of them—when he finds this trait of Morag's overwhelming. He should whip up the blinds, let the June sunlight in, see the sky through the windowpane, the comforting solid red bricks of the apartment building across the street.

"No. She told me yesterday that she had the day off. She was going hiking. With Flore. Why? Did you?" Morag's mouth cocks sideways, smiling.

Llewellyn colours a little. Puts his hands in his pockets. Shakes his head. Turns from his wife. "So, who was here?" He nods at the table. The crumbs.

"No one," she says. "Just lonesome me." And she reaches to kiss him again.

"Wait," he says, putting his finger on her lips then stepping past her into their small alcove of a kitchen. He returns with a single glass and fills it to the top with gin. He presses the glass, for a second, against her belly. A little gin spills over and runs, two dark rills, down her skirt: "A toast. To whoever he might be."

Morag takes the glass from Llewellyn's hand, raises it, takes a sip. "Or *she* might be."

How peculiar: he has never, until this second, considered the possibility of a girl. "Or she," he says. He studies his wife's face, then, more out of habit than anything else, he runs a single finger down her belly and back up the inner curve of her thigh. Morag makes that sound, soft, sensual. She hands him back the drink and begins to unbutton her blouse. Last week he wouldn't have waited. Last week he would have pushed her flat on the chesterfield and lifted her skirt. Now, he's cautious. He removes her blouse and slowly unlaces her camisole. He gazes at her breasts. She swears they are already heavier. He looks at each of her freckled shoulders then slides his hand over her collarbone and presses with his thumb on her sternum.

"Hurry up," Morag says, and she pulls him down to the floor.

He lies beside her, up on one elbow, just looking. He won't be hurried. Not Llewellyn.

8:15 p.m.

Some drunk bumps the woman's elbow just as she raises her glass to her mouth. This woman (Morag's sister, Isla's sister) is Georgina, the eldest, drinking Canada Dry Pale Ginger Ale with a slug of rye-whisky in it. She drinks surreptitiously—alcohol is not served at Medley Court—and, for the moment, alone. Now there's a liquid mess down her chin, her dress front, her shoes. She finds her handkerchief and turns, ready to cut the drunken oaf with one of her malevolent stares, but he's gone. She can see his brown suit jacket disappearing into the crowd on the dance floor. He grins back at her, his face pink, unrepentant.

Georgina is not really alone; the dance hall is full. And now, in search of a breath of fresh air, she is sharing the sidewalk with a noisy crowd that has spilled out onto the street with the same aim. But tonight's mob makes her feel alone, and old. The dance floor is busy, most of the cavorting fools younger than herself. And everything is too loud; she feels steeped in noise, tea gone tannin-bitter. Cold. Inside, Victor, her husband, is sitting at a round table of men in a smoky corner. He will be holding forth on his opinion of the Irish, Chinese workers, Catholics, women entering politics, the sins of the Liberal prime minister. Or, if he's feeling less surly than he was earlier, he'll be hoping to ensnare one or two of the lads in another real estate investment scheme. Her sisters—Isla, Morag, Harriet-Jean—are late, as usual. Georgina hates standing here by herself, but standing here by herself is better than sitting with Victor and his cronies. And much better than sitting home alone on a Saturday night, twenty-six and childless, while you age and the world passes you by, all the other, younger girls out on the flirt.

"Sorry, sorry, sorry, Georgie." It isn't the drunk, back to apologize, it's Morag. And there's Llewellyn. From the flush of her sister's face, it's clear she's in nearly the same state as the lout who is surely now cutting loose on the dance floor like a Stanley Park Zoo gibbon. (Pity the young woman who ends up with that fool.) Georgina turns and eyes Llewellyn. Llewellyn holds his liquor well; Morag, on the contrary, does not.

"Everybody here? Where's Isla?" Morag is peering toward the door, her fingertips tucked, Georgina notices with some distaste, into the waistband of Llewellyn's trousers.

"I haven't seen Isla or Harriet—" Georgina stops. Morag is bending in slow motion toward Georgina's ginger-ale-and-whisky-drenched chest. With a single finger on her sister's forehead, Georgina pushes her, as slowly, away.

"Just wanted to have a sniff. Did you have an accident?" Morag laughs.

"One of the dancing fools in there did it."

"A shameful waste of, uh . . . ginger ale," Llewellyn says, smiling. "Point him out, and I'll do him in for ye."

"Aye, that's why you love him, isn't it, Morag? Found yourself a crusader for worthy causes." Georgina glances at Morag, but her sister is gazing up at Llewellyn. "Nothing finer than the hairs in his nostrils, is there?" She turns away; the lovebirds aren't listening. "Ach, get yourselves a room," she says and heads back inside the hall.

Boredom. How insidious it is, the way it has crept into her breast and flattened the beat of her heart. It has made her life as dull and disappointing as Victor. Her husband: a tire puncture on one's bicycle the morning of a planned excursion, an empty jelly jar. She was fascinated by him once, the handsome man and his war medals and his one remaining arm. It was all so heroic, somehow. And she'd pitied him; there's the shameful truth of it. Now, two years into their marriage, how is beyond comprehension. But regret: Georgina Dunn will give it a pass. It is, she is certain, a pointless trough to wallow in. She knocks back the dregs of her drink. She'll ask Llewellyn to get her another. In her purse, her father's flask is empty. Surely Llewellyn will have something in his.

8:30 p.m.

The accursed shoes the girl has on are not appropriate for running. This one, rushing along in the evening's dusk in shoes that are contrary to her soul, is the little sister, Harriet-Jean, though, most often now just Harriet. The weather has done an about-face after a late, cool spring, and the night air is warm. Thank goodness, she is thinking, that I didn't wear my coat. She slows her pace before turning into the laneway and catches her breath. She can't stop smiling. Everything, *everything*, nineteen-year-old Harriet-Jean wants to shout, is beautiful.

At the side door she takes a look around—she's been trained to do this by all three of her sisters—making sure all is clear before she knocks. Harriet is late; Georgina will be annoyed. But it's their mother, Ahmie, who is to blame. Harriet-Jean is nearly grown enough to know that she is too old to still be holding her mother responsible for everything that goes wrong in her life. Another year or two will cure her of all that. But, for the moment, when Ahmie is overcome by her laudanum itch—damn that tincture of opium—Harriet does have a jarful of childish resentments she likes to carry on about. One: if Isla had been home tonight, Harriet would have been on time. Two: if Isla'd been home, it wouldn't have been Harriet who had to spend an hour scratching Ahmie's back with the Chinatown bamboo claw and reading aloud to her from her bedside copy of *Roget's Thesaurus*. (There is some compensation, although it is, as yet, underappreciated: Harriet's vocabulary increased tonight by a word or two while she cooed out a lullaby of synonyms, and their mother, too tired for her usual didactic commentary, drifted off.) And, three: well, just . . . three.

But Harriet's here now, isn't she, late but at the door, excited and out of breath and ready for a drink. *Saint Pete's* her sisters call this secret West End spot. After Pete Smith—an angelic-looking ex-soldier with eyes so placid they belie his postwar bitterness. Pete serves gin and rye-whisky and dreadful but potent homemade wine. And not just to anyone; Harriet feels smug, childishly so, about being one of the chosen few at Pete's speakeasy. She tugs at her dress. Tucks her bobbed hair behind her ears. Waits for someone to let her in. It's Paul, of course, whose eye and nose she sees through the door he cracks open. The tedious old flirt pretends not to recognize her and closes it again. She peers down the lane; someone is pissing against the fence of the house across the way. She knocks again, harder, and presses her mouth to the door. "Let me in. I'm late. Georgina's going to kill me." Or you, she thinks.

An interminable minute passes before Paul opens the door again, letting out the warm light and what she imagines are the gay sounds of her sisters and their friends inside. He demands his usual fee: a kiss. Harriet sighs. She's ready for Paul to have grown as tired of this game as she has, however unlikely that is.

"You're too old for me, Paul," she says. But the price—the kiss—is worth it, if only to get out of this darkening alley.

Paul feigns hurt. "And you, young human being, are cruel."

Harriet is young. Too young for a place like Saint Pete's? No one, certainly not Saint Paul (as the doorman insists the girls call him), is counting. The younger the better, according to Paul. He lets Harriet in but blocks her passage. She brushes her cheek against his and ducks under his arm into the living room. And there, smoking and drinking on Pete's stuffed chesterfields and divans, are a dozen not-so-saintly people Harriet has never set eyes on before. She looks into the kitchen. Empty but for

Pete's old dog, Butch, who looks up hopefully. Everything, suddenly, does not feel quite so beautiful. Paul grins at her.

"Where's Georgina?" she demands, cross as a four-year-old.

"Beats me," he says. "At Medley Court?" And the old reprobate performs what might be a few foxtrot steps. Second-rate, at best.

The skies are brooding; so is Harriet. It feels like rain. She may need a raincoat after all. Her good mood has slunk off, some feral cat to whom someone—not her, not intentionally at any rate—has given the boot. Georgina said they'd be at Saint Pete's. She is sure of that. She hesitates in the street, swamped by a feeling too complex to be understood just yet; she can only discern that she does not like it. It's clamorous, like a swarm of bees, shapeless, perturbing. And there's that longing, giving her an itch. The realization that she and her mother might suffer in similar ways is irritating beyond measure; what nineteen-year-old wishes to be even remotely familiar with the symptoms, or the causes, of their mother's woes?

She storms on, toward home, along Helmcken Street; it is quieter than either Davie or Nelson and, at this time of night, more than likely safer. She passes no one. Just one window-ledge cat, illuminated by the street lamp. It eyes her with such stark suspicion she can't help but laugh. And here, at Burrard, she decides: she'll go to Medley Court. Why not? Georgina and Isla and Morag may be there, and if not, she'll find a way to go in alone. She's old enough. She'll dance with whomever holds a hand out to her, even in these hateful, hand-me-down shoes. Before she reaches Davie Street, excitement has already skipped back into her heart. Moody, her mother calls her. What of it? A mood can't harm anyone, can it?

At Medley Court, she tags along with a group of others, strangers, and they let her into the hall, no Paul to pay. She stops at the edge of the dance floor. There Georgina is, leaning against a pillar with Fergal Doherty. This is not the first time Harriet has seen Fergal glued to her eldest sister (or vice versa), Georgina looking happy (uncharacteristically). Georgina's husband, Victor, is at a table, over there, to the right. Harriet sees him look up—what a grumbler—and turn back to his usual gang of bootlickers. There's Morag and Llewellyn, clutched in a lovers' embrace on the dance floor, barely moving despite the quick tempo of the music. Others are making stabs at the new dance steps everyone is talking about. Harriet shouldn't laugh; she is equally guilty of the same embarrassing gyrations. She scans the crowd for Isla. No sign of her sister. But there, oh God, is Isla's friend, Flore Rozema.

ꝏꝏ

Georgina has been staring at the floor, at Fergal's feet, at her own feet, while he tells her about his brother's move to Seattle. There is something dismaying about what he is saying, something that carves at her heart, a foreboding of loss. Now, she looks up, as if someone has whistled for her, and there is Harriet-Jean just inside the doors, dishevelled, flushed, coatless, with that look that is so often on her face—at once a brew of confusion and excitement and anger. Georgina chooses not to wave. Harriet will spy them soon enough. She looks to see what or who Harriet is watching so intently. Ah, Isla's friend Flore Rozema is dancing across the room. Georgina feels another tickle of distaste. She looks down and listens on, allowing her gaze to settle on Fergal's hands now as they float expressively, drawing her seductive pictures of Seattle's enormous market on Pike Street, the fishmongers, the bakers and butchers, the tall-masted foreign ships in the harbour. The Americans.

ooooo

A boy, the one Harriet danced with last weekend but whose name she can't recall, waves at her from the dance floor. Harriet shrugs at him, keeping an eye on Flore, and remembering how Georgina is always reminding her that finding a marriageable man should be her mission: *trousers and vests, trousers and vests*. Flore is crossing the room, edging sideways, being swept into twirls with one man here and another there, and then propelled off the dance floor, partnerless. Harriet watches her rise on tiptoe to kiss Georgina on both cheeks. Fergal's hand settles on Georgina's shoulder as he leans past her to kiss Flore too. *Roget's Thesaurus* has more than one word for Flore, but *cosmopolitan* is the one that suits best tonight. Harriet hurries over.

"Finally," Georgina says, "there you are."

"Here I am." Harriet risks a quick glance at Flore—she'd like a kiss from her too—then frowns at her sister. "You said you'd be at Saint Pete's."

"No, I said we'd be here."

It's a grudging thought, and it annoys Harriet to no end, but the word for Georgina and her long neck is *regal*. But also, *imperious*. And there's *old-fashioned* too; look at her with her hair still all pompadoured up with combs and pins, like somebody from the last century. Like their mother, in fact. Harriet smiles at Fergal. He's a bluebeard, handsome and dark and decidedly *trousers and vests*. "Where's Victor?" she says and scowls, as if someone else has control of her thoughtless tongue. (Harriet is still wrestling with her childish tendencies; guilt will not trot in on its little pony until later, perhaps only when she is falling asleep, tomorrow, in the wee hours of the morning.)

Georgina glowers at Harriet but nods in Victor's direction. "Over there. Pontificating. Dreaming of the good old days when we knew our place. When we couldn't vote. Or drink. Or smoke." Georgina raises her glass. "Don't you know women shouldn't drink, Harriet?"

Fergal laughs and asks Harriet and Flore what he can get for them. "Ginger ales all around?" he says with a wink.

"Where in the world is Isla?" Georgina asks Harriet.

"Didn't come home for supper. She had a fight with Ahmie this morning and went slamming out. I wouldn't have come home, either, after the things they said."

"Such as?"

"Oh, you know Isla and Ahmie."

Georgina frowns and sighs. "I do."

Harriet glances over at Flore again. She has chopped off her thick yellow braid since the last time they met, and her hair is bobbed as short as Harriet's now. Flore smiles at her. (Oh, what warm, liquid pleasure is this?) Harriet looks away to the dance floor and combs her fingers through her own unruly hair.

The girls at work talk of nothing but men. They'd all say she should be grateful that the one from last Saturday night, the waver, is approaching. Look at that boyish determination; it's the very portrait of *trousers and vests.*

She feels someone catch her by the hand.

"Dance with me, Harry?" says Flore.

SUNDAY, JUNE 25

In the early hours

The scent of the world after a downpour—dank, fertile. For as long as they've been here on the west coast, Harriet has been intoxicated by its earthy wetness: cedars drenched and fragrant, their rain-soaked moss-covered trunks green and springy under her fingers; bruised chestnut blossoms making pink and white streams along the streets; rain and more rain. And tonight, she *is* intoxicated, drunk as the proverbial skunk. They are walking, arm in arm—Morag, Flore, Harriet. Flore, in the middle, is insisting they sing some impossible children's song with her, in Dutch.

"The refrain, at least." Flore yodels mysterious vowels and consonants and they fly off, soft and misshapen birds, into the night. Harriet watches them go, up to the slipper moon. Flore stops, stamps her feet. "Concentrate," she demands.

Now Harriet's laughing so hard she's afraid she'll pee. She drops Flore's arm and braces herself against a dark storefront, legs crossed.

"If you have to piddle, go in the alleyway. It's what the men do." Flore bends over double, snorts with laughter.

Piddle. Harriet snorts, too, and squeezes her legs tighter.

Georgina, who has been walking behind them, catches up. "Shush. It's two in the morning." She tells Harriet she should have used the toilets at the hall, and it's true, Harriet should have. If she were anywhere near as prudent and organized as Georgina, she would have. But Harriet is not.

It can't be two in the morning. It's just past midnight at the most. "Oh, Georgie. Come on." Harriet stretches her hand out to her sister.

Georgina waves Harriet off and goes ahead. "The sidewalk isn't wide enough for four," she says.

"Sour as an apple in spring." That was Morag, in a stage whisper.

Harriet knows how it will go: Georgina won't jump to the bait. She'll only raise her arm to peer at the wristwatch she wears—their brother Roddy's wristwatch—then she'll say, wearily, ever the martyr—(is *martyrishly* a word?)—*I heard that*, and Morag will slap a hand over her mouth in mock surprise.

This is exactly what happens.

Contrite: it was a word in the thesaurus tonight. *Apologetic*, *humble*, *remorseful*. Harriet can't remember Morag apologizing to anyone, for anything, ever. She wonders if she herself is ever truly contrite. Maybe contriteness (contrition?) doesn't run in the family. Georgina certainly isn't known for it. Nor is Ahmie. Maybe it's a McKenzie flaw.

Flaw or no, the thought doesn't trouble Harriet for long. She relinks arms with Flore, and they make another attempt at synchronizing their steps.

Look down. Left, right, left, right. Now they've got it.

Even looking at Flore's feet puts an ache in Harriet's throat. She laces her arm around her, one hand low on her waist. She is too inebriated to be curbed by those ordinary inhibitions that would leave that hand higher, less inquisitive, more well-mannered. Later, in the stark light of day, she may or may not find herself thinking of the word *reckless*. She may or may not wonder whether it isn't spelled with a *w*.

Now, Morag has her arm around Flore's waist too. Under the scudding clouds they're three drunken sailors in the wake of Georgina, their stern but also-drunk captain.

Morag wants to know where Flore and Isla went hiking.

"When? Today? I didn't see Isla today."

"Oh? She said you two were going on a hike somewhere."

Flore shakes her head. She asks Morag why Llewellyn left so suddenly tonight, and so early.

"Police business," Morag says, so proud, losing the beat for a second.

"La-di-da. Important police business for your important policeman husband," Harriet says, because Morag's so smug. She calls ahead to Georgina. "Where'd Victor go, Georgie? Off to make patsies of another gang of hayseeds?" She's still poking the bear, this little sister. She sees Georgina flip her hands in irritation but slow her pace. Harriet looks up. The moon has come out again from behind the swiftly moving clouds, a golden crescent in a blue-black sky. For a moment, under its beauty, she feels ungrateful and mean. Here, finally, is contrition (contriteness?). But only a second's worth.

They walk along in silence for a while, subdued, Flore humming quietly, Harriet fuming in much the same way. *Trousers and vests. Trousers and vests.* It's not as if it's all that hard to find yourself a husband. *Trousers. Vests. Ties.* Now she's counting the number of blocks to Holly Lodge, Morag and Llewellyn's apartment building, and the five or so more blocks past that to Sylvia Court, where Flore lives. Georgina's surely not going to let Harriet walk Flore all the way home.

"Harriet, smack Isla for me, will you, for being a spoilsport," Morag says when they are parting. "And tell her to call over tomorrow. Today, I mean." She laughs. She is pulling Flore's hand, ready to cross the street.

But Flore is leaning back toward Harriet. Thanks for the dance, she is saying.

And here, finally, is what Harriet has been hoping for—a kiss.

"Come on, Harriet," Georgina says. "I'm tired. I want to get home." She stretches a hand out to her sister but drops it, with a sigh, when it is not taken.

She watches Harriet watching Flore. There's the Dutchwoman's blond head disappearing down Davie Street. Harriet is still and alert, like an animal, her hand on her cheek. What a quirky thing her little sister is. So tall and angular. Georgina feels suddenly furious with her. For what? For being youthful? Careless? She knows—it only takes a moment of contemplation—that her anger is about something else. Not Harriet-Jean. Not even Flore. "Too smart for her own britches, in my humble opinion," Georgina says anyway. Harriet turns to her, her eyes vaguely unfocused, the smile on her face as idiotic as they come.

ooooo

Harriet stands on the walk, watching Georgina go. 'Too smart for her own britches, in my humble opinion,' Georgina had said. She said she thought Flore was not only a *Bolshevik*, she was, even worse, a *Sapphist*. When Georgina said this, Harriet was only half listening. She was calculating just how much of her mouth Flore's lips had touched when she kissed her. Definitely not just her cheek. Her mouth. Maybe half her mouth? At least half. 'She's sweet,' Harriet said to Georgina. 'What do you know about sweetness?' Georgina replied, and she opened her handbag and took out a hat—Isla's lavender cloche. She'd pressed it into Harriet's hands, held them and the hat too tightly for a moment, scanning her face until Harriet looked down. 'I borrowed this from Isla,' Georgina said. 'Give it back to her for me, will you?' Harriet nodded. 'What's a Sapphist?' she'd asked. Georgina, walking away, didn't look back. 'A Sapphist is a woman who likes women,' she said. 'We all like women,' Harriet called after her, 'don't we?' Georgina's calm response had come: '*Instead of men.*'

Harriet looks up at the house now. The lights are out in their flat. Ahmie and Isla must be asleep. It annoys her, only a little, that no one thought to leave a light on for her. She touches her lips, then her cheek again, where Flore's hand had rested for a second. *Sapphist*. A wave of disquiet roils in her stomach. Nausea sweeps up her throat and she vomits into Isla's hat. She wipes her mouth with the brim of the cloche then holds the sodden thing at arm's length, astounded by the weight of it. Then she lifts the lid on their neighbour's trash can and drops the hat in.

Four in the morning

Last night, sitting on the floor, leaning up against the chesterfield and drinking straight from the gin bottle, his wife called him her salty dog. 'I'm not old enough to be a salty dog,' Llewellyn said. 'A salty dog is some old codger. Forty or something.' Morag laughed. 'Twenty-four is old enough to be a salty dog,' she said, 'especially when you start telling me you can tell the difference between the Pacific and the Atlantic just by a sniff.' 'Well, I can,' he said, and she whooped again with laughter. He'll never be able to prove it to her, but if the hand of God picked him up and put him out on the Strait of Georgia, even way up near Sointula, eyes closed, he'd know he was in the west. Not in the east, not on the Atlantic, where he spent half a year with his uncle Clyde. 'Well,' Morag said, getting onto her hands and knees and rising unsteadily, 'ocean is ocean, and saltwater is saltwater, and you'll never convince me otherwise.'

Now, Llewellyn leans back against the cabin of the boat, the *Queensolver*'s engine thrumming steady and comforting, night's chill still upon them. He should go into the cabin where it's warmer, where Abraham and Virgil are sharing a drink. But out here, the feel of the wind is as intoxicating to him as a woman's hand on the back of his neck. He's got a tune in his head from the dance last night and the smell of the early evening with Morag still on him. The tide has turned; they're going with it, back toward Steveston. They've made their drop; the crates of alcohol are gone. He takes a deep breath, filling his lungs with the salty air. An ordinary man might be embarrassed by the joy that fills his breast.

For a while the boat keeps lightly to port, avoiding U.S. waters, but there's a shift in its speed. Virgil's at the wheel. He must be keen to get home to Elinor. Llewellyn's uncle Clyde was like that—always impatient to get back to his wife. He smiles at the thought of Felicia. Llewellyn was still twenty-one when he was sent east to Clyde and his wife. Back then, in the spring of 1920, Llewellyn drank no more and no less than he does today, but to teetotalling prohibitionists like his parents, even a sip of gin was criminal. Anyone clever enough—and Llewellyn was that—could find his way around the Prohibition laws. But even clever men get caught up by the law if they are careless enough. That a child of theirs, temperance campaigners, should drink was bad enough. That one of their own might be caught at it was horrifying.

Though time has softened the shame, a pinprick of it comes back to Llewellyn from time to time, as familiar to him as his own left hand. He bowed so easily to their commands. It's not an excuse he would use now, but he did then: he was unemployed and dependent on them, used to their life—his life—of ease. His mother, as usual, delivered the news on the front porch. His father would have coached her on what exactly to say. He may even have been lurking in the parlour, listening through the open window to make sure she repeated his words exactly. They'd already purchased him a train ticket; he would be departing Tuesday morning, two days from then. Clyde would meet him in Halifax. Llewellyn put his feet down to stop the porch swing: 'But I've got a girl,' he said. His mother laughed, probably at the tepidness of his protest. She stood and looked down at him. 'The girl will have to wait,' she said. Then: 'Who is she?' she asked, an only half-curious afterthought. 'Anyone we would know?'

They would not have known Morag McKenzie. It was a laugh to even imagine that they might, or that she would run in his parents' social circles, as any girl suitable for Llewellyn should. And waiting? Morag didn't seem like the kind of girl who would wait for anyone. She was uncommonly handsome, with an eye for a good dance partner, and, thank God, that eye had finally settled on him.

As the boat churns toward home, Llewellyn pulls his cap down over his ears. Of all the crimes and misdemeanours his parents accused him of, there was only one, in his mind, that was truly criminal: he'd admitted to them that Morag worked at Leckie's. The look of disgust on his father's face had made his stomach turn. 'J. Leckie Company? The shoe manufacturers?' his father asked with his small, disdainful laugh. His father had golfed with John Leckie. His mother had played bridge with Leckie's sister. It wasn't for spite that Llewellyn had married Morag the year after he came back west, but it gives him some satisfaction to know that his parents think it was. Whether they were given too little notice about the small, courthouse wedding, or whether they simply chose not to attend, is still a matter of some dispute.

His parents, he thinks, are likely still as doggedly naïve as they were when they sent him away. 'Your uncle will set you straight,' his mother had said. His father laughed, not looking at him, speaking as though he wasn't standing in the same room: 'Straight? Clyde'll knock some sense into his dim-witted head.' But his parents must have been remembering a man of different character, because Uncle Clyde—his mother's youngest brother, who'd moved east from Ontario when the rest of the family moved west—had troubles of his own with the drink. And they'd surely never met his wife. Clyde had married a Lunenburg woman, Felicia Whynaught, and she and her brothers—Benjohn, Caleb, and Joseph—were rum-runners.

He almost laughs aloud now, remembering Felicia's fingers, light on his chin: 'You've a charming tongue, and just look at this wholesome, handsome mug. Those eyes! Those lashes!' she'd said, while her brothers and Clyde laughed. Llewellyn had blushed and rubbed his jaw and laughed along then, not knowing whether Felicia's smile was meant affectionately or as a challenge. 'Put it to use,' she said. 'A pretty bauble like you should be able to convince palms to be greased,' and she turned her back on him.

He could and he did. There were plenty of men out east who had that kind of palm. And if there was a cop or customs man or some do-gooder who didn't play the game, or who wanted more than his fair share, there wasn't a rum-runner's boat in town that couldn't leave the shabby police boats in their wake. Not then.

Within days of his arrival in Lunenburg, Llewellyn was out with his uncle and the Whynaughts, hauling liquor under eastern stars, from Saint Pierre and Miquelon, back to Nova Scotia or down along the Atlantic coast. Llewellyn looks up at the western stars, now fading as dawn's rays creep up to stain the mainland pink. Back here on the west coast there's no shortage of captains looking for crews of men to ride the waves at night, helping with deliveries in exchange for a bottle and some cash. In Canada, all that Prohibition mess is over. But the Americans are still sweating under their own Prohibition laws, and the demand for booze across the border is ferocious.

He has since cringed with embarrassment about the dread he felt that first night on the ocean with his uncle. He'd never been to sea before, but why, he thought, should Clyde and the Whynaughts know that? As he climbed aboard, thrilled, the sky was lit the way he imagined New York City would be, the stars a million streetlights. But away from shore, the ocean was black, its terrible depths unfathomable, the horizon no longer discernable.

They were on their way to the French islands, Saint Pierre and Miquelon, where, he had been told, no one aboard would be using one another's real name. The men were lighthearted and boisterous, sharing a bottle of champagne between them. Llewellyn, already queasy with seasickness, was doubly so when the fog came in, thick and sour as curdled milk. Clyde said it would pass soon enough; the nausea or the fog, he didn't say which. But they sat adrift, the engine cut. The boat lifted and dropped like a cork on the enormous, silent, invisible swells. He couldn't see the others, though they could not have been more than four feet away. For a while, that night, the men conversed, told the greenhorn sailor unnerving stories about the creatures of the deep, and then the fog filled their throats and stole their voices, and they drifted into silence. He was wet all over, as if the morning's dew had gone mad. He knew he was not alone on the godforsaken boat only by the smell of their cigarettes, though he never once saw the flare of a match. Once, when even the scent of smoke could not be detected, he called out, very quietly, for his uncle. No one answered, and in the silence, he heard his childhood preacher's fearsome warning about eternal damnation. He'd pressed his back against the gunwale, afraid to stand up, afraid he'd fall overboard into the dark ocean, unnoticed, as silently as one entered the grave.

Then, suddenly, he could see Caleb and Joseph Whynaught seated on the deck, asleep under a tarpaulin, their backs against the cabin and deathly still, as though the fog had killed them. Around the boat, the ocean's swells, black and glossy, appeared, and on them the red glow of a running light. Then Clyde in the cabin. The men stirred. Spoke. Called out to him. Benjohn started the engine. They said it wasn't two hours they'd been adrift. He'd swear it was three days. Dawn came and the night sky turned from ebony to deep blue, then a perfect line of orange drew itself across the curved horizon. And suddenly, brilliantly, there was the sun, rising out of the ocean, huge and the colour of fire—orange and pink and crimson.

A quarter of an hour later Joseph had shouted, and Llewellyn turned to see a behemoth rise straight up from the black depths. A humpback whale, flying in the now-amber light as though it had wings. Llewellyn stepped forward as the creature curved in a majestic arc and slammed back into the water. Spellbound, tears came. He knew then, just as he knew the sun rose every morning, that there was nothing to fear out there on the water, and everything to love.

Llewellyn smiles, remembering. Abraham sticks his head out of the door of the cabin for a second and taps Llewellyn on the shoulder with a bottle. "What're you smiling about?" he says. "Want a drink?"

Llewellyn shakes his head and Abraham retreats with a shrug. He keeps his eyes on the water, looking for killer whales now, west coast whales. The trip home is always sweeter. The bottles that, a few hours ago, were clanking about in their wooden crates, weighing down the boat, have been hoisted into someone else's hands. They're someone else's worry now. The *Queensolver* sits higher in the water, the dark ocean no longer threatening her gunwales. If they're stopped, the boys will be relaxed. Abraham and Virgil will be able to play innocent, shrug their shoulders, light cigarettes with steady hands. They'll tell the police, if Llewellyn doesn't know them, if he doesn't already have some kind of arrangement with them, that they were fishing, out after sockeye. A confrontation with a U.S. Coast Guard boat would be thornier; it might even end with a race across the waves if they'd strayed out of Canadian waters. But Virgil is good about staying clear of the Americans, both their waters and their police. And hijackers? Those bastards would know a boat heading this way would have nothing left on board.

Llewellyn pulls out his pocket knife and carves absent-mindedly at the wood of the gunwale. The tide is right; they'll be back at the mouth of the brown Fraser River before long. They'll drop him at Steveston. He'll return to the city in Victor's car, borrowed for the night, while Abraham and Virgil carry on up the river to New Westminster where Virgil and his wife live. Elinor's got one on the way, just like Morag. Their first child too. Virgil's a likeable soul, big as a house, and big-minded as well. Unlike the oceans, the men of the west coast, the men who make their living off the sea, are not so different from the men of the east.

Morag had another one of her strange premonitions last night. That can be the only reason why, when the lights of the Steveston canneries come into view, Llewellyn is warmed by an odd, short wash of relief. On the way to the dance last night she'd suddenly stopped: 'Someone is dead,' she said. Someone they knew. 'You're drunk,' he laughed. He kissed the frown from her forehead and they walked on. Morag calls her visions clairvoyance; she's seen things that proved true a peculiar number of times. Coincidence, Llewellyn always thinks, but she has made him shiver nevertheless.

Abraham comes out on deck as they approach the Steveston wharf. He stretches, then turns eastward, his eyes closed, his face lit by the rising sun. Llewellyn looks over at the captain;

that he himself may not be the only one who can get lost in the perfection of a Sunday morning makes him smile.

Abraham pulls a few bills from his pocket, folds them, and hands them to Llewellyn. "Thanks, Llew. We'll be home in time to make it to church."

Then Abraham reaches past Llewellyn and brushes away the wood shavings on the gunwale. He traces the letters Llewellyn has carved in the wood.

"Isla?" He laughs. "I thought your wife's name was Morag."

Shortly after noon

Not everyone is a churchgoer. And some people, Harriet supposes, will have gone to an early service so they could come to the game in the park at eleven o'clock, guilt-free. Then again—she looks at Rafe Margolis deep in conversation with Minnie Shapiro (they'll marry soon, no doubt)—not everyone here is a Christian. Harriet herself hasn't ever been to church, not as a worshipper, which some here think so scandalous she has stopped mentioning the fact aloud. Whatever the reason for the crowd today, there are plenty of players, enough for two full teams. Plenty of watchers, too, and none of the proselytizers who sometimes mingle with the Sunday morning crowd, urging them to come to God instead of to baseball. Harriet remembers the time their star player, Dora Tucker, now on third base, got converted and missed half a season. She was back at the end of summer, thank God, repentant in the right way and ready to whack a few more home runs.

Harriet, happy and on first base, having just now performed the most perfect bunt, surveys both of today's teams; they are a motley crew. Henry Burke and Alfred Stewart got into a fistfight last Sunday. Alfred, an ex-soldier, suggested that baseball uniforms were in order, or at the very least a dress code. Henry, a pacifist and a union steward, was all for keeping it a friendly game with anyone who wanted to play wearing 'whatever damn outfit they damn-well pleased.' Padraig Gleason, now at bat, is a good example of that kind of outfit: trousers cut off at the knee—neatly pressed and hemmed, mind you—and a white shirt. The umpire calls a strike, then a ball; Padraig tucks back a lick of his auburn hair that has escaped the Brilliantine, pushes his eyeglasses up on his nose, grips the bat, and whacks the next pitch clear over the head of the left-fielder. Harriet, running her fastest, is not quite home when Padraig catches up. He grabs her by the waist, lifts her off the ground—not an easy feat; Harriet's tall, Padraig isn't—and dances her feet like a marionette over the scored patch of dirt accepted as home plate. Laughing, he touches his own toe to the plate.

She's embarrassed and thrilled. "Padraig! God!"

"Hush, girl. It's the sabbath," he whispers.

Harriet smacks his shoulder.

"A bunt is so satisfying. So much more thrilling than a cracking good home run, isn't it?" he teases, out of breath. "The sound of the ball hitting the bat, the poor thing dribbling to the ground. Will it run foul? No, it's fair! Run!"

"Definitely more satisfying." Harriet is laughing. "A bunt requires talent."

They are cheered off the field, but despite Padraig's home run their team loses. The next player at bat strikes out. The innings are up. The game is over.

"Eighteen to seven. An ignominious loss," Padraig moans.

He says this every time he's on the losing team, no matter the score. He makes her laugh; *the ignominy*. Such a good word.

She has already recorded it in her word diary. She tucks her brother Roddy's old baseball glove in her back pocket and picks her sweater up off the ground and shakes it. "Are you taking the streetcar?"

"I rode my bicycle," he says. "Do you think my costume is appropriate bicycling attire? Am I fit to be seen on the streets? Do I court arrest?" He strikes a pose.

"Well, I would be arrested in that outfit, but on you . . . it's perfect." Over his shoulder she's surprised to catch sight of Flore Rozema sitting on the grass. Harriet's ears go pink; she's very conscious of the fact that she may have royally embarrassed herself last night. "Do you want to meet someone?" she says to Padraig.

"Of course I do." He gently flicks the blushed-pink tip of her left ear.

Flore folds up her newspaper.

"What are you doing here?" Harriet asks.

Flore looks amused. "I might ask you the same. I thought you'd still have your head on your pillow, or under it, considering last night. Besides, I'm allowed a little fresh air on a Sunday morning, aren't I?" She holds out a hand to be pulled up. Both Padraig and Harriet reach for it and Flore, hesitating for a moment, chooses Padraig, who gives Harriet a sly, competitive smile.

"Very pleased to meet you, Miss Rozema."

"Flore. Please," she says.

"Do you play?" Padraig asks. He tips his chin at the baseball diamond.

"Oh, never," she says, lifting her skirt a little. "Look at these short little legs. But I do like to watch."

"Well, you're welcome to watch us any time," Padraig says. "Especially McKenzie here, the master of bunts."

"I saw that," Flore says, smiling at Harriet. "She's good, isn't she?"

"Good? She's incredible." He punches Harriet's shoulder. "I hope you don't mind if I bid you adieu, ladies. I'm off to seek my Sunday fortune. And I will see *you* at work tomorrow. Don't be late."

"As if I ever would be," Harriet laughs.

She and Flore watch Padraig pedal off. Just before he turns the corner, he lifts his rear end from his seat and waggles it at them.

Flore laughs. "Don't you love a man with a sense of humour. Who is he?" she asks.

A needle prick of jealousy tattoos itself along some seam in Harriet's heart. "We work together. Well, not together. He's upstairs, I'm downstairs. At Woodward's. The department store."

"And never the twain shall meet?"

She doesn't know what Flore means but shakes her head anyway; it seems like a *no* kind of question. "We're just friends," she says.

"Just friends. Lovely."

Harriet watches Flore's mouth, the way her top lip curls up at its corners. "Are you going to the streetcar?"

"I thought I'd walk for a bit," Flore says. "Want to?" She tucks her arm in Harriet's. "Doesn't Isla play baseball on Sundays too?"

"She does, normally, but I didn't hear any signs of life this morning so I just let her be. I've made that mistake before, waking her up when she didn't want to be woken."

The sky is turning from blue to a brooding grey, quickly, as it does here on the west coast.

"Feels like rain. Shall we escape it before it arrives? Would you like to join me for lunch?" Flore says.

"Lunch?"

Flore smiles and tilts her head like the neighbour's cocker spaniel. "Yes. Lunch. We could find a restaurant, couldn't we?"

Harriet can count on one hand the number of times she has eaten Sunday lunch in a restaurant, each of them special occasions, and not since her father died. Some of the girls at Woodward's go to the food counter for lunch every day; Harriet brings her own from home. On Sundays, after baseball, she and Isla and Ahmie most often fry up a few eggs their own hens have laid and have a slice of bread and a cup of tea. Sometimes Ahmie bakes and there's scones and butter, and there's always blackberry jelly, though these days, Ahmie's scones are as rare as hens' teeth. "I should probably just get home to my mother. She'll be expecting me," Harriet says, though this likelihood, Ahmie awaiting her, is nil.

"Of course." Flore smiles. "Another time. My treat."

Harriet stops. She's changed her mind. But there is the streetcar rattling toward them, and here is Flore shooing her off. Harriet takes a few steps backwards, then turns and runs for the trolley stop. She could kill herself for being so foolish; it was only an invitation to lunch. By the time she has found a seat at the back, the streetcar is already halfway down the block and if Flore is still at the corner, she cannot be seen. Harriet sighs; imagine thinking that Flore would stand waiting to wave her off like someone's dearly beloved departing on a steamship for a foreign shore.

It begins to rain, softly at first, then it's pelting down, and around her people are slamming the streetcar windows shut. In his haste, the man seated beside her narrowly misses elbowing her in the temple. She leans left and doubts that his apology contains any true remorse, coming, as it does, with a grin and an appraising look up and down the length of her. Ahmie would cluck at the man or, if she had an umbrella handy, jab him; Morag would probably flirt with the idiot. Harriet stands and pushes her way to the front through the crowd. The windscreen wipers, shuddering back and forth, are hardly clearing the driver's view. All the world is grey now with rain. She hopes Flore has made it home.

And now, what has made her think of the girl who turned up halfway through her last year of high school? Beryl . . . what was her name? Gibson. Harriet's hand goes to the boney flat of her breastbone; she is flooded with remorse. Why had they shunned Beryl? They said she walked like a cowboy. That she didn't look "right" in her skirts and blouses. But that's not a crime, is it—walking like a cowboy, feeling awkward in a skirt?

Harriet thinks now of Flore's feet, her pretty teeth, and her mouth, and she remembers the day someone spread the rumour that they'd seen Beryl kissing a girl. They embroidered that rumour until it drove Beryl away. Looking out at the pouring rain Harriet shivers; she'd done it too. She looks down at her shoes, her socks, her dungarees and thinks: I'm like Beryl. Exactly like her. For a second, she is hollowed out by a glimpse of what she imagines is the only path ahead: life with a husband, or a life like Beryl's. She makes herself think of lunch instead. If Ahmie has not baked, she will.

A crowd gets off at Harriet's stop and they all disperse in the rain, running in every direction like marbles dropped from the sky. No one has an umbrella; the day tricked them, so blue-skied and promising this morning. When a man hurrying past holds a newspaper out to Harriet, she looks at him accusingly. But the man is benign as buttered toast; he smiles and shakes the newspaper at her and taps his hat as if to say, I'll be all right, I've got *this*. Harriet's father was this kind of man—one who'd give a woman his newspaper to protect her from the rain. With no ulterior motive. She'd seen him do it. Now, this stranger smiles at her the way her father might have, a king of courtesy. She smiles back.

In a minute she's wondering why men bother; the newspaper is sopped and drooping, keeping only the most ferocious of the rain drops from the crown of her head and leaving the rest of her soaked. She turns onto her street and drops the sodden thing, useless now, into the gutter. Back east, on the prairies, a rain like this would have made mud of the road that led to their little farmstead. Here, it is racing down the macadam and filling the gutters with swirling torrents. Sodden anyway, she takes off her shoes and dips one toe into the stream, thinking again of Beryl, then steps with both feet into it. She walks in the gutter the rest of the way home, the water flowing around each heel, surely ruining her socks. *Sapphist*, the girls called Beryl. She'd heard the word Georgina used before, of course she had; back then, in the schoolyard, it had filled her with dread.

Nearing the house, she lifts her head. There's a boy, his hands cupped to each side of his head, bending left off the porch to peer in their front window.

"Hey! What are you doing there?" Harriet shouts, rushing at him.

The boy starts away from the window and rushes down the stairs. "I'm Viola Jones's brother." The rain has slicked his hair across his forehead. He pushes it back. "My sister sent me with a message for you. If you're Miss or Mrs. McKenzie. I knocked, but no one answered." He steps forward, though not close enough for her to touch him, and stretches an envelope toward her. "Miss," he says, "here. She's at the hospital."

Harriet snatches the letter from the boy.

A quarter past one in the afternoon

Sunday mornings are sacred. Not for any religious reason; they are sacred because Georgina and Victor, a second ago dead to the world on rumpled sheets, are always hungover on Sunday mornings and any too-early interruption is considered inhuman.

"Why must the ring be so shrill?"

Victor grouses as if it were Georgina's fault the blasted telephone shouts so stridently. Or that she (not he) insisted on having it installed just outside the bedroom door. He rolls away, pushing at her with his feet and drawing some kind of mumbling parallel between telephones and hysterical women. Georgina doesn't catch the entirety of his sermon but, as always, the implication is clear, and here's her small bonfire of weary indignation, sparked again. She squints at the bedside clock: a quarter past one. Not remotely morning anymore. She has half a mind to stay where she is, to hell with Victor. If she waits, the emperor himself might actually rise. Or the telephone might stop ringing. It does not. Her pounding head insists, and, with a groan, she slides her legs over the edge of the bed letting her feet hang at the end of them like leaden fishing weights. Toes then heels to the floor. Steady, Eddy. She stands and makes her way into the hall.

The voice on the telephone, Harriet's, is hysterical. Georgina, suddenly sober and very much awake, puts her hand up as though Harriet can see it. "Stop," she shouts. "Where is she?"

Two o'clock

Georgina, Morag, and Harriet-Jean rush from one end of the hospital ward to the other. They stare at the occupants of the two rows of beds. Those who are upright stare back, curious or haughty. The prone eye them with dull suspicion. Georgina looks away from Morag's quivering chin and flooding eyes; to entertain her sister's hysteria would be to encourage more of it, and there is no point in that. Morag has already telephoned Llewellyn and foolishly insisted on calling Flore Rozema as well. What a waste of their time.

The ward reeks: sickness masked by disinfectant. Georgina finds her hankie in her sleeve but leaves it there.

She turns on Harriet: "You're sure the note said St. Paul's Hospital?" The question is illogical; a nurse has already told them that Isla is here, on this ward.

Harriet, looking suddenly nine not nineteen, holds the crumpled note out to her.

Georgina snatches it away but doesn't look at it. "Ask the nurse again," she commands, though she is already moving toward the corridor herself.

It is a sound that Morag makes that stops Georgina. Her sister is standing at the foot of a bed, one they have already passed twice. In it there is a body so still and so pale it cannot be living. It's Isla.

Georgina's composure abandons her; she has to steady herself against the bedrail. Isla is of such a strange pallor she is nearly unrecognizable. Her cheeks are hollow; her eyes, circled in a liverish mauve, are sunken and only slightly open. Her lips are the same colour as her face. If she is breathing, there is no perceptible sign of it.

"She's dead." Morag falls forward onto Isla's breast. "Oh, God. I saw this. Last night. I had a premonition."

Georgina roughly pulls Morag back; there it is, a pulse, rabbit fast, in Isla's neck. "You saw wrong," she says.

A nurse appears on the other side of the bed. "She isn't dead, but I'm afraid she isn't well. I'm Viola Jones," the woman says. "I sent my brother to your house with a note. I went to school with Isla—"

"What has happened? How did she get here?" Georgina interrupts.

"A man brought her in, apparently. Carried her from Stanley Park, he said."

"That's impossible. It's half an hour's walk from the park. What man?"

Georgina watches Viola's mouth flatten to a pinched line; she's offended. To be so sensitive, Georgina thinks, the woman cannot yet be married.

"I can only tell you what I was told," Viola says. "Isla was brought in yesterday. She was a Jane Doe until I recognized her when I came in for my shift today at noon."

"Yesterday?" Morag sounds like Harriet, nine years old too.

"Perhaps the man had an automobile," Viola says and squares her shoulders, her eyes still on Georgina. "Here's Dr. Oxford," she says. "He'll tell you more."

Dr. Oxford is short, sparsely haired, and cleanly shaven. He introduces himself. Softly shakes the hand Georgina extends to him. He nods a few times.

"Is there a husband amongst you? Or a father?" he says.

For a second, Georgina holds her breath, containing her rage. "I'm her sister. What happened to her?"

And there, suddenly, is the doctor's face registering relief at something or someone he sees behind her. Georgina turns. It's Llewellyn. Morag rushes to her husband and he pulls her to his chest, but Georgina sees his eyes over Morag's shoulder, wild as a horse's in a barn on fire. In a second, he untangles himself from Morag and bends over Isla, reaching toward her face with both hands. He pulls back before he touches her. His shirt is untucked, his shoelaces undone. He shoves both hands into his pockets.

"What happened to her?" he says.

The doctor leans toward Llewellyn and says quietly, "We believe that your wife attempted to cause herself to miscarry."

Morag cries out and clutches at Llewellyn. Even Georgina cannot stop the raw sound that rises from her own throat.

"She's not my wife, she's—"

"The feverish state she is in is a sign of septicemia. Given the blood loss . . ." Dr. Oxford pauses and beckons Llewellyn closer.

Georgina catches the doctor's sleeve, not gently. "Given the blood loss, what?"

The doctor glances at Georgina but speaks to Llewellyn. "Given the blood loss and what seems to be a very severe infection, it is likely that her organs will fail. Septic pneumonia is another probability. I'm afraid I don't have high hopes for the survival of your wife," he says to Llewellyn. "I'm very sorry."

"My sister's wife," Llewellyn says, then shakes his head. "My wife's sister."

Morag is sobbing again. Georgina tells her to shut up. She cannot think and she needs to. "Surely something can be done," she says to the doctor.

"There is not much more I can do. Our aim right now is to keep her calm and comfortable. Nothing else. Very few people return to health from the state this girl is in. I'm truly sorry."

Georgina wants to shake this man, like a terrier would a rat, to death. "You've given up on her then," she says. "Please," she adds, though the word does not come easily, "don't."

Again, the doctor addresses Llewellyn. "Depending on what has happened and how your wife, how she, procured the"—he hesitates, then says "abortion" crisply, quietly—"it is likely that her uterus or bowel or possibly her bladder has been perforated due to some form of mechanical interference. A perforation would be the cause of such severe infection and blood loss. Only an autopsy will determine—"

"Abortion? An autopsy?" Morag is shrieking now.

"Then she'll have surgery," Georgina says. She puts her hand to the thundering pulse in her temple.

The doctor finally faces Georgina, his face softening. He speaks slowly, the way one might deliver bad news, the worst news, to a child. "She is too weak. She would never survive surgery at this point. We have done a curettement to clear out what remained in her uterus. Are any of you aware of whether she had been taking some kind of drug, ergotine, for example?" He looks from Georgina to Morag, then to Harriet.

Georgina follows his gaze: Harriet is standing, like some alert bird—a heron, she thinks—in the corridor between the rows of beds.

"If so," the doctor continues, "unfortunately, this would make her even less able to resist an infection. We are, sadly, in the territory of hope and prayer."

He puts his hand in the pocket of his white coat and appears to be stroking something. A pipe most likely, Georgina decides, given the colour of his teeth and his moustache.

"An abortion. You think she has had an abortion." Llewellyn's eyes have no focus.

"Yes. The hospital Chief Superintendent has been informed. It will be up to him whether the police are involved."

"I am the police," Llewellyn shouts.

"Pardon me, I thought you were her husband."

Georgina knows one of the two men who have just arrived and are now standing behind the doctor: Andrew Morrison, the tall Scotsman who was with his pregnant wife at Morag and Llewellyn's wedding a year ago. They have four or five children if Georgina is correctly remembering the long, dull conversation she had with his wife about them all. He's a detective. He works with Llewellyn. The other man she's never set eyes on, though from the looks of him he's surely another policeman.

"Llewellyn," the other man says. He nods at the doctor but doesn't acknowledge anyone else.

"Webster," Llewellyn replies, vaguely, whether by way of greeting or introduction is unclear.

Webster approaches the bed. "An abortion?" he says. Without warning, he pulls back the sheet covering Isla and lifts her hospital nightdress.

"What are you doing?" Georgina grabs the sheet but Webster forcefully, painfully, stays her hand, as easily as if she were a child.

Isla's inner thigh, impossibly thin, the skin mottled and grey, has a huge purple bruise on it. And within that misshapen mark, two darker ovals, as if a thumb and a forefinger had seized the flesh there.

"Coincidence?" says Webster to Morrison, nodding at the bruise.

"No," says Morrison, his face scarlet, his eyes averted. He tugs the sheet out of Webster's hand and lets it drop. "That's not possible."

ooooo

Harriet hears Georgina say she'll go tell Ahmie.

She watches Morag draw an uneven breath.

"That would be nice of you, if you would. I couldn't—" Morag says. Morag doesn't look up. Her eyes, and everyone else's, are on Isla.

"I'll go with you," Harriet says.

"No, stay. You're of better use here." Georgina's right shoe taps the floor, light and fast, compulsive. Llewellyn's shoe answers. Tap, tap. Tap.

Harriet looks down: Georgina has a hold of her wrist. A wedding band, freckles, hangnails.

"No," Harriet says. She pulls away, steps back, rubs her wrist. Georgina's look is unfamiliar. Frightening. The light coming through the windows at the end of the ward is strange, as if the sun is grey-green now. As if it has never been bright or white and never will be again. Dr. Oxford has a stained-yellow moustache and long hairs sprouting from his eyebrows, like alley weeds. Viola Jones, standing on the other side of the bed, has a spot of blood on her sleeve, dark and spread open, a tiny sea urchin. Harriet has counted the white metal beds: twenty-one. She has counted the women: twenty. She looks around for the one who is missing. All the other women are held in place by white sheets. Six of them have flowers on their bedside tables. Two of the bouquets are nearly dead.

"I'm going. Keep Harriet here," Harriet hears Georgina say. No one is listening.

The crowded scene around the bed is a painting from some other century, a picture in a book Harriet borrowed from the school library once: Llewellyn hangs over Isla, one hand hovering close to her body but not alighting anywhere. Morag is draped on him, an arm around his hip, her cheek against his shoulder. The doctor, silent at this moment, clutches his hands together as if in prayer. The nurse, Viola, stares at the doctor's hands. The two policemen, shoulder to shoulder near the head of the bed, have their hands in grey pants pockets. Their heads bowed toward one another, their eyes on Isla, their conversation inaudible. Isla, between them all, the lifeless focal point, no stream of light from heaven illuminating her face. Harriet opens her mouth.

ooooo

Georgina raises her hands to her ears as Harriet screams. The sound is like the shot of a rifle, short and sharp. The ward has gone silent. Everything is still. Georgina reaches for her sister, but Harriet snatches her hands away and lurches back. Georgina watches Harriet's eyes go wide and dark; stones wet by a lick of the tide. "Harriet," Georgina says softly, to calm her, and Harriet screams again. This time Georgina snaps at her: "Harriet-Jean, that is enough." Georgina's own scream is caught in the back of her throat, wanting out.

ooooo

Everyone is staring. Harriet knows that she has screamed; there's still the red sound of it in the air. The doctor's mouth is open. The policemen, Llewellyn and Morag, the nurses, the twenty women in their beds, Georgina—everyone—is staring. She opens her mouth and the same brilliant noise comes out of her once more. Georgina shouts at her: "Harriet-Jean, that is enough." And Harriet is fourteen again, standing over her father's coffin. She can't breathe. She is swatting at the air as if grief is a solid thing, something she can beat away with her hand. She wants to remember her father's last words to her. And now she wants to remember whether she poured Isla's tea for her yesterday morning. Whether she took the last piece of bread and left Isla with none. Whether she sided with Ahmie or Isla during their fight.

She turns and runs. Flore is there at the door to the ward, reaching both arms out to catch her; but no one, not even Flore, can catch a body falling from the sky.

Past four o'clock

Aside from the scratched-up, short-legged table Isla and Harriet carried home like a couple of pallbearers—a discard found in some rich person's garbage—there are three pieces of furniture in Ahmie's front room. Georgina is perched on the edge of the mustard-yellow armchair, picking at stray horsehairs that have escaped the prickly fabric. Her mother, on the balding green-velvet settee, is dead asleep, her beloved thesaurus, slipped from her lap, open on the floor. God knows what is inside the third piece of furniture, a recent acquisition, a cheap sideboard missing a leg and supported instead by a short pile of bricks. Outside, a robin in a tree somewhere is repeating its song: *come, come to me.* Georgina slumps back in the armchair, closes her eyes. How lovely it would be to live like a small, winged creature, guided by instinct alone; a simple, repetitive life. *Come, come to me.*

She inhales deeply, but no manner of breathing has been able to ease the tightness in her chest, this jackboot on her throat.

Who nominated her to tell Ahmie that another of her children was going to die? Georgina winds one of the horsehairs tightly around her index finger and pulls until the coarse black strand snags, then she pulls again, more forcefully, until it breaks. She did. She nominated herself. 'I'll go home and tell Ahmie,' she said, and Morag mewled, 'That would be nice of you,' and then there was no option but to be nice and go home. And tell Ahmie. But it has nothing to do with being nice. Georgina is telling Ahmie because each of the McKenzie sisters has a role and this is hers. She's the organizer, the decision-maker, the fixer. The one who tells Ahmie. An inherited role, left to her by her father and brother—the responsible eldest sibling by default of death. And don't they call her *controlling*, when what they should say is *competent*. Could she not have refused it, bowed to any one of the others left behind—militant Isla, or even the charmer, Morag? All that was required was a quiet sidestep and Georgina could have entered a more peaceful territory where responsibility only plays second fiddle. But oh, the cost (how ironic): loss of control. It is simply too dear.

Ahmie stirs. Her eyelids flutter for a moment then are still, and Georgina is aware of the quick skip of her own heart. She still hasn't told her mother about Isla. Already, time has stretched to nearly an hour. Ahmie's body is restless, yet her twitches are languid; seaweed slowly undulating under water. The sweat sheen on Ahmie's forehead makes Georgina's hand itch for a handkerchief. But she won't touch her mother, not yet. Ahmie might only recently have fallen into restful sleep. Her breathing is shallow, like Isla's was. A ghost slides a cold finger down Georgina's back. She sees her sister in the hospital nightdress, her thin thighs, the bruise, a small stain of blood on the sheets. Barely breathing.

Untidy death, what happens when one breathes one's last? Does the red blood that once coursed through blue veins simply stall and congeal? Does the body let go? Urinate. Defecate. What, if anything, other than blood, has she seen oozing from dead animals—the prairie dogs Roddy shot, the moose felled by her father, the mice and birds delivered by the cat, the creatures she herself discovered in the woods—as they lie there, having let go of life?

The ache in her breast spreads down into her bowels, and she presses her hands between her thighs, bending forward, rocking. Georgina's not here because she is nice; she's here because she cannot bear to witness another death. Death has already wrung enough happiness from her; she is a rag, too many times washed.

Georgina thinks she remembers her father's last minute on earth as clearly as she might a summer Tuesday just passed. She doesn't. There were no women present at the moment of Angus McKenzie's death, yet she has painted a picture of that day: A coastal logging camp on Gambier Island. Lush forest. Salt smell. Blue skies. Moss and salal and huckleberry bushes. And amidst all that beauty, a boy named Freddy, an inexperienced young chokesetter, skinny, brown-eyed, and, ultimately, innocent. There's her half-deaf father, Angus, with his back turned to Freddy, a blue polka-dotted kerchief around his neck, forty-nine years old. There's the choke chain, wrapped by the boy around a log nearly half as thick as her father is tall, breaking and whipping free. An unintentional weapon. Tuesday, July 10, 1917, continuing with birdsong and the clatter of machinery and, later, the only slightly subdued talk of men playing poker, while fifty miles away as the crow flies, the dandelions in front of Ahmie's house close up and bow their tufted heads even before she hears the news.

Georgina's thumb finds and rolls the gold wedding band that Victor pushed over her resistant knuckle thinking, again, that even her finger knew it was the wrong man's ring. It is, this habit of ring rolling, a trick she uses to summon Stephen Salter, the man she would have married. Had he lived. The man who made her laugh. 'I've broken your defenses,' he used to crow, as she, denying it, grew more and more helpless with laughter. Then: his lips finding the warmth of her collarbone, his beautiful hands on the small of her back. His tan shoulder next to hers.

The persistence of regret is unbearably cruel. They had proudly—*proudly*, that is the bloody word for it—sent Stevie and their brother Roddy off to war. The news coming from the continent was horrific, already drawing a picture of hell. But they'd paid no heed. Only Isla had. While she declared the country's call to arms 'romantic propaganda,' they held fast, wilfully blind to the merit of her rants. What human ability is that? To ignore the truth, to be so ignorant of it, even while it stares you in the face.

Isla had railed at Roddy the day he signed up. She'd wept. She'd begged. She called him a stupid, stupid fool. Georgina had to drag Isla out onto the street, leaving a stone-faced Roddy alone with his wretched decision. But it was already too late. The war took Roddy and Stephen away. The war killed friends, and Isla's bombast lost them others. Co-workers, neighbours, old friends had eventually refused to give the time of day to the family of the Godless anti-patriot, the immoral pacifist, Isla. Georgina glances over at her mother. Even she and their father were shunned.

But what if they'd taken to heart Isla's words instead of being swept into the fiction of it—patriotism, adventure, glory, manliness. They'd have Roddy, she'd have Stevie. It was duty they felt. Duty! And there was the greatest irony of all: the three of them, Georgina and Morag and Ahmie, working at Leckie's Shoes for the last half of the war, stitching and lacing and polishing the boots other women's sons and lovers and fathers and brothers and nephews and friends would die wearing.

She rolls her ring again, remembering the day she heard the news. Stephen was killed six months into his service overseas, poisoned by gas or blown to bits or drowned in a muddy trench; his family thought it kinder not to share the details of his death with her, so it was left to her cruel imagination. Isla, raging again, called it state-sanctioned murder; a war of greed and corruption on every side. And Georgina, bereft and just turned nineteen, stopped believing she'd see her brother alive again. Why would any man return home when the remains of the man she loved would lie forever over the sea?

She returns her gaze to Ahmie. Her mother's dress is fading the way dark curtains will, black still, deep in the folds, but greying to brown at the shoulders and hips, as though Ahmie spends her afternoons gardening in the sunshine rather than prone on the settee. In 1917, her mother was shattered by the death of their father. She donned the clothes she has on now—this mourning outfit with a high black collar that recalls the past century—and clung to the belief that Roddy would survive the war. She waited, a patient dog promised a bone. She joined Morag and Georgina at Leckie's Shoes. And she worked and waited, and waited and worked. For months. Georgina thought her delusional, but never dared to say the word aloud. Isla had no qualms about that; she said it all the time, directly to Ahmie's face.

And then Roddy did come home.

His face was unmarred, his limbs intact, but there was something about his spirit, his Roddy vitality, that was sobered.

For a while he defended the war. Then, slowly, the humorous tales and the accounts of camaraderie between the men ended. The horrors he'd seen crept into his storytelling. Georgina had watched them poison him, Roddy's once sunny mind beset by confusion and wariness, nightmares and fear.

Georgina plucks at another horsehair and gazes absently around the room. He died here during the pandemic. Right here. In this house. Across that hallway. He survived the bullets and the bombs, the shrapnel and the mustard gas, the trenches filled with rats and mud and lice and the rot of men. Four stinking years at war. Only to die under clean sheets, surrounded by women in masks, safe home in his bed, but gasping for breath. Killed by influenza.

She stands, twisting the horsehair around the tip of her finger until the pink of her flesh goes white. This house that for a while she called home feels shabby now. Isla's absurd street-finds are everywhere: that ornate lamp with a curving swan's neck, a bright orange marble for its eye; a ratty peacock feather in a too small blue-glass vase; a garish crocheted blanket that should have made friends with the rubbish bin years ago, folded across the back of the settee as if it were some prize winner at the Exhibition. Living with Victor has changed her; what she once thought beautiful now seems cheap, dingy. She bites back her disgust—at the room, at herself—and her gaze falls on the only two photographs that exist of her brother.

Isla took one of them with her camera, the Brownie, just before Roddy shipped out. Georgina can't help but smile then weep at how perfectly Isla captured her brother's lopsided grin, despite the seething rage she was in, or perhaps because of it. The cock of his hip that dared anyone to take him on, those elephantine ears, one sticking out far more than the other.

With a finger, she traces Roddy's ear in the photograph. Ahmie blamed that queer ear on a cap he wore in the cradle, a story so long recited that the unlikely cause of the bent-forward thing became indisputable McKenzie lore.

The other photograph is of the five of them just before they left Carberry, Manitoba, lined up neither by order of age nor of height. She squints at them all, a new pang of sadness springing loose in her chest. Roddy would be sixteen then, Georgina fourteen and equal to him in height if not beating him by half an inch. He grew nearly a half a foot taller the year after that; at his new height he had no need of his cockiness, but what boy would give that up? To his left is Harriet, seven, an insistent imp in hand-me-down trousers perhaps saved for another boychild that thankfully never came along. Morag is eleven, a ribbon in her hair, ever the lady, and Isla, just twelve and already impatient to join the campaign for the vote for women or otherwise set the world on fire.

The only other photograph in the house is a small portrait of their father and mother on their wedding day. Georgina looks from the severe couple in the ornate oval frame to her mother and back. In the photograph, Ahmie is not wearing the small silver cross that now lies crookedly on her breast. The cross is an absurd remnant of her grief, worn in some strange, too late defiance of their father's atheism. And even more strangely, of hers. For a few months after Roddy died, Ahmie became a churchgoer. It didn't matter what denomination the church was, what manner of priest or pastor or preacher stood in the pulpit, nor whether he offered compassionate care or heartlessly condemned those who grieved as *sinners*, reminding them that it pleased God to take their dearly departed to be with him. On a hard pew, and more often on her knees, Ahmie sought the peace of believers. It was Isla, of course, who bitterly reminded her that one cannot *grow* belief as if it were a carrot or a little patch of sweet peas. Georgina sighs. How long did it take Ahmie to find another route to peace: doctor-prescribed oblivion in a bottle, blessed sleep in a tincture of opium, her laudanum? Not long.

Georgina glances at her wristwatch; it is the one Roddy wore overseas. There is a numb second in which it occurs to her that Isla might already be dead. She starts as Ahmie's arm slips from her lap, falling slowly, gracefully, swinging to a stop a few inches from the scuffed pine floor. Still her mother doesn't wake. A raised blue vein pulses slowly in the thin flesh of her dangling hand. As Georgina watches this thrumming evidence of life in her mother, rage freights into her chest, a train: What has Isla done? A baby. A baby! She stalks into the kitchen, whips opens the doors in the Hoosier cabinet, and rummages until she finds what she's looking for: a drink. There's a bottle of rye on the bottom shelf and behind it half a bottle of gin and two or three empties. Thank you, Llewellyn. She hesitates for a moment—it's twenty past four in the afternoon—then pours herself half an inch in the bottom of a teacup. She downs it quickly and pours another finger or two. Why should Ahmie be the only one finding comfort in a bottle?

Georgina stands at the window, smoothing her thumb along the teacup's chipped rim. *Come to me*, the bird sings. Where is that goddamned robin? She will shoot the blasted thing. It's not instinct, she knows, that governs the bird; it's hunger. A man, passing on the street, looks toward the window. She puts her cup down on the sill, ashamed. Then she picks it up again—how would he know what's in her teacup?—and that familiar assailant, grief, glides in, replacing her rage. Her eyes prick with more unwanted tears. She misses Stephen like the sea would miss its salt. She should be Stephen's wife, not the childless wife of Victor, a pinstriped fool whose selfish touch is more akin to a boy in his teens' than a grown man's. It had seemed so reasonable, so smart, two years ago, to marry him: he had an automobile, a spacious apartment, a promising future. She could leave the shoe factory. He'd take care of her. And all that pity. She'd been governed by it. His empty sleeve pinned down his side, so much of his pride lost with that hapless arm sawn off in a battlefield hospital. The help he needed.

The first rat off the boat. She turns to glare at Roddy in the photograph. Georgina, on her wedding day, heard but ignored her dead brother's voice: *The first rat off the boat.* He wouldn't have let her marry Victor. She faces herself in the mirror and is shocked by the pallor of her face. She lifts her arms, trying to bring air into her lungs. Her hair has come unpinned; it is unravelled, falling down over her shoulders. She thinks of Isla's pale face and, breathing hard, she makes a bargain. Not with God, as some might, but with herself: She'll cut her hair. If Isla survives, she'll cut it. She pulls her long near-black hair into her hands and ties it in a knot at her nape.

She slows her breath. Calmer now, she kneels on the floor beside the settee and touches her mother's arm.

"Ahmie," Georgina says softly.

ISLA

I heard moans, otherworldly and unnerving, men's voices issuing orders, women responding in obedient tones, the tap-scuff of feet treading surfaces unknown to me. Tap scuff. Tap scuff. There were two women speaking over me in quiet voices about the price of bread. One wanted to know whether some fellow named Robert would *ever* propose and whether she would accept after all. The other said that *God* must have performed a miracle for *this one* to still be alive. Me? I wondered. I felt the rough nap of the washcloth and the warm wet of the water as they washed me, lifting my arms and legs, prodding at my armpits. Then smell: that stale funk of perspiration, my very own stink. Their stink: disinfectant, ammonia, boiled meat.

My washers moved away, their conversation a soft, ebbing tide. I felt ancient. Beaten. I was thirsty. And so cold. I didn't know where I was. I let my eyes blink open. One second. Two.

And I remembered the man, his hat, his voice. My eyes leaked: warm tears draining into my ears, finding my jaw, pooling in the hollow of my throat.

RUE

That's them all, then. But for Gianluca, we've put names and faces to the cast of players. Patience: Gianluca comes in time. You will like him. I certainly do.

I myself was a few weeks away from meeting the McKenzie sisters and everyone who buzzed like honeybees round their curious hives. I still lived with my mistress, the one called Mrs. Zawerbny (and variously mispronounced) by most of the men who, at all hours, clacked the knocker on our front door on Haro Street. Some called her Rasia, but those so honoured were few indeed. Only her favourites were permitted this familiarity. (I, she often said, was her very most favourite. I would have called her Rasia if my tongue had allowed.)

When I was young, Rasia took to locking me in the parlour when her gentlemen called. (I use the word *parlour* here with some irony as, on my travels since, I have seen a few rooms significantly more suited to the word than was her tiny front room. Flore Rozema's, for instance. I use the word *gentlemen* with some irony as well.) I thought this punishment extreme, and sulked about it, as the crime that resulted in my banishment to the parlour, far from her bed, was most certainly not as egregious as some might think. I had only leapt upon the mattress and licked the hairless white buttock of a caller while it jounced up and down over my Rasia. She was amused; the owner of the buttock was not. Some men, Rasia later explained, do not like this kind of *interruptus*.

The (gentle)man called me a cur. A mongrel. A rogue and a scoundrel. He threatened to drown me and had to be calmed with a small dose of opium. *Pfui* to him. I am no cur. I am, I have been told, a beagle. (Who's a good girl? strangers ask. Who's a good dog? Don't ask again, for God's sake. I am.)

Another man called on Rasia once a fortnight. She called him Father, though he was not hers. He called her my child, though she was not his. There were no visits to the squawking bed on Father days. Instead, there were cream cakes and oranges (sweet treasures brought by Father) and coffee and conversation and a hand that scratched the spot in the centre of my back that I cannot reach. I mention Father not only because of his merciful hands, but because, were it not for this man in his long black cassock, I, too, would have gone the way of Rasia that morning when summer had come and all the world was out on the street. All the world but Rasia, who lay very still. I do not think I had ever seen the other man, the one who visited with his black satchel the day before Father had Mrs. Stachniak, our landlady, unlock our door. What the man had done to Rasia I did not know, but by the morning she smelled of blood and not much else.

She called me *Dama*, the word for lady in my mistress's language. It was Father's drear face that made me understand that

I would never again hear her whisper my name. They carried my Rasia out on a litter bed. The door was left open. Father, frantic, called after me—*Dama, Dama*—and still, I fled.

The woods were cool. The nights were dark and wild with animal sounds, unfamiliar and frightening. Food was scarce. I, being a domestic breed of animal, am no huntress. Who was I to snatch a goose by her neck or a drake by his? And if I had, what then? The very thought of it, even now, makes me queasy.

I thought I would starve. Worse than starvation: the blunt hammering of grief against my heart.

TUESDAY, JUNE 27

Mid-morning

Llewellyn drifts awake. Where was he? Bobbing on saltwater in a folded paper boat. Isla and Morag in ice skates, gliding across the ocean away from him, dark skirts flared, black hair flying. Alive as birds. Shiny dark crows. Now there's a frozen pond, silver fish darting beneath the surface, talking gibberish. Tiny ice-bubbles rising from their mouths. Where are the women? Gone. Thin white scratches in the ice, criss-crossing, their only trace.

It is the doctor's voice, loaded with offense, that pricks at Llewellyn's fog: "My patient is dying. This is not the time to be questioning her."

Llewellyn stands, wobbles with fatigue, one hand clutches the green metal of the chair back for balance. The fish are still there, shouting at him now in shrill voices: Who is dying? Who?

There's Morrison. And beside him, another man. Equally tall, very well fed, brown hat, gold watch chain. The doctor, Oxford, has positioned himself between the two men and the foot of the bed, his arms spread as if to protect his patient. A useless gesture as the man in the hat has only to tilt one way or the other to stare around the doctor at Isla, which he does.

"Does she know she is dying?"

A stab of rage lifts Llewellyn from what remains of the fog. "Who in hell's name are you?"

Morrison's mouth opens like the fish in Llewellyn's dream, but the man in the hat steps forward and extends his hand. "Dr. Clarence Driscoll, Coroner's Office." He is silver-tongued, a man's man. His smile says: *I'm sure we understand one another*. His mouth says: "We are here to obtain an ante-mortem statement from your wife."

Llewellyn doesn't take his hand. "This is not my wife. She's my wife's sister."

"Pardon me," Driscoll says. His eyes make it clear: asking pardon is not one of his habitudes.

Driscoll still has not removed his hat. Llewellyn wants to smack it off his head.

Oxford continues his protest, arguing with Morrison: "She is in no condition to answer your questions. I cannot let you disturb her."

The coroner's man gestures at Isla with his chin and asks his question quietly: "Is this your handiwork, Dr. Oxford?"

Oxford recoils. "What do you mean? Certainly not."

"Then I'll ask you to inform your patient that she is dying. The court will only accept her statement as evidence if at the time of questioning she knows she is going to die."

"I know the law," Oxford tells Driscoll.

"Would it not be wise, then, to help me get a proper dying declaration from this woman." It's a command, not a question. He gives Oxford a fraudulent smile.

Oxford says he'll have a nurse summon the hospital's Chief Superintendent. "We'll see what he has to say."

Llewellyn watches the doctor. His face is confident, smug. He's a man not used to being challenged. He steps away from Isla, arm raised to catch the attention of a nurse whose attention, it seems, will not be caught, not without shouting.

"It was your Chief Superintendent who summoned my office, sir," Driscoll calls out drily to the doctor's back.

Oxford turns, defeat in the thin hard line of his mouth. He returns and stands beside the bed, his hands slack. Driscoll and Morrison confer quietly for a moment. Morrison is nodding, his expression grave. Llewellyn hears him utter the words *unmarried* and *murder.* Someone, thinks Llewellyn, should murder them both.

ooooo

Pausing for a moment in the ward's doorway, Georgina sees Llewellyn raise his arms then drop them in some gesture of defeat. He looks like the rag man next to the two tall men at Isla's bedside. Like a sidelined player. Dr. Oxford looks the same. One of the tall men is Andrew Morrison; the other, Georgina doesn't know. She approaches. Glares at Morrison, then at the man in the hat, and correctly assesses which one of them she should address. She lifts her face to him. "What's going on here?"

ooooo

Llewellyn watches Georgina eyeing Driscoll's hat. Harriet, Morag, and Flore have also arrived, smaller boats, bright in Georgina's formidable wake. Llewellyn nods at her. He doesn't mind her scowl; the arrival of a fresh, fully armed regiment of Allied Powers soldiers would not have been more welcome just then. Georgina turns on Driscoll. Asks him: "What's going on here?"

Morrison answers for him. "This is Dr. Driscoll, from the Coroner's Office. He is going to question Isla before she dies," Morrison says. "It's the only way to find out who this monster is who—"

Georgina interrupts him. "Dies? What monster?"

"The one who killed your sister's baby. And has killed her too." Morrison's tone, initially mournful, rises to indignation. Neither approach, Llewellyn knows, will sway Georgina.

"Killed her? She looks alive to me," Georgina spits, though Llewellyn sees her glance quickly at Isla as if to reassure herself that her sister is still with them. "What possible reason could there be to question her now?"

"Mrs. Dunn," Morrison starts, "I hardly think—"

Georgina turns back to Driscoll, ignoring Morrison. "Take off your hat. There are women in the room."

The coroner's man has kept his tongue until now. He briefly touches the brim of his hat but doesn't remove it. "We're seeking an ante-mortem statement from your sister. When one is dying there is no motive to utter falsehoods," he says coolly. "If your sister is about to meet her maker, her last words will be the truth."

Georgina practically caws: "Her maker? You don't mean God, do you? If you're imagining that Isla believes in God, you would be very wrong."

Morrison looks stunned; that was expected. But Llewellyn also sees a momentary flash of incredulity in Driscoll's eyes.

"That's not possible," Morrison says, a half smile on his lips.

"It most certainly is, you sanctimonious fool." Georgina's hand flies up and snatches at Driscoll's hat. He dodges, but she wrests the hat from his head and flings it down the wide corridor between the ward's beds.

Oh, the surge of satisfaction in Llewellyn's chest. He watches, nearly grinning, as Driscoll pats at his awry spikes of Brilliantined hair as if he were in front of his own bedroom mirror.

"I'll give you your declaration," says Georgina. "My sister isn't dying."

Driscoll's words curve out of his mouth and wrap themselves, a sinuous snake, around Llewellyn's neck: "From all reports, she is."

Llewellyn falls back onto the bedside chair and drops his head between his knees.

'How would you like to die?' Isla had asked. They were at the beach. It was May. The tide was low. The third-quarter moon not yet risen, the Milky Way a white blaze in the heavens.

'Me?'

Isla laughed at him. 'That would be the meaning of *you*, I think. Or maybe you think you're immortal.'

How lovely she was. Her small teeth, the long space between the bottom of her nose and the top of her lip. He slid a finger down the beautiful indentation there, over her lips and chin, then along her jaw. She pressed her head hard against his hand, a cat.

Then she lifted her mouth, kissed his knuckles: 'Truly, how?'

'Here, with you,' he said. 'I want to die in your arms.'

She made a sound with her teeth and her tongue which he took to mean he should take her seriously.

How would a man like to die? He had contemplated, briefly, on his first night at sea with his uncle Clyde and the Whynaughts, how he would *not* like to die. But never how he would.

'Not at sea. Not by fire. Not being run over and cut in half by the streetcar,' he laughed.

'So, not painfully or bloodily, then.'

'No.'

'Is any death not painful?' Isla rolled onto her back and stretched her arms and fingers toward the stars.

'Not if you die suddenly.'

'But the shock of it. A sudden death. Awful, I think.'

'But you wouldn't be around to know that it was sudden,' Llewellyn said. 'You?'

Isla lay quiet for a minute. In the dark, he'd waited, struck, as always, by the workings of her ever-curious mind.

'I think I would like to die in a fall from a great height. Off a cliff,' she said.

'Ach. But then you'd have all that falling time to know that you were going to die.' He leaned, propped up on one elbow, and traced the line of her forehead, her nose, her chin, this time with his eyes.

'So suddenly is better than slowly?'

'I suppose,' he said. 'Think how awful it would be to die slowly. Of consumption or some other wasting malady.'

Isla nods soberly as if she is actually contemplating the awfulness of such a slow death. After a while she says, 'You could die of embarrassment.'

'Or shock.'

'I'd like to die laughing,' Isla said. And this made her laugh.

Her near-black eyes, her black hair. She is mine, he thought. 'And after?'

'After? Like floating around in heaven playing the tuba in God's orchestra you mean?'

'No, your body. What would you want done with your body?' he said.

She smiled and rolled toward him and laced her arm through the crook of his elbow. With both hands she drew his head to hers and whispered to his mouth: 'Take me up in an airplane and throw me out of it somewhere in the mountains. Let the mountain lions eat me.'

Someone has touched his shoulder. Llewellyn lifts his head. The coroner's man—and the rest of them—are watching him. He's seated on the bedside chair. He makes himself stand. "Sorry. I'm a little light-headed," he says.

He sees Driscoll glance for a second at his hat, an upended turtle under another woman's bed two down from Isla's, kitty-corner, then turn to the doctor. "This girl has been tampered with, Dr. Oxford, I'm sure we all agree. You have no wish to lose your medical licence nor to see this hospital's name in the newspapers, tied to an inquest surrounding a dead girl. And your cooperation will ensure that you are not charged as an accessory for keeping the details of this crime quiet."

Driscoll and Oxford are dogs in a standoff. In girth and manner, they may seem equally matched, but one is the kind that bites; the other only growls. Llewellyn knows this is not his fight. He's a third dog; the third dog would be a fool to do anything but hold his tongue and watch. Under Driscoll's glare, a chastened look slowly settles on Oxford's face. Llewellyn feels the shame of Oxford's capitulation as though it were his own.

Oxford looks from Llewellyn to Georgina, then he reaches out and gently touches Isla's hair.

"No," Georgina says, but quietly, as if, as it has for Llewellyn, curiosity has won over indignation.

When Isla opens her eyes, Llewellyn sees nothing of her in their clouded darkness.

As Georgina has assessed Driscoll, so Driscoll assesses Georgina: "Tell your sister that unless she cooperates, she won't get any more medical treatment. The doctor cannot help her unless we know what happened."

"You've just said she's dying," Harriet cries, her words disappearing to a whisper, *dying* barely audible. Morrison reaches over and pats at her hand on the bedrail. She snaps it away.

Driscoll glances sourly at Morrison as if it is Morrison who is hindering his investigation. It occurs to Llewellyn that Morrison *is* the engineer of this madness; he has likely promised Driscoll something—a passive family, a compliant doctor, easy answers. Driscoll has evidently not been warned about the McKenzie women.

The coroner's man speaks in a tone that makes Llewellyn think of his father. "I will ask you all to leave if you continue to disrupt this interview," he says. Driscoll glances at Morag. She is sobbing softly. He shakes his head; even he must know how pointless it would be to insist on her silence.

"Miss McKenzie, do you understand that you are dying? That you have no hope of living?"

Isla's eyes roll toward Driscoll, then back toward Morrison who is bent over her.

"Say it, Isla. Say 'I do,'" Morrison says.

She opens her mouth and the tip of her tongue licks at her upper lip.

"Are you of sound mind? Do you understand that I will be asking you questions related to the condition in which you now find yourself?" Driscoll says.

"She nodded," says Morrison.

"She did not!" Harriet pulls at Georgina's arm, who shushes her.

"State your name please."

Llewellyn closes his eyes and hears the surprising word come out of her mouth, murky and wet: "Isla."

Morag's sobbing is now some frantic bird bashing at windows in the ward's hush. Everyone else seems to be waiting, the women in their beds, the nurses, even the pigeons on the windowsills, silent.

"Isla what?" asks Driscoll.

"McKenzie."

"Mc or Mac?" The coroner's man has his pencil ready.

"Oh, for God's sake." Flore pushes past Morrison and takes Isla's hand.

"Mc." Isla closes her eyes.

"Good," Driscoll says. "She is of sound mind." He smiles across the bed, at Georgina, as if there is some likelihood that she will smile back. He touches his hatless head. He clears his throat. "Isla, did you, sometime in the past few days, go to an abortionist in an effort to produce a miscarriage?"

There's a mass to Driscoll's questions, like Llewellyn's fishing weights, each one rolling off the bed and dropping with a dull thunk on to the floor: *What is the abortionist's name? Who told you about him? Where did this take place? How did you get to your appointment? What instruments did he use to induce this miscarriage?* But there are no answers.

A single tear has appeared at the corner of one of Isla's closed eyes. It doesn't fall; it rests, a glittering jewel in a crease that Llewellyn has never noticed before. The coroner's man tells Oxford to wake her up again, and Llewellyn flinches as the doctor presses a hand on Isla's shoulder.

"Can you tell us, Miss McKenzie, was the person who did this to you a man or a woman?"

When Isla opens her eyes, Llewellyn is sure she is looking at him. A tiny smile flickers across her mouth. He can't let his breath go; he cannot trust it to come out quietly. 'How would you like to die?' she'd asked. She'd kissed his knuckles. Held his face. Not this way, not this way.

Morrison bends over, blocking Llewellyn's view of her, his mouth too close to Isla's ear. "Isla, you're dying. Tell us before you depart this world. Who got you into this trouble?"

Llewellyn shoves Morrison out of the way, but Isla's eyes are shut again. This tiny smile, he believes, is the last he will ever see of her, and it is gone. Memories flash past him—the meadow on the north shore; bread, butter, and honey picnics on the boat; tea in floral cups; nights under the hanging stars—as if it is he, not she, who is breathing his last.

ooooo

"You are not married, Miss McKenzie. Were you taken advantage of then? Have you any idea who the father is?" To Georgina, each question is a fresh cut. The man wielding the knife slices at Isla, and Georgina feels it in the softest parts of her own flesh—her inner arm, the back of her knee, the underside of her breast. Tears rise and rim her eyes and she wipes them away with a furious hand. The coroner's man asks whether Isla has been with more than one man. "Two? Three?" Is he goading? Llewellyn lurches forward, bellowing, knocking Flore aside. He grabs the big man by the lapels, attempting but failing to knock him down. He manages to pull him sideways, but the doctor's feet go wide and he remains solidly planted. Mr. Morrison shouts and pulls Llewellyn off. A ripple of gasps erupts from the women and nurses on the ward, sounding almost musical, broken ice, tinkling against the shore. The coroner's man rights himself, smooths his suit jacket, puts a hand to the knot of his tie, then lets it drop; Georgina can see that the shock that had troubled his eyes a moment ago is already gone. His calm enrages her, yet she recognizes his studied equilibrium in herself; what does it cost him to have this much control?

He tilts a grave face at her as if he knows her mind. "Shall we continue?" he says.

Llewellyn is red in the face, breathing hard. He shakes Andrew Morrison off, jams his hands into his pockets, and turns away. "Sorry," he says. Georgina watches the sharp intake of his breath lifting his shoulders as if he has suddenly run a mile.

It's Isla who ends the questioning; she turns her head and from her mouth comes a foul-smelling dribble of bile. Mr. Morrison presses a handkerchief to his mouth.

Dr. Oxford, summoning a nurse says, "That is enough. Leave the girl be."

The coroner's man persists: "Without her declaration, it will be impossible to prosecute whoever put her in this state. Let us get this over with."

"No." Dr. Oxford, it appears, has found his backbone; he shoulders Dr. Driscoll and Mr. Morrison away from the bed. He stands face to face with the coroner's man. "Get out," he says.

Dr. Driscoll folds shut his notebook. He glances down the ward to where his hat lies, then looks at Mr. Morrison. For a second Georgina thinks that Mr. Morrison might retrieve it for him, like some kind of lap dog.

"Excuse me," Dr. Driscoll says to Georgina. She is in the way. He waits; slowly she steps aside, her heart thundering.

"No fond word of farewell?" she says. She wants to give him a taste of the caustic vinegar in her throat, but she knows now that he is immune. He smiles; he may as well have stabbed her.

Mr. Morrison, clutching his own hat, follows him out.

Dr. Oxford sweeps his arms at them all, his calm flown. "All of you. Out!"

A nurse hurries after Mr. Morrison and Dr. Driscoll, the doctor's hat in her hand. Georgina is reminded of the small scurrying rodents in *Alice's Adventures in Wonderland.*

ooooo

Llewellyn stops Georgina—she is clearly enraged—from following the men down the hall. They're arguing near the exit doors at the end of the corridor. Morrison has a hold of Driscoll's elbow. Driscoll looks up, sees them all watching, pulls his arm away, and pushes the door open. Morrison, like a begging hound, follows Driscoll out.

"We can't leave her. Someone has to be with her when she dies," Morag says. Her cheeks are blotched red. She reaches into Llewellyn's pocket and takes his handkerchief; instead of blowing her nose, she covers her whole face and bends over, sobbing into it.

Georgina is already turning on Morag. Llewellyn can see it in her expression; she will not be kind. But he sees her stop herself, first the indecision, then the choice, as if she is swerving to avoid hitting an animal on the road.

"She's not dying," Georgina says flatly.

"Let's wait outside awhile," Llewellyn suggests, putting an arm around Morag. "Then one of us can go up to be with her."

One of us. He can't breathe. He is the one. He should be the one with her when she dies.

On the front steps of the hospital, it's windy. He looks up at the clouds, bright white and scudding across a searing blue sky. The wind is carrying the smell of the harbour; it is salty, rotten. Familiar. How can this day be beautiful? How can he be alive and Isla be dying? As they stand, quiet on the steps, he imagines a cluster of chessmen. Pawns. Lowly, powerless pawns.

Georgina breaks the silence, growling. "Are those two likely to be back?"

Llewellyn takes a breath, looks away from Georgina; he cannot bear the pain and anger in her eyes. "It's possible. Knowing Morrison. If Isla dies, there will probably be a coroner's inquisition. They'll want to find the person who did this to her first and then . . . That's why they want the dying declaration."

"An inquisition?" Georgina says.

Morag looks at him vaguely. She wipes her nose on her sleeve. She still has his handkerchief, clenched in her fist.

"An inquest. It's like an investigation. The coroner calls a jury of men," he says, putting his hands in his pockets.

"No women?" says Flore. She immediately puts her hands up and shakes her head, as if offering Llewellyn an apology, a half-hearted one.

"And that jury is to decide whether or not charges should be laid and the man tried in criminal court, and what charges they might be. It's complicated. There would only be an inquest if the coroner has reason to believe that the person who died—"

"Isla." Flore again.

"That Isla died under circumstances that require investigation."

"She's not going to die." Georgina has sat down on the top step, head in her hands.

"If she doesn't die . . ." Llewellyn's voice breaks. He waits a moment then continues. "The dying declaration won't work anyway. It's unlikely there'd even be an inquest. Unless we find out who did this to her."

"Do you think they're praying for her?" Morag says.

Llewellyn looks at his wife's forlorn face.

"Yes, because prayer really helps, doesn't it, Morag?" says Georgina.

"Shrew," Morag says, but with little conviction.

"Who did this to her?" Harriet suddenly asks, and everyone turns toward her.

Llewellyn shot a rabbit with a homemade bow and arrow when he was young. When he finally found it in the tall grass, after searching for half an hour, it was still alive, the arrow pierced through its hind quarters. Harriet's eyes, dark pools, are that rabbit's now.

"We don't know, Harriet. Not yet," says Llewellyn. "But we will."

Georgina asks: "Will Isla be charged or tried? For what she has done?"

"It's unlikely. Juries don't seem to want to punish the women. They'd rather punish the abortionists."

"They shouldn't be punished," Flore says. "There are good people who—"

Morag turns on her, aghast. "Whoever did this to Isla should be."

"Well, yes, in this case, but . . ." Flore flushes, opens her purse, extracts a cigarette, then seems to change her mind about smoking it.

They're quiet for a while. The wind is soft. Morag takes Llewellyn's hand. He watches her fingers intertwine with his but he can't feel them. When she looks up at him he knows, at once, what is coming; he squeezes her hand, too hard, a warning. She raises reproachful eyes at him and pulls away. He shakes his head at her, signalling, pleading—this is not the time. She will be alone with her announcement. He's already sorry for her, but she cannot be stopped. He inhales deeply, her scent, or Flore's, and waits.

Now Morag's weeping again, rawly. "I'm pregnant," she says.

ISLA

I blinked again. Someone was there, behind a newspaper.

A woman touched my face. She lifted my hand to her mouth and kissed it. Flore.

My voice was a whisper. 'You won't tell, will you?'

'Dear God, Isla, no.'

I slept again, for days, they told me later.

He'd made me close my eyes. We drove for a minute or two then he pulled the car to the curb. There, he put his hat on my head then tipped it down so it covered half my face—my eyes, my nose. I could have fled then. I didn't. When we stopped again, he took back his hat. I blinked in the bright sunlight. Where we were I could not have said. The neighbourhood was unknown to me. He unlocked a door to a ground floor room and led me inside, his arm gentle around my waist, as if we were some loving couple, going home.

Naïve me: I'd imagined he would have something kind to say, some words of comfort or encouragement. But he hadn't opened his mouth once in the car, other than to tell me to close my eyes, nor did he speak when he took my money and counted it and tucked it into an inner suit coat pocket. In the room, nearly everything was spoken in gestures. Only a few words, curt and impatient: *Hang your cardigan here. Lie down. Not there*—as I went to lie on the sagging bed—*over there*. I lay on the thin, stained towel he'd unfolded on some sort of low dresser. I realized I was still clutching my handbag. I held it out to him and he took it and placed it with an odd preciseness on the bed, perfectly lined up with its edge. I was uneasy, close to changing my mind—not about what I was doing; I mistrusted *him*—and this precision, even the gentleness of his gesture, had flooded me with hope. But then he'd indicated that I should push my dress up over my hips, bend my knees, and slide toward him, down to the end of the dresser. He smiled at me as he undid then pulled my stockings down, then my underpants, leaving them so they hung around one ankle.

I closed my eyes, held my breath, endured the sudden scouring pain without making a sound. He grunted, just once, at the moment of my most excruciating pain. Then, just as I was sure I was going to die, he pulled away. Wiped his hands on the towel between my legs. Got off his knees. He was done.

My face and chest prickled with hot sweat and still I had to bite down hard to stop the chatter of my teeth. But the relief was staggering, bright as a new penny in my palm. It was done. Oh, God, it was done.

The man washed his hands in a basin in the corner of the room, then knelt and packed his instruments away into his satchel. He stood, rolled down his shirt sleeves, put on his suit jacket, and came back to where I still lay, shaking. He put his hand on my knee, to calm me, I thought. Instead, he ran a firm finger down from my knee to my groin and across my sex, then pinched the skin of my inner thigh, hard. 'Now, you won't get yourself into that kind of trouble again, will you?' he said, holding tight, not releasing the pinch.

I will never forget his voice. It was reedy and immature, like a boy of thirteen. I brought my hand down on his, enraged. 'I will not, doctor,' I said. He laughed and pinched me harder. 'I'm not a doctor.' Then, as if the idea of being one appealed to the peacock, he let go of my thigh, straightened, and cleared his throat officiously. 'Everything will come away in the next few days. If anything goes wrong, you will not contact me. Nor will you mention my name anywhere or to anyone.' 'I don't even know your name,' I spat, and I turned my face to the wall. It was grimy and looked flecked with spit and blood and made me think of who else might have lain there. The other women or girls I had shared that 'bed' with. I turned back toward him. He lit a cigarette and blew smoke toward the ceiling. 'So much the better,' the man said. Then he asked if he'd seen me down at the Castle Hotel. 'Lots of modern girls down there,' he said. 'Flappers, like you.' He had a lewd grin on his face. *Flappers. Like you.* My God, the man had just been between my legs with some sort of sharp instrument and now he was flirting with me.

He stood, watching, grinning, while I pulled my dress over my thighs and closed my eyes to the humiliation of my dangling underwear. 'I'd like to stay here awhile,' I said. I felt sure I wouldn't be able to stand.

He let out a huff. 'You have five minutes to clothe yourself. I'll wait outside.'

For the better part of the car ride he put his hat over my eyes again. He dropped me exactly where he'd told me to wait for him that morning. 'You can catch the streetcar somewhere along here, can't you?' he said, taking his hat back. He leaned across me to open the passenger-side door and brushed his arm across my breasts. He jerked his chin at me and raised his eyebrows. 'Out,' he said. 'We don't want any blood on the upholstery, do we?'

I was too shaky to think of an insult to shout after him, though plenty came to me once he'd gone, of course. They still do, lying awake at night dreaming of what I might have said. He tipped his hat at me and drove off. I leaned for a long time against the brick wall of a building, waiting for the strength in my legs to return and thinking, bizarrely, how beautiful the brilliant blue colour of his hat's band was.

I still wake in the night, the smell of his hair oil, that gamey sweat of a man's head, in my nostrils.

I have retraced the steps I took that morning a hundred times, in my head and with my feet, trying to understand what animal instinct made me walk into the woods instead of to anywhere I might have been helped. I'd boarded the streetcar then missed my transfer stop and was carried along toward the park. At the Stanley Park loop, I rose with the few passengers left on board. There was a woman. She touched my arm. Leaned in like a co-conspirator. She gave that knowing nod to the back of my skirts. Something wet was already seeping through. If only she'd understood what and had taken me under her wing.

When we were younger, Ahmie used to bring us to the park to feed carrots to the elk. There was a caged paddock where the lawn-bowlers are now, tossing their little balls about on those sleek green lanes. I could have sought out the bowlers. I could have gone up through the trees and made my way to English Bay, to Flore at her apartment in Sylvia Court. To a shop, to Almond's Ice Cream, to a sunbather, a delivery boy, anyone. Instead, I cut right, into the woods, around the west side of the lagoon. I suppose it was because it was a path I knew. It led to that grove of old trees they call the Seven Sisters.

I turned down another path, one I also knew well, toward the lagoon. I recall picking a few huckleberries, thinking that they'd quench my thirst. There was a bird singing nearby, perhaps a mating song, though no other bird replied. I remember hearing it just as the first excruciating cramp bent me in half. And the next one and its nauseating pain. I threw up. I can recall sinking down against a stump near the water and staring at my feet, my brown shoes, splayed inches from the shore, while the cramps continued in waves, like white flames. The water, the forest, the dirt—everything had the iron smell of blood. I remember thinking I would die in that place. That I could die. And that it would be fine if I did. Death would be better than the pain.

Though I could take you to that exact spot now, I remember nothing more of that day, nor of the ten that followed.

Bleeding, dying woman, carried in by Good Samaritan. What a newspaper headline that would have been. Of my saviour, I remember nothing, and I hold no hope of ever being able to thank that kind soul who left the hospital without giving his name. I owe him my life.

I lost my handbag and one of my good shoes that morning. Someone must have carried off my purse, but I imagine that shoe lying soaked in the rain somewhere, kicked under the bushes, carried off by an animal perhaps. Unwanted. And yet, still lost.

TWO WEEKS LATER, SUNDAY, JULY 9

11 a.m.

How bewildering that this paltry collection of clothing has such extraordinary powers. That a swatch of stitched and hemmed cotton or wool can make Harriet-Jean feel so second-rate. Dresses and skirts and blouses that would look so smart on Morag and Isla seem to have something against her. Morag, the queen of fashion, knows when to wear white and, more specifically, when not to (not that Harriet has anything white to wear, or ever would). But even when Morag is there with her big-sisterly advice, even when Harriet's blouses are not too short-sleeved or tight across her back, clothes are akin to a defeating army. And shoes? Let us not talk of shoes. Shoes are simply ridiculous.

Harriet is, thus, still in her underwear when, through the curtains, she sees Flore pull up out front in an automobile. Flore is at least fifteen minutes early or it is possible, of course, that Harriet herself is fifteen minutes late. She pulls on her blue dress, finds her grey cardigan—which she will not need—and hurries to the door without a second glance in the mirror. She does not even think of whispering goodbye to her mother who is dozing in her usual spot, wrapped in blankets on the settee as if, for heaven's sake, it is cold out. Harriet opens the door and there is Flore, leaning up against the automobile in a pair of belted trousers, a white shirt, and a man's straw boater.

Flore leans into the car and honks the horn, a wolf-whistle, the kind of swaggering admiration that the boys who loiter outside the butcher shop lay at the feet of Morag when she passes (though not usually at Harriet's; she's not quite girl enough). Men love Morag, Harriet thinks. How wrong this dress is, she thinks. What a chump I am, she thinks. Could I be more foolish? But Flore sweeps her arm out: "Step into my runabout, ma chérie." And Harriet does.

Flore's hands tap a beat on the steering wheel. "Where to, mademoiselle?"

Harriet's vocabulary has fled; Flore laughs as if there is nothing more delightful than having a lunkhead in the passenger seat. But it's Sunday; Isla, they say, is on the road to recovery; and all the world—most of the world, including Harriet—has the day off. How extraordinary, she thinks, that she will spend it with Flore Rozema.

"I know where we can go." Flore pulls the car away from the curb without looking over her shoulder. Another car honks its horn and swerves around to pass. The two men inside the car shout *Women drivers, off the road.* "Horses arses! Macaronis!" Flore shouts after them, shaking her fist and laughing. The car's front tire leaps the curb; she spins the wheel and they bounce back down into the road. "Oops!"

There's a traffic jam on the road into Stanley Park. When they pull up onto the grass to park—the parking lot is already filled with cars—Harriet is disappointed to no longer have the warm wind in her face. She has already tossed the grey cardigan into the back. Harriet has been paying little attention to whatever Flore has been chattering on about—some labour union rally and the vindication of someone or other's rights. Harriet has been contemplating other things, the pretty curve of the back of Flore's neck, for one.

"Is this actually your car?" Harriet asks. It's the first thing she has said since getting in the automobile, unless nods count as speech.

"It's my brother's. Well, actually, my father's. Or maybe mine now," Flore says. "My father bought it for my brother, and when Hadrian was killed, I suppose, maybe, it became mine."

"Your brother died in the war?"

"No. In a bar. In San Francisco."

Harriet stares. What kind of response does this require? Flore is waggling some knob or lever back and forth and looking down at her hand on it. And now the moment has passed and Harriet thinks it is too late to ask Flore how her brother came to die in a bar in San Francisco. Flore looks up, smiles—oh, God, are her eyes wet?—and walks two fingers across Harriet's knee. "Shall we?"

Flore tucks her arm in the crook of Harriet's. The beach is crowded: shrill children, women and men corralling them or ignoring them; roving gangs of young men, their eyes peeled for gangs of young women; slow strollers like themselves.

"Wouldn't you love to know what everyone is talking about? I want to know who they are and where they've come from. Like that man there in the striped outfit." Flore leans into Harriet, narrows her eyes, and points toward the beach. "Isn't he gorgeous in his stripes and his pink skin that's about to turn red as a lobster."

Harriet peers at the fifty or more pink-skinned men in bathing costumes of various stripes. She feels suddenly hopeless. Hopelessly unequal to Flore, who is clever and beautiful. A dullard, Harriet is, seated at the mathematics exam with no pencil at hand. Why ever did she agree to this? Holding back the flood of feeling that would normally bring annoying tears to her eyes, she points her chin at three nattily dressed men who are leaning over their bicycles to talk to a group of young women lying on a beach rug. "What do you suppose they're talking to them about?"

"They're fops. And of no interest to those women," says Flore, dismissively. "But from the look of the girls' skirts I'd say that someone will summon the police to measure the length before too long. Or do they do that in Vancouver? Can you imagine how many women drowned in those old head-to-toe woolen bathing costumes women used to wear. Did your mother?"

"Ahmie? Wear one?" Harriet hasn't seen her mother out of her mourning clothes for five years. Did Ahmie ever swim? She doesn't think so. When they lived in Manitoba, Ahmie hiked, took them sledding, ice-skating even, but swimming? "No. I'm probably only alive thanks to Old Joe who taught me to swim after we arrived in Vancouver."

"Joe Fortes? I heard about him. He died, though, didn't he?"

"Yes. In February. We all went to his funeral."

Flore sighs. "Let's get away from this madding crowd, shall we?"

And there it is, Flore's hand, reaching out to take Harriet's.

"I'll show you something special," Harriet says. And now she is—how mortifying—four years old again.

But Flore waggles her hand at her and smiles. "Something really special?" she says, the perfect reply to a child.

Harriet feels the heat in her cheeks again. She will give the cat her tongue until she can think of something less mindless to say. She leads the way into the woods, Flore's soft hand in hers, like something sweet and edible.

"Ah," says Flore when they stop in the circle of majestic trees. "The Seven Sisters? Isla told me about them, but I've never been here."

"We each have one. This, the tallest one, is Georgie's," Harriet says, without having to look upward. "And that one is Morag's. This is mine." She smacks a tree. "And this one," she says, going to another and stretching her arms around it, "was Isla's."

"*Is* Isla's," Flore says. Around the other side of the tree, she spreads her arms, touching Harriet's fingertips with one hand, and stretching but unable to reach her with the other.

Harriet presses her forehead against the rough bark, closes her eyes, and inhales its pitchy scent. "Is," she says quietly. She turns and leans her back against the tree. The doctor says that Isla will survive, though Harriet will have to see it to believe it; Isla still looks like a corpse.

Flore circles around the tree and plants herself in front of Harriet. "You don't blame her for what happened, do you?"

And there's the brooding thing, finally surfacing: "Why wouldn't I? Isla nearly died, and it was her own fault."

Flore doesn't speak for a minute and in the silence, Harriet has two terrible thoughts: what Isla has done is awful; Flore might not like her for thinking so.

"I can't imagine being in that boat. How distressful it would have been." Flore is speaking slowly, guardedly, taking the measure of each word, Harriet thinks, as she might take the measure of a person, of her. "A child out of wedlock is a prison sentence for a woman. And not only that, she'd be a victim of society's disapprobation for the rest of her life. Both Isla and the child would be."

Disapprobation. It annoys Harriet that she has never heard this word before, that she does not know its meaning, though she can guess at it. She squints at Flore.

"Society's scorn," Flore says quickly. "Its judgement."

Harriet rubs at her forehead—a habit her mother abhors—and scratches at the ground with the heel of her shoe. She feels for her handkerchief in her dress pocket; the tears are that close. But all she can find there is her stubbornness. And then, true donkey that she is, she is going ahead and making it worse: "Well, how did she get in that state? It's not like it happened by some kind of miracle. She had . . ."

"She had sexual relations with someone. Yes, she did. Dreadful, isn't it?"

What kind of smile is that?

"I . . ."

"Unmarried women do, you know, Harriet, have sex with people sometimes. It happens. Probably more often than you and the rest of the good old world thinks. And the unfortunate thing about having intercourse with men is that women can become pregnant. It's as simple as that."

"Why do they do it?" The question is ironic; hadn't Harriet, not many minutes ago, been imagining kissing Flore?

"Because they want to." Flore's fingers gently entwine with Harriet's, and for a moment she is smiling. Then she is not, and her eyes change, the softness there turning dark. "And sometimes they don't want to and it happens anyway," she says.

Harriet squeezes Flore's hand; she wants this storm in her eyes to depart.

"Do you know who it was? With Isla, I mean," Harriet asks.

"I might have asked you the same thing," Flore says.

This, Harriet thinks, is not a fair answer and she is about to say so when Flore suddenly grips Harriet's arm and cries out: "My God. What is that? A fox?"

Harriet looks to where Flore is pointing, through the clearing and into the woods. The animal crawling on its belly toward them is mostly orange, but it is not a fox. It's a dog. A little beagle.

"Are you lost?" Harriet says, crouching down and reaching out to the animal. Harriet loses her balance as the excited dog climbs into her lap. Stretched flat out on the ground, she cradles the animal to her chest. "I can't believe you thought it was a fox. Big city girl," Harriet teases.

"He's obviously in love." Flore sits down cross-legged beside them.

"Either that or *she*'s very hungry," Harriet says.

"Ah, the same kind of passion, I think," says Flore.

Flore's apartment overlooks English Bay. Harriet, at the window, hears the soft clamour of people—down in the street, on the beach, the pier—drifting up on a breeze. She sticks her tongue out to see if she can taste salt.

"Is it like this just on Sundays?"

"Like what?" Flore is on the chesterfield, her feet tucked beneath her, one hand stroking the dog's belly. The beagle—she has been named: Rue—is asleep beside her, having finished off the plate of chicken hearts and livers that were meant to be Flore's supper.

"I don't know." Harriet is following a car's passage along the street, six storeys below. Its top is down. The four people seated in it—two men in the front, two women in the back, the women's knees angled toward one another—are all wearing hats. Two circles, two ovals, two light, two dark. A woman in rose is crossing the street in white shoes. There's a delivery boy on a bicycle pulling a wagon—a circle followed by a square. "Like this. So . . ." The word she wants won't come. It is as elusive as the *unknown* in Mr. Potoski's algebra class. What, Harriet wonders, is the opposite of grey?

Harriet roams the apartment, like the women health inspectors who occasionally visited their old neighbourhood did. She eyes the handsome furniture, the burgundy carpets, the art hung on the walls. More remarkable to her is what she doesn't see: there are no water stains on the ceiling, no cracks in the plaster, no laundry lines hung over the stove. In the kitchen—a large room painted a sunny yellow—there's a gas stove, an icebox, a dish cabinet, and, oddly, a bookcase jammed with books. Regular books, not recipe books.

"How can you afford this apartment?" Harriet says and blushes. "Oh, sorry, was that rude?"

"My father pays for it. He doesn't like imagining me unmarried and living on a bookstore clerk's salary in some big old house converted into wretched apartments."

"Like ours, you mean?" Harriet sits on the chesterfield and rubs Rue's belly. Flore looks embarrassed. She touches Harriet's arm. Harriet shrugs and smiles. "Where does he live, your father?" she says.

"San Francisco."

"And your mother? Is she . . . ?"

"She's back in Holland now. In Rotterdam."

"They're divorced?"

"No, they're just living separately. She likes it better that way." Flore laughs. "Surprised? You're a little bit innocent, aren't you?"

"Innocent!"

"Naïve, then?" Flore pauses. "You're darling, actually." She pinches the hem of Harriet's dress and lifts it an inch or two above her knee then lets it drop. "Come with me," she says and gets up.

"Where to?" Harriet's eyebrows rise in alarm.

"The bathroom," says Flore.

The bathroom. The rush of relief is unsteadying and is followed swiftly by another rush, of fear this time. What does Flore want with her in the bathroom? Harriet hears the sound of water flowing.

"Harry? Coming?"

In the small black-and-white tiled room, Flore sits Harriet on the edge of the bathtub and kneels to unlace and then remove Harriet's shoes. She reaches up under Harriet's dress and unclips one of her garters.

"Off with your stockings."

Harriet unclips them both and pulls them off.

"You know what we're going to do, Harry?" Flore takes the stockings from her hands and tosses them behind her.

Why does that casual toss send such a thrill down her thighs?

"What?" says Harriet.

"We're going to shave your legs," Flore says. "Everyone's doing it."

And here is Harriet-Jean McKenzie, her feet in a few inches of warm bathwater. Flore Rozema, kneeling on the floor, is sluicing water up Harriet's legs. Now Flore is lathering up a shaving brush and gently soaping Harriet's left leg from ankle to mid-thigh. And here is the razor gliding down from top to bottom. Harriet looks up at the ceiling and closes her eyes. Agony, the sweetest.

RUE

This is your new home, the one called Harriet-Jean told me. Tucked uncomfortably under her arm, she gave me a tour, brief and with little fanfare, though the tone of her voice was ceremonial: parlour (larger than Rasia's); kitchen (small); privy (smaller); three bedrooms (crowded with what I would deem extraneous furniture). Outside, out back, Harriet made known without showing me, were chickens, a kitchen garden (tended mostly, allegedly, by the second eldest sister, Isla, who was, without explanation, *not at home*), a fenced yard, and a gate that gave out onto the lane. The lettuce has bolted, Harriet said, dramatically sad, as if neither she nor any other family member had the foggiest notion of what to do with a vegetable intent on going to seed.

The household consisted of the mother, Ahmie (at first glance a hateful lady, possibly with unnatural habits); the second eldest sister, the aforementioned not-at-home Isla; and the youngest,

Harriet-Jean, whose acquaintance I had obviously made. These women rented the main floor of this dwelling on Comox Street (minutes from my old home with Rasia on Haro). Upstairs, on the second floor, I was told, dwelt a Mr. Rex Barker (good Lord) and his wife, Irene, along with their three children (whose names were not revealed to me then) and, from the smell, what I presumed to be a cat (or two). There was also a third-floor tenant, an elderly bachelor with the alliterative name of Johnny Johnstone. An undertaker. Truth be known, Harriet said, we do not see much of Mr. Johnstone.

The girl could not possibly have known the state of my heart that day, but I knew hers: terrible sorrow. That, among other, selfish, reasons (starvation, to name one), is what drew me from the woods toward her. But there was something else, not quite as fatiguing, though nearly. I guessed the tender and sometimes troublesome upheaval of love.

MONDAY, JULY 10

Morning

Llewellyn hates Morrison. The man is bent over, elbows on the railing, and his face is twitching. He's got something on his mind. It's there in the muscles of his clean-shaven jaw, as if he's chewing on something small with his front teeth. Rat-like, but not as fast. Morrison's more rabbit-like in nature, isn't he? Llewellyn hates Morrison, but he hates the morgue worse. He has stepped out for a smoke, and Morrison has followed him. He knows the man isn't a smoker but he has, perversely, offered to roll him one anyway. Morrison, of course, has refused. He never joins the boys, not for drinks, not even for a cigarette. 'Off you go to your vices, I'm a churchgoing man' is Morrison's line. He says it pleasantly enough, but still, he's made a laughing-stock of himself. Most of them go to church with their wives of a Sunday, but not one of them but Morrison takes all those homilies about men's vices to heart. Or brings them to the station on Monday mornings, as Morrison does.

Morrison's tie is hanging down over the railing, that red plaid one his wife made him. Who wears a tie in clan tartan these days? Especially a homemade one. Llewellyn checks the little noise of irritation surfacing in his throat. His hands are shaking. He jams one of them into his pocket but that does no good; the sight of the dead woman has left him rattled.

"What's her name again?" he asks, tossing the cigarette.

Morrison rises, all six-feet-four of him, and Llewellyn wishes he'd stayed bent over.

"Maria Veltri. They found her in a rooming house, in Grand View. Her eldest, a five-year-old girl, knocked on a neighbour's door to say there was something wrong with her mother. The neighbour woman came and took one look at her and ran for the police. She thought she'd been stabbed, all the blood. When I got there the child was lying on the bed with the dead woman. Bled to death. There are two other little ones. Heaven knows what will happen to them all."

"No father?"

"Seems not. No one was very clear. Italians. You saw the bruise on her thigh?" Morrison rattles the loose change in his pocket.

"Yes," Llewellyn says. "I saw it. What does it prove?"

"It proves that there's someone out there with the devil in him. Killing babies and leaving his mark."

Llewellyn stares down the street. He knew a holier-than-thou kid like Morrison when he was younger. They nicknamed him the Dire Warner, always humping a big old Bible back and forth to school and talking about Lucifer and the prophesied beast that was coming. That kid, whose real name he doesn't remember anymore, even looked a bit like Morrison, all raw-boned and lanky. Llewellyn looks back at the man and his tartan tie and, just for a second, his heart stalls; just for a second, he envies Morrison's calm blind faith.

"Llewellyn, this is the sixth dead girl we've seen with the same mark in a little more than a year. Shall I remind you of their names."

"No," Llewellyn says, but there's Morrison, afire with righteousness, already pulling out his notebook.

"Eva Collings. Rasia Zawerbny. Edith-Mae McEwan. Margaret Irwin. Honor Braga. And now Maria Veltri." He snaps the book shut. "And your sister-in-law. Same bruise. Same devil's calling card."

"Isla's not dead," Llewellyn says.

"By God's grace." Morrison's eyes look sorrowful now. It's one of his tacks. "Your wife's in a delicate condition. Just imagine that tiny little baby growing in her."

Llewellyn grunts. Whatever's growing in Morag can't be much bigger than a kidney bean because she's as flat-bellied as ever. But small as it may be, Morag's already in love with it. She's got a list of names picked out for the bean: Emil or Daisy. Rufus. Emma. She's annoyed with him because he isn't cooing over it, infatuated like some dove. Asking him to love something that is smaller than a pea pod and utterly unknown is like asking him to love the man in the moon; he doesn't believe in it. Not yet. And there's Isla. Even Morag's excitement is countered by that bloody mess.

"Sounds like you're more concerned about the babies than the women," Llewellyn says.

Morrison clears his throat. "The unborn are innocent."

"The unborn," Llewellyn says. For some reason he can't put his finger on, his father comes to mind, as he so often does. He hasn't told his parents about the coming child. If he had his way, he never would. He puts his hat on and tells Morrison he's got an errand to run. The unborn, he thinks, are . . . unborn. "So are the women," he says to Morrison. "They're innocent too."

Llewellyn mounts the hospital's front steps two at a time. He's halfway through the front doors before he realizes that the woman sitting on the steps outside, smoking a cigarette, was Flore. Beautiful Flore, normally impossible to miss. He goes back out and sits beside her. That wry smile of hers; she knew he'd be back.

"A woman smoking in public," he says, holding back a smile. He doesn't say what he's thinking: a woman smoking in public, on the steps of a Catholic hospital with black-robed nuns strolling the grounds and the hallways. His mother would have said that Flore was vulgar. It strikes him that the cigarette defines Flore somehow. Not in any way he could easily explain, if asked, at least not well. Certainly not vulgar. She and Isla are cut from the same cloth—opinionated and fearless, and defiant. He likes them; he's confused by them. And the rumours about Flore and women—even more confounding.

"Indeed," Flore says, as if she knows exactly what he's thinking. She smiles and blows a puff of smoke at him.

"Would you have said anything if I'd not noticed you?" he asks.

"I didn't, did I?" She blows her smoke away this time. "Going up to see Isla?"

Llewellyn nods. He bounces one knee, his right, and taps his feet up and down, a nervous habit, one learned in childhood. He rolls a cigarette—this time with steady hands—and offers to roll her one after lighting his, a force of habit, but decidedly an afterthought. She laughs, shakes her head, and shows him the tailor-made one already burning between her fingers. He grins, shrugs.

"How is she?"

"Better. Exhausted. Now that she knows she's going to live she's . . ." Flore waves her arm in the air. He can feel the exhaustion in her gesture. ". . . happy?"

Llewellyn taps his feet again and stares at his hands. He sneaks a peek at Flore's shoes—black, low heel, a leather flower at the buckle. Isla's got a pair just like them, only in brown. Or she had a pair. The hospital has only one of her shoes. "Why would she do this?" he says.

Flore swivels her knees toward him for a second. He catches her look of weary contempt before she swivels back. "Oh, yes. Why *would* a twenty-four-year-old unmarried woman in this day and age risk her life to rid herself of a pregnancy?"

Her sarcasm is stinging-nettles sharp. But he doesn't want to pick a fight with Flore. He'd lose. "She could have done something else," he says.

"She likely already did," Flore says.

"What?"

"Home remedies. Gin. Quinine. Pennyroyal. Rum. Laxatives. Castor oil. Rue. Turpentine. A fall down a flight of stairs . . ." Flore's counting on her fingers.

"That's not what I mean," Llewellyn says.

"A boiling hot bath. Blue cohosh. Oil of cedar. Jumping off the kitchen table forty times."

"Enough," he says.

Flore keeps adding to her list. "Did I mention turpentine? A punch to the stomach? And if none of that works, there's a trip to the abortionist. Or she could have done it herself. With a knitting needle."

"For the love of God, stop. She could have had it," he says angrily.

"Had it?"

"Yes. Had it."

Flore is silent, looking down while she grinds her cigarette out on the dusty granite powder on the steps. Then she faces him. "And be seen as a fallen woman. By virtually every human being whose feet trod this earth. Lose her job. Be sneered at and judged by even the *shortest* pillars of society. The self-righteous, the hypocritical. All those good folks?" A curl of her blond hair has come loose; it bobs like a live thing against her cheek. She tucks it back behind her ear in an almost violent gesture.

"A fallen woman." Llewellyn doesn't mean to sound so snide.

"Yes, Llew," she says, raising both her voice and her arms and shaking her hands at him. There are sweat stains in the armpits of her dress. "You know what I like to imagine? I like to imagine the streets lined with all earth's fallen women. Everyone else having to pick their way through the streets, stepping over them. That would be some kind of justice, wouldn't it? All those women blocking the path of the sanctimonious bastards who knocked them down. And there would be a lot of us."

A priest and two nursing sisters are mounting the stairs toward them. Llewellyn starts to rise, but Flore puts a firm hand on his arm.

"You're getting up for them? They think women who get into trouble are lesser beings, and they think the same of the children they bear—that they're not only morally but physically and mentally inferior."

Llewellyn nods at the priest as he and the nuns pass. Catholic or not, his Presbyterian father would have cuffed him for not standing up for the women. Flore has at least lowered her voice.

"And how would anyone imagine that Isla could afford to raise this child? Live with her mother for the rest of her life? Ahmie would love that. Ha." Flore spits out a noise, more a caw than a laugh.

"Not that Ahmie would necessarily notice," Llewellyn says. His small laugh dies as Flore glares at him.

"And I don't see a man rushing to Isla's bedside to declare his paternity or his everlasting love for her and what would have been her poor little bastard."

"She didn't tell you about anyone? A man?"

"Silent as the grave," Flore says. "Oh, God, sorry. Not funny." She covers her face with her hands. She shudders as though she might be crying.

"How in the world would she have found this abortionist?" Llewellyn asks.

There's a single tear on Flore's cheek. She wipes it away. "It's not hard, Llew. You know someone who knows someone. A druggist, a dentist, the florist, a midwife, the boarding house matron where some friend of yours lived. A doctor, even. Word of mouth. Check the ads in the back of the newspapers. I just don't understand why she went to . . . I told her . . . I—" Flore looks away. She fumbles in her handbag for a cigarette or a handkerchief or . . .

Llewellyn clamps a hand on her shoulder. She shrugs it off. "You knew?" He's shouting.

She turns to face him, defiant. "I gave her the names of two women who were recommended to me. Two good women who are willing to help women in need. I don't know how she found the person she went to."

Llewellyn stands up. "My God, you advised her to have an abortion."

"I did not advise her to have an abortion." Flore stands up too. She's shorter than he is but she mounts two steps so he is forced to look up at her. He resists the urge to take a step up as well, to dominate. "I respected her wishes, that's what I did," she says.

"Who is he? Tell me his name, Flore, or so help me God I'll—"

"Don't you dare threaten me. And don't you dare threaten her. I don't know his name. Isla made her choice, God knows why him, and she has suffered because of it. It's over. Over! I'm grateful she's alive. We all should be. And it's not your business what she did."

"I'll make it police business." Llewellyn points a finger at her.

She slams his hand away. "Making it police business will do nothing."

"Why?" When Flore doesn't answer, he grabs her by the elbows. "Why?"

She jerks her arms up. "Because finding this one man will not make it any different for women." He sees her fierceness drop a notch. Her eyes look suddenly sad. "We need to be able to prevent pregnancy in the first place. That's what we need. Education. Proper birth control. Don't you understand, Llew? In the meantime, if there are people willing to help, praise be. You will not put any of them, including whoever harmed Isla, out of business until we have some choice as to whether or not we get pregnant at all. And even then . . ." She bends and gathers her handbag and cardigan off the stairs.

"This man is not your good midwife, Flore, getting women out of a jam. This is not the nice lady next door helping when you're in trouble. This is a butcher. This is someone who doesn't give a damn about what happens to the women he touches. He's in it for the money . . . or—"

"He's punishing them, Llew." Flore takes a few steps down the stairs then turns to him. "Don't look so surprised. Go ahead then, find him," she says. "Then do something so that we do not to have to resort to butchers like him in hotel rooms or back alley kitchens. Look at the price Isla paid, just for having sex with someone. Is that what she's due? Women having sex is not a crime. And the hypocrisy of you men's one-sided morals is staggering. As if you were a virgin when you married Morag." Flore's face is dark with rage again. "Though I hear *she* was."

Llewellyn is speechless for a moment, but Flore's anger doesn't stop the momentum of his own. "A couple more dead women turn up with that mark on their thighs, and you'll give me his name."

Flore is almost at the bottom of the stairs. "I don't know his name," she screams.

"You want to hear *their* names? The dead women's? The ones he's killed?" He tries to draw the names in Morrison's notebook from memory, shouting after her, getting them wrong, knowing it. "Maria Veltri. Eva Collins. Edith-Maude. Honor. Rasia. Margaret." And, nearly, Isla McKenzie.

"How about these names: Gin. Turpentine. Pennyroyal. Rue." Flore is shaking her hands at him, in a rage. "Hat pin. Crochet hook. Knitting needle. Bicycle spoke."

ISLA

During those weeks in the hospital, the way the nursing sisters treated me—how they touched or bathed me—made clear their opinion of what I'd done. The ones who found me morally wanting, guilty of a heinous crime, the ones who couldn't hide their judgement, gave me what I came to think of as the sinner's scrub. To them, I was a murderer. Deserving of the worst form of punishment, and wouldn't they love to be of help with that, sending me, with their rough washcloths, along my way to hell. Some nurses were indifferent: We've seen it all before, their competent hands said, you are nothing new. A few, not many, maybe three or four, indicated by the smallest gesture that they understood how such things could happen. Or I hoped they did. And in the dark one night, a girl's voice confessed in my ear: 'There but for the grace of God go I.'

You came often, Llewellyn. Eyes closed I could tell it was you standing at my bedside. I could smell you. You were salty, as though you were born in the sea. You were christened there, I know, though not as a child. Your true baptism, you told me, happened out east, on the Atlantic Ocean. I knew you, too, by the way your footsteps sounded in the ward, the way you slowed before you came near, so unlike the nurses who padded about, swift cats arriving unannounced and departing as silently. The first time I was conscious of your presence I listened as you pulled close the chair that Flore had been warming a few minutes earlier. You took my hand, and you lay your forehead in my open palm. It was instinctive, perhaps for both of us: I slid my fingers up into your warm hair. Your warmth, Llew. It was the thing that slayed me.

Occasionally, I manage to convince myself that what happened between us only started in April that year, on that Sunday when the will of our bodies triumphed over our rational minds. But it wasn't April, was it, Llew? It wasn't a picnic day on the North Shore. And it wasn't one night's mistake—a flask of gin meeting a bottle of rye. It started the second Morag introduced us, months and months earlier, before you went out east. Another autumn. Do you remember that quiet pause? We shook hands. You held my gaze and I held yours just a second longer than potential in-laws should. An adulterous second. No? When, then? Isn't yearning just as much adultery, even if it isn't acted upon?

There came a point, after you'd come home, where we should have known that being alone together would tip the whole damn apple cart. I can't pretend to be so naïve that I didn't know that. Your voice alone made me stupid with love.

And I can't blame Morag, though I am often tempted to do so. She was infamous for backing out of plans, as she did that day. She left us alone. We who were a loaded freight train with brakes made, at best, for that apple cart. 'You two go,' she said, so trustingly. 'Have fun.' Go, we did.

We took the ferry across the inlet to the North Shore, and we hiked away from the water, then followed a trickle of a stream up into a wooded area where we sat to have our lunch. It was so quiet, that little park. Remember? So cool, green, and far away, thank God, I said, from the hordes of beachside walkers in their Sunday best. I can still hear you laughing. All right, I was exaggerating. There weren't hordes; I just have never liked a crowd of any size.

How different things might have been if we'd stayed nearer to those "pious phonies," as my father used to call them, fresh from their Sunday sermons. Forgive me. I'm only quoting my pa. I don't have anywhere near as dark a view of churchgoers as he did, although I don't understand them. I must ask Ahmie again what made him turn so irrevocably from the Church. She said once that they'd both lost what faith they'd had after the death of Baby John. But for Pa I think it was something else. Something bigger. Their terrible loss, but everyone else's too. The oppression endured by men and women of his class. *What God*, he might have asked, *would let people suffer such hardships?* Or maybe I'm talking about my own lack of faith. Whatever it was, Pa was born a Presbyterian and reborn an atheist before most of us were even a gleam in his eye.

Morag, on the other hand, had an endless fascination with all things churchy. Did you know that, Llew? She must have told you how she went to the Presbyterian church with a neighbour girl for several years when we were young. But did she also tell you how Pa barely tolerated her going? He never forbade it. But the antidote, it seemed, was to feed her scientists and philosophers, poets, Shakespeare, the dictionary, and the thesaurus for lunch when she came home every Sunday—to the benefit of us all, I should say. It was strong competition, Darwin versus Jesus, new words versus the Almighty Lord's. But Morag was often seduced by the conventional. No, I don't mean you. You never fell into that category. In our family, being conventional was more or less the equivalent of breaking the rules. You knew that when you married a McKenzie, didn't you?

God or no God, I can no longer remember how it was that your thermos of tea got spilled, up there in that pretty spot by the stream. I suppose you might have done it on purpose, though there was never much of the schemer in you. Did you do it on purpose, Llew? You took off your shirt and rinsed it in the stream and there it was, hanging from a low hemlock branch, the sleeves of a scarecrow. And there you were, half naked. You were—and this is the only word for it—radiant, though that men can be such a thing is a wonder. We talked about Morag, attempting to create a barrier between us by evoking her presence, I suppose. But that barrier was paper-thin. 'Ironic,' you said, 'that she, of all of us, would have loved this picnic spot most.' 'Indeed,' said I. Blah-di-blah-blah, on we blathered. Did you ask permission to lay your head in my lap? I don't remember.

I dozed, you slept, or seemed to. When we woke, your arms were wrapped around my thighs, my hands were in your warm hair. I bent and kissed you. In a while, we climbed farther up the mountainside until we found a clearing, that beautiful glade with all the wildflowers in bloom, as if they knew a pair of star-crossed lovers was coming. O, traitorous flowers.

You made love to me. And after, you lay there, contented, smiling, the dappled sun kissing your beautiful body. I watched a bumblebee as it buzzed heavily above us, languidly, as content and innocent as you seemed. I confess: for a moment I wanted to kill that bee just because, like you, it was so untroubled. I shivered in the soft breeze: How would I ever face Morag again?

But did the thought of my sister mean I never again held your head in my hands?

On your first visit to the hospital, the first I remember, that is, I asked, 'Do you know what day it is, Llew?' I drew my hand away from yours and slid it under the blanket.

'July tenth. Why?' you said.

Your face was clouded with the kind of misery that very little, certainly not words, can wipe away.

Oh, Llewellyn. You poor, dear man. How merciless, I have learned, regret can be—as ruinous as cutting stone with a knife. And revenge, you would learn, is doubly so.

'My father died five years ago today,' I said.

You were supposed to offer your condolences. You were supposed to look sympathetic, hold my hand, ask how my mother would get through the day, tell me how Morag had been reminiscing about our father earlier. But you were angry. You could not begin to fathom what I had done.

I tried to laugh when I told you that the doctor had tested me that morning, asking if I knew what day it was. I'd failed.

You weren't in the mood for laughter. 'My God, Isla,' you said. 'You should have told me you were pregnant. When did you know?'

And there I was again, on the floor of my employers' upstairs bathroom, face to face with the thing I could no longer deny.

'When?' I said. 'I was on my hands and knees scrubbing the Westcotts' toilet.'

I thought it would give me some satisfaction to see the anger in your eyes give way to shame. It didn't.

The moment of my full surrender had come that day in the Westcotts' bathroom in their Shaughnessy home. For two weeks I'd been pushing the nagging thought away. Like the insistent flickering of a hallway lamp, I could just shut the door on it. And then, I couldn't. I stood. I finished cleaning the toilet. I bent and wiped the little Westcott boys' pee drops off the tiled floor. I rinsed the rag in the sink, wringing it until it was nearly dry, avoiding looking at my reflection in the mirror. One edge of the cloth was frayed, and a few long, annoying threads dangled from it. I opened the medicine cabinet, something I had never done before, in search of a pair of scissors to cut the threads. Instead I found Mr. Westcott's razor. I ran the razor along my thumb and might have pressed harder to raise some blood had I not turned to find little Jamie Westcott at the door, holding the front of his pants.

'Why don't boys and men just sit down to pee?' I asked you. 'It's about pointing, I suppose. You can point, so why shouldn't you, is that it?'

You made a dismissive noise, a horse's whicker.

'The thing that matters to me,' I said, 'isn't what I have done. It's what you and I have done.' I lifted my arm in an attempt to draw a line between us, then let it drop. I was infuriatingly weak.

'Why didn't you let me help you?'

'How? You would have stopped me,' I said.

'Was it mine?'

If I'd had the strength, I would have bashed your head in.

'I'm sorry,' you said immediately.

I'm sure your remorse was sincere. You were deathly quiet for a minute, and, cruelly—I'm sorry now, Llew—I let you soak in your misery, unforgiven.

'We could have sorted something out. My God, Isla, there are other ways.'

I looked up at you, exhausted again. 'Other ways? What other ways? Your own wife is pregnant.'

Your mouth opened and then closed, a little like a fish before it is gaffed.

'Your wife. My sister,' I said.

The woman in the bed next to mine turned her back on us. You said I was imagining it, but her condemnation felt tangible, vinegar on my tongue. The whole ward—all the women in their beds, their faithful husbands and brilliant, well-behaved children, the dutiful nurses, the self-important doctors, even the poor beleaguered man who mopped the floor—knew my story.

You reached for my hand, and I didn't have the strength to keep it from you. You kissed it and lay your head in it again. When I looked up, Georgina was standing at the foot of the bed.

'Georgina,' I said.

You stood quickly and shoved your hands in your pockets. My Pocketman, I used to call you. I doubt I will ever again know a man who makes such use of his pockets.

Georgina brushed past you, and I let her touch my forehead.

'You're much better,' she said.

I nodded and pushed her hand off. 'I am. And we'd better get me out of here before we all have to give up our firstborns to pay my hospital bill.' I waved my hand dispiritedly at Georgina. 'Oh, God. I'm sorry, Georgie,' I said.

Georgina dodged your kiss. You cast me the most heart-breaking look, like a mournful dog, and you left. Sorry for all the animal metaphors. I always thought of you as part of the animal world. Georgina was another creature: an imperious bald eagle. I have never understood the battleground that must rage inside my sister, whatever it is that makes her so rarely soft, so rarely amiable. But who am I to judge? What good, I wonder, is a woman who is only soft? What would such a woman ever get done besides the ironing of the sheets?

You left us. Georgina stood beside the bed. Her hands wrung the low iron rail that barred my escape as if she was strangling someone, or wanted to.

'Would there be anything you need to tell me, Isla?' she said.

'No.' I was sure a lecture was coming. She took an overly long time before she spoke. I waited. I'd become good at that.

Why, in the end, is all she said, and her voice broke as she said it.

'Why?' I repeated.

'What were you thinking?'

'I was thinking,' I said, 'that my life was over. That I would lose everything.'

'Lose everything?'

'I don't know. My life as it is. My family. My job. My future,' I said.

'You have lost everything. You nearly lost your life. You'll lose your job. And God knows what future you'll have. Not one with children.'

I stared at the ceiling, counting those so-familiar tiles, tracing the criss-cross of the pipes. Georgina would never understand how desperate I'd been. Not the devastation I felt as I lay there on that dresser, that awful man between my knees. Nor the relief. None of them would. 'It was worth the risk,' I said, dully.

'Worth it? Could you not have thought of anyone but yourself?'

Here was the lecture. I turned angrily back to her, ready to say 'I was, I was thinking of someone else,' but Georgina's eyes were soft with a rare bewilderment. We were silent, each taking in the other's pain. I watched her struggling to hide hers. Finally, when she knew she couldn't, I suppose, she looked away.

'I would have taken the baby,' she said quietly.

I felt a confusing stab of remorse. I'd sat with Georgina each time she miscarried. The last time, a few months earlier, had been her third, long weeks into the pregnancy.

'You've cut your beautiful hair,' I said, reaching up and touching Georgina's head.

'Oh, for God's sake, Isla,' Georgina said, pushing my hand away. 'Did you hear me?' When I didn't answer, she bent and rested her forehead on the bedrail. In a while she said, 'Victor says you'll go straight to hell.' Her shoulders were shaking. She might have been crying, but she could have been laughing too.

A noise made us jump. The woman in the bed to the right of mine, the back-turner, had fallen asleep and the Bible she was constantly reading had slid to the floor, landing with a solemn whack. The woman, a Mrs. Adelaide Tenpenny, read all day, rustling the book's thin paper, smoothing her fingers down the gold ribbon bookmark that she brought forward every time she turned the page. She moved her lips while she read, and when she wasn't reading, her lips still moved, in prayer I suppose. Later, she wasted a sunny morning telling me about everyone and everything she was praying for, including her stern-faced husband who came every evening with their five-year-old, Davy, a child as solemn as his father. She'd been praying for me, too, she told me. *Don't bother*, I'd wanted to say. *You're twenty-four years too late.*

Georgina leaned down, picked up the Bible, and handed it back to the woman.

'God bless,' Mrs. Tenpenny said, sleepily.

'I would have raised your child,' Georgina told me. Morag said the same. Can you imagine that, Llew? Your little twins, closer to true kinship than my sisters would ever have imagined.

When we were little we used to have staring contests. Georgina always won. She never laughed. Never blinked. No one could beat her. Not even Roddy. That day, Georgina put her palm on my cheek and held me, intently, with her eyes. Wouldn't she make a good politician? If only she'd put that fierce, unwavering stare of hers to good use. Conquering totalitarian nations. Disarming the enemy. Dealing with the government naysayers. There in the hospital, I broke the connection by pulling her hand away from my cheek and placing it, instead, over my eyes. This was not like the knuckling under of my childhood. I wasn't giving up; I was just refusing to play. She bowed her head eventually and sat down again in that bedside chair. God, how I came to hate that chair and its daily inhabitants.

I think, sometimes, of the child my pregnancy might have produced. I wonder whether it would have been like you, Llew, or like me. A boy or a girl. Green-eyed or black. I would have been the kind of mother that nibbled on toes, squeezed fat little thighs, gave bellies the raspberry. And still.

I have never told anyone, Llew, and I never will, but I could not have borne having someone else raise our child. Not a stranger, leaving me to imagine, for the rest of my life, that child out there in some unknown family. And not even Georgina and Victor, or you and Morag. No one. Is that wrong? I don't know. I am certain, most days, that I did what had to be done. What a terrible secret we would have had to keep. And if it had been revealed, how many hearts would I have broken.

The bleak moments do come, very occasionally, at night, and I am swept under, imagining how it might have been different. What if I'd chosen someone other than that terrible man. What if I'd chosen to keep it. But not a soul on earth has the gift of foresight. And hindsight? Clear as mud, dear Llew.

FRIDAY, JULY 14

After work

Bets are on, but what are the odds? Harriet gives him two to one he'll catch the streetcar. That's generous, given that it's Padraig. Seated in the streetcar's back row, she watches him come out of Woodward's, see the trolley, and start running for the stop. She's rooting for him, but no amount of rooting will make any difference if he runs to the stop on the wrong side of the street. *This side*, Harriet mouths, waving and rapping at the window. He can't see or hear her. And now, there he is, at the wrong streetcar stop looking so satisfied with himself that Harriet laughs out loud. She watches him tuck a large brown-paper parcel under one arm, open his book, and, with his middle finger as always, push his eyeglasses up on his nose. For some, clearly, old habits die hard; the traffic direction changed half a year ago. How Padraig can fail to remember that the whole world is driving on the right-hand side of the road now is inexplicable. She hoots and claps her hands when she sees him finally realize his mistake. He takes off at a sprint, dodging traffic, and now here is Padraig high-stepping it after her streetcar, book in one hand, brown-paper package in the other.

How pleased she is that six months ago, in front of the door to the ladies' staff room in the basement of Woodward's, she met this funny man. She'd finished her shift and was searching her change purse for car fare. He seemed to be doing nothing better than loitering. But she somehow knew him to be, she understands now, friend and not foe. It was his socks—they were yellow argyle—that made her curious, made her brave enough to ask, 'Waiting for someone?' He bent forward, bowing it seemed, and said, 'You?' He glanced up as a man came out of the men's staff room opposite them. The man paused, just for a second, his puzzled gaze moving from Padraig to Harriet and back, then he disappeared up the stairs. 'Padraig Gleason,' he said to Harriet, holding out his left hand. 'I think I've just been stood up.'

She knows Padraig has seen her now, waving in the back window of the streetcar. He's pink-faced from running, but his mouth opens in laughter and he holds up the package to her. When the streetcar stops he catches up and leaps aboard. He makes his way to the back where he slides into the seat beside Harriet.

"Lavatory Lady," he says.

"Don't remind me, Top Salesman of the Month," she says.

"I can't help it if they flock to me," he says.

"Like bees to pollen, all those ladies," she says.

"Hoping to make their husbands look smart," he says.

Harriet snorts. "They flock to me, too, you know. Can't visit Woodward's without a trip to the lavatory. There's such a nice girl down there, keeping things tidy, handing out towels."

"Oh, she's a sweetie, I've heard, that Miss McKenzie," Padraig says. "You're just lucky you don't work in the men's lav."

"What's this?" Harriet asks, plucking at the string on the package he's carrying.

Padraig slides the parcel onto her lap. "Just take it straight home," he says. "You can thank me later."

Harriet gives the package a squeeze and Padraig puts one long finger on her wrist; *wait*. She rustles the paper, laughing, excited. He holds his hand down harder on her wrist and gives her a mock warning look.

"Or thank Woodward's men's wear department. Better yet, thank the clever fellow who tried on a new model and walked clean out the door in it, without paying. He left this in the dressing room. I thought it would suit you perfectly. I can't wait to see you in it." He turns to face forward, giving her his freckled profile.

Harriet smiles to herself. She does not know why sitting next to Padraig Gleason makes her feel as though all will be right with the world one day.

"How's Isla?" Padraig asks.

His question dumps her happiness on its head. Harriet shrugs. "They say she's getting better, but she won't be home anytime soon."

"Ah, the notorious 'they,'" says Padraig.

At his stop, Padraig hangs on the pole by the door, arms spread wide, then drops off the streetcar. "Tomorrow night. Saint Pete's. I'll meet you out front. Nine p.m." He tips his hat.

At home, Harriet sits cross-legged on the back steps. The brown paper, now lying discarded on her bedroom floor, contained a suit. A man's suit. The trousers a bit bagged out at the knee, a long oily stain under the left lapel of the jacket, the tie dotted with shiny egg yolk, the vest and shirt smelling distinctly of the sour sweat of men. She spent an hour scrubbing everything in the washtub and there he hangs now, a thin man, on the washing line.

She closes her eyes. She herself is hanging on that line, naked for all the world to see.

RUE

Harriet slipped out the back door that evening, unusually attired and without so much as a head rub for me.

She smelled of fear. I did not presume to know why.

SATURDAY, JULY 15

Nine p.m.

At Saint Pete's, Paul lets Padraig and Harriet in without any of the usual harassment, though he's ready with a sneer for both of them. Padraig leans his face, all charm, all innocence, close to Paul's. The doorman recoils. "You don't have to let us in, you know, Paul," Padraig says.

Paul sniffs. "Bad company," he says. His eyes linger on Harriet.

Harriet can taste it: the bitterness of his suspicion and, worse, his disgust. She is sweating in her suit. There's a squirrel gnawing in her gut; it's ferocious. Her father's cap is too big for her. It hangs low on her forehead. Her shoes aren't right, of course they aren't. But they're flat. As is her chest beneath this vest, bound with a panel of cotton and secured with safety pins. (What an ordeal.)

Flore—(in a pretty dress, oh God)—is in the kitchen sitting close (very close) to a man Harriet has never seen at Saint Pete's. Padraig's gentle hand nudges Harriet through the doorway. He leans for a kiss from Flore then introduces Harriet as his friend Willie. (Oh, he will pay for that.) Harriet is now glad for the too-large hat; she is blushing to her roots. Flore introduces her companion. "This is Maxwell," she says. That's a gentle hand she lays on the man's back.

"Ah, I see my competition has arrived," Maxwell says, standing and giving Harriet's hand a manly shake. Harriet looks down at their firmly clasped hands: so this is how it's done.

Flore, still seated, stretches her hand out to Harriet. There's an endless second during which Harriet is certain she should never have come, it is time to go home, time to take off this ridiculous costume, but then Flore's mouth opens. The word *oh* is sitting right there on her red-rouged lips. She slips off her chair and flicks Harriet's tie with one finger. Harriet follows her into the living room.

"You sexy thing," Flore whispers. Now she has her arms around Harriet.

Harriet bends to Flore's ear. "Can't take the hat off."

"We'll get you one that fits," Flore says. "Now take me dancing, Harry."

And here, in these clothes, with Flore, Harriet is finally home. Relief, a spring river, floods every one of her bones. Every single one of them.

By eleven o'clock, they're all drunk. Padraig, on the chesterfield, is beguiling the two women seated on either side of him.

"Who's your darling friend, Padraig?" asks the woman to his right.

All eyes are suddenly on Harriet.

Harriet feels a surge of anxiety, but Flore lifts her chin: "Well, whoever he is, he's all mine."

"Lucky you," says the woman to Padraig's left.

"Who's lucky?" Maxwell, returning with another glass of rye, signals for Padraig to get up. "Not your type, are they?" he says to Padraig, then squeezes himself in between the two women on the chesterfield.

"Isn't he sweet?" Padraig says to Flore, with a nod at Harriet. "I thought you might like him."

"Sweet!" Harriet says.

"Sweet!" Padraig mimics Harriet's high squawk. "You're going to have to work on your register, Willie." Padraig clears his throat. "La, la, la, comme ça," he says, his voice descending a step deeper with each *la*.

"Willie. Ach," Harriet says. "I can't be a Willie."

"Yes," Flore laughs, "I think 'Harry' will do."

"Harry it is, then," Padraig says, looking over Flore's shoulder at a handsome man who has poked his nose into the living room. The man smiles at Padraig. "Excuse me, my friends," Padraig says. "I believe I have to see a man about a dog."

It's midnight now and the world is spinning. Harriet, leaning back in her chair, legs kicked out and spread like a man's, sits forward and grips the edge of the table until, finally, the spinning stops. She leans back again, smacks her heels against the floor, so happy; she could never do this in a dress. She grins at Flore, but Flore does not seem to be grinning back. Is she nowhere near as drunk as Harriet? Wasn't Flore keeping up to her, drink for drink? No, it seems. It seems Harriet has been keeping up with Padraig.

Harriet can hardly bear to look at Flore, she is that beautiful. She feels a bumblebee buzzing in her breast, a careless joy; it makes her smile idiotically. She'd like to kiss Flore, right here, in front of everyone. She will. She bends toward Flore; her half-filled glass falls and smashes on the floor.

Flore frowns, and Pete's there, frowning too.

"Shall we go home?" Flore says, standing. "Sorry, Pete."

"Home?" Harriet rises. She wobbles, her carefree heart now pinched in a vise.

Out on the street, Flore pulls Harriet's hat off with a sharp tug.

FRIDAY, JULY 28

Noon

Llewellyn blinks at the man across from him. His eyes are as pretty as a woman's. He'd forgotten how good-looking Bill Hogarth was. His stomach heaves with the queasiness that has plagued him for more than a month now.

"Are you sure you can do it?" he says.

"Of course," Hogarth says. "I'm an actor. You saw my last performance, didn't you? I'm the real McCoy, my friend."

Llewellyn nods. A vaudevillian wasn't exactly the kind of actor he'd had in mind. His mother used to take him to the theatre when he was young. All those tedious amateur productions about humanity's vices. There wouldn't have been an actor among them suitable for the role he's asking Hogarth to play.

"What name do you want to go by?" Llewellyn asks.

"Something double-barrelled, I think. You need that hoity-toity touch for a coroner."

"How about Dingwall-FitzPatterson," Llewellyn says with a cheerless laugh.

Hogarth laughs uproariously, as he always did at school, all teeth and tongue and that thing that hangs down at the back of the throat. "That's too over the top, Llew."

"You come up with something, then," Llewellyn says. "You're the creative one. Let me know and I'll get Morrison to bring you to the house."

"This Morrison, is he in on it?"

"No. Absolutely not. Call him at the number I gave you and tell him you're from the coroner's office. Don't make him any the wiser about what we're up to."

"And you just want me to see if I can get anything more out of them than what you've told me. I'll do some research before I come. Gotta get wise to the topic."

Llewellyn's gut heaves again. "Yes. Where, who, how. You're sure you can do it?" Someone has opened the door to the café; a refracted ray of sunlight hits Llewellyn in the eye. In that blinding second, he knows how lost he is.

Hogarth leans forward across the table. "Trust me. I'm your man."

TUESDAY, AUGUST 1

Before noon

"I don't know what all the fuss is about."

Ahmie is upright in the horsehair chair, a poor man's Queen Victoria, nursing a cup of tea that went cold an hour ago. Isla, home at last, is in Ahmie's usual spot on the settee, wrapped in the old crocheted blanket. She's small, the colour of yellowed ivory. Georgina has been watching her sister obsessively since before Ahmie's tea grew cold. The pulse in the blue veins that have appeared in Isla's temple and the one down the centre of her forehead is slow and mesmerizing. Isla's cheekbones, the round sockets of her eyes, and the bones of her mouth protrude oddly, the rest of her flesh hollowed back. She looks starved, yet her eyes are strangely incandescent, her pupils and irises a glittery black. Georgina is listening to her mother's endless drone with only half an ear; she's not convinced that Isla won't die if she takes her eyes off her.

"In my day," Ahmie says, "we never thought anything of it unless you'd felt the quickening. If you lost it before then or, frankly, found a way to get it gone, it was no spilt milk to cry over. Such a fuss. Such a fuss." Ahmie puts her teacup down. It rattles in the saucer.

"Ahmie," Georgina says. It's only a tepid warning. She is trying to be pleasant though her patience departed hours ago. Earlier this morning, she had convinced herself that Ahmie had always talked this compulsive and tactless way—when she is awake, when there is an audience, even when there is only one person whose ear she might bend. Now, she sees her mother's bewildered eyes and reminds herself that Ahmie only lost her way when their father died. Then there was their brother Roddy's death. And what she has had to endure in the past five weeks has only made it worse. Ahmie has been wandering from one valley to another and back again, trying to make sense of what she has been told about Isla, refusing to allow that Isla might have died. Be generous, Georgina, she tells herself. Be generous. Somewhere inside that pale, twitching, sweating woman sitting there in that hideous chair is your funny, protective, opinionated spark of a mother. She taps her wedding ring on her own empty teacup.

"When is the coroner's man coming?" Ahmie asks again.

The coroner's man. Isla isn't dead, but a man from the coroner's office is coming nonetheless. Llewellyn has explained: it is to determine whether there should be an inquest. But nothing about the visit makes sense; no one is dead. 'If you are up to something,' Georgina has warned Llewellyn, 'I will kill you. Then there really will be an inquest.' They've all had enough.

"At one," Georgina tells her mother. "He's coming at one."

There has been no sun all morning. Just rain or threatening rain. The house feels cold and dark. Ahmie rattles her teacup again, and Georgina stares at her. Let me not be this at sea when I am fifty-four, she thinks. Her mother half smiles—a rare occurrence—and shows her teeth—even rarer. They are the same colour as Isla's skin. Her hands are idle, but they twitch as though she has a needle and embroidery floss in her lap.

"The quickening happens at about three or four months. I remember feeling Rodric's first little kicks. It was like a butterfly was flitting about in there," Ahmie says. She places her hands on her belly where they finally lie still.

Isla pushes out a loud, obviously intentional sigh. "And Georgina's, and Morag's, and Harriet's little butterfly kicks," she says drily. She goes quiet for a second. "And mine. My little kicks, right, Ahmie?"

Ahmie looks surprised, as if she had forgotten Isla was here. "Oh, yes. Did you feel it too?" She brightens, sits up. "The quickening?"

"No."

Isla lies back and covers her whole head with the blanket; Georgina panics. "Isla," she says, and Isla pulls the blanket back down and rolls her eyes. They are rimmed with tears.

Georgina turns away, the foreignness of tears pricking in her own eyes. She felt the quickening once. One of her own pregnancies, one of three, lost to miscarriage. "Would you like some hot tea, Ahmie?"

Ahmie's gaze wanders from Isla to the front window to Georgina's hands and back to her teacup. "I just remember

Rodric best. You always remember your first best. I know exactly where I was. Your father was chopping wood and I was piling it. And then I felt it. Little Roddy."

God help them; now they'll be deluged by Ahmie's Rodric recollections. Georgina bends forward to touch Isla's foot, the only part of her not covered by the blanket. She is wearing a pair of woolen socks, darned to death—Pa's or possibly, and more ironically, Roddy's. More ironic because, after his funeral, Isla told Georgina she never wanted to hear Roddy's name mentioned again. And here she is, wearing his socks. There is no comparing degree of heartbreak, but if one could measure such a thing, Isla would have been the winner. There's no prize, of course, for the most inconsolable. For the one most crushed by the filthy mess of it: heartbreak, regret, guilt.

Ahmie sighs. "Rodric was the most beautiful baby."

To Georgina's relief, it is Isla's patience that cracks first. "Ahmie, that is enough," Isla snaps.

Their mother looks confused. In the past she might have snapped back. But Ahmie only shoots a dagger look, not at Isla, at Georgina. How unfair it is, but it has always been this way. Georgina shifts uncomfortably, resentfully, on her hard chair. It has been a long time since Georgina fought with Ahmie, and even then it was only bickering. Isla and their mother fight like alley cats. They're fearsome together. And yet they love each other just as fiercely. Theirs is a love Georgina has never experienced, not with her mother. Isla is not entirely to blame for the fighting; Ahmie is increasingly testy. But all this Roddy chatter today is more than just tiresome; it's upsetting. They loved Roddy and they miss him. Worship his memory the way their mother does, they do not. Georgina stands but doesn't move from the room. She'll ask Victor if Isla can come and stay with them. This is no place for her to recover.

Ahmie is in a sulk now. She'll be silent—punishing someone—until she forgets why. The slight flush of pink in Isla's cheeks is undoubtedly some of her hellfire returning. Georgina decides it's safe to leave her alone with Ahmie while she makes a pot of tea. She wants this leak of disquiet in her chest to dry up. Gin will help.

In the kitchen, bent in front of the Hoosier cabinet, a thought comes, gentle as a kiss: Isla isn't still heartbroken about Roddy. Isla has just never forgiven him for going to war. It doesn't matter that it was the flu that killed him; Isla blames the flu on the war too. It's not heartache that Isla wins at. It's unforgiveness. An enduring rage of it.

Georgina pours three cups of tea and adds a slug of gin to hers and Isla's and returns to the front room with the teacups on a tray. Her sister takes one, sips. The movement of her lips is almost too small to recognize as a smile.

When they collected her from the hospital on Saturday, Llewellyn and Victor wrapped Isla in a greenish-yellow car rug and tucked her between Harriet and Morag in the back seat of Victor's automobile. At home, on the street out front, it seemed as though the men were planning on carrying her from the car, fireman style, still bundled in the ridiculous blanket. 'For God's sake, I look like a banana slug,' Isla said, making everyone laugh. 'And I can walk. I'm not a corpse.'

The laughter turned nervous at that. If only Isla knew how familiar they all are with her as a near corpse.

For the past three days, Georgina is beginning to understand, they've been overdoing everything: Did Isla want tea, buttered toast, broth? A coddled egg? Should someone make biscuits? Yes. Is there any blackberry jam left? Yes. Was Isla warm enough? Yes. Too hot? No. Where should Isla sleep? Who would keep watch over Isla? Shhh. Today, calm has descended. The others are elsewhere, for now. Georgina is content to be here, alone with Isla. And Ahmie.

Isla has been fired. A letter from the Westcotts was delivered by hand yesterday as if there were some special telegraph system out there in the city that had informed her employers that Isla was finally home. *We thank you for your years of service, however* . . . 'Lovely timing' was all Isla said, tossing the letter aside. Georgina read it and was furious: a fine send-off from the people Isla has served for five years and whose sons she has known—and loved—since they were infants. Wasn't it? Wasn't it? Isla only sighed. 'I'll find myself a better job,' she said. She asked Lim, the man who brought the note, what news he had of the Westcott boys, Jamie and little Will. 'They are sad,' he said, his face grim. 'They miss you. I will miss you too,' Lim said. 'Farewell,' Isla shouted from the porch as he left. Farewell. Fare well? How would Lim ever fare well? Georgina thought, watching him go.

Yesterday, after Lim left, Victor had leapt on his little soapbox, ranting about how it was incomprehensible that the Liberal prime minister had not yet stopped the tide of Oriental immigration given that everyone—businessmen, trade unionists, veterans, even the clergy—were all in agreement: it should end. Stop the tide? Georgina shakes her head. Talk to the moon about that. Standing at the window now, she wishes she had Isla's courage; Isla had told him to shut up.

Georgina hears a car pull up out front, then Flore's laughter. She pulls aside the curtain in time to see Harriet reach for

Flore's hand. Flore lifts it to her mouth, lets it drop. Flore, in a dress, and Harriet, in a pair of dungarees Georgina has never seen on her before, burst in. The ridiculous little dog Harriet has adopted is hot on their heels. Aren't they a triad of excitement. And isn't Harriet making quite the day of it, after complaining about having to ask for time off at work. Flore goes directly to Isla and perches on the edge of the settee. The dog does a round of the room then girds its loins in front of Ahmie, ready to leap, obviously in hope of a warm lap. Ahmie gives it a sharp kick and it skulks under the settee. There, beneath Isla's feet, it fixes Ahmie with its droop-eyed stare, either indignant or curious, Georgina would be hard-pressed to tell.

"The others are right behind us. We passed them at the corner," Harriet says, hands in her pants pockets, just like a boy, and barely suppressing a smile.

Harriet's birth is Georgina's earliest recollection. If, at seven, they'd spared her the experience of listening outside the door while her mother panted and swore and screamed, it might not have usurped every other childhood memory Georgina had. The cause of her mother's pain, this babe, dark-eyed, red, lying like a smug conqueror in her exhausted arms. Georgina was supposed to love her. Even when, at nine or ten, Harriet became the spitting image of their father with her tomboy posture, that little swagger they shared that everyone so loved, Georgina found it difficult.

And speaking of conquerors: Victor, sweeping in, tips his chin at her, as if that is greeting enough. Georgina sighs. Not for the first time she wonders whether his parents recognized something in him as he lay as yet unnamed in the bassinette, or whether he rose to the destiny of someone saddled with a name of the defeater of rivals. She gets up to open a window, despite the drear outside, and opens the door instead to Llewellyn and Morag. She can't help herself; she scans Morag's belly for evidence of what is growing inside her. Nothing yet, really. She lets them pass and stands for a moment in the open doorway, leaning against the frame, taking a breath of the rain-scented air. The damned gin's not having the desired effect. A few of them crab at her: 'Shut the door, Georgina.' They can all go to hell.

The coroner's man will arrive at one o'clock. During lunch, without consulting Isla, they argue over whether she should be present at the interrogation. The argument is fierce, the split predictable: Morag and Victor against (it will be too upsetting for Isla); Flore, Georgina, Harriet all for her presence (how else will she defend herself). Isla smiles, listening, as enigmatic as a cat. Llewellyn is strangely mute, Georgina notes. Ahmie, rambling about undecipherable things, is, wisely, ignored.

Just before the hour strikes one, Isla rises and wraps the blanket around her shoulders. "He'll need somewhere to sit. Georgina, I'd like another one of those teas you gave me earlier. I'll be in my room."

Llewellyn stands and makes to follow Isla. Georgina needles him out of the way.

In her bedroom, Isla takes the teacup from Georgina's hands and tells her to leave the door ajar. "I want to hear," she says.

The man, who arrives at one sharp with Andrew Morrison, should be a florist, not a coroner. He has huge blue eyes that are dewy and soft, with black lashes fit for a girl. His hands are long and thin, tanned as the rest of him. A tennis player, no doubt, thinks Georgina. He has the jaw of a movie star. He's young. Too young, surely, to already be a doctor? Mr. Morrison introduces him: Dr. Emerson-Gray. There is some confusion as to whether Emerson is his first name. This is clarified by Mr. Morrison. The coroner's man is double-barrelled. He shakes hands with the men, nods at the women, as does Andrew Morrison. He has, Georgina notes, removed his hat.

She imagines him to be the trustworthy kind of man whose mouth might produce poetry. Until he opens it. How deceiving those red, angel-carved lips; Dr. Emerson-Gray is an unflinching man who clearly imagines himself to be in the company of inferiors.

"I am working on the assumption that you will cooperate in helping me find out who put your sister in this compromising situation. That is a given. If you are all as forthcoming as my friend Mr. Morrison suggests you are, we'll soon sort it all out." Dr. Emerson-Gray takes a quick look around the room and into the kitchen. "Might I have a chair?" he asks.

Kitchen chairs are brought, though not enough for everyone. Georgina imagines her mother's house through the doctor's eyes. She sees him eyeing the tawdry, mismatched furniture, the ratty rug, the kitchen Hoosier they hauled from Isla's employer's when they were done with it, to replace an even older one. When he intently looks her way, she drops her gaze, feeling as tawdry as the rest of it and hoping he's not a mind reader. It was a mistake to allow him to come to this house. They should have set the meeting at her and Victor's home. Or not permitted the meeting at all.

Dr. Emerson-Gray takes the chair Mr. Morrison offers him and, after a moment's hesitation, places it in a spot that must be to his liking, opposite Ahmie. Mr. Morrison lowers his frame onto another kitchen chair he has placed just to the left of Dr. Emerson-Gray, then moves a few inches farther away. The rest of them form a semicircle across from him, Morag, Harriet, and Georgina squeezed side by side on the settee, Flore standing at the kitchen door, Llewellyn on another chair that Flore has refused. Georgina is not surprised when Victor places himself slightly behind the coroner's man, standing, as though he is on the opposing team.

The coroner's man speaks as if they are in a classroom, not a crowded parlour, and as though, Georgina thinks, they are children. "We'll first determine who is responsible for your sister's condition, the father of her child, as well as the abortionist. Both can be charged under the law." He pulls a notebook and pencil from an inside pocket of his jacket with a dramatic flourish. "Of those present, who actually lives in this house?"

A hand is raised in a tentative schoolgirl's gesture. Georgina experiences a pang of tenderness for her youngest sister as the doctor swivels on his chair, away from Ahmie, to point his knees at her.

"This is Harriet-Jean McKenzie, the youngest," Mr. Morrison says in a low tone, bending near to the coroner.

"Hello, Harriet-Jean. I'll get straight to the point: Does your sister have a sweetheart? Someone with whom she was having sexual relations?"

Georgina looks over at Llewellyn, who has made an odd, strangled sound. "Good Lord," she says. Morag has spared her the necessity of putting her arm around Harriet, but she already would like to shove the man off his chair and show him the door.

Harriet's eyes widen. "Isla?"

The coroner's man looks around the room then back at Harriet. "Yes, Isla."

"Not that I know of," Harriet says.

The man taps his notebook. "I believe she has been involved in various labour and protest movements."

Harriet glances over her shoulder at Flore.

"Why would you need to know this?" Flore says.

Dr. Emerson-Gray apparently doesn't need an answer. "Was someone from one of these organizations courting your sister? Would you call Isla a good-time girl?"

"What do you mean?"

"Well, is she a girl who likes to offer a kiss or two, or something more, in exchange for a drink or a dinner out?"

Llewellyn clears his throat. "What kind of question is that?"

"I am simply trying to get to the character of your sister, Harriet-Jean," the coroner's man says, then regards Llewellyn with a quizzical look.

"Do you and your sister go out on dates together? With men?" he asks, and when Harriet hesitates, he adds: "You, too, could go to jail, Miss McKenzie, for not answering honestly. Tell me the God's truth. With whom was your sister having sexual relations?"

Llewellyn stands up. "For God's sake, man."

Harriet turns scarlet. "With whom?" she repeats.

Georgina sees the doctor and Llewellyn exchange an odd look. The doctor frowns then carries on: "Had she talked to you about her delayed menstruation? Do you know this word?"

"No. Yes."

The doctor cocks his head. "How could you not have known, sharing a small flat such as this one, that your sister was pregnant?"

"Isla has her own room?" Harriet says.

"So, you were completely unaware that she planned to rid herself of her troubles by employing an abortionist."

"I was. I didn't know she was pregnant."

"Did you see abortifacients in the house, of any sort?" He turns the pages in his notebook and reads: "Excessive amounts of alcohol? Herbs or concoctions? A rubber catheter? Anything unusual?"

Georgina stands, thinking of the empty gin bottles at the back of the Hoosier cupboard.

"I expect that one of you cared for your sister when she came home after her abortion."

Georgina says, "The first we saw of Isla was in the hospital. After—"

"Please speak only when you are spoken to," the coroner's man says in an overly calm voice. He turns back to Harriet. "So, you did not see her at home."

"No. She didn't come home for supper the night before we found her in the hospital."

"Where were you that night that you didn't care enough to see that your sister had not even returned home to her bed?"

"I was with friends, at a dance."

"A dance. And you didn't see her in the morning?"

"I've already told you, I didn't. Isla didn't come home for supper, but I didn't know she wasn't home when I got home, or the next morning. Not until the boy came with the note from the hospital."

"Who is the man who brought her in? A friend of the family?"

"How should I know?" Harriet says. "We've been told a man carried her from Stanley Park, but nothing more than that. He must not have told the hospital his name or you would know it, wouldn't you?"

"Don't be insolent, girl."

Harriet looks astonished. "I'm not being insolent, sir. I am just telling you the truth."

Dr. Emerson-Gray stands, as if to pace, though it is immediately clear that there is no room for that. He circles around and places his hands on the back of his chair. Victor moves back, just a step or two. The dog emerges from under the settee and sniffs at the man's trousers. Georgina watches as the man's expression softens. He makes a clucking noise that seems completely out of character, and bends and fondles Rue's ears as gently as if he were in love. When he rises he composes his face and says, "I'd like to speak directly with Isla."

"Isla is sleeping," Morag says, rising from the settee.

"Can't we wake her?" Llewellyn says.

"No," says Morag, looking daggers at her husband, "we cannot."

"One of you must know the name of the person who aborted Isla's baby?" Dr. Emerson-Gray says.

Georgina's mouth drops open. Does the man think they will suddenly admit they know everything? No one speaks. No one even shakes their head.

"And not one of you can tell me the name of the father."

Morag answers for them all. "No. Because we do not know who the good-for-nothing is."

Mr. Morrison stands. "Is Mrs. Maria Veltri a friend of yours?" He looks from Harriet to Morag to Georgina. The coroner's man looks confused.

"Who is Maria Veltri?" Georgina asks.

"A dead woman," says Mr. Morrison.

Dr. Emerson-Gray starts to speak, but Mr. Morrison interrupts. "We believe Mrs. Veltri and several others died by the same hand—that of whoever did this to your sister."

This? Georgina meets Andrew Morrison's gaze with a steely version of her own.

"Well," Dr. Emerson-Gray says dramatically. "Hasn't this been a waste of my time." He tucks his notepad back into his jacket and puts on his hat. To Ahmie he says, "One needs cooperation to move forward with an inquest, and I am not finding any such thing here."

Ahmie starts and glares up at him.

"Well then, there's the door. You may as well make use of it," says Morag.

Georgina could kiss her sister. She goes to the door and opens it. The doctor, followed by Victor, Llewellyn, and the righteous Mr. Morrison step outside. She notes, with pleasure, that it is raining so hard that the raindrops are bouncing off the sidewalk. She closes the door and turns the lock.

"He must be as popular as a skunk at a garden party," Ahmie says. For a moment she smiles up at her daughters, and Georgina loves the look of complicity in her eyes.

Morag bursts into laughter and bends to hug their mother.

From the bedroom Georgina hears the sound of Isla laughing too.

ISLA

A skunk at a garden party. We laughed. The old fire obviously still burned bright somewhere in our mother.

I remember that day . . .

Morag flops onto my bed. 'What a creep.' She picks at the counterpane. 'Handsome though. Movie-star handsome,' she says, grinning. Classic Morag. My shameless sister. Practically batting her eyelashes.

'Was he?' I tease, and pinch her. 'You're married, sister.' A pinch in my own heart.

Morag laughs, blows on her hand, and fans her face. 'Yes. But really creepy,' she says.

Georgina stands, sober-faced at the door, her shoulder against the jamb. Classic Georgina. Angry ambivalence. Which will it be, lady? In or out?

Why in hell's name was this bloody Emerson-Gray here, she wants to know. Then she says what she has already said, many times: 'An inquest is for the dead.'

Dead. *Dead.*

'Llew says not always,' Morag says. 'Llew says an inquest can be held to help find the person who . . .' And her bright expression fades. Has she just been reminded of why I am lying in bed, scrawny as a backyard hen? I can see it in her eyes. She'll only ever half forgive me. There'll always be the tiny hard uncomprehending rattle of a stone in her heart. But she puts a warm hand on my arm and her eyes have gone tender and Do you remember, I want to say, but I can't remember what I want her to remember. My sister, this beautiful dark rose. God forbid she ever know the enormity of the forgiveness I'd have to ask of her. Beg of her.

Georgina makes a face. She has her doubts about Llewellyn's explanations, as do I. 'Hogwash,' she says. 'I don't believe him. Does anyone know Maria Veltri?' she asks, invoking the sudden, searing image of this dead stranger lying in the same place I had, her stockings around her ankles, her purse at a tidy angle on the bed. Someone knew Maria Veltri. Someone loved her.

Morag shakes her head.

Georgina comes in—doesn't sit, but stands, the skeptic at the end of the bed. 'Isla's not dead and—'

I close my eyes, exhausted beyond measure. *Isla's not dead, and.* And?

I imagine the quiet of the grave, although it is not really death I want. I want the peace of the hospital ward; there, despite its ceaseless rattle, I could pull those clean white sheets up over my head and be ignored. I am aware of the irony—hospital as sanctuary. It is not. But here, oh, the endless hovering. It's unbearable. For three nights, Georgina has slept on a chair at the foot of my bed. I've lost count of the worried glances exchanged across my bed, over my body. And the number of cups of tea I've been offered; legion—necessitating endless trips to the privy. A sailor could drown in the gallons of pee I am producing.

I lie there, wishing them all away. Them, their worries, their suspicions, anger, judgement, pity, and confusion—and their cups of tea. And then, suddenly, I am aware of the deathly silence in the room. Everyone must be holding their breath. A hand takes firm hold of one of my feet. I open my eyes. It's Georgina, checking, surely, to see that I am still alive. Harriet makes a sound; her eyes are big as walnuts. I hold out my arms and she falls into them. She presses her mouth against my shoulder to stifle her sobs. Why won't I tell, she wants to know. Everyone wants to know: Why? Flore combs her hand through Harriet's hair, tucking a lock of it again and again behind my sister's ear as she weeps. It may as well be my own ear, so comforting is the gesture.

There is nothing to tell. I say this, but it's not what I mean. I say that I don't know who he is, that I don't know where he took me, or where to look for him. I mean that I don't want to look for him because I don't want to find him. Because I cannot bear the thought of— What? Seeing his face, hearing his voice? No. *Smelling* him.

Harriet sits up and wipes her nose with the back of her hand; sorrow has bruised her face. She cannot understand. 'But he's killed people,' she says.

And I am standing on the street corner, watching him give me that tip of his hat before he drives away, leaving me, intentionally or not, to die.

I hear Flore promising my little sister—because I am not, because I cannot—that we will find him. That we'll stop him from ever hurting another woman. Soon, no woman will ever again have to go through what I went through, she says. Change is coming, she promises. Change is coming. I feel the conviction, and the anger, in Flore's voice; she is so convincing.

'Why are women so angry?' Victor once asked Georgina. I smile at Georgina, remembering her telling me. Her face that day, her tired laughter, and the despondency in her eyes, not as hidden as she thought.

Then I smile at Flore. I want to believe her. But mostly I just want the world to spin on as before. Harriet and I will play baseball again on Sunday mornings. I'll meet Flore for coffee and march with her in labour rallies, see Morag's pregnancy bloom, dish the dirt with Georgina about her upper-class women's group and her tiresome husband. I'll stain my fingers and the kitchen counter purple making blackberry jam with Ahmie. Wash the floors and scrub the toilets and sweep the floors at some rich person's house, forever if need be. And not love Llewellyn. *Not love Llewellyn.*

On the floor, Harriet's little dog—ignored too long it seems—utters a string of short high-pitched howls, a perfect reflection of the feelings in the room. I want what Rue wants: Indulge me, please. Let me lie about, moaning and whimpering, weeping and howling, just for a while, until I have let it all out. And while I'm at it, for heaven's sake, someone, just rub my damn belly.

Georgina doesn't like Rue, though I'm not sure why; she has never been averse to animals, even dead ones. Morag has to pick the wee beastie up and Georgina gives an Ahmie-like cluck of disgust as Morag puts the dog on the bed. Rue gives her a doleful look (true: Rue's looks are always doleful) and makes her way across the bed, stepping gingerly over me, to get to Harriet. Does Rue love Harriet best? Or does Rue know that Harriet needs her most. Or is it just that Harriet is the one who feeds Rue? My sister lies back beside me and the dog climbs onto her belly. She puts her grey muzzle on Harriet's breastbone and, with a shuddering sigh, closes her eyes.

Ahmie appears then, at the bedroom door. Though she is tall, she looks tiny, hovering there in her antique dress, like some apparition, thin and lost and old. My heart swells with love for her.

'What is it, Ahmie?' Georgina says, going to her.

I don't hear Ahmie's reply, but Morag leaps up.

'What did she say?' I ask Harriet.

Harriet heaves a sigh and slides Rue off her chest onto the bed beside me. 'Probably Rue threw up somewhere.' She rises, smiles at Flore, and I witness her sliding a hand across Flore's back as she leaves.

Rue stretches and regards me with an indignant curiosity that makes me laugh, then puts her snout down on the bed again and closes her eyes. Flore comes and sits beside me. She strokes my arm. She strokes the dog.

'I'm glad you're home,' she tells me.

I lie: 'Me too.'

She asks me if I'd like a cup of tea.

It was cold the night I first set eyes on Flore. The fifth of February. It was still winter and the gods had decided to drop both snow and rain on us, but I'd seen in the *Western Clarion* that Vancouver Local No. 1 was hosting a propaganda meeting at the Royal Theatre at which one J.D. Harrington would be giving a lecture—Revolution and Counter-Revolution in Early Peru—and I was curious. I'd found a place to sit and was taking off my coat when a woman in a yellow hat and a pink scarf entered the room and took a seat in the front row. At propaganda meetings at the Royal Theatre, women did not normally appear in the crowd of greys and navy blues and sit, like a bouquet of flowers, in the front row. Women generally sat toward the back of the crowd. There are a few more of us now, and we've dared move closer to the front, but we were so few then. And we were most certainly not daffodils or azaleas or fully bloomed roses, as this woman was. She took her seat and the men around her hunched left or right, away from her, toward one another, turning to matters of much greater importance than the rose growing in their row. She flung her long blond braid—rather unfashionable but somehow defiantly so—over her shoulder, and all my fervent young men friends were suddenly as old and rumpled as their fathers' caps.

At the break, while the women served coffee, the woman in yellow and pink fell into an argument with one of the organizers. He offered her a smile and condemned her with it: *She's too well dressed to be behind the cause. Look at her shoes. Is that scarf silk? How did she come by that fancy coat?* 'I don't know what they do in San Francisco,' I overheard him say, 'but here we—' And the flower woman gave him his smile back and shredded his argument as effortlessly as she might a chunk of cheddar cheese: 'What about women? Imagine thinking you'll bring about the emancipation of the human race when you're only concerned with one half of it? Not to mention your exclusion of Asian workers. You don't want them undermining the unions with cheap labour, but you won't let them unionize. It's completely illogical. To quote a friend: *There is no alien but the capitalist.*'

I had no idea until then that I was just waiting for a woman of this sort to turn up in my life.

I found the courage to introduce myself. The woman had, it turned out, a name that matched her hat and scarf: Flore Rozema.

Within a week of meeting her, I had decided that emulating Flore in every way possible was the only path to a truly fulfilling life. And because Flore drinks coffee, not tea, I tried to pick up the taste for that bitter dark bean. I tried hard. But coffee and I are not a happy match; heart palpitations, indigestion, the list goes on. And so, I stick to my milky cups of tea. She'd laugh if she knew I still imagine myself a disappointment in her eyes—an inexperienced, provincial, small-minded tea drinker. Hero-worshipping? Guilty as charged. Just a wee bit though. Vicarious living? Probably more that than anything else.

'Do you want a cup of tea?' Flore asks again.

'Yes, but Georgina's recipe please,' I say.

Flore smiles. 'Georgina's recipe? You mean gin in a teacup then? A little early in the day, but coming right up.' She pats my hand and moves toward the door.

'Flore,' I say. She doesn't turn. Perhaps she knows what I am going to say. Perhaps she expects it. 'Don't break her heart.' I see her head drop forward, a small nod, and she goes off to the kitchen.

Rue lifts her head and she narrows her eyes and regards me with what can only be profound suspicion.

'What?' I say, and I squint back at her.

That was summer. The mid-point of it. Flore and Georgina and Harriet wanted justice. Llewellyn wanted revenge. I wanted them all to go away. My desire for any kind of just deserts for the man who had nearly killed me took weeks to surface and, even then, it had work to do. It had to push up through my fatigue. It had to obliterate my need to forget.

RUE

A curious notion, a skunk at a garden party. Though the others laughed and the one called Ahmie looked pleased with herself, I could not see how the black-and-white scourge I came nose-to-nose with twice during my days of starvation in the park could be the cause of such hilarity. The stink of them. True, the guise of the beaver with its long orange teeth is more hideous than that of the sweet-faced, myopic-looking skunk, but I would rather meet the former than the latter in a dark alley any day.

The one called Isla was unhealthily coloured for a human. She was like a four-day-old bruise, the kind I occasionally saw on Rasia's arms. I was not certain that my presence next to her on the bed was pleasing to her. Twice, her fingers touched my thigh, the tap-tap, perhaps, of one not particularly well acquainted with dogs. I lay still, waiting to determine whether this was, at least, a gesture of curiosity, if not friendship. But her hand lay still, too, and I took my cue.

(I made a note to myself from my aging knees: it was a long way to the floor from atop Isla's bed.)

The one-armed one named Victor, with whom the sister Georgina was obviously in an unhappy alliance (The man cleans his ears with the dull end of bobby pins. Publicly. What more need I say?) had to be let in out of the rain. He was followed into the salon by the sad-eyed one they call Llewellyn..

Victor the one-armed has stammering speech. I have met a few stammerers in my lifetime, but none so many as the ex-soldiers who called on Rasia after the Great War (such an odd name for an armed conflict where, from all overheard reports, men in one uniform are hellbent on the death of men in another). A psychological wound—shell shock, Rasia called it. (I abashedly admit: until she explained further, I paid careful attention to where I placed my feet when walking with Rasia on the shell-strewn beaches near our abode, lest I be shocked.) When these stammering men left Rasia's bedroom, she often pressed the money they had placed on the table back into their hands. Only the nice ones, she promised me, as we cuddled later. The nice ones, I presumed, were those I had heard weeping in her bedroom, most assuredly in her arms. I do not think Rasia would have pressed money back into Victor's hands.

'Do you suppose she could have been violated? Raped?' Victor inquired.

In the salon, the silence was absolute; in fact, I shook my head, fancying the sudden onset of deafness.

Victor spoke again; the man was most certainly inept that day at reading the cues: 'It could have been someone at one of the political organizations she's so f-f-fond of supporting. Or'—and he said this slyly, as if he had received a tip on a horse that was sure to place at the Hastings Park races—'that houseboy at the Westcotts. If it had been him, I'd find this abortion of hers so much easier to forgive.'

Call me an opportunist: in the furious mêlée that ensued, I found myself a warm spot upon the settee.

WEDNESDAY, AUGUST 2

Half past six in the morning

"Is this it?" Llewellyn steps toward the door, unsure. The building is anarchic, not particularly old, but already tilting. This second-floor hallway reeks of cooking. And of what must be a communal privy.

Morrison nods. "Yes. Apartment 2B. How did you find out about him?" he says, almost in a whisper. He stands back, as if expecting something violent to rage out the door.

"I asked around. People like to talk," Llewellyn says. "It sounds like he's been playing husband to Mrs. Veltri for quite some time."

"Well, let's do it then, shall we?" Morrison steps in front of him and knocks. Officious, but still soft enough to be polite. It is so early in the morning.

Down the corridor, a door opens, a head emerges and quickly withdraws. There are disgruntled thumps from the room across the hall. A dog barks. Someone yells *shut up*. Watery sunlight filters through a small window at the east end of the building. It illuminates nothing but the dark poverty of this place. Llewellyn's pulse is a thud in his temples and he feels sick to his stomach, again. He puts his ear to the door. "I can hear something. He's in there."

Morrison knocks again, a little harder this time. "Give him a minute, Llewellyn. It's early."

It is Llewellyn's self-doubt that sparks the violence: enraged by his uncertainty, he slams his shoulder against the door. The frame splinters. In a second, he's in the room. And there he stops, a brutal intruder, for here is a scene of quiet domesticity: A small kitchen table. Bowls of porridge. Bread. Butter. Jam. Three children, one of them in a high chair, the other two clasping cups of milk. They have milk moustaches, for God's sake.

The man at the table, rising cautiously, reaches for the baby, whose face goes red and then opens in a piercing shriek.

"Who are you?" the man says. He puts his hand on a knife on the table, beside a loaf of bread, but leaves it where it lies.

The girl sits frozen. The other child, a boy, slides off his chair and runs to grip the man's leg.

"Gianluca Padula?" Llewellyn says. He had hoped to sound commanding.

"Yes."

"Whose children are these?" Llewellyn asks. He knows already whose children they are. Why hadn't he counted on them being here? If Morrison were not standing stiff as a ready hunting dog behind him, Llewellyn would back out the door. Apologize and flee. He wants to be lying on his back in a rowboat, Isla beside him, gazing up at the stars, drifting, nothing more than that.

The man shifts the baby so that it is facing away from the strangers. It continues to twist toward them, screaming. "They are the children of my . . ." He stops. He looks at the girl, still as stone across the table, then down at the boy pressed against his thigh.

Llewellyn sees the boy's pointed little shoulder blades shaking beneath his nightshirt, and he is felled by regret. Their grief—the man's, the children's. His own.

". . . the children of my friend," Gianluca says.

"Was your friend Maria Veltri?" Morrison asks.

"Yes. Maria. Why?"

"You are aware she's dead?" Morrison says.

Llewellyn has to lean against the wall as a wave of nausea floods him.

"Yes," Padula says. His eyes fill with tears. "I know Maria is dead. Who are you?" The big man is holding the squalling baby in one arm, stroking the hair of the little boy with his other hand.

Morrison answers: "You need to come down to the police station for questioning."

"You're the police?" Padula scowls at Morrison. "Why? I have to go to work."

The contemptuousness on Padula's face unleashes the rest of Llewellyn's uncertainty. A familiar weight climbs onto his shoulders and perches there, a burden as old as childhood. He needs to sit.

Morrison has taken charge. He is someone's stern father: "Because we think you were involved in the death of Maria Veltri."

"Involved? How so?"

Llewellyn interrupts: "Is there someone to take the children?"

"Maria's mother is coming soon. She stays with the children when I'm at work."

They wait. The baby is calmed, the silence broken only by a few shuddering hiccoughs now and then until eventually even that sound dies away. In the quiet, Llewellyn locks eyes with the child at the table. He hadn't meant to look at the girl. But he has, and she has caught him, a fish on her hook; she has no intention of setting him free. In her eyes: hatred. Why ask a child to spare him? Why should she? She has lost so much. Here is her fish club—fishermen call the damned thing a *priest*—ready to administer the last rites. Let her, Llewellyn thinks. Do it, he wants to tell her. Kill me.

The woman at the open door now is small, her features dark and sharp, a startling stripe of grey at her temple. She comes in, carefully, cautiously, her fingers lingering on the splintered door frame.

"Gianluca?" For a second, the little girl at the table shifts her gaze, but it is too late for Llewellyn; she has already destroyed him. She stands and moves toward her grandmother, all the while sure, Llewellyn knows, of his terrible slow fall.

Padula speaks to the woman in Italian.

"Speak English," Morrison says.

"She doesn't speak English," Padula says, with just enough derision to bring a flush of red up Morrison's jaw. Padula continues in Italian, calmly handing the woman the baby. He says something to the children and rubs the little boy's head again and takes the girl's chin in his fingers. She nods, but her eyes do not soften.

Padula takes the time to button up his shirt over his undershirt and tuck it in. He takes a cap from a peg on the wall. He looks back at the grandmother and the children, touches his lips with two fingers, then walks past Llewellyn and Morrison out the door. He makes a sucking sound with his teeth as he passes through the splintered door frame, glancing at the shards of broken wood.

"It wasn't locked," he says.

Llewellyn raises his hand; he imagines it on Padula's back, shoving him. He feels more than remembers his father's hand hard on his own back and, grey with shame, lets his own drop.

Chief MacIntyre seats himself on the edge of the desk, as always. He does this, Llewellyn knows, so that he and Morrison must look up at him.

"What's this about, Morrison?" the chief asks, his eyes on Gianluca Padula.

"This man seems to have been romantically involved with Mrs. Maria Veltri. The woman who died a few weeks ago. Of an abortion."

The chief addresses Padula. "You're not her husband?"

"No."

"He says her husband left her a couple years back," Morrison clarifies.

"He didn't leave her. He—" Padula starts.

Chief MacIntyre interrupts. "Were you having an intimate friendship with Mrs. Veltri?" He grins.

Padula glares at the chief, but his eyes betray him. Llewellyn can see the thin line of fear etching across them.

"So, the child she was attempting to rid herself of was yours. Were they divorced, she and this husband of hers?" the chief continues.

"Her husband has been missing for nearly two years," Gianluca says.

Morrison's voice is full of judgement: "Had you promised to wed her then? Is that why she had intimate relations with you?"

"Since no one knows if her husband is dead or alive, Maria is still married to Franco," Padula says, calm again. "Was. I would marry her except for that. I would have married her. I don't believe Frankie's coming back. Something must have happened to him. And there's the children. I . . ."

"Frankie? You sound very familiar with her husband," Morrison says.

Irritated by Morrison's incredulity, Llewellyn stands. He crosses his arms then shoves his hands in his pockets.

"Yes, he was my friend," Padula says.

The chief smiles over at Llewellyn. "While the cat's away, eh?"

Llewellyn stares at the chief, expressionless.

Morrison turns back to Padula. "Did you force this woman, your girlfriend, to suffer a miscarriage? Or perhaps it was you who did it for her."

"What?" Padula starts to stand. His face is wracked with revulsion and his eyes are wet. MacIntyre places a hand on the man's shoulder and Padula sits.

"There was another bruise. On her thigh, Chief. The same as we've seen before," Morrison says. "Same as the one on Miss McKenzie and the other girls."

There is an almost imperceptible change in the chief's expression, a small flash in MacIntyre's pale eyes; Llewellyn sees it.

MacIntyre stands. "Let him go," he says. "Unless you've got some kind of proof of his involvement, we can't hold him."

"Chief," Morrison protests.

MacIntyre smacks the desk with the flat of his hand. He smiles. "You're free to go, Mr. Padula."

"But the bruise. It's the sixth we've seen," Morrison says, standing now too.

"It's nothing. Maybe bruises happen easily. You know, all that fussing around down there." The chief waggles his hand at crotch level, and Morrison goes red.

"This man must know something," Llewellyn says.

"He might. He might not. You know where he lives. If you need him again, you can find him. Good day, Mr. Padula."

Llewellyn blocks Padula's way. "Chief, I'd—"

"I said leave it, for God's sake," MacIntyre says.

Llewellyn pulls open the drawer of his desk and slams it shut again, thinking of the look Padula gave him as he went out the door. Pain all wrapped up in anger. He clasps his hands around the back of his neck, at the base of his skull, and pulls down for the stretch. His head aches. When he looks up, Morrison is standing in front of his desk, that alert hunting hound again, obviously disappointed. His long arms dangle at his sides.

"The coroner wasn't able to get much information out of your family, was he?" Morrison says, frowning.

"Who?"

"Emerson-Gray, the fellow from the coroner's office."

Llewellyn can't help the laugh. It's bitter.

"Something funny?" Morrison says, smiling too.

Llewellyn gets up. "No. No, he didn't," he says. "Maybe there's nothing more to get."

"That, I cannot believe."

Llewellyn looks up into Morrison's indignant face. "No?" He pulls on his jacket. He needs to have a word with Bill Hogarth.

SUNDAY, AUGUST 6

8:10 a.m.

Eyes closed, ears pricked, lying on her messily made bed, Harriet strains to hear what is going on in Isla's bedroom. Twenty frustrating minutes. And now, her guilty conscience, which has been mounting by the second, finally peaks. She slides off the bed and dresses for the baseball game. What in the world is Llewellyn doing in there? She lingers by Isla's door for a moment, and the voices go silent. (Georgina would say *It's none of your beeswax, Harriet-Jean*. The hypocrite.) She tiptoes quietly into the front room, taking her frustration with her. She peers into her mother's bedroom. Rue is asleep, stretched across Ahmie's belly. Though Ahmie's eyes are shut, she must sense Harriet's presence; her arms tighten around the dog. It's ridiculous how completely they've taken to one another in the past week, Ahmie and Rue. Isla even calls them Rhumie. Harriet-Jean is almost jealous.

She pries away her mother's hands and lifts the warm, sleepy dog into her own arms, sniffing at Rue's soft neck. Her mother makes a disgruntled noise but lets the animal go. Outside, an early morning breeze, still cool, softly billows the sheets left overnight on the clothesline. It ruffles Harriet's hair and Rue's ears too. Autumn is coming. She puts Rue down and sprinkles a handful of seed for the chickens and tips a pail of kitchen scraps into their new, makeshift enclosure. The pen, built by Harriet and Flore, was necessitated by Rue, who has proven untrustworthy where chickens are concerned. The hens race at the offering, fighting over the potato skins, carrot and parsnip parings, and an apple core. Not so appealing, it seems, are the cabbage leaves, or a few mushed and moulding blackberries. Harriet is not surprised to see some crushed eggshells stuck to the bottom of the pail. Ahmie doesn't like to give the chickens eggshells. She says it's impolite to give them back the remains of their own production. But Isla says the shells are good for them, calcium or something or other, so she sneaks them into the pail, often hidden in cabbage leaves. Harriet explains all this to Rue who seems to be listening with at least half an ear. Harriet gives the pail a whack against the fencepost and flakes of white and brown shell drop onto the ground around the birds. Snow.

"Strange creatures, aren't they?" Harriet says, as she and Rue watch the hens peck alternately at the shells and at each other.

Harriet's curiosity feels like the strongman at the Pacific National Exhibition. He's twisting her arm: *Would there*, he asks, *really be any harm in crouching beneath Isla's window for a minute or two? It's open, isn't it?* The strongman loses the arm-wrestle, but barely. Harriet ties the rope to Rue's collar and they go out the back gate. She doesn't want to contemplate what Morag would have to say about Llewellyn being in Isla's room so early on a Sunday morning. She doesn't want to contemplate Llewellyn being in Isla's room at all. It has already laid the annoying burden of a secret on Harriet's shoulders.

Morag used to listen to Ahmie and Pa's conversations through their bedroom wall in the old house on Keefer Street. She used a drinking glass, rim pressed to the wall, ear pressed to the glass's bottom. She swore she could hear everything. Ten-year-old Harriet pretended along, reporting conversations between her parents much more preposterous than any of Morag's tales, though she'd never really heard anything more than the muffled murmur of Ahmie saying Pa's name and Pa saying Ahmie's. And she was forced to block the memory of the time she hid in their bedroom wardrobe and heard noises—sighs and whispers and moans—she never wanted to hear made again. This morning, she could hear the argumentative tone of Isla's and Llewellyn's voices. One needn't put a glass against the wall to hear that.

In the laneway, she decides to let Rue choose the direction they'll take. She drops the rope leash, and the dog wanders across the lane to sniff at a pile of abandoned cogs rusting in the weeds. Rue half squats and half lifts her leg to pee on them.

"You're not supposed to lift your leg, girlie. You're not a boy dog."

Rue tilts her grey chin at her and cocks her head as if to say *What in the world are you talking about?*

The dog turns left. Harriet smiles. Flore's is left. "Who's a good girl," Harriet says.

Ahead, up the lane, there's a gang of children so hobo-like Harriet can't tell whether they are boys or girls. They're coming her way, armed with arrows held high over their heads. Their weapons, Harriet sees as they come closer, are giant fern stalks, trimmed to a few feathery green fronds at one end, their points sharpened with someone's pocket knife at the other. Harriet's father used to make her fern arrows like this; she'd traipsed with her friends through alleyways in the East End, just like these children. *Guttersnipes*, Pa affectionately called Harriet and her friends. Harriet laughs, imagining that some of their neighbours might have been frightened of her little gang. Though there are some gangs, made up of older boys, that are best avoided, the members of this grubby troop are not old enough to be feared.

Rue barks and rushes forward. The children drop their arrows and swarm the dog, ignoring Harriet. Rue rolls on her back in the dirt then flattens onto her belly and snuffles at their dirty hands and knees. Then suddenly, though Rue hasn't, they've had enough. At the command of one of them, the children grab their arrows and, hoisting them aloft, race off down the laneway, a flock of dusty crows. Rue canters after them on her stiff legs.

Harriet steps on Rue's trailing leash. "Oh no you don't. This way, unfaithful beast."

What a day: The wild children. The beautiful coppery colour of the rusted cogs. The sky, still cock-crow blue. The dandelions, both yellow-headed and gone to seed. Pink-tinged bindweed, purple thistle, a small patch of blackberries. She picks a handful of berries for Flore, then eats them, one by one, swearing she will not eat another as she puts the next into her mouth. Flore won't know, she thinks, until she looks at her stained-purple palm. How in love is she? "Oh, let me count the ways," she says aloud to the last blackberry, kissing it first then popping it into her mouth.

"We are all slaves to the capitalist system."

Harriet lets Flore talk; she herself is concentrating on undoing the tiny buttons on Flore's blouse.

"An article in the *Western Clarion* said that . . ."

Harriet knows the *Clarion.* It's the Socialist Party's paper. Isla brings it home from time to time. Another button.

"In Winnipeg at the general strike, all they wanted to do," Flore says, "was improve working conditions. Collective bargaining. Unions. The strike wasn't about fomenting a bloody revolution! Though one is due across the whole country, if you ask me. It was about making life better for the workers. A share of the means of production. And here we are, three years later, and what has changed?"

Flore looks down. Harriet sees her notice, finally, that she is down to the last button.

"Oh, you're insatiable," she says. Her eyes, still hard with indignation, soften a little.

"And you're lovely. All these words when all I want is to see your beautiful breasts and—"

"God, what have I engendered?" Flore laughs then sighs and opens her blouse herself, slipping it off her shoulders. "Conspiracy to overthrow the government! Such bunk. The 'Hello Girls'—the damn telephone operators, for God's sake—walked out. Those women, revolutionary conspirators. Ha! It was revolutionary, but . . . Oh, Harriet, when I think that while we are just sitting here, across this country and around the world there are atrocities happening that we will never know about, I just . . . How can we dance? How can we laugh or find anything funny?"

Harriet kisses her midriff, and Flore rests her hands on the back of Harriet's head, pressing it to her and holding it still for a moment. In a while, when Harriet thinks that Flore might have moved on to less weighty thoughts, she lifts her head and kisses her ribs.

"I almost cannot bear it," Flore says.

After, Flore, lying with her head on Harriet's shoulder, her hand tracing patterns on Harriet's belly—hieroglyphs, Harriet thinks—interrupts the sweet silence: "Do you ever think about children? Having children, I mean?"

Harriet sweeps her left hand back and forth across the Persian carpet, erasing the flutter of hearts she's been carving in its soft plush.

No rises to her lips, but she stops it there.

She tries to blink away the memory that lurches up of the baby she'd minded for a neighbour woman when she was twelve or thirteen, his bulging eyes, poppy-red face, screaming and soaked through to his nightie. They'd left no clean diapers, no bottle, no pacifier. He'd wailed until, rattled to her bones, she gave up trying to soothe him and simply drew the curtain between the bassinette and the rest of the room and put her fingers in her ears. She waited, weeping herself, for the mother to come home. All that for a penny and a wet kiss from the drunken husband.

"Not really. I haven't really ever thought about it." Her hand trails along Flore's back and down her thigh as Flore gets up. Harriet holds her ankle for a moment, and Flore smiles down at her, then, with a shake of her leg, takes her beautiful naked body out of the room. Harriet rolls over onto her belly to watch her go. The squalling Barker children upstairs come to mind. And the wild ones she saw in the lane on her way to Flore's, off to war with their fern arrows.

From the kitchen Harriet hears the rattle of the kettle and then Flore: "I do."

Harriet sits up to take the cup of tea Flore is holding out to her. They sit on the floor, side by side, knees up, their bare backs against the chesterfield. The biscuits are sawdust in Harriet's mouth; they taste like they were made for the dog. Rue takes hers from her hand with a gentle snap. Flore sips her coffee. Harriet does not know what to make of this silence, rooted as firmly as a dandelion.

"Someday," Flore finally says. "Someday I'd like to have a child."

Harriet's cold now. She stretches for but can't quite reach the blanket on the chesterfield.

RUE

The injustice! Blaming the disappearance of that chicken on me. It still rankles after all this time. They might have taken pains to enumerate the more likely suspects. I know the act of a weasel when I see one. (Though let us not discount the possibility of a human weasel entering the yard by night and later regaling himself with boiled hen for supper.)

But who was I to hold grudges when there were digestive biscuits to be had at Flore Rozema's.

The laneway was rich with scents that day, as always: I smelled cat, the fawn-coloured one who had no left ear; and there was dog—the Spaniel next door, no doubt (a neglected animal who had taken to expressing his melancholy in the wee hours of the morn)—on the abandoned cogs and on the second fencepost. There was also the scent of the ubiquitous rat; the city is rife with them. They raid the compost and strew about the contents of garbage cans. God knows if an appropriately sized pack of them may also successfully carry off a chicken. The mental image is too disturbing to contemplate.

There was always human piss in the laneway, male human piss—against the rocks, the fenceposts, the walls, the vegetation. With the male of the human species, we dogs have a commonality: we like to piss on things.

But on to more important matters: silence, that grand barometer of the state of human relations.

Poor Harriet. The look on her face. Though I was already very fond of Flore, I will not deny it: her approach was clumsy if not careless. Breeding, particularly for the purposes of the creation of small human beings, is not a concept to be tossed about offhandedly.

I was bred once, the corollary being, in this case, I was once a mother. This was not Rasia's fault. Rasia was fastidious; on my fertile days my leash was short. I, however, was more single-minded then, that most common characteristic of my breed, and so preferred a carefree romp with the neighbourhood dogs to a bridled walk. What can I say? I was young. I am led by my nose. I am a beagle. You remember that, of course. On that romp, I was joyously set upon by several dogs of various breed. The end result: six puppies, born sixty days later on the end of Rasia's bed, five alive and one dead. For eight more weeks, the (my) little gluttons exhausted me. And entertained Rasia, it should be said. One of her (gentle)men offered to put them in a gunnysack and toss them in the Fraser River. Rasia most politely declined; when he'd gone she promised me that he would never again darken our door. Then one by one my puppies disappeared, given into the hands of people who may, or may not, have been fine custodians of my brood.

We picked more blackberries on the way to Harriet's baseball game that morning, both women keeping their own counsel, until, I suppose, the whacking of the ball—and many gentle taunts from the charming Padraig Gleason—loosened Harriet's heart and tongue and all seemed normal again. Or as near to normal as could possibly be. I do not mean to leave you in suspense, but I shall. I know the future, and you do not.

And, look, I truly do not mean to dwell on the chickens. But if I could not kill a wild duck whilst starving in Stanley Park, the idea that I might eat one of its kind raw while I am amply fed indoors is ludicrous. I suppose, were I so inclined, it would not be difficult to catch one by the tail feathers; they do seem to be among the least intelligent creatures on earth. I have met miniature poodles with greater mental capacities.

ISLA

It was early, not quite yet seven o'clock. I even remember the date: the sixth of August. We crossed each other in the front room, our sleepy heads still in love with last night's dreams. Ahmie on her way back to bed from the privy, me on my way there. 'You need to find a job,' Ahmie muttered. Our mother, the queen of well-timed understatements. 'I've scarcely been home for a week. Can I not be forgiven for taking a day of rest? It's Sunday, for Christ's sake,' I sniped back, wasp mean. The day had hardly begun and there we were, miaouling at one another, a pair of alley cats. I went to stalk past her, but Ahmie's hand whipped out and caught me by the wrist. She pulled me to her with a strength that was shocking. I flinched and, curiously, braced myself for the sting of her palm, though I had never in my life been hit by my mother.

There was no slap. She reached up and gently took my face in her hands. I watched her eyes searching for something in mine. 'I don't know you anymore, Isla,' Ahmie said. 'Where have you gone? Where have you gone, my darling girl?' I was crying before she finished. My dam broke. Appalling noises came out of my mouth. Ahmie pressed my forehead to her shoulder and held it firmly there as I wept. It was Llew I was weeping over, my beautiful Llew.

With her other hand, Ahmie tapped my back, her fingers and thumb writing some consoling story in indecipherable Morse code, just as she used to when we were young, and when she was young too. Then, in her sweet, thin voice, she began to sing a song Pa had loved—"The Last Rose of Summer." I sobbed harder as she sang, remembering him listening to it, remembering her wiping the tears from his reverent face. Finally, Ahmie faltered, her throat constricted by her own gathering sorrow, I suppose. She let me go, pushing me from her and turning away as if she'd embarrassed herself or was embarrassed by me and the guttering sounds I was making. She went into the kitchen without glancing back. I felt fully abandoned and full of remorse, if those two sentiments can be suffered in the same moment.

A movement drew my eyes to the front door; through the window I saw Llewellyn's dark head. He blinked at me with his mournful eyes.

They saddle the heroes in romance novels with eyes like Llew's—sombre, beautiful, wistful. His sadness wasn't new. I knew it wasn't about us or about me. He was sad before Morag met him, those grey-green eyes full of a private despair that would not be concealed, no matter the effort taken to do so. It's no wonder Morag, our resident romantic, fell for him. But I did, too, and it wasn't the first time I'd fallen for someone with eyes like his. The first time was over a boy the year I turned twelve, the year we moved from the prairies. The boy, a classmate, had been inexplicably (ha!) spurning my advances of friendship. It's curious that I can't now conjure the boy's face—though I do remember his name, Gerard—when, at the time, his rejection of my feelings, those tender green shoots of love, was enough to nearly drown me in the notorious Slough of Despond. What I do remember well were his dark brown eyes and the unrelenting sorrow in them. Imagine the dramatic speculation in the heart of a twelve-year-old reared on a diet of nineteenth-century authors and poetesses: Was he being beaten at home by a heartless father? Did his poor consumptive mother lie dying? Or was he desperately in love with some cruel girl who would have nought to do with him? Whatever the cause, I was sure I could cure Gerard of whatever troubles had set his sorrow there.

Lesson not learned: we thought the same of Llewellyn, Morag and I. I sigh now, thinking of that hopeless ambition—curing someone else's sadness.

I unlocked the front door. Llewellyn thrust his handkerchief at me and followed me to my room. I got back into bed.

'Shut the door,' I said quietly.

It could not be helped; we shared a smile despite my tears. How many times had I said *Shut the door*, to which he had replied *Je t'adore*? Say it aloud.

He perched on the edge of my bed. His hands fidgeted for a while with the worn satin trim of my blanket. I longed to still his hands; instead, I folded and refolded his handkerchief in my lap. He had something to get off his chest.

'Why were you crying?' he asked.

I shook my head. 'What is it, Llew? Why are you here?'

He stood. 'There's going to be an inquest.'

I sat forward, stunned. 'What? About me?'

'No. About another woman. The one the coroner, Emerson-Gray, talked about. Mrs. Maria Veltri. But I want you to testify—'

'You cannot be serious. How could her case be related to mine?'

I might have understood much earlier what Llewellyn was planning if I'd paid more attention to the colour that rose in his face. He was a dreadful liar. He stood, his hands jammed in his pockets. 'It's the bruise. Mrs. Veltri had one too.'

I shook my head. On my thigh, there wasn't a trace left of the mark that had taken so long to heal, turning from that livid purple to blue to violet to yellow, and finally disappearing. How many times that summer had I lifted my nightgown to examine my bruise, watching the progress of that ugly reminder. 'No,' I said.

'Help me find him, then.' He was pleading.

'I can't.'

I'd convinced myself that when the bruise was gone, all the fury I felt would be gone with it. For good. But Llewellyn had come in the door, hand-in-hand with the ghost of Maria Veltri that day; and there she was, Maria and her bruise, sitting beside me, an utterly blameless spectre, reminding me of my own dark mark. I didn't understand then, not yet, that it would never be over. That she would never leave me, and that I would never let her go.

'This isn't like you,' Llew said.

'Promise me,' I said, 'that I will not be called to testify.'

He was silent.

'Promise!'

'I promise.' If he'd still been a boy, he'd have crossed his fingers behind his back, a schoolyard betrayal.

I would like to be able to say that I didn't watch his lovely back as he stood and went to the window and lifted his arms to pull the sash shut.

'Leave it,' I said. 'Leave it open.'

In the week since my return home, Ahmie was forever stalking in and closing the window, or shouting for Harriet to shut it for her. My poor mother's imagination grew so fearful that summer: she had murderers climbing over the sill, day or night, to dispatch us all. To convince us of this probability, she'd read aloud the newspaper stories about the so-called fisherman thief. This (clever, I thought) man had been stealing purses through open windows with the aid of a fishing rod, hooking them off bedside tables like leather rainbow trout. Not a likely transition, from fisherman thief to murderer, I'd said, but to Ahmie it was a short path. She changed tack eventually, turning from murderers to fatal breezes: I'd catch my death through the open window, she said. It was impossible to make her understand that I'd rather risk dying of cold than ever be feverishly hot again.

I recall the rest of that day with a clarity that is bittersweet:

Llewellyn is standing in the soft morning light by the window. It is like a whisper around him and I am suddenly stilled, remembering the curve of his armpit, the sinew of his muscle there, the colour of his skin. And his smell, the sweet, bready scent of him between his legs.

'I should go work in a logging camp,' I say.

'Why?' he asks.

To get away from you, I think. From these thoughts. 'I don't know,' I say.

'What would you do at a logging camp?'

'Cook?' I say.

'I'll come with you,' he says with such little conviction we both laugh.

'The only things you're not good at, Llew,' I say, 'are singing and lying. Oh, and being a cop.'

'You don't think I'm good at being a cop?' He's wounded. Those eyes.

'No, you're too . . . soft.' I do not use the words *too sensitive*, but they would be appropriate. I don't dare tell him everyone in the family thinks the same. He frowns and I tilt my head at him, trying to soften the blow.

I hear Harriet come out of her bedroom and pause for a moment outside my door. I can picture her, holding her breath out there, head cocked like the dog's. Inside my room, we hold our breath too. Then she leaves, with Rue, going out the kitchen door. For a few minutes she's in the yard, talking to the dog, or to the chickens, or to herself. And then the hinge on the gate squawks and I know she's gone.

'Harriet?' Llewellyn whispers.

'And her ever-faithful companion, Rue the Magnificent.'

We both snort with laughter.

'I can't say I am particularly fond of that dog,' I admit.

'Oh, she keeps the mice and rats at bay,' Llewellyn says, 'doesn't she?'

'Mice, yes. Rats, she doesn't know what to do with.'

'I love Rue.' He smiles. 'She'll grow on you. Dogs do.'

'Possibly,' I say. 'She's grown on Ahmie. I might prefer cats.'

'Cats.' He huffs and comes away from the window. 'Come out with me,' Llew says. 'I have a car.'

I want him to mean, *Come away with me. Forever.* It is only a tiny part of my heart that disapproves; it tells me to stop. I imagine that part beating faster than the rest. Or slower. Or stopping altogether. Or being cut right out.

'A car? Victor's?' I ask.

'My own,' he says, like a little boy. 'Second-hand. I got it for a song.'

'Oh yeah?' I say, smiling. 'What song did you sing?'

We drive out to the Endowment Lands, the distance between us on the front seat as healthy as a wide-hipped chaperone. His arm hangs out one window, mine out the other; he's drumming the outside of the door with his fingers, proud of his new old car.

He drums and I hum and the car rattles and the wind soughs through the trees on either side of the road. For forty minutes, this is our conversation.

This conversation, I know, is our farewell.

Llewellyn could identify every species of wild mushroom that grew in the fields and forests around the city. Which were edible and which—he used to clutch at his throat and mock tumble to the ground—would result in an immediate and painful death. He knew the birds by their songs. The trees by their needles and the droop of their crowns. Flowers, weeds, berries, snakes, frogs, insects, sea creatures. He knew them, and he loved them. He would be virtually euphoric while telling me which owl—the barred, the snowy, the great horned—had expelled the pellet that he was poking at with a stick, and whose bones and fur or feathers were in it. Which eagles were female. Where the crows flocked to at night. Whose scat that was. The immense value of a nurse log. 'Where did you learn all this?' I asked him once. We were south of the city, near an arm of the Fraser River, exploring a bog, hoping to catch sight of an American bittern. 'My father,' he said. 'He fancies himself a botanist. A naturalist, really.' I'd never before witnessed even a trace of the cavernous bitterness I heard in his reply that day. Morag had warned us not to ask after his parents. I knew he was estranged from them, but not why. 'It's quite a gift, this knowledge,' I said, pushing, only a little, I carelessly thought. 'And you're reluctant to acknowledge the source of it? He can't be that bad.'

We fought.

He explained—angrily, impatiently, as if he'd had to tell me over and over again—that it wasn't just that he blamed his father for pulling strings to keep him from going overseas during the war. There were many other reasons. Lots of them, he said, the childish words of a hurt ten-year-old boy. He wouldn't say what those other reasons might have been, or how they might justify his rancor, so his anger excited my belligerence. I said that I was all for the strings his father must have pulled with people in high places to keep him on this side of the Atlantic. 'Without him, you'd be over there, with all the other victims of the war's slaughter, beneath the poppies. Or six feet under, like my brother,' I said. I waved my arm about, pointing left and right, unsure in the face of the vast bog which direction was east. He'd walked away, leaving me standing before the creeping shrub he'd identified before our quarrel—bog cranberry, *Oxycoccus oxycoccos*. 'I suppose I'll never meet him,' I'd called after him. 'I will make certain you never do,' he'd replied.

As much as he loved the fields and forests, the only place in the natural world where Llewellyn appeared to be without even a trace of resentment was on the water. Once, out in a skiff off Kitsilano Beach, I said, 'Your father wasn't a water man, I take it.' 'Fortunately not,' he said and smiled.

Here's a regret: I didn't understand Llewellyn's bitterness toward his father. I didn't understand, until it was too late, how justified it was.

He parks his new car on the verge and we follow a steep footpath that leads down through a primeval forest of ferns to the beach.

'Are there civet cats around here?' I ask.

'Civet cats?' He laughs. 'No. They're from Asia. None around here, trust me.' He asks me why I want to know about civet cats.

'My father saw one once,' I say, the sureness in Llew's response already causing doubt to colour mine.

'Well, unless your father spent any time in the Orient, I don't think that's possible.'

I feel a small pain in some other part of my heart at the thought of my father being wrong. 'Couldn't one have secreted itself on a boat? You know, from the Orient. And snuck off it in the dead of night. With the rats.' I am writing fiction now, I know. I try to remember my father's story. A long-tailed black and white creature, slinking along the dock. Was it the dock or was it the forest? I can't remember, and now even the name *civet cat* seems wrong. A pole cat?

He smiles at me, his face sweet and sad, and I am undone.

Down on the beach we skip stones and pop dried kelp between our fingers. Innocent as children, we roll barnacle-encrusted rocks up to reveal hermit crabs and starfish, mussels and limpets. There are two men, naked as jays, sunbathing on the sand; they ignore us, we ignore them. The waves salt our bare feet. Two seals play, just offshore; they stop to watch us with their huge, curious eyes. In a tidal pool, a circus of orange sea anemones moves with such hypnotic slowness it is hard to look away. We stand six feet apart and scan the strait, ever hopeful for whales. The ocean is grey and calm.

'What do you think it was?' he says.

I know what he means. He means: Was it a boy or a girl? I have run down that road already. I don't want to go there again.

'It wasn't,' I say.

We take a different path back up. It is steeper and our hands stretch out for branches and tree roots to pull ourselves up. Ahead of us, something flushes out of the bushes with a squawk, and in my alarm I let go of my handhold. I have to scrabble fast to catch another. Llew, ahead of me, is excited to report that it was probably a female sooty grouse. I slow behind him; he is oblivious. Over his shoulder, he tells me a story about a pheasant that used to fight with its reflection in the glass door of their backyard greenhouse when he was small. 'They were so rare in those days. But it infuriated my mother to have a mad pheasant making a mess of the door. I loved it,' he says.

This hill is too much for me. I am breathless. He glances back, he waits for me, but he doesn't give me his hand. We have moved out of the realm in which handholding is allowed.

We get in the car and we drive.

I imagine this: We keep driving. We head east, cross the Rockies, traverse the prairies. We never stop. There are our feet in the Atlantic Ocean.

I glance over at him, and his eyes meet mine. We are sharing the same thought, but we have long ago passed the turnoff that would have taken us that way.

I have closed my eyes. The temperature of the wind on my face changes, half a degree cooler, and I know we are crossing the bridge. When I open my eyes, I see a swallow rise beside us, elegant and swift, then swoop out of sight again beneath the railings. Below us, the inlet sparkles in its dark way. On the sidewalk, two women, twins perhaps, in matching pale-blue dresses share a sudden laugh. A man passing in the opposite direction stops and whistles at them. I imagine that they laugh harder. On a billboard at the end of the bridge there's a girl's pretty face, shilling for Nabob coffee.

Llewellyn speaks to the dashboard. 'What if I never get over you?' he says.

I don't reply.

I ask him to drop me off before we are home. I want to walk, I tell him. He leaves me on the corner of Granville and Davie. I watch him: He drives away. He does not tip his hat. But a thread of me is caught in the car's door, a thin line of blue that will unravel and unravel until I am naked on the corner.

Second Trimester

THURSDAY, AUGUST 17

Mid-afternoon

Sinking ships. Drownings. Houses on fire. Hangings. Fistfights. Fatal automobile accidents. The list of miseries that people will turn out to gawk at is endless. The public has a macabre fascination with dead women too. And abortionists. So the coroner's courtroom is packed. There is Llewellyn, at the front, sweating in his brown suit. Even from there, the crowd in the hallway can be heard jostling to be closest to the door should any courtroom seat be vacated or one of the standing-room-only spots at the back come free. Watchers have brought their lunches—sandwiches wrapped in tea cloths, sulfurous hard-boiled eggs, sweets, thermoses of coffee or tea. A few have flasks of something more potent in their pockets, and these are being surreptitiously sipped. The newspapermen are here, their notepads ready on their knees. (They are the ones with the flasks.)

The fish stench is in Llewellyn's imagination; the room only smells of humans.

The man addressing the jury is not Morag's long-lashed movie star, Dr. Emerson-Gray, of course. He is Dr. Lester Gilchrist. The jury members have already been asked if they will "diligently inquire" into the death of the victim, and they have sworn to do so. The chosen foreman, Will Brown, is a merchant. Ben Lee is retired, as is Justin Marshall. Andrew Judd is a logger; Mason O'Reilly, a roofer; Marcel Thibodeau, a dining-car chef. The jurymen are both solemn and eager, like bird dogs on point, thinks Llewellyn. The foreman, Brown, has a tic, an upward shrug of his left shoulder every twenty seconds or so; Llewellyn wonders how the man can live with an annoyance like that.

Dr. Gilchrist has told the jury members that an autopsy was performed on the victim. They have learned that under *Cause of Death*, the doctor who signed Maria Benedetta Veltri's death certificate has written *Criminal Abortion*. Dr. Gilchrist has explained that Mrs. Veltri suffered death by exsanguination due to a perforation of her womb; this perforation occurred a day prior to her death through the introduction of an instrument used to cause a miscarriage. The doctor has also indicated that the damage suffered is not likely to have been self-inflicted. Very unlikely, in fact. Maria Veltri was thirty-three years old. The post-mortem report, Gilchrist says, describes Mrs. Veltri as having been 138 pounds, five-feet-four inches tall. Hair, brown. Eyes, brown. Teeth, healthy with the exception of some rot in the molars and one missing second bicuspid on the bottom right. She had a number of pockmark scars on her lower abdomen associated, the doctor believes, with either the chicken pox or smallpox, though more likely the former. There was also a large bruise on her upper inner left thigh.

"Mrs. Veltri's identity was confirmed by her mother, Mrs. Giuseppina Occhipinti." Gilchrist stumbles over the name, pronouncing it slowly in flat English. "The person who performed the abortion on Mrs. Veltri is unknown; however, the police have taken a Mr. Gianluca Padula into custody. He sits before you." The coroner points with his chin at Padula and gives the jurors a moment to take him in before he continues. "This coroner's inquest is being held to determine whether Mr. Padula, who has admitted to being Mrs. Veltri's . . . *beau*, for lack of a better word, should stand charged with being an accomplice to murder by abortion." Llewellyn frowns at the restless audience members. They have gasped, the hypocrites, as if they were unaware of the charges. Llewellyn's already well-tested faith in human beings drops by another degree.

"For observers who may not understand the nature of a coroner's inquisition, these members of the coroner's jury will make this decision using any evidence given during the inquest. During this process we may unearth other pertinent information and determine whether anyone else can be implicated in the death of Mrs. Veltri."

Llewellyn presses his left shoe hard to the floor to stop the bounce of his knee. Isla used to put her warm hand there: bounce; stop; bounce-tap; stop; bounce. Stop. He knows she is in the back row and that Flore and Harriet are with her. He saw them come in. Victor and Georgina are back there somewhere too. He has promised himself he will not look for Isla again. In a minute he turns around. There she is; his knee starts up again.

"Mrs. Veltri has a sister and a mother in Canada, and I believe her mother is in attendance here today. Apart from these relatives and her three children . . ." The coroner pauses and reaches for another document. ". . . Mariana, aged five,

Salvatore, four, and Angelo, two, Mrs. Veltri had no other living relative in Vancouver. The children are currently in the custody of Mrs. Veltri's sister, Mrs. Isotta Colombo." *Eye-Saw-Ta.*

For a second, Gianluca Padula closes his eyes. He shakes his head, almost imperceptibly. Llewellyn watches the man then scan the room, taking in the jury, the coroner, and the crowd. His gaze comes to rest on Llewellyn. He reads the expression on Padula's face: it's not fear, it's disdain. Padula shakes his head again, slowly, this time more noticeably, his eyes locked on Llewellyn's. Llewellyn is the first to look away.

"Mr. Padula has admitted that he and Mrs. Veltri had a relationship of an intimate nature. *Ergo*, the child Mrs. Veltri chose to rid herself of was presumably the product of their union," says Gilchrist.

Padula's lawyer clears his throat and raises his hand, but when Gilchrist looks expectantly at him, he lowers his head and shuffles some papers on the table. Llewellyn can't bear the sight of the young man. From a distance, he seemed slick enough, a man in a good suit and hat, and Llewellyn was relieved to see that Padula had found himself a competent lawyer. Close up, however, he sees that the young man's cheeks are still pimpled with the acne of youth and his nervous eyes say he is way out of his league.

Padula is the first to be questioned. He is invited to the stand. He places his hand on the Bible and is asked whether he swears to tell the truth. Llewellyn's mouth goes dry as Padula calmly says, "I do."

"Mr. Padula, do you consider yourself to be mentally and physically well?"

Padula exchanges a perplexed look with Maria Veltri's mother, who is seated in the second row.

Gilchrist enunciates slowly: "Do you understand my question? Do you speak English, Mr. Padula?"

"Of course I speak English. I was born in New York."

"Well then, do you consider yourself to be well? Do you have any diseases or mental illnesses?"

Padula looks as if he might stand and walk out of the room. Now there's much more than disdain on his face.

"I am well, sir."

"I raise these questions because I am mystified by your relationship with Mrs. Veltri. Did you know that she was married?"

"I did."

"And yet you had sexual relations with her."

"I did," Padula says.

Gilchrist faces the jury. "Had you promised to marry Mrs. Veltri?"

"I would have married Maria if I could've."

"If you could have? What prevented you from doing so?"

Padula seems unable to stop the look of contempt that flickers across his face. "She was already married to Franco Veltri?"

There are a few titters from the gallery.

"I'm sure you are by now aware that you could spend many years in prison for your complicity in this matter, so the way in which you answer my questions is of great importance. What made you think that extramarital relations are an acceptable practice, in this country?"

"Normally I wouldn't have been with a married woman. In this country," Padula adds, the trace of sarcasm unmistakeable.

"Normally?" The coroner raises his eyebrows at the jury.

"Maria's husband, Frank, went back to Italy two years ago to visit his dying mother, just after the baby was born. He never arrived, and no one has heard of him since. For all we know he's dead. In fact, that's what we all think because Frank loved Maria, and the children. He wouldn't have run off. But wherever he is, he's not here. And Maria needs help. Needed help."

"A fine helper you seem to have been." He faces the crowd and gets another small laugh for his line. "Were you present during Mrs. Veltri's operation?"

"I was not."

"And yet you knew about it."

Padula glances at his lawyer. "I did."

"Did you do it yourself?"

Padula pales. "No."

"Am I right in assuming you are not a wealthy man, Mr. Padula? What is it that you do for a living?"

"I'm a longshoreman."

Someone in the audience calls out, "Planning on going on strike anytime soon?" and the room explodes with laughter.

Strike! What unmannerly boor has said this? Georgina leans forward and looks past Victor, down toward the end of their row. The man, in pinstripes and greying at the temple, is enjoying the attention, smiling and bowing in his seat. What a buffoon.

Georgina sits back and crosses her arms. "It's like they think they're at the circus."

"What?" Victor says.

"A circus," she repeats impatiently. "A bloody circus."

She'd like to see Mr. Padula give them a real performance. She'd like to see him stand up and roar and tip the table over with his longshoreman hands. Right here, in front of the portrait of King George and his stupid, swooping moustache.

"Leave him alone," she says, under her breath.

"You're not cheering for Mr. Padula, are you?" Victor says. He squeezes her hand.

She pulls her hand away and finds her handkerchief. God, what is happening to her? She is leaking tears all the time now. This time it's over Mrs. Veltri's children. She wants to know, as fiercely as the coroner does, who did this to their mother, but not at the cost of destroying this man.

The coroner puts a hand up and waits for the laughter to subside then goes on with his interrogation: "A longshoreman. I see. The cost of an abortion is significant, is it not? Not the kind of sum a man on your wage comes by easily, is it? Where did you and Mrs. Veltri get the money?"

"We borrowed it. From a friend."

The coroner follows Gianluca Padula's searching look at the people in the gallery. "Oh. Is that friend in the courtroom today?"

"No." Padula addresses the table. "He's gone. To Oregon."

"Has he now? I suppose it is of no use to us to chase down that friend, Mr. Padula, to verify your statement. It would save us all a great deal of time if you would simply tell us the name of the person who performed the operation on Mrs. Veltri. The person who killed her."

Padula shakes his head. "I don't know it."

"What can you tell me about him, then? Was he a doctor? Some kind of snake-oil salesman? A plumber?"

The pinstriped man in the audience seems helpless with laughter now. Someone shushes him, and the room quickly quiets. Georgina's annoyance has turned to rage; her heart thumps wildly.

"You'd be surprised. We've had people of any number of occupations involved in the abortion business," the coroner says.

That repugnant smirk. Georgina clenches her fists: Now's the time, Mr. Padula, Knock it over!

"What?" Victor says again.

She hasn't spoken aloud, has she?

Georgina is carried back to the dog days of late summer, years ago, their prairie schoolyard. A fistfight, another one. They've circled the two boys who are grappling, sunburnt in the dust. Fists swing, bare feet shoot out to injure, knees and arms rise protectively. Her stomach is roiling. She feels tears pricking in her eyes, yet she cannot leave, cannot stop the fight. Suddenly, in one of the boys, the fury is gone. She feels his submission; he's losing. Resignation; he has lost. There's blood, and tears. In triumph the other boy tugs the loser's shirt up over his face and calls him a baby. She's horrified; she cheers and chants with the others—*baby, baby*. Later, she's sick in the bushes behind the schoolhouse.

The silence in the courtroom is broken; the thrum in the hallway intensifies. All heads turn to see what is happening. Andrew Morrison enters. He is followed by a man Georgina knows only from the newspapers, Llewellyn's boss, Chief MacIntyre. The two policemen find a place to stand, leaning against the back wall, and the coroner calls the court to order. The door hushes shut. The sounds of the disappointed rubber-neckers in the hall are diminished but not gone.

Mr. Padula is the only one who has not looked up. Georgina imagines his rage to be as potent as hers. She sees Llewellyn in the front row, his head bowed, the nape of his neck, somehow vulnerable. Vulnerable or not, he is to blame.

ooooo

Birds of prey. They hunt to kill; they eat their catch. It's a fact of nature, and nothing that Llewellyn has ever been sentimental about, not particularly. Llewellyn's a country boy. Big birds, big animals, eat smaller ones; they eat rabbits and field mice and all manner of creatures that have no defence other than speed, or agility, or the ability to hide. Fairness plays no part in it, as his father always used to remind him. It's an eternal law: *Nature, red in tooth and claw.*

Now, seeing the grief in Padula's eyes, the weight of it bowing his big shoulders, Llewellyn feels his notion of the justness of that law of nature sliding away. Llewellyn gave this inquest life—he harnessed Morrison's zealousness to his own desire for revenge—despite Chief MacIntyre's explicit orders not to; it has gone awry, and he no longer has the power to stop it. It will march along of its own volition and come to flawed conclusions. Gilchrist is a man with a machete, bushwhacking, with one aim in mind: to crucify Padula. Crucifying an innocent man was not Llewellyn's intention. It was a name he was after, one name. Padula does not have it, and that much, now, is very clear.

"Mr. Padula, why, if you knew that your lover was undergoing an illegal procedure, did you still help her to do so? Did you understand the risk she was taking? Not to mention the laws she was breaking?"

Padula seems to wipe a tear from his cheek. The courtroom is parched by a long, unbearable silence. Llewellyn can hear only the deafening roar of his own guilt.

"Please note that the witness does not choose to answer," the coroner says quietly, as if he might have decided that some kindness, in the face of Padula's emotion, might be observed. "We will record that as *No answer.*" He nods at the court stenographer, whose poised fingers return to her machine, and Gilchrist continues, Padula's grief clearly of no concern to him.

"Mr. Padula, why didn't you accompany her that day?"

"She was told to come alone."

"And you accepted that? What made you obey that order?"

The colour of shame slides up from under Padula's collar.

Beside Llewellyn, a man taps the woman next to him on the arm. She leans toward him. "Italians," the man whispers. "Can't keep their gospel-pipes in their pants. Gotta obey the Pope."

Llewellyn pulls his police badge from his pocket and puts it far too close to the man's face. "Get out," he says.

The couple's low laughter stops and the man pulls back, squinting. "What've we done wrong? We haven't done anything, have we, Alma?" he says. His hands grip his chair and he doesn't get up, though the woman named Alma, wide-eyed, tucks her thermos into her bag.

"You're"—*dreadful people*, Llewellyn wants to say—"disturbing the peace. And I need your seats. For other police officers."

The two of them gather their things slowly and leave. Now Llewellyn is obliged to turn and signal the availability of the seats to Morrison and MacIntyre. As he does, he sees Isla; her face is stone.

"So, where were you while your lover was bleeding to death?" Gilchrist asks.

Padula doesn't raise his head. "I worked that night. She seemed all right when I left in the evening. She was just tired. And a little weak. When I came home the next day, she was already gone. And the children had been taken too."

"Alas," Gilchrist says.

In the silent room, the word sits like a lone crow atop a forest snag.

Gilchrist has eviscerated Mrs. Veltri. She is immoral and selfish, a woman who, when her husband went missing, chose a life of promiscuity, the inevitable result of which was her death. She chose, he has said, to involve herself with a man who has as little regard for life as he has for women's duties of marriage and the responsibilities of motherhood. If Gianluca Padula had any respect, either for truth or for justice, he would have given this court the name of the person who killed his *sweetheart*.

Padula's lawyer does little to dispel Gilchrist's grim portrait of Maria Veltri and Gianluca Padula as enemies of all that is good, all that is moral, patriotic, Canadian.

"I believe we have time for one more witness today," the coroner says, and a Miss Nancie Twiname is called.

Chief MacIntyre, next to Llewellyn, grunts. He stands and leaves.

Llewellyn's heart sinks as the elderly woman shambles up to the stand. Gilchrist will make mincemeat out of her too; they might as well have enclosed a stout old doe on its last legs in a cage with a sleek mountain lion.

Nearly 6 p.m.

Twelve years in Vancouver, nearly half her life, and Georgina is still astounded. This city, it is a gift. To be able to do this, to stand a few feet from the water's lap at the shore, to breathe cool salty air. Georgina inhales, her face lifted, eyes closed, inviting all the shoreline's sweet stink—the tidal ebb of fish and green vegetal rot, even the human fetidness. Evening on the prairies at this time of year is golden, harvest time, beautiful in its own way, but a prairie summer can be so oppressive, all heat and no relief. Ahmie and Morag grumble about the west coast winter—how grey it is, how drizzly, how damp. Georgina prefers the grey to the endless months of bitter, nostril-freezing cold and ice of Manitoba. *Pease porridge hot, pease porridge cold.* Here, it is neither one nor the other; *some like it* . . . never too hot, never too cold. And the ocean, this grand thing: whatever it brings in or takes away, it has her in its thrall. She'll never tire of it.

There is something down there amongst the jetsam, black, unidentifiable from this distance, wedged between the seaweedy rocks close to the water's edge. Georgina leaves Victor above on the path and steps down through the bushes and over the rocks. The black thing is the body of a mink, its brown eyes open, glistening, but unseeing, its fur still lustrous. She crouches down.

"What is it?" Victor won't come down to the water's edge. (His shoes, the salt.)

"A mink."

"Well, d-d-don't touch it."

Georgina slides her finger along its smooth back and over the small round nubs of its ears. She feels a pulse in her groin at the silkiness of the animal's fur. Then, an ache; this is such a raw, exposed death. Another one. She shakes away the coroner's impassive description of Mrs. Veltri's body.

"Georgina."

She stands, resigned to whatever is next for the mink. The tide will take it, make it an offering of food for some other creature, let it sink to the bottom of the harbour, eventually scatter its skeletal remains.

Victor is shaking his head. "You shouldn't touch things like that."

"Why not?"

He wipes her hand with his handkerchief, roughly and gently at the same time, she the child, he the paterfamilias.

"I had a strange dream last night," he says. "You were in it." He gives her lower back a forgiving pat then crooks his arm: *Take it*, says his lone elbow. They'll walk awhile now. Victor likes to set his pocket by the church bells that ring at six o'clock. She'll hold the watch; he'll adjust the time, if necessary. He's not stammering this evening, not much. The familiarity, the repetitiveness, setting his watch this way; it always calms him.

"And this dream?"

"We were, you were, at the grocery store."

"Which one?"

"I don't know. The one you go to."

Georgina laughs, and Victor has the humility to do so too. He knows nothing about this chore of hers. If he were forced to fend for himself at home, her husband would starve.

"In the dream, you were outside the shop. That Irish friend of yours—what's his name? Fergal?—he approaches you with a big silver tray covered in cookies shaped like the letters of the alphabet."

The smile on Georgina's lips fades. Victor glances at her; she keeps her eyes on the path ahead. Fergal's name in Victor's mouth feels like an accusation.

"Fergal is bizarrely shaped," Victor continues. "As wide as he is short. He tells you that you may enter the store only if you have the letter *A*. If you have the letter *B*, or any other letter, you would not be allowed in the store. So the chances are slim.

Fergal closes his eyes and feels around then picks up a cookie in the shape of an *A* from the tray. Then he opens his eyes and hands it to you, delighted. But right away he snatches it back from your hand and nibbles at the legs of the *A* until it is just a triangle. 'No entry for you, I'm afraid,' your Irishman says with a sad face." Victor pauses.

Georgina makes herself laugh. "And then you woke up?"

"And then I woke up."

"So, what do you make of all that, Vic?"

"I thought you'd have some clever analysis, Georgie. You're the dream girl." He squeezes her arm against his body. He kisses her temple. "D-d-on't you?"

Georgina shakes her head. These rare offerings of affection are always surprising. This one may be, she thinks, interpreted as true fondness, or a jealous warning, or it may be that Victor knows how to love her today, as he does now and again. Just as now and again a mink will be found dead on the shore.

"Not really. School grades? But the eating of the *A*'s legs . . . Perhaps it has something to do with what we receive being taken back. The vote?" she says, leaving Fergal out of the interpretation. "You'd like that, if we lost it." Now she's being mean. In her stomach there's a tiny spill of acid. Victor doesn't reply. Oh dear, how mortally has she wounded him now? She looks quickly up at him. His face is turned toward hers, his eyes soft with affection, a smile on his lips. At their wedding he'd had tears in his eyes; that was unexpected as well.

"I wouldn't deny you that, darling," he says earnestly. For a moment he is generous Victor, the version of her husband who enticed her to wed him, on a Tuesday, "for wealth," as the old rhyme goes. And then he is just Victor: "Not so long as you vote the right way," he says.

"The right way. Yes." Georgina loosens her arm from his and bends to pick up a rock. She bounces the weight of it three or four times in her hand then tosses it in the water, wondering what Fergal's stance on women's suffrage had been. At the last dreadful meeting of her dreadful women's group, Lydia Reid had said the same thing, or its equivalent: *I'll vote with my husband, of course.*

There's no one left from before; Georgina's old circle of friends has disintegrated. The girls at the shoe factory, a few school chums—that death knell rang the minute she married Victor and found herself, like one of those charlatans who claim to be able to levitate, rising up to another class. It's disconcerting: she is now a woman who could employ a servant—if she knew how exactly that was done. She thinks of Gladdy and Betty and Lillian, still working at Leckie's, still stitching sturdy leather shoes so that they may put food on their plates, help with the rent, pay whoever minds the children. They earn in a month about what Victor paid for last winter's coat, and their husbands don't make much more. Gladdy and Laird Horan over for tea with Victor? Georgina almost laughs aloud imagining her husband asking Gladdy's husband what he does for a living or if he has a few hundred to invest in Victor's latest enterprise. Georgina rolls her wedding ring with her thumb and thinks of Stephen Salter. Then she thinks of Fergal Doherty's lovely blue beard. *Make new friends*, Victor keeps saying, as if making new friends is like picking humbugs from a jar.

At least she'd made Isla laugh when she told her what she'd nicknamed the group: the DWG. The membership of the Dreadful Women's Group—not so long ago thought of as possible *new friends*—meets in the parlour of Mrs. John Clarke.

Mrs. Clarke—Evelyn—is the "dear wife" of one of Victor's business associates. Mrs. Albert Reid—Lydia—is the "dear friend" of Mrs. Clarke. Other dear missuses include Mrs. Elmer, Mrs. Christopher, Mrs. William, Mrs. Tom, Dick, and Harry—a.k.a. Ruth, Laura, Mabel, Anne, Vera, Dora, and Honey, who are all "dear friends" of Evelyn. And Georgina, not really vying for dear friend status, *not really*, takes tea with them all on Tuesday afternoons.

Mrs. Victor Dunn. Georgina laughs aloud. We now present the award for Most Unenthusiastic Member of the DWG to Mrs. Victor Dunn. Suddenly, sorting out how to politely extricate herself from the DWG is what must be done.

"What are you harrumphing about?" Victor says.

"Nothing," she laughs.

"Would you explain again your aversion to moving to Shaughnessy? Your ladies group is there. The Clarkes. We are so behind the tide, sweetheart."

Georgina doesn't answer. She will never move to Shaughnessy, and nor, she thinks, will Victor. As much as he dreams of it, he is not of the class of people who have moved to Shaughnessy, not financially, and not in other ways as well. Victor does not belong. They, the Dunns, do not belong.

"Not a pleasant day at the inquisition, was it?" Victor says when she does not reply.

"Not pleasant, no. But surely, it's not meant to be. Surely, it's meant to harass some poor soul until he confesses, whether he understands what he is confessing to or not? Poor Mr. Padula."

"Poor Mr. Padula? Abortion is serious business. Why you insist on attending this inquest to watch these shabby people . . ." He pauses. "Padula is guilty of something. And must you always be so prickly, Georgie?"

Prickly. Dismissive. Judgemental. No, she does not always have to be. She stops herself from asking, *Guilty of what?* Living, possibly. Victor kisses her forehead this time, and she is once again determined to be a better person. A kinder person.

"Not very cooperative, that woman this afternoon . . . Mrs. Twinall—" Victor says.

"Miss Twiname," Georgina snaps, thinking of the stout old woman in her battered hat, who, on the stand, was not to be rattled. The coroner had explained to the jury that Mrs. Veltri had been to see this witness, Miss Twiname, sometime before she met the abortionist. He demanded to know the purpose of Maria Veltri's visit to Miss Twiname's home in the East End. 'To bring on her monthlies, of course,' the woman said. 'Are you aware that abortion is illegal, Miss Twiname?' 'I'm not sure that I knew that, mister, or that I'd agree with that,' Miss Twiname said, 'but I was not giving her an abortion. I was only helping her to bring on her monthlies, like I said, giving her some herbal remedies, so I'm not quite sure what you mean.' 'Whether you agree with the laws of the Dominion, Miss Twiname, we are not circumnavigating the globe,' the coroner said. 'You understand that it was your duty to report to the police this transgression of the law?' Miss Twiname stood firm: 'There was no circumnavigating the globe on my part, mister, and the only transgression that I know of is that someone did Mrs. Veltri in, and it weren't me.'

"I don't suppose we can expect anything better of people like Mrs. Twiname," Victor says. "The lower classes have no sense of how to behave in situations like that."

Georgina looks down at his shiny shoes. "I am lower-class people, Victor," she says. And so were your parents, she thinks.

He seems not to have heard. “Nearly six o’clock,” he says. He pulls his pocket watch out and snaps the lid open.

The bells begin to ring.

Georgina’s heart beats high in her throat; she has promised to love, honour, and obey this man, and she is incapable of doing even one of the three. She bends again to pick up another rock. This one goes into the current as well, this time more violently. And as she tosses it, a longing seizes her—for Fergal Doherty, for his Seattle dreams, for anything other than this life with Victor. But then, softly, another thought comes. It slides in sideways, there on the shore, twenty yards from the nine-o’clock gun, ten feet from the sea: perhaps, in being childless, she has been spared.

ISLA

Llewellyn was left-handed, and he had unusual toes on his left foot. The second and third were fused. Two normal toenails, side by side, but the rest of it, smooth and double-wide with only the slightest indentation. It made me think of the webbed feet of that dusty, taxidermized platypus I'd been fascinated by in the old City Museum at Main and East Hastings.

'You must swim well,' I said, inspecting his foot one day. 'This is your only imperfection.' I bit his toes, gently. Why does love make us hungry, and those we love so edible.

Head to toe in the boat's narrow bunk, the light of dawn barely illuminating us, warm beneath our grey wool blanket, he held my feet and kissed them, one toe after the other. 'And you have none.'

No imperfections. 'Well,' I said.

The first time we walked along the tilting dock at dawn, I hadn't asked whose boat it was, only whether we wouldn't suddenly be disturbed by its owner, some portly, red-faced fisherman in a slicker and sou'wester, I imagined. Llewellyn had taken my hand, and we went over the gunwale and down into the neat cabin. 'Does it smell like anyone has anything to do with fish here?' he said. It didn't. It was clean and tidy, outfitted with a tiny galley, with—and this was odd and amusing—floral-patterned bone china teacups swinging on hooks. Its compact cupboards contained two plates, two bowls, tea and coffee, sugar, and a sack of porridge oats. A bottle of honey. A brass oil lamp hung above a table on which a large map of the Strait of Georgia was unfurled under glass. There were stout homemade candles, too, which we preferred and always lit; I loved their soft guttering sound and the amber light they cast, turning our skin golden. Two narrow banks on either side of the table folded down and converted into a bed just big enough for two. Sometimes we'd fall asleep there, wrapped in one another's arms, and we'd awake, entwined as the roots of trees.

Women talk about knowing the very moment they conceive. I could hazard a guess, but, I assure you, I never found myself in any state of dreamy contemplation about it. More like abject terror. The morning I discovered Llewellyn's strange toes may have been the day we conceived. It was the only time we were that careless. Did I realize he'd lost the will to withdraw in time? Did I hold him to me, for God's sake? Is it infidelity that makes us so reckless? The sex act itself? Or is it love that overpowers us?

That morning, the moment at which I usually began to feel a mounting tide of ruefulness had not yet arrived. We were still in that light-headed, stupid fever of love. In fact, we were so lost in it that I didn't think about our carelessness until much later in the day, well after I'd sponged the smell of him, the taste of him, off in the tub. Prudence and Remorse—always so late to the ball.

For him—though he swore he was no philanderer, and I believed him—it may have been as intoxicating as stripping a woman of her gloves, then one stocking, and the next. He took as much pleasure in doing so with me as he took in hiking in his beloved wilderness.

It has taken me all this time to understand why I loved him. Why I would have so heartlessly and so brazenly betrayed my sister: Llewellyn stripped me of my rage. He wrested it from my breast. He made me leave it panting in the dirt, crying out like some naked and abandoned creature. And this, this made me surrender. This made me love him. When we were together, he softened the pain of loss—of Roddy, of Pa, of those we had lost in the hideous war. He tempered my sense of powerlessness; he calmed my fury over the corruptness of our politicians, their willful ignorance, their immorality. He was a human balm against all that. I don't know if he gave me hope, but he made me soft. Softer.

And yet, what good can come of being soft? Is it akin to preferring the 'nice' side of Georgina? Does anything change without the power of anger? I don't know anymore.

Nothing could ever have come of the Maria Veltri inquest. Llewellyn must have known that. There'd been no dying declaration. No evidence but for the body of Maria and her bruised thigh. As for Gianluca Padula—Llewellyn used the man. On the first day of the inquest, the heartlessness of the coroner's questions cut open a fresh wound of anger in me. No one believed Gianluca had anything to do with Maria's death. Not even Llewellyn. Gianluca was just a deeply grieving man. Not calculating. Not concealing. But Llewellyn, in his desperation, saw in Gianluca a route to the man who'd hurt me. He wanted Gianluca to know something, to admit something, that precious bit of information that eluded us all—the man's name. In the end Llewellyn got what he wanted, but he left devastation in his wake.

During his testimony on the first day of the inquisition, Gianluca hadn't given anything away, and who can blame him for being wary about doing so. He wanted to protect Maria and the friend who had told her where she might get help. He'd told the coroner what Maria had told him: Someone at the sugar refinery where she worked—Gianluca said he didn't know who—knew a woman who knew a woman who knew a man. Maria had met that woman in a café near the train station. She'd given Maria a card with only a telephone number on it. When Maria had rung the number, the man who answered told her to bring the card, and like he'd done with me, he'd asked for it back before he knelt between her legs with his little bag of tools. Gianluca's voice broke as he told the court that, in the car, the man had covered Maria's eyes with his hat.

My heart seized: Hat. Bruise. Desperation. What else had Maria and I shared?

On the second morning of the inquisition, sitting in the back row, Flore and I waited to see which poor soul would be called next to testify. Gianluca and poor old Miss Twiname had been more than adequately tormented the previous day. Surely no more. 'Who will their next victim be?' Flore had leaned toward me and whispered.

It seemed that Llewellyn was finding the floor between his shoes very interesting as I stood and laid my hand on the Bible.

Odd to swear on something you don't believe in. Odder still that others believe in something so profoundly that it doesn't matter to them that you don't. I stared at Llewellyn as I said 'Yes.' He looked in desperate need of sleep. No mercy, I thought.

Dr. Gilchrist started off in a gentle voice. 'A simple question,' he said, and he smiled. 'How much did you pay for your abortion?' I told him: 'Sixty-five dollars.' 'Where does a housemaid get such an astronomical fund?' he asked, looking not at me but, as was his habit, at the jurymen, eyebrows raised.

Victor provided the most. He carries a surprising amount of cash in his wallet. I did have a few dollars in savings, but the rest I stole. From Victor, Llewellyn, my sisters, my employers. Dime by dime, dollar by dollar. This was, of course, not what I told the coroner.

'I had savings,' I said.

'Really?' the coroner said. 'Where did you go to have the procedure done?'

I could be honest about that: I didn't know. I told him how I had waited on Cordova near the CPR terminus. That we drove to a building, no more than twenty minutes away. No, it wasn't a hotel. No, there wasn't a street sign. No, I didn't recognize the neighbourhood. No, I didn't notice the make of his vehicle; it was just a black car with tires and a steering wheel. 'A Model T Ford?' I said, a guess. It was the only make of car I knew. No. No. No. The coroner didn't like my answers.

'Surely you can tell us what this man looked like?' he said, all business now. I hesitated; I could not. I could hear his voice and see the room, the dirty wall, him rolling his shirt sleeves back down and putting his jacket on. The sink in the corner.

My purse on the bed. The wrinkles in the knees of his suit. His shoes. My blood on the towel. The water-stained ceiling. Mouse or rat droppings by the door. I could not recall his face.

'I can describe his hat,' I said.

'A whole lot of good a hat is to us,' Dr. Gilchrist said. 'What instruments did he use to do the job?'

'That,' I said, 'I was not in a position to see.' Dr. Gilchrist didn't like that answer either.

He asked if I'd felt the quickening before the abortion, and I didn't answer. I hadn't, but it was a tack Flore suggested he might make use of to taint Maria Veltri and Gianluca Padula in the eyes of the jury. Here he was using it on me. I caught Gianluca's eye; I'd never before seen a more mournful man.

'Put *No answer*,' Dr. Gilchrist told the court stenographer, and her fingers flew on, marking down my silence in the official court record.

The coroner gazed at me for a long time after that, a disappointed expression on his face, as if he was assessing the crimes and misdemeanours of his own daughter.

'When preventing pregnancy is so easy . . .' he finally sighed.

From the back of the courtroom, I heard Flore howl. She was not alone: People laughed. Women mostly. Someone hissed, and a lone voice booed. Dr. Gilchrist, God bless his ignorant soul, flushed a little and called for order.

'When preventing pregnancy is so easy,' he continued, 'one need not resort to murder.'

Dr. Gilchrist's next tactic changed everything: 'Did no one go with you to meet this man, whose hat you remember but nothing else?' he asked. 'What kind of man would put you in this compromising position and not accompany you to your appointment?'

I bent my head.

Gianluca rose then, slowly and quietly; the coroner noticed the courtroom's murmuring hush first, then turned to see Gianluca standing.

'I think his name is Granville,' Gianluca said.

'Granville?' the coroner repeated.

'Maria just wanted to bring on her flow,' Gianluca said. 'She had three children already. We didn't want another. We could barely make ends meet. The woman at the café, the woman who gave Maria his card, she said *Granville*. *Granville* could help Maria.'

Gianluca turned to me. 'Why didn't I go with her?' he said. 'Why didn't I see who he was, at least, before I let her drive off with him? I'm sorry. I'm so sorry,' he said, as if he could have stopped the curve of time and my unlucky spot on that line as well as Maria's.

Llewellyn rushed from the courtroom, a fleet-footed fox. Where he was running to, God only knows. The telephone directory? City tax rolls? He would not find anyone called Granville there, not one who matched our man's description.

The coroner dismissed me. 'Now, a name,' he said, 'is a whole lot more helpful than a hat.'

SATURDAY, AUGUST 19

Late morning

Ahmie tips her chin toward the back door. "The blackberries are ripe," she says, and Llewellyn knows exactly where Isla and Harriet will be. Ahmie won't mind if he cuts through the kitchen and out the back gate; Llewellyn knows Ahmie loves him. She's making blackberry jelly. He stops at the stove for a moment to peer over her shoulder into the dark pot of simmering berries. On the kitchen table hangs a cheesecloth bag, tied between the four legs of an upended chair. Deep purple juice drips into a bowl beneath it. He can already taste the blackberry jelly on one of Ahmie's famous scones and says so. "Patience," Ahmie says, and she shoos him out the door.

He lets the back gate latch close quietly and stands in the alley, content to watch for the moment. They're down by the empty lot, Flore, too, tin pails in hand. Last winter the house there went up in flames and burnt to the ground. The blackberries have already taken over, spreading so quickly and so densely that there remains no evidence of the charred house but for a half-tumbled chimney that juts up, black and uncertain, a prisoner of vines.

The lane weeds and grasses are bent, still heavy with last night's rain, the droplets of water on them glistening now as the clouds disperse and the sun breaks through. He is face to face with a hollyhock that is nearly as tall as he is. He finds himself bowing to this flower in Ahmie's magnificent patch of *Alcea rosea*. Their seeds—he has been told many times now—were brought all the way from Manitoba by dear old Ahmie. With one finger, he tips a collection of water from the pink hollow of a blossom.

Down the lane, the women drop berries into their buckets, every other handful going straight into their mouths. He can taste these sweet fat Himalayan blackberries, *Rubus armeniacus*—so disdained by his father for not being the native variety—in their laughter. He has, for many years, taken a contrarian's pleasure in the breakneck speed of their growth, all those "foreign" brambles overtaking vacant lots, smothering the footings of bridges, defining and encroaching on the borders of rural pastures, and his father's yard. (Their housekeeper made both jam and jelly with the invasive berries, neither of which his father ever had any trouble spreading on his bread.)

Flore is surprisingly ethereal, the late morning sun on her golden hair. Surprising because *ethereal* is not the word that normally springs to mind when Llewellyn thinks of Flore. But there she is, almost fairylike in the filtered light. He watches as she bends her knees then springs upward. Quickly he changes his mind: she's a goddess, not a fairy. Then she catches a berry-laden vine and "Ouch," she cries and shoves her prickled fingers in her mouth. Flore is human after all. Harriet, in trousers and easily taken for boy at this distance, is like some tall, slender youth, also from a Greek myth, not yellow-haired but golden as well. She reaches up and easily pulls the vine down toward Flore, who, perhaps in gratitude, pops a berry into Harriet's mouth. Llewellyn walks closer, hoping not to be seen yet; he loves the sight of them, these women he is so enchanted by, gleaning.

Rue gives him away.

The old dog shouts a warning bark, then, recognizing him, yips her pleasure and rushes bandy-legged down the lane toward him. Flore and Harriet wave; Isla does not. He had not expected a warm reception. She turns her back and disappears, seemingly into the brambles. Harriet, in what must be sisterly allegiance, follows her.

"So now we know his name," Flore says.

"Yes. Now we know." Llewellyn nods too many times. He makes himself stop.

Flore faces him. "Have you found him then?"

She's not even remotely ethereal anymore. More like the goddess of war, Athena. Llewellyn shakes his head.

"No?" Flore says. "So we're no closer to righting the world's wrongs, are we? Or whatever it was you thought you were doing."

Llewellyn looks over briefly, remembering that Athena was also the goddess of wisdom. Her face is placid. This, he thinks, is what fools people about Flore, the way she can look so much like someone's darling spaniel when in reality she is a German shepherd.

"Not really," he says. He's rather fond of German shepherds, but he would happily be somewhere other than next to this one.

They have wandered down to the beach. Flore tied Rue to a fencepost in the alley, hung her blackberry pail out of the dog's reach, and shouted to Harriet and Isla, silent in the brambles, that she would be back. Now they are seated on a driftwood log, twenty feet from the shore.

"What you did was horrible. She said you promised she wouldn't be called to testify."

Llewellyn shakes his head and furrows a channel in the sand with the toe of his shoe. Of one thing he's sure: he can better stand Flore's anger than Isla's.

"It's unlikely she'll ever talk to you again, you know," Flore says. "What on earth were you thinking?"

He shrugs. It would, he knows, be wiser to acknowledge that he had no idea what he was thinking. He should admit that he was that proverbial drowning man clutching at whatever proverbial straw happened to be floating by. Nonetheless, what he says next is a lie: "I thought she must have known something more than she was admitting."

Flore snorts. "You're joking."

"I'm not." He's digging in now, that hole into which liars fall getting deeper.

She turns her whole body toward him. Her hands are palmed together, as if in prayer. She taps the tips of her fingers once against his chest. "For Christ's sake, Llew, everyone questioned her. The police. The coroner. You. And you think she's going to come out with something new because she's under oath? You cannot possibly know Isla very well if you thought that."

He can't know Isla very well? He wants to tell her that no one could know Isla better. No one. To stop himself, he bends and sifts a purple mussel shell out of the sand. He finds another shell, small and white, and places it in the mussel, cupping them in his hand, letting the grains of sand drain between his fingers.

He loved this beach when he was a child. They used to come to the city, the annual family trip to pay homage to Rose, an ancient great-aunt. About this time every summer. His father so proudly drove his new car—a Flanders 20—ten miles an hour at the most, which meant the trip often took them two or more hours. He once got a beating for telling his father that the twenty in the automobile's name might be a better driving speed. The reward for the long, silent car ride, however, weather permitting, was a trip to the beach at English Bay. His mother, head held high in her huge hat and fashionable frock, his father no doubt sweltering, even in his summer suit, strolled along the pier, avoiding, as best they could, the unruly throng they looked down upon. Llewellyn, shoes and socks off and pants rolled up, longed to run wild with all the other children, strangers who plunged joyously, endlessly, into the salty water. Oh, to swim out with the others to the slide. To be able to glide like a real swimmer, rather than paddling like a dog. He would stand there, water lapping his white calves, shivering, watching, afraid to go any deeper. Then it was time to have tea with the great-aunt and begin the long, tiresome drive home.

He remembers now, with only a pinch of the original pleasure, the time he witnessed old Joe Fortes dive off the pier. He turns to Flore. "You knew something," he says to her. It's not an accusation. It's simply a statement, though one he hopes might derail her from the attack he is anticipating.

"Me? About Isla? Very little. Not much more than you did."

A gang of boys, tan and lithe, has suddenly appeared, eleven- or twelve-year-olds, parading like soldiers through the water at ankle depth, knees high, their voices as deep as they can make them—*left, right, left, right*.

"You knew she was pregnant. I didn't," he says.

"Why would you?" Flore says dismissively, watching the boys.

He remains silent. When Flore looks back at him his face flushes; he doesn't look away.

"Oh my God."

"Flore—"

"It was yours? It was yours."

Flore stands, slides her hands over her ears, and palms her cheeks. She is staring at the sand, her back to him, shaking her head.

On a shouted command, the boys turn in the reverse direction and troop past again, less disciplined now. Before long, they fall apart completely, shoving one another over in the water, diving beneath the waves, shouting. Llewellyn watches them. What is this ache rising in his chest? Sadness, regret, relief. He needed to tell someone. Who else but Flore?

"I . . ." he starts, then stops. He lets her wrestle with this news; there's no need for his commentary. When she finally turns, he is shocked to see that she's not angry; it's tenderness he sees in Flore's eyes.

She puts her hand on his arm. "I am so sorry, Llew," Flore says. The relief makes him laugh, though tears come to his own eyes. "I don't know what to say."

"Nothing, I guess," Llewellyn says. "It's over."

Flore nods. "Does Morag know?"

"God, no," he says. His heart constricts.

"I suppose that's for the best," Flore says.

"You'll keep it quiet too?"

"Of course."

"Even Harriet?" He watches something slide into her eyes: apprehension. "Even Harriet," he says again, wrapping her hands in his.

"Yes," she says finally.

They sit silently for a while, watching the soldier boys who have tossed themselves like eulachons onto the warm sand.

"Would you have wanted her to keep it, if you knew?"

Llewellyn picks up the two shells again and bounces them in his hand. "Of course."

"Really?" she asks. "How would that have worked?"

ooooo

Harriet stands watching. What are they talking about? A minute ago, she'd seen Flore suddenly stand and turn her back on Llewellyn, her face in her hands. Then she turned back to him and touched him, his arm. Llewellyn took both her hands in his, some secret pressed from him to her, or from her to him, between their palms. Their eyes were locked, their faces sober. Harriet will be excluded from whatever was shared; she already knows that. There's a gang of boys in front of them. They emerge from the water and throw themselves noisily down on the sand. Harriet looks down at her shirt, stained purple, a berry massacre on her belly. Rue barks. She pulls on her leash and the handful of blackberries Harriet has brought as an offering fall into the sand.

ooooo

Llewellyn looks up and there is Harriet, her white shirt stained purple, as if she has been using it as a bucket.

"This is where you got to," Harriet says. She's sullen as a child.

"Yes, here we are," says Llewellyn.

Flore taps the log: *Come sit.*

Llewellyn stands, turning away from the hurt on Harriet's face. He calls to the boys: "Atten-shun!" They leap to their feet and snap their arms up in salute. How joyous they are.

RUE

No fruit falls more into perfectly into the domain of the gods than the blackberry. Am I mistaken? I think not. The peach, you suggest? A close second, but for its skin, textured much like that of a vole's, which, in a fruit, is surely a failure of nature. (If I live a thousand years, I hope never to relive my Lost-Days-in-the-Park encounter with a vole. Be assured: even the little ones are not at all tasty.) Not the fallen plum, nor the apricot, pear, apple, or unobtainable huckleberry, and especially not the ridiculously flavourless and watery salmonberry. (Have you ever seen anyone wasting sugar in the making of salmonberry jam? That is correct, you have not.)

Some will say that my predilection for blackberries comes from the fact that I am able to glean them myself, which is, indeed, at least a partial truth. Before I was a year old, Rasia had taught me this foraging skill. Even today, as my eyesight fails, I am expert at determining which berries are ripe, which are likely to be sour, and which will leave prickles in my muzzle.

I approved of Harriet's thoughtful gesture that day—bringing Flore blackberries as a gift—and was (I am not overly ashamed to say) elated when, after a tug on my leash, her cache of berries cascaded onto the sand. Ruined for her, I found them quite delectable, even if gritty. (There were plenty more left on the vines.) But I am negligent in my duties, focussing on the pre-eminence of the blackberry when there are more important tales to be told.

And yet, as I ponder this now, I wonder what I would have been able to tell you right then. Something secretive, obviously, had taken place between Goldilocks and the sad-eyed one on that log on the beach. But even I, in front of whom the humans speak embarrassingly freely, had no inkling (then) of what had just been shared.

That blackberry season, there was a strange mix of emotion in the air. In some of the pack, I sensed sadness. In Isla, sadness *and* relief. There was love. Longing. And anger. And some seemed particularly plagued by extreme versions of that nebulous emotion, worry. In the sad-eyed one, Llewellyn, I sensed the impatience and the restlessness of the hunter.

But mostly, I believe, everyone seemed to be caught in a limbo of sorts, waiting. Waiting. Not for something to happen, perhaps, so much as for what had happened to drift away and become part of the past. Tick tock. Time hurrying past. As you know, it is never so simple as that. A slow meander through a forest was a better description of the nature of time just then.

ISLA

August went; September came. People love spring, that tender prophesier of summer. I love September. Sunny, still warmish, but with its first lick of coolness at night. Like someone holding fast, brave and enduring, before the grey rains of October and November. And before winter bashes in. September is a month that, if it was human, I'd be in love with.

'You're quiet,' Flore said, leaning across the table.

We were at the restaurant Morag had named the Hateful Café. She had, by then, refused to ever again darken the door of that establishment on East Hastings. I don't know if I ever knew the café's actual name. It's gone now. We knew it simply as 'the one on the corner with the green door' until Morag came up with its apt nickname which we all, immediately, adopted. Flore and I took perverse pleasure in being served by the surly waiters and waitresses, and in giving the evil eye to the skinny supervisor who lorded it over the staff.

His Skinniness, we called him. He was clearly the source of all the peevishness.

'Quiet? Am I?'

'You look good though,' Flore said.

I narrowed my eyes at her. I'd passed the mirror in the front room too many times not to know that I still looked like a stick-figure drawing. *Pinched*, *peaked*, *wraith-like*, to list a few of the annoying if valid descriptors that Ahmie had been tossing around. I'd gained a few pounds, but where those pounds sat, I couldn't say. My appetite was nil. My stomach felt the size of a walnut.

'All right. You look like you got run over by a trolley, then limped off to the woods where you've been living off fiddleheads, blackberries, and perhaps a roast mallard or two for a couple months,' Flore said, poking my forearm with her fork. 'But definitely better than a week ago. Have some pie. It'll help with the barn owl pallor.'

I laughed. She reached across the table and picked up my fork and put it in my hand. Normally I'd eat my pie and half of Flore's. (I still don't understand how she can leave anything on her plate. Clearly she's never had to worry about whether there will be enough to eat. We who have, know to scrape our plates clean.) But that day in the café I wasn't hungry. 'Glad I can count on your honesty, Flore. Thank you. You're as sweet as my mother.'

'You're very welcome.' She tilted her head toward me in a courteous bow. 'So,' she said.

'So, what?'

'So, how are you really?'

I stared out the window. The traffic in front of the Hateful Café was always endless. Your usual passersby—businessmen, shoppers, workers, women pushing prams and towing small children by the hand. Delivery boys. Cars and trucks, the rattling trollies. Always a few vagrant men panhandling outside and sometimes a huddle of ladies of the night, even if it was the middle of the day. Occasionally a fistfight, the participants male or female. The constant churn of humanity. Life goes on, even if you're not sure it should. I felt, then, as though I was waiting for something, God knows what.

Flore looked back over her shoulder to see what I was staring at. 'Helloooo?' she said, wiggling her fingers in front of me like a hypnotist.

I swirled what was left of the tea in my cup. 'I saw Gianluca Padula last Sunday.'

For a moment, Flore didn't say anything, wise woman, although that may have been a sharp intake of breath I heard. She took a bite of pie and didn't look up. She swallowed. 'Oh? Where?' Casually, quietly.

I lied. 'I ran into him. He and the children.'

Flore just kept on eating her pie.

'They were in the park. Out for a Sunday stroll, I guess,' I said, attempting to sound as casual as possible myself.

'How is he? How are the children?'

'Fine. At least I think fine. Grieving, of course.'

'Poor soul, what he endured. What they endured.'

'Truly.' I put a forkful of pie in my mouth but wished I hadn't. My dishonesty was rising like bile in my throat.

It was easy enough to weasel Maria Veltri and Gianluca Padula's address out of Llewellyn. Llew was so happy to hear my voice and happier still to hear I'd forgiven him. Not entirely a lie. Not exactly the truth. And of course, he couldn't have imagined that I would call on the man.

The building was in Grand View, on a side street just off Powell. Gianluca answered my knock, flinging the door to their two-room apartment wide open and standing there like a puffed-up grouse, albeit a grouse with a hunting knife in its hand. He peered up and down the hall making sure, perhaps, that the police were not skulking there. He dropped his left hand, pressing the knife flat to his thigh, and indicated that I should come in. 'Shut the door,' he said, and I did.

The three children, playing on the floor, eyed me cautiously. The two eldest turned their backs. The baby, Angelo, ran and clung to Gianluca's leg. Gianluca humped over to the table with the child still attached, and he and his knife went back to the work he'd been doing—chopping carrots and potatoes. He must already have fried onions in bacon fat or lard because the room was fragrant with them. In Italian, then with a *please* in English, he sent the girl, Mariana, for water. She left with an empty pot and returned with it a few minutes later, filled at a communal tap somewhere, I presumed. There was a sink in the room; Gianluca caught me looking. 'Tap's on the fritz,' he said. 'Sit down.'

Angelo gave up Gianluca's leg in exchange for a little cup of blackberries; he waddled off with it to the farthest corner of the room. Gianluca salted the water and added the vegetables and scraped in a pan of onions. He set the pot to simmer on a hotplate. Then he pulled out a chair and sat next to me.

And there we were: the one left behind and the one who'd survived. Gianluca's eyes explored my face with the questioning vagueness of the recently bereaved, as if I was someone he used to know but couldn't quite remember. I regretted my intrusion. I thought I knew why I'd come, but there at the table, the fabric of whatever my intention had been began to fray. 'I should go,'

I said. 'I'm sorry.' But I couldn't stand; I lowered my face to my hands like a child hiding behind its mother's skirt, eyes closed, world gone, not the subject of Gianluca Padula's unfocussed gaze. What really was I sorry about? Maria mostly. The inquest. Llewellyn. He touched my elbow to get my attention and I lifted my head.

'If I find him, I'll kill him.'

A dog started howling, and we sat listening to its tale of hardship as though it would be rude to interrupt. Someone down the hall or upstairs or out in the street finally shouted at the dog; there was a yelp then a whimper and the howling ceased.

'I understand,' I said.

'For Maria. And for you,' he said.

Mariana and Salvatore played quietly at our feet, he with a rag dog and some marbles, she with what looked like a handmade game of knucklebones. Occasionally, while Gianluca and I talked, the children peered up at me with shy eyes. After a while, the baby crawled into Gianluca's lap and placidly gazed at me with an open-mouthed stare. Then, suddenly, he stretched out his arms toward me, and I instinctively lifted mine. Gianluca, the heartbreak in his eyes deepening, hoisted him onto my knees. Angelo, his face cocked up to look at mine, seemed wary but curious; his eyes never left my face. I murmured and smiled at him, reassuring him that he'd be all right on this stranger's lap, until, at last, his warm little body relaxed against mine, his breathing deepened, and the dark lashes fell. I buried my face in his hair, smelling him. I thought of the little Westcott boys and their sweet heads. Were they, I wondered, missing me as much as I was missing them?

Gianluca rose to check on the soup pot. He came back to the table and put his hand on my shoulder.

'Join us for supper. It's just soup . . .'

'I didn't bring anything to offer you,' I said.

'Next time you can bring a loaf of bread,' Gianluca said.

Next time.

We sat at their small table, Angelo now in his high chair, beside Mariana. The little girl and Salvatore mostly kept their heads down and spoke in Italian to each other, though their glances at me were braver now, longer. Gianluca put a bowl of soup in front of me. It was delicious. The children scooped the last bits of carrot from the bottom of their bowls and then there were more blackberries for dessert.

Angelo cried when I left. I was not foolish enough to imagine that his sobs had anything to do with me. They were the cries of a child who has met the monster who lives under the bed.

We stood in the hallway. Mariana held Angelo. He buried his wet face in her hair and she stroked his back, a child comforting a child. Salvatore, beside them, was silent, stoic. Gianluca and I shook hands, like businessmen agreeing to a deal. It was an absurd way to say goodbye, though I suppose we had agreed to something unspoken. I could still hear Angelo shrieking *Mama*, even once I was out on the street.

Flore tapped my empty teacup with her fork.

'Can I ask you something?'

She was nervous. The vein ticking in her temple kindled a hollow feeling in my gut. I knew what she was going to ask. 'Go ahead,' I said. I was ready to confess.

'I'm not judging you,' she said. 'It's just . . . Why didn't you go to one of the women I told you about? Why did you choose this Granville man?'

It was not what I was expecting. I thought she'd ask me the question only the coroner who had visited our house ever dared ask. Everyone in the family seemed too leery of the possible answer: Who was the father?

Looking up, I stiffened. Behind Flore, a customer rising from her seat was backing blindly into a waiter passing with a tray laden with clean coffee cups. I expected a spectacular sound, cups and saucers falling, smashing, spreading across the floor, the tray bouncing, once, twice. But I heard only muted thumps, as though the floor was made of moss. The waiter was hot red, hands on hips, mouth working in an almost soundless fury. The customer, a pink-faced woman, bent toward him, conciliatory and apologetic. The waiter kicked at the broken pottery, scattering it everywhere. Under my feet. Against the wall. He whipped his apron hard across the woman's table scattering more dishes and cutlery. He flung the café's door open. It slid quietly shut behind him. In the hush, I was outside of myself, inside of him, feeling the satisfying heat-flush of his rage. The waiter had done what I had been longing to do for weeks: explode.

Flore took hold of my arms and gently pulled my hands away from my ears.

I laughed. I felt exhausted. I wanted to cry. 'I'm sorry,' I said.

His Skinniness appeared. 'Who's going to sweep up this mess?' he shouted. A few customers laughed. One man said, 'Well, not me.' A waitress came out of the kitchen with a broom and handed it to her boss. When she stripped off her apron and threw it in his astonished face, nothing could have been more satisfying.

'Time to go?' Flore laughed, putting on her hat.

Outside, she took my arm. We walked awhile in silence. The smell of fall was sharp in the air. The five-o'clock crowds were on the street, hurrying, before the shops closed, to buy provisions for their Labour Day picnics, hurrying to get home and dressed for their Saturday-night dates. Just hurrying. Me, I wanted never to be in a rush again.

I knew Flore wasn't satisfied. I hadn't answered her question. I also knew she wouldn't insist. Why did I choose the man named Granville? In June, when I'd asked, Flore had given me two names, without comment and with just the right amount of commiseration. I'd telephoned both women. The first—Mrs. Lukins—never answered. I called several times, and the phone rang and rang. Finally, I'd given up.

'I called your friend's aunt too. Mrs. Daniel,' I told Flore. 'She was willing, but she said she was working out of Seattle. She wanted me to go there. I didn't have the money for that. And even if I had, I don't know how I would have gotten back on my own,' I said. 'Afterwards, I mean.'

'I would have come with you,' Flore said.

It wasn't reproach I saw in her face. She was hurt. I'd hurt her.

'I don't believe that people should have to do hard things like that on their own,' she said.

'Nor do I.'

'But you did. This. You did it alone.'

I shook my head. 'I was desperate, Flore,' I said. 'I'm sorry. It truly never occurred to me that anything would go wrong. Stupid, I know.'

'No need to apologize. I just wish you'd asked for help.' She stopped and said, 'It all went so wrong.'

'My fate, I guess,' I said. I watched a wave of anger replace the hurt in Flore's eyes.

'Your fate could also have been the same as Maria Veltri's.'

I shrugged, though that dismissive gesture belied what I felt. I hated hurting or angering Flore. 'I suppose,' I said.

'Do you regret it?' she asked.

I laughed. 'What part of it?'

Regret. I am overly familiar with that useless sentiment; it is my constant companion, frowning on the sidelines like a disappointed parent, that pointer finger asking whether I might not want to follow a better path next time. Tap, tap, tap.

Here is my list of regrets: I regret betraying my sister. I regret getting pregnant. I regret choosing Granville. I regret not choosing to ask for help that day (and therefore nearly bleeding to death on the shore of Lost Lagoon). I regret losing my damn shoe. (No one wants one half of a pair of shoes, except maybe a dog. It is a dreadful waste. This, on the scale of regrets, is small, I know, but good shoes do not come easily for some of us.) I regret worrying my family.

Here's what I know about regret: It changes nothing.

Here is the list of what I cannot bring myself to regret: Having loved Llewellyn.

Flore and I wandered into Government Square—it's Victory Square now—and a flock of pigeons flew up, away from us, grey and white and that iridescent pink. We watched them circle one of the maple trees planted in the square and alight instead on top of a building.

'I regret going to that bastard,' I said.

'I'm afraid of what will happen if Llew ever finds this Granville,' Flore said.

I wondered what she and Llewellyn had talked about, and she looked down, as if she knew what I was thinking. 'I know. Gianluca Padula too. He wants to kill him.'

'They think that if they put an end to villains like Granville they'll have solved all the villainy in the world, don't they?'

'They do,' I said.

Flore leaned against the trunk of the maple and sighed. 'I had one, too, you know.'

I didn't have to ask 'one what?' I understood.

'I should have asked my father's business partner, *ex*–business partner, what he found attractive about a fifteen-year-old girl.'

'Oh God. What happened?' I asked.

'To him? Not much. He went his way, and my father went his. My father found someone to take care of it. Of me. When you've got money, it's so much easier.'

'I'm so sorry, Flore,' I said. Out of my pocket I pulled a shiny brown horse chestnut I'd found that morning. I gave it to her.

'So pretty,' she said quietly.

There was nothing more to say.

That was Saturday.

On Sunday morning I took another glossy chestnut from my pocket and handed it to Gianluca. 'Pretty,' he said. He smelled it and shined it on his vest, then he pocketed it.

We were standing at the corner of Cordova and Seymour. For more than an hour that morning we'd waited, patient as bird-watchers, hoping to catch sight of our Mr. Granville. After that, there were rainy Saturday afternoons, windy Sundays, quiet weekday mornings or Tuesday evenings. We brought thermoses of tea, biscuits, sometimes an apple that Gianluca would slice in half with his penknife and then carefully cut the core out of, as one might do for a child. A few times he brought the children; we called it a walk. For weeks we kept up our vigil. When we stopped meeting on that downtown corner and started meeting indoors instead—the library, the lobby of the train station, the aisles of department stores, and, eventually, Gianluca's flat—we told ourselves it was because of the weather. Too rainy, we said. Too cold, we agreed, not quite looking one another in the eye. Neither of us wanted to admit that we had given up. That we were tired of being disappointed. And there was something else: we'd bonded like birds do. It wasn't love, not at first; it was the terrible thing we shared. We'd become dependent on each other. By Armistice Day, I'm sure neither of us felt that we would survive without the other.

SATURDAY, SEPTEMBER 23

Closing time

The girl had slammed past Harriet, head down, hat like a shield—though misery like that could never be hidden, even by a low-brimmed cloche—and locked herself in a toilet stall. And now the noises coming from behind the door are not happy sounds. How long does one wait before one taps on the door to offer help of any kind? Or should Harriet just mind her own business and have a hand-towel ready? For all she knows the girl will bawl it out and appear at the sink, calm, dry-eyed, ready to put on her lipstick, and smile at Harriet as if to say *No, nothing's wrong, why on earth do you ask?*

Harriet has seen her share of tear-stained faces in the lavatory at Woodward's department store. The suffering seems epidemic—every few days, another girl, sobbing her heart out in a bathroom stall. When they emerge, most have little to say; they go off with their woes, lonely and private. For those few who do spill the beans, there is always a man involved. Always. Harriet wipes the counter again and dabs at a spot on the mirror even though she knows that small rusty mark is permanent and she has already done her final tidy-up. Her shift is over in five minutes. Flore is waiting for her outside, at street level, under the Woodward's sign. For a second, Harriet feels just a tiny bit smug—no man will break *her* heart. Then she catches her reflection in the mirror. She turns left and right, examining her profile. What in God's name does Flore see in her? She grimaces at herself and pokes her tongue at the little gap between her two front teeth. Flore says she loves that gap. Harriet clamps her mouth shut and turns her back on the mirror. Flore's nuts.

The girl in the stall lets out a terrible sob. It's depressing how lonely human beings can be. Since Isla—Harriet thinks of her life this way now: *since Isla*—girls crying in the toilet stalls is much more disquieting. Before, they were in there crying over some liar or cheat. Now, they might be bleeding to death from poking themselves with something sharp. Or someone else might have done the poking. Harriet leans against a sink and crosses her arms. She'll give the girl two minutes, then she'll knock. One, one thousand, two, one thousand, three, one thousand, four.

When the outside door to the lavatory opens, Harriet expects to see the night watchman, Mr. Hirst, whose job every night is to make sure no one is loitering in the stalls. But it's Flore.

"I thought I'd come collect you," Flore says. She tucks her hands into the pockets of Harriet's smock and lifts her face to be kissed just as the stall door smacks open and the weeping girl emerges, red-eyed, hat off. Harriet shoves Flore away. The girl's eyes widen and she makes a sound of disgust. She leaves without washing her hands.

"Well," Flore laughs. "Not so friendly, that one."

"It's not funny. I could lose my job."

Flore leans against Harriet again and kisses her this time. "You won't lose your job. And you didn't have to shove me quite so violently," she teases. But tears spring to Harriet's eyes. "Oh, my girl. It's all right. She's got more on her mind than who's kissing whom in the Woodward's lavatory," Flore says.

"You don't understand. If I lost this job, who'd pay the rent?" Harriet says, brushing away the hand Flore puts to her cheek. "And I don't know why she was crying."

There's a knock on the door and it opens, just far enough for half the watchman's face to appear. Harriet gives Flore another rough push.

"Time to clear out, ladies," he says. "Store's closed."

"We're on our way, Mr. Hirst," Harriet says.

"Am I forgiven?" Flore asks.

They're crossing Government Square, where Roddy once took Harriet to see the recruitment marquees, so long ago, at the start of the war. "No," Harriet says.

Flore takes Harriet's arm. "You're lying," she says, and Harriet laughs. How could she not forgive Flore?

On Pender Street, Harriet says, "Did I ever tell you how we used to play the wiener game?"

"Argh. I'm not sure I want you to. By 'we' whom do you mean?"

"Mind out of the gutter, Flore." She nudges Flore's shoulder with hers. "The whole family. We used to do it on the streetcar."

"Ack!" Flore laughs. "It gets worse! And here I thought you were a wholesome bunch and you a perfectly loveable girl."

"Wait! You'll laugh." Harriet points at the signage on the Universal Knitting Company building. "See that? All you do is replace one word in a sign with the word *wiener*. So, you have Universal Wiener Co. Ltd. And up above, at the top." She points. "Makers of Canada's Finest Wiener Coats."

"For Men, Women, and Wieners," Flore laughs.

"You've got it."

"This is going to make my walk home much more amusing. You should tell Padraig about this. He'll love it."

"Nugget Wiener Polish."

"Undertakers, Embalmers, and Wieners."

"Grandma's Wiener!"

"You're ridiculous."

"You are."

They're not halfway home when Flore presses Harriet's arm more tightly against her side and asks, "Do you think I'm too old for you?"

"Why? Do you think I'm too young for you?" A ship is sinking in Harriet's belly: Was it the silly wiener game? Was it too immature?

"I'm just asking. Some might think—"

Some might think we shouldn't be together at all, Harriet could remind Flore. "I'll be twenty next year," she says instead.

"Um-hmm," says Flore. "And I'll be twenty-four."

They take the alleyway. Harriet unlatches the back gate. Georgina had said she might come for a visit after work, but her bicycle is not here. Come and gone already, Harriet supposes. She hopes that Georgina has snuck out with her friend Fergal Doherty, he who is so preferable to Victor Dunn. One of Ahmie's hollyhocks, still flowering though bedraggled, leans at her, over the fence. She breaks off the top of the stalk of dark-pink blossoms and gives it to Flore. Isla has hung the laundry on the lines that criss-cross the backyard. Mrs. Barker, upstairs, must have hung hers, too, because every line is in use. Rue, who was sleeping in a patch of sunlight between the shadows of their sheets and towels and undergarments, rises and stretches, pitching tail-end back first, then nose forward. She yawns and Harriet bends to pick her up. At least Isla hasn't hung their menstrual rags outside, as she's been threatening to do in some declaration of women's emancipation, encouraging Mrs. Barker to do so as well. Harriet hopes if her own rags are anywhere, they're inside on the rack above the stove. Or better yet, already dry and folded away in her dresser drawer. It seems it's only Harriet who bleeds now. No one has been particularly clear with Harriet on whether Isla will ever get her flow again. Now she realizes that she'd give anything for Isla to have rags to hang on the line.

As she rises, Rue in her arms, Flore is standing there, under the clothesline, with the legs of a pair of old-fashioned underpants hanging over her shoulders. Flore lurches to the left, then right, as if she is playing chicken in the schoolyard, someone on her shoulders, like the boys used to at Lord Strathcona Elementary. Look who's being silly now, Harriet thinks. That sinking ship in her belly seems to have righted itself. Harriet laughs. "Those are Mrs. Barker's!"

Ahmie is stretched out on the settee, asleep. They let her lie, but Harriet taps gently on Isla's door. No answer. Isla is never home. Where does she go? She's out every day, though she still doesn't have a job.

Flore has a hold of Harriet's hand now and is pulling her into her bedroom. Now they're falling down onto the bed and Flore is kissing her.

"My mother," Harriet whispers.

"No, your lover," Flore says. "Your mother's the one out there in a laudanum-induced sleep on the divan."

Lover. How is it that Flore is always so calm?

Flore slides her hand up beneath Harriet's blouse and exposes her white midriff. She kisses her belly. "You're like an English milk maid."

"What? A milk maid?" says Harriet. "Don't you think I'm manly?"

They both laugh, and Harriet rolls Flore onto her back. "I think *you're* the milk maid," she says.

"Ah, everyone always wants to be on top, don't they?"

Nothing in nature is as soft as Flore's skin. Only rabbit's fur. Or the plant that grows in the garden next door—*lamb's ear*, they call it. Harriet slides her hand under the waistband of Flore's skirt; Flore responds with a sweet exhalation and closes her eyes. Flore's hand finds Harriet, too, and they lie, face to face, their hands moving gently, until Flore curls forward with a moan. Harriet gives her a minute, then rocks gently against Flore's still hand. Flore takes the hint. She leans in to kiss her.

"Harriet?" Isla is at the door.

"God!" Harriet pulls Flore's hand out of her pants and sits up. She tucks in her blouse.

"Don't be so nervous, Harry," Flore says, lying back on the bed. She smells her own fingertips then puts them in her mouth.

"You are very wicked, Flore." Harriet says, but the pulse between Harriet's thighs is exquisite.

Isla's knocking.

"Get up," Harriet whispers. She tosses Flore a book from her bedside table and picks one up herself.

"Coming," Flore calls out and laughs.

Ahmie is up, rustling around the kitchen, searching the cupboards with the frenzied energy of a red squirrel.

"What are you hunting for Ahmie? Can I help?" Isla asks.

"A nut she buried last winter," Harriet whispers to Flore, who frowns disapprovingly.

"The tea." Ahmie, having pulled a few items out of the Hoosier, is now putting them back in.

"It's over here, where it always is, Ahmie, in the tea tin." Isla picks up the old tin box from the counter. It has followed her mother from Scotland to the Prairies to Vancouver.

"Your father gave me this," she says, taking it from Isla and working with her fingernails to get the lid open.

"Yes, that's right. He bought it for you in Inverness, didn't he?"

Ahmie has the lid off now and is spooning loose tea into the pot.

Harriet leans toward Isla. "Time for a dose of laudanum?"

Isla ignores Harriet. "I'll put the kettle on," she says.

"Thank you, dear." Then Ahmie turns and looks from Harriet to Flore. "So, what is it you do, anyway?"

"What do you mean, Mrs. McKenzie? Do you mean my work? I have a job in a bookstore."

"No, no, no. I mean, what do you do in the bedroom? There's nothing that fits together with two girls, is there?"

Harriet is a brilliant scarlet colour. Isla has turned her back and is shaking with laughter at the stove.

Flore puts on her hat. "I think I'll leave this one to you, Harriet." She bows slightly at Ahmie, hands her the hollyhock, and lets herself out the back door.

RUE

It was apparent to *me*, that lovely end-of-September afternoon, that Ahmie did *not* think it *in*appropriate for Morag to wander unaccompanied through the streets—she and her burgeoning belly—though clearly not to Morag, who, as she bent and buckled my collar, accused her mother of 'old-fashioned' thought. My belief (I stand by it to this day) is that Ahmie simply did not want to be alone. And there was Morag, 'borrowing' me, as she had said, for an hour or two, so that she herself might not be alone on her walk. Misunderstanding: humans are the kings and queens of it. What a good counselor I would be, if only I could speak.

We gazed our farewells to one another, I, by my forlorn expression, attempting to reassure Ahmie that I would miss her as much as she would miss me.

'Imagine if I'd told her I might like to bicycle,' Morag said as we descended the front steps.

I scowled at the round-bellied one, but I'm sure I was not understood. My facial expressions are, doubtless, too subtle for human interpretation.

But Morag was bedevilled by a more pressing dilemma that day, of which she quickly apprised me. She had in her handbag, she told me, a letter. Addressed and stamped it was—she later showed me the envelope with its green two-cent stamp and orange one-cent war-tax stamp, both adorned with the King's mustachioed portrait—and ready to be mailed. But should she post it, she pondered aloud. Did she have the right? *Should I, or shouldn't I?*

Who, I would have asked, had I been able, is the addressee? She left me in the dark for longer than necessary while she rambled on about a dream she'd had in which a baby was being held aloft by an old man. The old man was joyously happy, the dandled baby as well. 'Could this be,' she asked me, 'my baby's grandfather?' Her dreams, she explained, were as nigh to premonition as could be. And if this were a premonition, the letter should be posted. 'They should know,' she said.

To whom, I howled, is the damned letter addressed, and what is its content?

If hindsight were foresight, I would have found the letter and torn it to shreds ere she ever posted it, for the addressees were the mother and father of Llewellyn. The contents of the letter: the news that Morag and her husband, their child, were themselves with child.

She did not post her epistle that day, though she did stand indecisive in front of the postbox for several minutes. Finally, a man, perhaps not noticing her condition (or perhaps not caring that she was nigh five months gone), smiled at her with the eyes and mouth of a flirt. He offered to open the postbox's slot for her himself—men do love Morag—and she flushed and smiled and dropped her gaze and tucked the envelope back into her purse.

'I'll think on it,' she said as we continued our walk.

If only she had been more prudent with her thoughts. Three cents of postage stamps be damned. If only she had tossed the letter forthwith onto a coal grate—any coal grate—and incinerated its contents to ash.

FRIDAY, SEPTEMBER 29

Midday

A strange notion, Georgina thinks, as she passes a plodding bicyclist, this idea of letting go of one's anger. Morag, yesterday, all benevolent philosopher queen, had taken Georgina's hands in hers: 'You're so angry, Georgina. Let it go. Let it fly off, free as a bird.' But to what end, Georgina wants to know. Each hard, angry pump of the bicycle's pedals is as satisfying as flight. She is nearly flying after all. And isn't there so much to be angry about? Her mouth opens for breath and now she's laughing; oh, the joy of it, this speed.

Then, someone whistles at her from the roadside and there's a sudden rent in the sky. She has a vision of her skirts tangling in the spokes and the ensuing spectacular crash. She lifts her feet from the pedals and they spin without her. The bicycle slows, and there she is, just a woman whose heart is thumping, now more with confusion than with rage or with joy, cruising at moderate speed down the road toward the library.

The world is falling to pieces: she is being driven mad by the thought that it may have been Llewellyn who was Isla's lover. The thought of them together, making a baby, twists her mind like the honeysuckle vine on the back gate at Ahmie's, but not so prettily. Morag, blind to all of it, is strutting about as plump and smug as some Shaughnessy matron's prize rose. Their mother is becoming increasingly peculiar. And Flore, that short little Bolshevik, has Harriet in her sway.

But wasn't she herself, just half a bloody hour ago, swooning around in a reverie about running away to Seattle with a man who is not her husband? Georgina sighs. She has brought a gift for Fergal; why, she cannot say. He surely will not have brought her one. She walks her bicycle up onto the sidewalk and decides that the gift in her pocket will stay there. It's only a little thing, a small amethyst geode that has been gathering dust on her dressing table for years. She'd forgotten how lovely it was, all shined up.

She mounts the stairs and peers into the library through its big glass doors, and when she draws back, she sees, in the doors' reflection, Fergal, standing close behind her. For a moment, without turning, she closes her eyes; she sees herself, a contented wife, shopping for fish for supper, in Seattle.

"I've never seen you in the daylight," Fergal says.

His eyes are a dark hazel, not something she has ever been able to discern in the low lights of Saint Pete's or Medley Court. Brown, she had thought. They are beautiful.

"Nor me you," she says, though that is obvious.

Fergal holds the door open for Georgina and then, his hand hovering near her back but not touching, guides her to a corner at the back of the main hall where there are two large leather chairs and very few patrons. Georgina hesitates; this corner of the library seems private and, perhaps, forbidden.

"Are we, you and I, permitted to be here?" she whispers.

Fergal grins. "Yes. You and I are. Women *and* Catholics," he whispers back. "We're allowed."

"That's not what I mean." She's flustered. "I mean here in these chairs. It feels . . . sanctified or something. Some kind of men's club, or . . ." Georgina laughs, and there is more heat in her already flushed cheeks. She strokes the smooth leather of one of the chairs. "And can we talk?"

"Yes, but quietly I suppose." He laughs. "Have you never been here?"

"Not since I was in school," she says.

They are still standing; Fergal, Georgina knows, is waiting for her to sit first. As impulsively as a sixteen-year-old, she pulls the geode from her pocket. She has wrapped it in a plain white handkerchief and tied it with a red ribbon. Immediately it seems a ridiculous thing to have done, to have brought this gift, to have wrapped it as though it is something special. Still, she holds her hand out toward Fergal, her arm rigid.

"Take it," she says, almost annoyed, as he continues to stare at the small lumpen offering in her hand.

"Thank you," Fergal says, and he picks it from her palm.

"It's just a little thing. I don't know why it made me think of you." But she does know why it made her think of him; like his eyes, it is beautiful.

Fergal unwraps the package and almost immediately pockets the geode and the ribbon. He folds and presses the hankie flat and hands it back to her. "Thank you," he says again, not looking at her. He fishes the ribbon out of his pocket, winds it up, and holds it out to her on one finger.

They sit silently for a minute; she is thinking, and she imagines that he is, too, that they have gone too far, meeting like this, in daylight.

"How was your DWG meeting?" Fergal says to his feet.

"Dreadful." She laughs, flooded by relief.

"That bad?" Fergal smiles and looks at her, finally.

How humiliating it would be to tell him that, last Tuesday at the Dreadful Women's Group, Evelyn Clarke's grandmother scolded them all for having too few children. 'You may stop having children, but the immigrant races won't,' she said. 'Soon there will be fewer of us and more of them.' Race suicide, she called it. 'And Catholics.' She said the word as if it were dirty. 'Breeding like . . .' She left the rest unsaid. Georgina felt every eye in the room on her as Evelyn's grandmother cast her that sideways glance. Georgina herself, the grandmother's eyes said, was a perfect example of the kind of woman responsible for the downfall of their race. As if she were purposely barren. The subject was changed, by Evelyn, though not soon enough for Georgina, and the grandmother was gently shown the parlour door.

At the Tuesday afternoon meetings, the Dreadfuls talk about their womanly skills as society's nurturers and men's helpmates. They bemoan the plight of the poor. Debate the causes of poverty (laziness, uncleanliness, lack of faith, undesirable hereditary traits, too much drink). They plan small charity picnics in their own backyards (where their husbands drink too much). And at every meeting the conversation quickly and with obvious relief turns to happier subjects: Their husbands' successes. Their gardens. Their children. The quantities of socks they knit to send to soldiers overseas during the war. (Georgina hated knitting socks and therefore knit very few. This she does not admit.)

The women who clean their foyers (not well enough). The cost of butter (high). And church. 'Where do you go?' Evelyn asked Georgina at the first meeting she attended. 'Where do I go?' Georgina asked, smiling blankly, not understanding the question. 'What church do you and Mr. Dunn attend?' It took more than a second or two for 'First Presbyterian' to find its way to Georgina's tongue. It was only half a lie. Victor's family went there when he was young. Evelyn looked blank. 'At Hastings and Gore,' Georgina explained. 'So far from here,' Evelyn replied, with a pitying look.

The DWG does not discuss fathers who are atheists, women who miscarry, sisters who have abortions, Darwin, birth control, women's rights, Socialists, the war dead, men with one arm, anger. Last Tuesday, Georgina sat quietly in Evelyn's parlour, she herself a fine example of that class of person for which the DWGs are sure there is no cure. And she smiled and nodded her head.

"They call themselves reformers, but I don't think they actually want to reform anything. I think they just want to protect their own little worlds."

"They're doing their best, I suppose," Fergal says.

"You're always so generous, Fergal," Georgina says, more disdainfully than she'd intended. "The problem is, I think they'd rather just cleanse the world of certain people rather than help them. People like my sister. They don't think much of girls like her." Or of the people who take care of their children, who make their shoes, hand them a clean towel in the Woodward's lavatory, deliver their groceries, and do their laundry. Or of Catholics, she thinks.

"Do you mean Isla?" Fergal asks.

"Isla," she says. "Harriet-Jean. My mother." Me.

"Well, what can you expect from the wives of Victor's friends?" Fergal's hands reach out instantly in embarrassed apology, but Georgina laughs.

"It's all right. He deserves your contempt. Go on."

"They're not attempting to set the world on fire and change the status quo, and neither are their husbands. They're happier just having a game of bridge or golf. Why don't you make a graceful exit? There must be groups of women doing more worthy work. What about Flore Rozema. Aren't Flore's politics more palatable than your DWG's?"

"Flore? Flore's out to crush the capitalist system and have the Bolsheviks run rampant over us. She'd burn Evelyn and her friends in their beds first chance she got."

Fergal looks surprised. "Would we call Flore a Bolshevik, then?"

"I would. Just this morning Isla invited me to some lecture she and Flore were going to. A woman speaker on—" Georgina stops. The lecture was to be on birth control. "On rebuilding the Socialist Party," she says.

Fergal's eyebrows lift ever so slightly. "No DWG attendees, I presume?"

"Not a one." Georgina has to laugh.

Birth control. She had snapped at Isla: No, she did not want to attend a lecture on *birth control.* In truth, she immediately regretted saying no. She would never acknowledge the hypocrisy of her response, but she'd have been fascinated by a lecture on that topic. Barren. Hypocrite. What else is she? At the moment, unbearably dispirited.

"Flore's a little rabid, for me," she says, her disgust for the woman rising again. How could a woman so privileged as to be able to go to university throw it all away and drop out three months before graduation as Flore did?

"I see. Middle ground you'd prefer, then."

"Middle ground." She's surprised by how flat the words feel. "They hate Catholics too," she says bleakly. She doesn't miss the irony of how like a Catholic confession this must sound.

"The Bolsheviks?"

"No, the DWG."

"Of course they do," Fergal says quietly.

Georgina feels sick. How long has she been in Evelyn Clarke's group? How long has she known they hate Catholics? And yet, there she sits every Tuesday afternoon, sipping tea, eating cake, silent, complicit. What would Pa have said?

Fergal nods several times, as if he knows what she is thinking. But then he shrugs. "Any news of this Granville character?"

"None," Georgina says. "Llewellyn's on the hunt though. I fear for my brother-in-law." And she is struck suddenly by the memory of an early morning drive to the country with Llewellyn and Morag and Victor to listen to the spring peepers. Llewellyn's near ecstasy at the beautiful sound of the frogs, 'like a million little bells chiming.' The Pacific chorus frog, he called them. 'Why is the world so beautiful?' he'd wondered aloud. No one had replied, though she had wanted to weep with joy at the beauty of the frog chorus. She picks at a small hole in the arm of the leather chair, a smooth round burn from dropped pipe tobacco perhaps, then stops picking and smooths her hand over it. The library smells stale and old, like Evelyn Clarke's parlour and grandmother. "Can we go somewhere else, Fergal?"

Fergal gazes at her. She cannot mistake the declaration in his eyes. How differently men love, she thinks.

"We can go anywhere you want, Georgie," Fergal says.

As they walk, Georgina keeps an eye out for any of Victor's cronies. She is about to suggest that they find a quieter place to walk when, ahead on the sidewalk, they are startled by an explosion of feathers. Before them stands a beautiful hawk, and in its talons, the not yet lifeless body of a pigeon. In three or four frenzied bouts, the raptor plucks feathers from the pigeon, then plunges its beak deep into its breast.

"Good Lord," Fergal says, as the raptor lifts its bloody face and peers up at them. Georgina can feel Fergal's consternation in the touch of his hand on her back. "Shall we cross the street?" he says, pressing harder.

But Georgina wants a closer look. She is reminded of the bones of animals she used to bring home as a child. Skulls, backbones, rib cages, claws—the remains of creatures found in the copse near the farmstead. Her mother would help her lay the animals out, reconstructing the skeletons, identifying every creature, large or small. She'd seen the innards of the farm animals they raised for food, of course—sheep, cows, chickens—and the deer and moose their father and Roddy brought home every fall. But rarely had she found a wild bird intact. She had wanted to see the shape of their organs—the liver, the heart, the lungs. She'd longed to dissect an owl's brain.

Fergal's hand is insistent and now they are on the other side of the street.

Georgina says, "I used to think I might go to university and study biology or zoology."

Fergal laughs.

What a small sudden ache this is, this disappointment. Like laundry left on the line in the rain.

"Oh dear, you're serious," Fergal says. "I'm sorry."

He's silent for a while. Georgina hopes that he is tormenting himself with at least a small amount of guilt.

"It's just that I never thought about going to university myself," he says finally. Then adds, "It's expensive, isn't it?"

"A bit," Georgina says. She makes herself smile at him. She will leave it lie for now.

Fergal tells her that his brother Carey has finally managed to set up a hardware store in Seattle, and their cousin Connell will be joining him there soon. "Seattle's really nice," he says.

"Nice," she repeats. When she is relatively sure that the sadness settling in her breast will not manifest itself in her voice, she says, "You'd go there, then, to Seattle?"

"My brother wants me to come," Fergal says. "But I'm not really keen on being in a city. I'd like to live somewhere rural. Get myself a small farm, maybe."

"A country boy, then." How, after all this time, can she know so little about this man? "Where would it be, this small farm? Somewhere near here? Overlooking the ocean?"

He laughs. "A farm on the ocean? I don't think so."

"But that would be perfect, wouldn't it?" Georgina can't imagine leaving the ocean. "Would you actually be a farmer? A real farmer?"

"Well, I'd have a vegetable garden."

Georgina laughs. Fergal is so sweet. "A kitchen garden."

"Yes, exactly."

"Have you ever grown anything, Fergal?"

"Not really, but I can learn how it's done."

"Any animals on this farm of yours?" Georgina asks, laughing again.

"Of course. Goats, I think."

"Good God. Goats eat everything. And I can't bear the smell. We had goats in Manitoba."

"Then there shall be no goats," he says. "Isn't it just the billy goats that smell bad, though?"

"True enough," she laughs. "They're the worst. Anything else?"

"Sheep, chickens, a cow, a donkey."

"I know you, Mister Soft-Hearted. You'd have them all living inside during the winter or whenever it rained."

"Yes, sleeping on the chesterfield," Fergal laughs.

"In your bed, more likely. How about rabbits?"

"Oh, no. Not rabbits. Have I never told you my rabbit story?"

Fergal and his sister Brigid, he tells Georgina, had two rabbits when they were children, given to them by a favourite aunt.

"As pets," he says. "*Pets* is the important word here. Brigid's was black and white and mine was brown. I named mine Charlie. And Brigid's was Puffy. We loved those rabbits. Brigid even made them harnesses and we took them for walks."

"I can picture it," Georgina says. "Pretty sweet."

"Sweet, initially. But about a year in, Puffy started getting aggressive."

"Aggressive how?"

"Biting, scratching, riding roughshod over poor Charlie. Then one day we come home from school and Puffy's gone."

"Escaped?"

"That's what my father said. Gone off to be with the wild rabbits, wasn't he? But that night at supper, Ma sets a tasty-looking stew in front of us."

"Oh, no." Georgina groans and covers her eyes.

"Meat was a luxury, so there's Brigid and me, digging in. But Ma's hesitating and Da's got a big forkful just hovering in front of his mouth. And Brigid pipes up, bright as a daisy: 'Is this Puffy?'"

"What did they say?"

Fergal nods.

"So, what did you do?"

"We ate Puffy." Fergal's trying on a mournful look. "I didn't think about it for years. And then when I was about seventeen it struck me how awful that was. I remember having a big row with Da about it."

Georgina says, "No rabbit stew since, I suppose."

"Actually . . ." he laughs.

Georgina swats at him. "All right. You won't be raising rabbits, but you seem to know what you want. Farm, garden, animals, away from the city. Old Macdonald."

Fergal is looking straight ahead, but his hand is there, she feels it, his knuckles almost imperceptibly brushing hers.

"I think you know what I want," he says.

SATURDAY, NOVEMBER 4

10 a.m.

They're warm beneath the blankets. So warm. A sleepy Saturday morning, rain against the windows, soft as a distant drum. Harriet is awake, just, and now, up on one elbow, she watches Flore sleep. Flore is, Harriet imagines, in that place that lies between the dream world and the understanding that the warmth beside you in bed is the body of your beloved. Soon Flore will stretch out her arms and draw her in.

She checks her new wristwatch on the bedside table, a gift from Flore. It's not a ladies' watch; its strap is thick brown leather, its face large, and the numbers on it bold. Pulling it from its wrapped box last night, she'd felt a happiness she has never before known. Now she feels it again. It's after ten: not too early to wake Flore. Under the covers, she walks her fingers across Flore's belly. Flore, eyes still closed, puts her hand on Harriet's and holds it still. Harriet persists, her hand slipping out from under Flore's, roaming a little higher. Flore's eyes are open now. In them, there's an emptiness that hammers a cold nail into Harriet's heart.

Harriet cannot stop herself. "What's wrong?" she says.

What Flore says will write itself somewhere on Harriet's skin, sharp as the tattooist's needle. Seven words. They will be found there, even if Harriet lives to be a hundred. They will be found on her decaying skin after she is dead. A few minutes from now, standing outside in the rain with Rue, she will think that those unimaginable words would never have been uttered if she had not asked 'what's wrong.' Weren't her own words the invitation to heartbreak?

Flore says: "I don't think I can do this."

"Do what?" Harriet asks. She is still smiling, but now there are two cold nails in her chest.

"This. You and me. Us," says Flore.

Three nails. Four. Flore's eyes belong to someone Harriet has never met. Someone terrible. Someone cold. There is water rising in them, frozen water.

Five.

Harriet stands. She's naked. She puts her hand to her breast where the nails are. Surely there will be blood.

Flore pulls the blanket up to her chin and stares at the ceiling. "I'm sorry."

I'm sorry?

Harriet stares. Quiet thunders in her ears. The end of them: it has been brewing, not so far beneath the surface. Sooner or later—and she understands now that she has always known this—Flore would choose a man. Real trousers, real vests.

"You gave me that wristwatch last night," Harriet yells. Rue startles from sleep and jumps off the bed.

Flore remains stone-faced.

Harriet understands. It is brutally simple: the watch was a parting gift. This was premeditated. Flore apologizing for the preplanned murder of their love. With a gift.

Harriet says it aloud, her voice an accusation, quiet and cold: "You're scared."

"I am," Flore says.

"But you're not scared of anything," Harriet says.

"I'm afraid of this," says Flore.

"Look at me," Harriet says.

Flore closes her eyes. A tear falls. It is, Harriet is sure, the only trace of warmth in the room.

"Chicken," Harriet says. She picks up the watch and slowly winds it. She dresses, gathers everything that belongs to her in the apartment, including her thesaurus (another gift a few weeks back) and Rue, and goes out the door, leaving it hanging wide open.

Flore's words, a howl, follow her down the hall and nearly fell her: "I want a baby."

They wait at the corner in the rain, Harriet and Rue, and her book and her watch, for a funeral procession to pass. The motorized hearse, the row of black cars, the flowers, the veiled widow, the children, the fortunate man laid out in the sealed box he'll rest in for all eternity. That fortunate, fortunate man.

RUE

There is a perennial that Rasia adored. Lamb's ear, she called it. I had, on occasion, seen Rasia go so far as to leap low fences or stroll, nonchalant as a visiting priest, through the gates of some stranger's pleasant garden just to pluck a lamb's ear growing there. Then she would rub that leaf against her cheek. Oh, the moans of pleasure. The delirium! I freely admit my jealousy. In a fit of pique one day, I destroyed a leaf of lamb's ear she had carried home and had left within reach on a low-ish table. (All right, it wasn't a low-ish table. It was high-ish. A high table. I had to leap for it.) Rasia, the beneficent woman, of course knew my heart: 'Oh, Dama,' she said. 'A dog's ear is also beyond compare.' (That was not the end of her lamb's ear thievery. I was, however, thenceforth adequately reassured of her love.)

All this preamble to explain how, the afternoon of Harriet's Great Departure from Flore's, I was required to lift my snout a dozen times before Harriet's hand descended on my ears.

Alas, she found no comfort there. Inconsolable, she was. She lamented, rather puzzlingly—*trousers and vests*—and resumed her rivers of tears.

I rolled onto my back, and she ran her hand over my rib cage, down my pink-spotted belly. She has, occasionally, called my hind legs (which she gently pulled that day) drumsticks. I am assured, at this point, that she has no intention of ever roasting me like a chicken and eating me. But I would have sacrificed a hind leg that day to be able to give solace to my heartbroken girl.

Third Trimester

ISLA

'Some people call the operator just to talk,' Miss Mansfield confided from her seat beside me at the telephone exchange. 'Do not spend any time on that sort of folk.' Miss Mansfield, my supervisor, and the woman who trained me, were of one mind; all three had issued the same warning. But I came to know 'that sort of folk,' the ones who call just to talk, as lonely or lost—the widowed man, the isolated housewife, and the children, good God, whispering questions that would crack open even the iron heart of a despot.

I took to walking after my night shifts at the exchange. Alone, not too far from home. Wearing my father's cap—if Harriet didn't have it—and sometimes his old jacket, for anonymity, for safety. I'd learned this walking habit from Llewellyn. He liked to go out after the sun had set, though not in the city. He loved places where it was truly dark, away from civilization—the forest, the edge of the bog, the banks of the Fraser

River. I'd walked with him in those places, and I'd learned that my eyes would adjust to the dark, my feet would eventually grow confident, however rough the terrain. And that I could walk alone. Let go of his hand.

That fall, in 1922, on my solitary city walks, all those faceless voices from the telephone exchange came along with me, wandering the city streets, filling the Llewellyn-sized void in my soul with their lonely chatter: 'I can't remember the words to the song my wife adored. I know the chorus but not the verses. Do you know it, miss? It goes like this.' Or, 'Do you think all women should know how to mend socks? My husband says so, but I didn't ever learn. My husband, he makes me feel so ashamed of myself.' And, 'Is it my fault, what my uncle does to me?'

And one night, a new voice: *Why'd you do it?*

I stopped and spun around, though I knew I'd find no man behind me. The one who'd spoken no longer had a working tongue. I hurried on, my skin all gooseflesh. Eventually, I slowed, knowing I'd never outpace him; he was loping along behind me on his long legs, just as he had often done when he was alive. For months I'd felt my brother near—in the hospital, and afterwards. I'd kept him silent. Made him sit in a dark corner. That night, I surrendered. I answered him.

'I was desperate,' I said.

I don't mean that. *That was obvious. That I understand.*

'What then?'

Your affair with Llewellyn. What made you do it? my brother said.

'Love.'

He made a small sound. Noncommittal.

He'd loved, hadn't he? He'd understand love's fierceness. And its stupidity.

'You would have loved him too,' I said.

Kicked the bucket too soon, didn't I?

God. My conjured ghost of a brother was making flippant jokes. 'Oh, plenty too soon,' I said sourly.

Llewellyn and my brother had never met. Roddy died in January 1919. Morag met Llewellyn that September. Nine short months too late for these men to know one another, to love one another.

Don't be churlish, Roddy said.

'Churlish? You're *my* ghost,' I said. 'You can't tell me how to behave.'

But I allowed my ghostly invention to laugh.

Sometimes, back then, I felt as though I was being erased. Some great invisible hand was reaching down and slowly rubbing out parts of me. My body first and then my memories. Sometimes I couldn't remember what Roddy looked like. Or the colour of his eyes. Or a memory would come back to me—my father reading to us at Sunday lunch, for example—and I'd realize I'd forgotten those lovely, unhurried afternoons when we were all still alive. But there Roddy was, beside me, seemingly as substantial as any living, breathing mortal, with his funny ear and his lanky arms. I looked down at his hands, and I wanted to weep.

'Georgina got your watch,' I said.

My brother didn't reply.

'I wanted it,' I said. An understatement; I'd desperately wanted his watch.

But you said you didn't want anything of mine. He waggled his face in front of me, mocking. I turned away. *Ah, look at her. The girl cuts off her nose to spite her face*, he said.

He passed me and walked a few steps ahead, his hands clasped behind his back. He was still in military uniform. I didn't have to dress him that way. He could have been in civvies. Or why not the damn flannel pyjamas he died in. 'Go away,' I shouted, stepping on his heels as he slowed.

Not until you tell me you forgive me.

I growled into the darkness until my brother began to fade, and when he did, I wanted him back. He whistled a few notes of a shared childhood tune and a long-forgotten memory drifted up: the pair of us, just children, me nine and he thirteen perhaps, sitting on chairs my father had set up in the farmhouse's open door, watching sheet lightning flash across the prairie sky. We are eating sticks of rhubarb, dipping them into a small, shared cup of sugar. Roddy says: 'Do you think people are beautiful, Isla?'

I wanted to ask him if he remembered that day. I wanted to answer his question, to tell him that yes, people are beautiful. And some even more beautiful than most.

May I add to my list of regrets?

You cannot tell the dead how much you loved them.

I thought I was completely alone, standing there like a fool on the sidewalk, but farther down the walk I spied Rue. Sitting, waiting. The strange little beast often followed me. It was oddly comforting. She made me feel just a whisper less lonely.

RUE

She talked to herself.

Less so now, but then, constantly.

I used to follow the bruised one as she wandered the neighbourhood at night, her hands waving about, stopping, starting, stomping off as if mid-argument with someone invisible to my then not-yet-failing eyes.

Lady Macbeth came to mind the first time I witnessed Isla conversing with the air. (I do hope I did not just hear you guffaw. I am *very* well acquainted with the play, thank you. Rasia read it to me often and I was enraptured, both by the words of the Bard and by the stellar performance of my mistress who was once an actress in her native land.)

But I have grown forgetful. Remind me, please. Where was I?

Ah yes, *Lady* Macbeth.

It was, perhaps, inaccurate to liken Isla McKenzie to that miserable soul.

First, I did not sense in Isla even an ounce of the wretched ambition that so perverted the mind of Lady M. (Though I did discern some small-to-middling degree of guilt in Isla. I knew for a fact that she had not murdered anyone. Nor had she incited anyone to murder. But this guilt, it surrounded her like a strange fog, one that might have quite properly engulfed Birnam Wood on an autumnal morning many centuries ago. Of course, we could not guess, then, at the source of her guilty conscience. And to this day, there remains only two of us who know. And I will take her secret to my grave, naturally.)

Second, Isla lives on in all her loveliness, unlike Macbeth's wife who was *neither lovely, nor a queen*.

FRIDAY, NOVEMBER 17

11 p.m.

In the dark space where the circles of light cast by the street lamps do not meet, a man calls out after her: "Good evening, miss."

"Bugger off," Harriet says and hurries on, past the loitering men puffing on cigarettes, past the showy women.

"Oh," the man laughs, "some lady you are." He follows her, his pace as quick as hers. He reaches for her arm and grips it as if "bugger off" were an invitation to dance.

Later, she will only remember that one minute his hand was around her waist, his fingers clutching at her, the next she was on the other side of the street. She flew, she thinks, and twenty seconds of her life cannot be accounted for.

And now she's running, fast, almost as fast as she can skate.

"Harriet. For God's sake, stop."

A bicycle clatters to the ground beside her, the wheel still spinning, the spokes glittering beneath the street lamp's light. Harriet can drop her fists: it's Padraig.

"What in the world happened? I went outside for a smoke, and when I came down you were gone. I've been riding all over the place looking for you," he says.

Now she's soaking the front of Padraig's suit jacket. Her mouth is leaking. Her nose bubbles. Embarrassment, apparently, is no match for grief. Grief always wins.

He is patting at her back: one, two, three, hard, soft, soft. "Tell me, now. Tell me."

"Flore," she says, and cries harder.

Padraig pats harder. "Oh, Harriet," he says.

It is exhaustion that eventually makes her loosen her grip on him. She wipes her nose, lets out a last shuddering sigh.

"What happened?" he says.

"You didn't hear Maxwell's announcement?"

"No, I didn't realize he was there. Was Flore too?"

Harriet nods. "Maxwell clinked a knife on his glass, then he put his arm around Flore and he said, 'I'm taking a wife. And to my surprise,' he said, 'she has agreed to the taking.'"

"Maxwell? That was extraordinarily fast." Padraig tsks. "A handsome man, but not all that bright, in my opinion. I prefer witty men to the beautiful ones. Maxwell is monied, dear Harry, but I can't see how she'd prefer him over you."

He rights his bicycle and glances down the street. "Let's get away from here. Your friend across the street back there might be heading this way with an avenging army."

"I think I hit him," Harriet says, remembering, suddenly, her fist coming down hard on the man's nose.

"Oh yes, you hit him all right," Padraig says. His voice is sombre. "You might not want to make a habit of that, Harriet. Hitting men on the street. Hitting men who are big enough to kill you can be very dangerous."

He taps the crossbar of his bicycle. He means for her to get on. But Harriet's feet are a crate of beach stones.

"Why didn't I guess? Maxwell was always, always around." She stares at her immovable feet. "She wants babies," she says.

Padraig twists his mouth. "Now, that is a problem."

"There are ways, don't you think?"

"Such as?" he says.

"An orphan? Adoption?"

Padraig smiles benignly, and she knows how pathetic she must look. Again.

"Kidnapping?" Padraig swings a leg over the bar of his bicycle. "Get on. I'll double you home."

Harriet climbs onto the crossbar. The bicycle's tires make a soft, shushing sound on the wet pavement.

"You can trust me, Harry," Padraig says quietly.

She relaxes, leaning back into his arms. People are sleeping. People are dying. People are making love.

"Will you be all right now?" Padraig asks.

She shakes her head. It's too cold to sit outside, but there they are, anyway, shoulder to shoulder on the front steps. Padraig leans into her.

"Poor, dear Harriet. It sounds trite, but you will love again. It's heinous what Flore has done. But you'll survive, I promise you. There are other Flores out there. I swear to you, love is worth the pain of loss."

"I'd rather fall in front of the streetcar," Harriet says morosely.

"Don't do that. I'd miss you too much. And what a mess you'd make, all that blood. The guts. Ugh."

Harriet is too heartsick to laugh. "How do you do it?"

Padraig shrugs. "Carefully," he says.

She thinks he is mocking her. Then she knows he is not; she has seen the rage in his eyes, behind his good humour, his irreverence, his mirth. It's there now.

"Flore said she's afraid."

"Well, aren't you?" Padraig asks.

The question is so blunt it feels like a slap.

He puts his hands over her ears and gives her head a tender shake; his eyes are fierce. "Find the place where you belong. Then you can stop pretending. Stop performing. There, at least some of the time, you can be yourself." He lets her go.

"Do you have that? A place?"

"With some friends. With you, and Flore, I do. I did. There are some places where I don't have to be quite so vigilant all the time. And some where I get to be as queer, as they say, as a good old three-dollar bill."

"And otherwise?"

"I behave myself. Sort of."

He smiles, and Harriet thinks he is the loveliest friend she's ever had. She rests her head for a moment on his shoulder. She feels something akin to hope. It is, she may know, the hope of that lone, lionhearted daffodil bulb that decides winter is over when it is not.

"Let's just put it this way," Padraig says. "You'll never have to walk up the steps of a church as Miss Harriet-Jean McKenzie and walk back down with some monstrous moniker such as Mrs. Harry Butt."

"Keep all the Mr. Butts away from me," she laughs.

"What's Maxwell's last name?" Padraig asks.

Flore saw her. She knows it. While Maxwell was making his announcement, Flore lifted her head and saw her. And Harriet saw the terrible, shamed look that came onto Flore's face.

"Vanderbilt," says Harriet.

Padraig rolls his eyes. "God save me," he says.

FRIDAY, DECEMBER 22

Late afternoon—early evening

Llewellyn lingers in the toy department. He picks up a small cast-iron tractor, shiny with green enamel, and then a palm-sized cannon on wheels. He had a toy like this as a child. He puts them back—who knows if the baby will be a boy—and buys a Teddy bear instead. For Morag, leather gloves, pale and soft. He has them wrapped. While waiting for the earnest, birdlike salesgirl to finish, he is reminded of a fine little Bewick's wren he once saw, her striped tail pointed skyward as she sang at him, scolding. 'Where's your mate, little bird?' he'd asked the wren. The salesgirl looks up and he blushes, thinking he may have spoken aloud. But she is just offering a smile. She goes back to her undertaking, the tip of her tongue between her teeth. Concentrating, just as Isla does. This pain that floods his heart, he doesn't really want it to ever wane.

Here, doing nothing more than watching a girl bite her tongue, the wave he calls *Isla* comes again: remorse, anger, yearning, grief, heartbreak, love. Never in the same order. *Isla* is a ball of wool after the cat's been at it—no beginning, middle, or end.

There is another thread in that tangled ball: vengeance. Or it may be that vengeance is its own miserable mess, an entirely different ball of wool. Whichever it is, this is the thread that consumes him.

"Sir," the girl says, holding out the package to him. She smiles again, her eyes not quite meeting his, shy, or coy, a girl looking for a husband. I am taken, he thinks. He thinks of Isla on the boat, her teeth gently biting his shoulder, her tongue leaving a wet trace, cool to the air, on the inner curve of his hip bone. How welcome this shiver of heartache is.

With his packages, he takes the elevator up to Ladies' Wear. He'll buy a gift for her too. For Isla. The salesgirls here eye him with avid interest; one approaches. Just looking, he signals with his hand, and there's another smile, this one not at all bashful. They all want husbands, he thinks, and he remembers what Flore once said, angry as a hornet: 'They all *need* husbands. Otherwise, what woman would allow herself to be yoked in marriage?' And yet, Flore is marrying. He asks the woman for directions to Men's Wear, though he knows exactly where it is. There will not, cannot, be a gift for Isla.

Padraig Gleason is there in the men's department, his back to Llewellyn, folding cardigans with his long-fingered hands. Doing a precise job of it, no doubt. Llewellyn stands near a rack of neckties, wishing he'd stayed in Women's Wear, or the toy department, or better yet, left. He is not up for an encounter with Padraig. The man will have him suited up in something pinstripe and expensive before he knows it, and God knows, with a chunk of Llewellyn's salary going to help pay Ahmie's rent, pinstripe and expensive is not in his budget. Llewellyn slides his fingers down a blue-and-yellow striped necktie and looks down at his own. How dishevelled it looks. Morag has been complaining about having to iron it. 'Shouldn't a tie just lie flat?' she said this morning as she pressed it. The thought of a trip to Housewares for a new electric iron crosses his mind until he imagines Morag's scornful response to such a gift for Christmas.

"Pinstripe," Llewellyn mutters.

"You have something against pinstripes?"

Llewellyn starts. Padraig is standing behind him, that smile of his suggesting, as always, something more than hello.

"Never liked the look," Llewellyn says, reddening.

"What've you got there?" Padraig rattles the paper Woodward's bag Llewellyn is carrying. "Gifts for the girls?"

"No. Yes. For Morag. And the baby," he says.

Llewellyn watches Padraig size up his rumpled tie; his hand goes up to the knot in a protective gesture.

"No blue-and-yellow stripes for you, Mr. Policeman. Too flashy. You're a plainclothes cop. You need something simpler. A little more *you*." Padraig pulls a mossy green tie from the back of the rack. Wool, not silk. "This one."

The soft green reminds Llewellyn of the quiet afternoons of his childhood, escaping the house, lying in the moss, dappled by sunlight and the shadows of vine maple trees.

"I'm not sure how much longer I'll be a policeman anyway," Llewellyn says, surprising himself.

"Oh?"

"Just something I—" He stops himself from saying what he was going to: Just something Isla said.

Padraig raises his eyebrows. "Well, with that necktie"—he points at the one Llewellyn is wearing—"you wouldn't even get a position in Floor Coverings here, so don't quit your job without a plan." He's already heading to the cash register, the perfect mossy tie in his hands.

As Llewellyn tucks his purchases into his desk drawer, careful to put the package containing the tie on top so it won't rumple, Webster appears from out of nowhere and smacks his hand on Llewellyn's desk.

Llewellyn jumps. "Christ, Webster," he says. "You'll give a man a heart attack."

"Sorry, Llew. It's just that some fella called and asked to leave you a message. He said to tell you that tonight's off." Webster cocks his head and grins. "Fog, the guy said. Didn't leave his name. Said you'd know who."

"Thanks." Llewellyn sits and picks up a pencil and taps it lightly on his desk, as if he has a great deal of paperwork to do. Webster takes the hint.

"Right. I'll just go back to my desk. Here I go," Webster says, ever the comedian.

Llewellyn nods without looking up. It had to be Virgil. Not Abraham. Virgil's a good soul, but Virgil's also the sort of person who might just turn up at the front desk if their plans had been scuppered and, while there, strike up a friendly conversation with Chief MacIntyre. *Don't you worry your pretty little head, Llew, my boy,* Virgil always jokes. Leery Llewellyn, he calls him. Call him what you will, in Lunenburg Uncle Clyde promoted one rum-runner rule of law: an excess of caution does no harm. If Virgil's too careless, he'll end up at the bottom of the sea, and Llewellyn has no desire to join him there.

There'll be no extra cash in Llewellyn's wallet tonight, but even so, he feels a wash of relief. Since *Isla*, not even being out on the ocean helps take his mind off the mess that is his life. He'll find a place to have a drink, he decides, then go home. Webster is whistling at his desk. The detective isn't someone Llewellyn normally likes to drink with—he's boorish and a blowhard—but he's here. Morag's mother would likely have something wry to say about beggars not being choosers. Llewellyn swivels around in his chair to face the detective.

"Drink, Webster?"

Webster stops his whistling and looks up, clearly surprised. "Really?"

The lonely hope in Webster's eyes makes Llewellyn instantly regret having asked the older man to come along. He's barely coping with his own lonely hope. A drink by himself, a chat with a nameless bartender, that would have sufficed. But it's too late now. Webster's already on his feet.

"You bet, Llew. I was just packing up."

Webster's wife left him last year. She packed up the kids and took the train to Portland, Oregon, where she was from. Her sudden departure was followed as quickly by a letter in which she requested a divorce. Webster made light of it for a few weeks, bandying the letter around the office and asking the men to place bets on how long it would be before she came begging him to take her back. It was embarrassing, Webster airing his dirty laundry in public, but the cockiness, at least on that topic, is long gone now. His wife never did come back. Llewellyn watches as Webster tidies a few papers together and puts his pen in his desk and locks it. Webster has to be forty. Llewellyn wonders what he'll look like at that age. Webster looks like hell.

"Ready?" Webster says, his face eager, earnest, and for a second Llewellyn is ready to forgive him all his barnyard behaviour. Then the boor is back: "No reason to go home for me. Although you've got a good one. Or has the coming baby put the kibosh on getting a little Friday night . . ." He rubs his hands together and whistles through his teeth. "You know . . ."

It's not something Llewellyn would ever tell Webster, but Morag, pregnant, is keener than ever to make love. Some men make a habit of sharing these things about their wives. Llewellyn isn't that kind of man. Webster, Llewellyn guesses, probably always was. Wives don't run off to Portland for no reason at all.

Webster's taken him to an underground bar in Chinatown. Tonight, Webster will pocket a bribe from the management; he'll offer to share it with Llewellyn. And neither one of them will pay for their drinks. Next week, they'll likely have to raid the place, pretending they didn't already know they were serving alcohol illegally. Llewellyn can't wait for the city's laws to catch up with the city's nightlife. Prohibition is long over here, for God's sake.

Webster raises his third glass of gin in a sloppy toast then looks away without clinking. Llewellyn examines the detective—his yellowed shirt collar, the hairs in his ears. He's a wiry man, thinner than he was last year. When Webster turns back toward Llewellyn, his look is intent.

"Something you want to get off your chest, Webster?" Llewellyn asks.

But Webster drops his gaze, apparently not ready to spill the beans, and takes another swig of gin. Llewellyn will wait. Not much else to do.

"Your sister-in-law . . ." Webster says finally, his eyes still focussed on something down at the end of the bar.

Llewellyn puts his drink down.

"She had that bruise, right?" Webster's talking slowly. "I'm not judging. I'm not like your pal Morrison. He's way too much of a Papist for me, that fella. But maybe you haven't heard the story. About Chief MacIntyre? Kind of before your time on the force. Even before Morrison's." He pauses and looks behind him and down to the other end of the bar, the caricature of some detective from the movies.

Llewellyn wants to shake him. He takes a breath, presses his fingers to his drink, and wipes the condensation off the glass with his thumb. "No, I haven't heard anything."

This is Webster's cue to disclose the news he's obviously dying to share. "So, Chief MacIntyre, quite a few years back now, he's got a mistress, right? And doesn't he get her in the family way. Story goes, she wants to keep the baby and Chief doesn't, being married and all, so he arranges for this fellow to take care of it for her, if you know what I mean." He nods until Llewellyn nods too. "You never heard this from me, right?" He waits for another nod. "Anyway, apparently there's a whole lot of arguing, and she's pretty far along by the time she changes her mind. I don't know what makes her. Change her mind, I mean. Maybe MacIntyre finally strong-armed her. But doesn't she up and die after the—"

Llewellyn has been rolling the bottom of his glass in circles, making patterns with the wet rings. He puts a hand up and stops Webster. "What's this got to do with me and my sister-in-law?"

"This is all hush-hush, but that bruise your sister-in-law had?" Webster whispers.

"Yes?"

Webster's hand slides beneath the bar to tap his own leg. "MacIntyre's gal had the same bruise on her thigh."

"What was her name?" Llewellyn asks, expecting it to be one of the names that Morrison carries around in his little notebook.

"Fox. Aileen Fox."

It isn't one of Morrison's. Llewellyn looks hard at Webster. It's painful to see how happy the detective is to be out with him; the man's so drunk he can't keep the gratitude out of his eyes. He leans toward Llewellyn and says, "MacIntyre was tight as a drum about the name of the man. But if I can find anything out, pal, I'll let you know." He swallows, like he might vomit. "You can trust me, my friend," Webster slurs. "My friend," he says again, as if he is tasting the word.

What a weaselly little man, Llewellyn thinks. "Chief never did anything about it?" he says.

"What could Chief do? The guy's got something on him, don't he?"

Morag always leaves a lamp on for Llewellyn, just inside the apartment door. If it was spring or summer, there'd be a small vase of sweet peas beside it, flowers she steals from neighbourhood gardens. Through the late fall and winter, when free flowers are less abundant, the vase is filled with other items: sprigs of holly, blackberry vines, braided stalks of dried marsh grasses, and, once, a long plait of Morag's cut hair. Tonight, Llewellyn sees that she has tied four coloured pencils together with a pink ribbon, their pointed noses in the air. The posy of pencils makes him smile until he notices a letter, addressed to him in his mother's handwriting, leaning up against the lamp.

Llewellyn's deep breath doesn't soften the dread that fires in his chest. He touches the envelope with one finger, tilting it forward for just a second to see if it has been opened—it hasn't—then leaves it where it is.

Morag doesn't wake when he enters the bedroom. She's too used to his late-night returns. He stands beside the bed and looks down on his wife. She's only half covered by the sheet, the counterpane already pushed to the foot of the bed. Too hot to sleep with the covers on during these final months of her pregnancy, she says. He bends close and inhales deeply; he loves the smell of Morag. He pulls the sheet back, gently—he doesn't want her awake self yet—and sits in the small rocker beside the bed. It's his secret joy, watching Morag sleep: the rise and fall of her chest, her nipples, larger and darker than before, discernable beneath the white of her nightie, her hands wrapped protectively around the hard roundness of her belly with its new brown stripe down it.

'I love this baby so much,' Morag said in bed this morning, sleepily, her hands stroking her belly. And suddenly, sitting in the dark beside his sleeping wife, Llewellyn understands: He'll love it too. He'll love this child, whoever it is, as much as he loves Morag. He loves it now. He is, for the first time, in love with the thing inside her, the thing that is half him.

An image comes to him: a child playing, collecting shells on the beach, climbing trees, searching for owls in the woods with him. A boy, a girl? Dark-haired, hazel-eyed? And now he imagines what might have been. Two children. Half-siblings. He puts his hands to his face. Oh, God, what did he do to Isla?

He reaches to touch the halo of curls around Morag's head on the pillow. He misses her long, beautiful hair. But even without it, Morag is still his overgrown garden, voluptuous and warm. Isla's different. Isla is architectural; she's like walking into a beautiful building, all intelligent lines and fine details. Different and the same: They both want him to stop his search for Granville. And the trips with Virgil and Abraham. 'When the baby comes, that's your last time out to sea with those two,' Morag said last week.

Gazing down at his wife, he makes a silent promise to her, to himself. Once the baby is born, he'll stop. He'll tell Abraham it's over. But finding Granville. That's another matter.

Llewellyn stands and removes his clothes; he slides naked into bed and runs his hand along Morag's thigh. She exhales that sweet moan of hers and pushes her bottom toward him.

"How did you know it was me?" Llewellyn nips her shoulder.

"Oh, it's you. I thought it was my other lover," she softly teases.

They move together, setting a slow rhythm.

"Did you tell my parents you were pregnant?"

"Yes." Morag says, reaching an arm back to pull him closer. "I wrote them."

She's unapologetic. He's not angry. And he's not surprised. Now that it's done, he knows that it's exactly what he expected Morag to do. "Well, nothing like a grandchild to bring them around again, I guess. I might have done something right for once," he says. "Though I suppose I'd better read the letter first. Wouldn't want to make any false assumptions."

He pulls away and rolls Morag over onto her back. She's so sleepy and soft. He loves her this way. He comes to his knees and pulls Morag close, lifting her legs against his chest.

"Oh, Llew," she says.

"Oh, my sweet girl," he says. He could weep.

ISLA

Apartment 2B. I laid my hand flat against the wood of the door, as one might against a man's broad chest, and rested it there for a minute. I'd come to tell Gianluca something: I'd seen Granville.

When at last I knocked, it was Salvatore who answered the door. He stood before me, Sal, the earnest little man, probably thinking—as many adults do with people who do not speak English, for example—that I'd understand if he just repeated the words many times over, slowly and loudly.

'Hai un albero di Natale a casa tua?'

I recognized *Natale* and *casa*—Christmas, house—but nothing else.

'Do you have a Christmas tree at your house?' Gianluca translated without turning from the pot he was stirring on the hotplate.

'Sì,' I lied.

Christmas was upon us. The city's shop windows had been trimmed. Cedar garlands, lights, tinsel—everywhere, it glittered at us. I remember that winter; for the first time in my life I found the festiveness overdone, almost unbearably so. The joy was missing; the tinselry made me sad.

I twitched Sal's ear and he bared his sweet baby teeth at me, threw his arms around my hips, and, before I could hug him back, skipped away. He smacked a small fist against Gianluca's backside as he danced past.

'Thank you very much,' Gianluca said. 'Now I'll have to get a tree too.'

'You should. You've got children.'

He raised a single eyebrow and tilted toward me, Angelo on his hip. 'They're not really something we do, Christmas trees,' Gianluca said. 'Here, take him. This baby's getting to be a real lug.'

The little boy came into my arms willingly, his big eyes steady on my face. 'Not a baby anymore, are you, Angelo?' I asked solemnly.

Angelo shook his head, just as solemnly, then wanted down. I put him on the floor, and he ran off too.

'Any news?' I asked with a nod toward the children. Gianluca replied with his familiar *tsk*.

My own news sat like a knife on my tongue. *Wait*, my head said; my heart said otherwise.

After Maria died, her sister Isotta had been appointed guardian of the children. There was no fanfare. The powers that be hadn't kicked up much fuss about the fact that Maria and Franco had left no specific instructions about guardianship. (What woman imagines that her husband will mysteriously disappear, for God's sake? What woman expects to die at thirty-three?)

The authorities must have decided there was no point in adding three more souls to the care of the Superintendent of Neglected Children, not if there were family members willing to take them.

Isotta and her husband, Joe, were unmistakably relieved when, after his acquittal by the jurymen at the inquest, Gianluca told Isotta he wanted the children. Isotta already had three of her own and another one on the way. Giving her sister's children back to Gianluca was easy. Making his guardianship legal was not. Chief among the barriers was his friend Franco; although officially missing, Frank Veltri wasn't officially dead.

'It is as it is,' Gianluca said, taking my coat and sitting down with me. He tapped the table near my hand with his middle finger a dozen times or more, a gesture, I had by then learned, that means he is hurting. He still does it, although not quite so often now.

'Which means no?' I nudged the tin of scones I'd baked toward him, wanting to tap my own middle finger on the table, hard.

He opened the tin, plucked one out, and took a huge bite, consuming most of it. 'Yes-sh,' he said. He looked sheepish, as a boy might, pushing what remained of the scone into his mouth. When he'd swallowed, he laughed.

'It doesn't really matter. The children are mine,' he said. He wiped away the crumbs, but not the oceans of grief still in his eyes.

I love how Gianluca laughs. I love that he can laugh. Even in that miserable time, I suspected a lightness in his personality, buried then beneath his sorrows, an irreverence for the rules that only the youngest in the family gets away with. He reminded me of our own rule-breaker—Harriet-Jean. I have not been proven wrong. The Padula brothers grew up on the streets of New York before the turn of the century, but only the four older boys did what was expected of them: they have jobs, wide-hipped wives, homes near their parents, children who are not children anymore. 'What happened to you?' I asked Gianluca when we were getting to know one another. He was thirty-three when we met—a decade younger than his next oldest brother—and he'd scarcely settled for more than a season in one place. Until Vancouver. 'Frank happened to me,' he said.

Franco Veltri, whose family still lives in the apartment across the hall from the Padulas in New York City, was the lure, and Gianluca the big fish that bit. It was 1906, he'd told me. They were seventeen. 'Every state in the nation,' Franco had declared the morning they set out. 'We'll see them all.' They'd managed twenty-three, hitching rides on trains, cars, hay wagons, working here and there, for two months or six, often in restaurants, then moving on. 'And why not Canada?' Franco had said. Gianluca's good friend Franco, who never ran out of gas. Until he did, somewhere still unknown.

In Vancouver, the war stopped them. The war and a woman: Maria Occhipinti. Like thousands of other men from the United States, they signed up to fight with the Canadian forces, with men like my brother, and with men who would soon be dead. Or they tried to sign up. Franco was short-sighted and that, and the curve in his spine, made him ineligible. Heartbroken and ashamed, he'd tried to bribe a recruiting officer after being refused, Gianluca told me. Gianluca, big, clear-eyed, and straight of spine, was sent first to Valcartier and then overseas. I laughed when he told me he'd spent most of his time on the continent as a cook in the camps near the front lines. I had to explain my laugh: belated relief, I said. Gianluca and I don't agree about the war. We don't agree about the concept of the 'ultimate sacrifice.' I don't hate the young men who became soldiers, I tell him. I hate what was done to them. Mostly, we agree not to talk about it.

They had both fallen for Maria in 1914. By 1918, Franco, left in Canada, had won her. When Gianluca returned to Vancouver at the end of the war, looking for his dear friend Frank, Maria Occhipinti was already Mrs. Veltri. 'The lucky dog,' Gianluca said.

I watched him finish off another scone, imagining him at seventeen. How different life would have been in a family of men. Sisterless men. I looked over at Mariana and she smiled up at me. It was unimaginable to think of a world without my sisters. Gianluca smiled at me, too, and tilted his head. A penny for your thoughts, his eyes said. I was glad he hadn't touched me. I was shaking with my Granville news. A single finger on my wrist would have triggered an avalanche.

He called the children to come get a scone.

'I want one, Papà,' Salvatore said.

I watched Gianluca's eyes go soft, and tears pricked in my own. Angelo, the baby, called Gianluca 'Papà.' But Sal had, until that day, only ever called him 'Zio'—Uncle.

'Yes, Sal,' Gianluca said, and he scruffed the little boy's hair back on his forehead.

If Mariana felt betrayed by Sal, nothing in her expression that day said so, but it took many more months for her to stop calling Gianluca 'Uncle.' I watched her make the decision. And it was hers to make; no one ever asked her to. Gianluca fiercely respects the few hazy memories Mariana has of her first father. Whatever it meant to her to let it go, I will ask one day, when she is older. If she remembers.

Plates, butter, a knife. A pot of jam. Un cucchiaio, too, please, Mariana, for the jam—a spoon. These were set on the table. Chairs were pulled out; pushed close. How sweet the children's small impatient hands were, I thought. How lovely their faces. Gianluca smiled at me. Again, that tilt of his head: What are you thinking about? it said.

Whatever deeply buried grain of wisdom stopped the bitterness in my mouth from spilling onto that table, I am grateful to it. One would think the children alone would be stoppers enough. They were, in part. But it was what I knew of Gianluca's mind that most made me bite my tongue. His dreams of revenge were as familiar to me by then as my hairbrush or my shoes. And far more dangerous, not just to Granville. To himself. He and Llewellyn shared the same, singular ambition: 'If ever . . .' they swore. 'When . . .' they said. It had not occurred to them, nor to me, not once, that I might be the one to come upon Granville. And that I might be alone. What then?

I'd been to Flore's bookshop that morning. She and I had browsed the shelves for something for Ahmie. We'd sighed—or had we cordially argued?—over my still heartbroken little sister. I'd left her, looking oddly contrite for Flore. Or possibly just indecisive. I was standing at the corner, waiting to cross the street, already immersed in the book she'd pressed into my hands as I left—*The Age of Innocence*, ironically. It was the pair of shoes on the feet of the man standing next to me at the curb that made me look up. A momentary glimpse of an ordinary pair of shoes. They were brogues, oxbloods, but the laces were mismatched, one dark brown, the other black. A hardly noticeable difference, but I knew where I'd seen them before. I turned and looked into the face of the man who wore them; it was him. Granville smiled at me. It was not a smile of recognition. He was flirting. He made that clicking sound men do, out of the side of his mouth—a verbal wink. And he spoke. Granville said something to me. 'Pardon?' I asked, as if we were having some pleasant conversation that required me to respond. But the only sound in the world was the blood rushing in my ears. He winked, with his eye this time, and he stepped into the street. For the second time, he left me at the curb.

I felt only one thing: fear. I went straight home. I made scones.

Over the flour and sugar and buttermilk, the fear slowly left me, but it was replaced by something worse: shame. Why hadn't I chased him across the street? Called the police? Shouted his name? Where was the rage that had devoured us all for months?

I found a tin and put the warm scones in it, put a tea cloth over them, found car fare for the trolley, kissed Ahmie. I'd go and tell Gianluca, I decided. It was Saturday, two days before Christmas; they'd be home. Salvatore answered the door and disarmed me with his question. Mariana with her smile. The baby with his sweet smell. And at Gianluca's table, that tin of scones between us, I changed my mind. I changed my mind about ever telling him that the man who had killed his lover had been walking down Robson Street that morning, merry as a fucking lark.

I could feel him sitting at the table beside Gianluca, breathing, almost tangible, tarnishing this sweetness.

I changed my mind because, just for a second, I had pictured Gianluca in the BC Penitentiary. Because I'd had to blink away the image of Gianluca swinging on the gallows.

'Let's go get you some Christmas trimmings,' I said.

SATURDAY, DECEMBER 23

Almost midnight

"Marry me, Harry."

Harriet snorts and punches Padraig's shoulder. "What in hell's name are you talking about?"

"Wouldn't you like to marry a nice Catholic boy from Wexford, Ireland? A little bit fey, but awfully nice. Intelligent. Handsome. Now, the Catholic bit, I know. That makes it a bit sticky. And Irish. Lordy! You never know whether I'll keep my job and if I lose it whether I'll get another one. But you ruling Scots are in charge of that. Maybe you could make a special dispensation for me?"

"You're drunk, Gleason."

"You're drunk, too, McKenzie."

"Am not."

"Walk a straight line then. Up ye get."

"I'm not going to walk a straight line. You walk one!"

"Aw, come on." Padraig walks his fingers along the chesterfield in the space between Harriet's thigh and his. "If we were married, we'd be respectable. You could do whatever you wanted with whoever you wanted. And I . . ." Padraig says, taking a long, slow, appraising look at a man in a dark-blue suit passing in front of them, "could do the same."

Harriet watches the man turn back and give Padraig an almost imperceptible grin. Padraig, on the other hand, offers up a conspicuous wink. With a finger on his jaw, Harriet turns Padraig's face toward her. He makes a comical show of tucking his tongue back in his mouth. She wonders if it's just the drink that is making her think that marrying Padraig might actually be a brilliant plan. "Where would we live?"

"Well, not with your mother. And not in my little boarding house. Mrs. Gallagher is getting a little ornery in her old age. Lots and lots of lovely shacks in Hastings Park for us. I bet you there's more than three-thousand homeless fellows living there now. Room for a couple more."

"Hastings Park? You'll have to do better than that if you want to marry me." She feels a fat shred of excitement. Sitting before her may be the perfect, albeit drunken, solution to her *trousers and vests* problem.

"Me do better? You're being pretty presumptuous about my role as a provider, aren't you? Just because I'm the man."

"So, I'll have to wear the pants?"

"Well, looks like you're already pretty comfortable in pants," Padraig laughs. "We'll be looking after one another. Playing house."

The thought sobers Harriet somewhat, but she can picture it: a little apartment somewhere, maybe over in Kitsilano, a couple of bedrooms. The alternative is so much drearier: Ahmie for life, God forbid. Or life in a boarding house, an equally odious plight. All those single girls moving in and then out, eventually, as they each find their very own husband. And she, a spinster, old as Ahmie, probably left to run the house as the years pass. She shifts her gaze away from Padraig's. He's smiling too intensely. The hope inside him is showing and so, possibly, is hers. And there's something else, shining in his eyes and even more frightening—desperation.

She's shocked to see an old school friend standing by herself in a corner of the speakeasy. She's leaning against a wall, smoking a cigarette, a drink in her hand. Harriet can't remember the last time she saw Jessie Smedley. Jessie tilts her head slightly, acknowledging Harriet. Harriet nods back. Jessie's skinnier than she used to be, if that is possible. Harriet can see the jut of her hips beneath her trousers. Her hair is short and sleek, cut blunt at the chin. They got on like a house on fire, she and Jessie, until the eighth grade. Now, pretending to not understand what happened to their friendship when they turned thirteen would be hypocritical. Harriet knows: It ended the moment they saw something in each other that neither one of them wanted to acknowledge in themself. They liked girls. Not one another. They liked the ones who braided ribbons into their hair. Better to stop being friends than to look into your classmate's eyes and be reminded, every day, of that dreadful desire. The September she and Jessie stopped being friends Harriet had imagined that the only way to put an end to her shameful longings was to leap off a bridge and take them with her. Or to never let her friend remind her of them again.

Harriet stands up. "Let's go," she says to Padraig.

"Gotta piss," Padraig says. "I'll be with you in two secs." He stands and wavers for a second, then grins. "Does this mean you've accepted my proposal?"

Harriet snorts and sits down again. She looks over at Jessie. She thinks, for a second, that her old friend is smiling at her, but Jessie's smile is meant for the woman crossing the room toward her. Jessie and the woman kiss, a little too long on each cheek, and Jessie's hand rests on the woman's hip for a minute, her fingers firm around it. The woman turns and leans against the wall beside Jessie, and they share her cigarette. She is pretty but not soft, the way Flore is pretty but not soft. Jessie catches Harriet looking. Her face is full of plain satisfaction. A cat in the cream jug. Harriet stands and puts on her coat. She'll keep this forgery of a smile on her lips until she has turned her back.

The stars are out. It's cold. The sidewalk's puddles are layered here and there with thin ice. Their delicate patterns glimmer under the street lamps. Padraig takes Harriet's hand in his, and they march along singing, swinging their arms, such a pair of fools.

"Oh, look. A lost glove," Padraig says. When he bends to pick it up he loses his footing and falls flat on his back. They are both too drunk and helpless with laughter to care if Padraig is injured. Harriet tries to pull him up, at least to a seated position, and is just about to call him a great lump of potato—his own favourite insult—when she notices two men, one of them the man Padraig winked at earlier, approaching.

"Oh, sir," Harriet laughs, "could you give me a hand getting my friend up?"

Padraig snorts with laughter. "Yes, sir, get me up, please." He stretches an arm back. "Your hand if you will . . ."

As he arches his neck to see behind him and hold out his hand, the gesture is met with a boot to the side of his head. Padraig curls up tightly, quickly, as a second blow hits his back. There's another then another, to his ribs, to his head, around which he has wrapped his arms. Both men are at it now, battering the soft flesh, the hard bones. Harriet stands, paralyzed, silent, five feet away, a scream caught in her throat. One of the men delivers a final brutal blow, and they're done. They smile at one another and brush past Harriet on the sidewalk, calm as cats.

"Fucking fairy," one says, the words floating over his shoulder, softly, as though he is just politely saying goodbye.

Padraig lies curled, a small, still circle of human flesh in the dirty puddle. He's too still. Harriet falls to her knees, crawls to him, and frantically tries to uncurl him, straighten his legs, his arms. She pushes at his knees, pats at the blood on his face with the hem of her coat. She takes his twisted eyeglasses from where they lie on the side of his neck and tries to put them in their proper place. She finds his cap and presses it onto his head.

Padraig takes his glasses off, a ginger movement. His tongue finds the blood at the corner of his mouth. "That was unkind," he says drily.

"You need a doctor," Harriet says, crying now.

"No. I deserved that."

Harriet recoils. "You did not!"

Padraig manages to roll onto his front and get up onto his hands and knees. "I winked at him, Harriet."

"So?"

Harriet helps him stand. He staggers a few paces, his legs unsteady. He looks down. Harriet follows his gaze and her heart stops. There's a long dark stain down the front of his trousers. Blood?

"Oh, Harriet," Padraig says, "I think I've pissed myself."

Flore runs a bath. They strip Padraig of his clothes and she and Harriet get him, one foot then the other, over the edge of the tub. He moans as they help him down into the warm water. He sits rigid, upright, his hands cupping his genitals.

"We've seen a set of family jewels before, Padraig," Flore teases lightly, though her eyes are dark with worry. "Or some of us have."

Harriet averts her eyes and runs the wet flannel over the raw welts and bruises that are blossoming purple on Padraig's skin. Blue. Black. Soon the washcloth is red and the bathwater pink with his blood. Flore brings a folded tea towel, filled with cubes of ice, and, hesitating for a moment, deciding where best to put it, finally holds it to his jaw. He lifts his hands and takes the tea towel. Pressing it against his eyes, he rocks forward. And the tears come. Harriet and Flore bend over him, holding him, while he weeps.

"Those bastards," Flore says.

"Those bastards." Padraig's words echo Flore's, but with none of the anger. His voice is weary, resigned. He leans back, finally, his freckled knees bent and splayed against the sides of the tub. He touches Harriet's hand on the edge of the tub and turns a gaze so anguished on her she cannot meet his eyes.

"It wasn't the first time, Harriet," Padraig says.

Flore pulls the plug and lets the pink-tinged water drain out and fills the tub again. She goes to the kitchen for more ice. "Where do you want this?" she asks when she returns.

He takes the bundled cloth from her but the ice cascades into the water, as if the weight of it is too much to bear. "Do you think it will ever happen, Flore?" he says.

"What, Paddy?" she asks, touching his cheek, tucking his hair behind his ear.

"An ordinary life. That people like us will have one," he says. "As ordinary and normal as everyone else's. As I am. Me just being me. And not getting the hell beaten out of me for it."

Harriet stares at the walls in the bathroom. The walls stare back, noncommittal, neutral.

Padraig breaks the silence: "Harriet won't marry me, Flore."

Flore's eyebrows lift and she tilts her head. Harriet's gaze drops down to the thing between Padraig's legs and the copper-coloured flowering of hair there. Now she's certain; she'll never marry a man.

"No. Listen to me. I have a proposal," Padraig says, closing his eyes, his arms relaxing into the water. His voice has the serious tone of a determined drunk, though it is impossible that there is still any alcohol left in his blood. "I'll marry one of you, and we'll all live together. You two can carry on as you wish, and so will I. Not with you, of course. Oh, God, no." He opens his bruised eyes for a second and laughs, then closes them again. "And if you want, I could give you babies. Somehow. We could do it, if you wanted, Flore, couldn't we? Either one of you. Both of you. I want babies too," he says.

Flore had answered the door in her nightgown, sleepy and flushed. "I'm sorry," Harriet had said, her arm around Padraig. "I didn't know where to bring him. He won't go to the hospital."

Harriet stands now in the middle of the parlour, her stockinged feet feeling the fat plush of Flore's Persian carpet. "I'm so sorry," she says again.

"No. I'm glad you came here. It was the right thing to do, Harriet."

"Isn't Maxwell here?"

Flore glances up but says nothing. She goes to the kitchen, makes a cup of tea for Padraig, but returns from the bathroom with the cup.

"Asleep," she says.

"Can he drown?"

"No. The tub's too small for that. He'll just get cold. Eventually."

"I stood there. I did nothing while they beat him," Harriet says. She lifts her eyes to Flore's. She should have hurled herself at them and scratched their eyes out. She should have screamed. Why hadn't she? "He said he deserved it," Harriet says. The weight of those words; she's under water, drowning.

Flore shakes her head. "Fear can make you hate yourself."

Harriet wants to leave now, to slink like an animal, back under the fence, to the privacy of her own guilty little den. She's cold. She's filthy, covered in blood and dirt. She lifts her hands and examines them; they're the only unsullied part of her, washed clean in Padraig's bloody bathwater.

"A pill bug. He was curled up like a pill bug," she says, her throat constricting. A painful sob rises in it.

Flore shushes her gently. "Come on. Let's get you out of your wet clothes too."

Flore helps her undress, tossing her muddied garments onto the kitchen floor with Padraig's until Harriet stands naked. Flore holds the bottom of a flannel nightgown open for her. Compliant as a sleepy child, Harriet inserts her head and arms and finds the sleeves. Flore tugs it down, over her hips. Then she takes Harriet's hand and leads her to her bedroom and her unmade bed. She tucks her in, under the blankets, and then climbs into the bed herself. She opens her arms and Harriet, unsure, sees Flore nod.

They lie quiet for a while, Flore stroking Harriet's back. Then: "What is it that makes them know it's over?" Harriet asks.

"What do you mean?"

"Beating him. I mean, what makes them stop? Are they thinking they might kill him and that would be going too far? Or are they just . . ."

"Maybe. Or maybe they think there's no point in flogging a dead horse. You can't hurt a dead man. Best to leave him in pain."

Harriet closes her eyes. She's so tired. She feels Flore's mouth against the top of her head.

"I've missed you," Flore whispers. "So much."

ISLA

We liked Padraig. Not that liking or disliking should matter when a human being, any human being, is nearly beaten to death. But it felt so . . . personal. We knew him. Padraig was our friend.

Flore and Harriet had kept watch over him the night of the beating, bathing him, holding him. Raging with him.

The rest of us only learned of the assault the following day—Christmas Eve. Harriet was all grief and guilt, a gushing river of it. It seemed to me as I looked into her face in Padraig's bedsit, that she wasn't a girl anymore. Overnight she'd aged. In the city she loved, she'd seen evil. Flore was, by turns, mute with rage or frothing with it. Fear—for Padraig, for my sister and Flore—took hold of me; how much more dangerous the world suddenly seemed.

Were we naïve then, not to imagine that things might go awry at Georgina and Victor's Christmas Eve supper that night?

How did it fly so out of control? And might it all have gone down a different path if Georgina hadn't insisted that Harriet come for supper (and if Harriet had actually spent the evening with Padraig, as she had wanted to)? Or if Flore's surprise appearance hadn't been sprung on Georgina at the last minute, necessitating the rearranging of chairs, the setting of another place, the counting and recounting of potatoes?

Never discuss politics at the supper table: who said that? Surely it depends on who the diners are—the amiable or the quarrelsome, the compromising or the unyielding. Whoever made up that mostly disregarded edict must have had a blowhard like Georgina's husband in mind. Before we'd even sat down to eat, Victor had already gotten up Flore's nose a few too many times. To be fair (if we must), he'd likely say the same of her. They'd been arguing, with a steaming politeness, about universal suffrage. Flore, her mood already crisper than a burnt matchstick, pounced on a comment Victor made about the prime minister—ironically, they both hated Mackenzie King, though for entirely different reasons—and the restrained civility was abandoned. Victor eventually called her, and I remember this very clearly, so I'll quote him: 'an imbecilic ignoramus.' 'Such big words, Victor Dunn,' Flore said, and she let out a tinny, derisive little laugh that could not be misinterpreted. She loathed him. *Such big words, Victor Dunn.*

Georgina emerged from the kitchen. Red-faced, harried, she called us to the table. Her voice was tight, a terse storm warning; she sent Victor to his chair, and she fired her childhood glare at us, as if we were at fault, as if we should have known better than to whip up the dust. It wasn't yet six o'clock, and she'd already had enough. 'Sit,' she commanded.

We found our spots, dutifully, silently, by way of the little cards Georgina had placed on the tablecloth. She gestured toward the cards and her face went redder still. 'Oh, just find your own,' she said, as though we'd all been smirking. She pointed at a chair. 'You're there, *Miss* Rozema.'

Had Georgina studied some 'Perfect Hostess' manual that Victor had bought for her and sat up the night before (while Padraig was being beaten), hand-writing the little cards? Poor Georgie, she was trying so hard, then, to get it right.

Victor was at the head of the table (of course). She'd seated Flore, safely (in theory), to her right, at the opposite end of it, no place card for our friend.

Peace lasted but a few seconds. As soon as the last chair scraped in Victor was back on his soapbox. Which of his bugbears was he on about? He had so many. Immigration, most likely. Then Georgina slammed the ham down in front of him and handed him a carving knife, and for a few seconds, our one-armed brother-in-law looked up at her in confusion. Georgina growled—another perfectly interpretable utterance (she loathed him too)—and she shoved the ham and knife toward the only other man in the room, Llewellyn (because only a man can carve a damn ham).

That brief lull left room for the peacekeeper, Morag, to jump into the frothing fray. She'd move us all onto *sweeter* topics, even if it cost her an arm and a leg. 'Did I ever tell you the story of my eyelashes?' she asked. I sighed. She had, Llewellyn reminded her. And he sighed too. No amount of sighing would have stopped Morag. She retold the story of how, when she was fifteen and I sixteen, I'd apparently told her that if she cut her eyelashes they'd grow in longer and thicker. To this day, I swear, I have no memory of doing so. But Georgina, at the end of the table, was nodding, laughing even (someone had to) and confirming again that I had and that Morag's lashes did no such thing.

Family lore is told with a laugh on the storyteller's lips, isn't it? Morag *was* smiling, and she did bat her eyelashes at me, but in the retelling of that old story, there lurked the familiar trace of a long-retained grudge. In spite of that, the ham was sliced, the vegetables passed. Bread shared and buttered. Ahmie's pickled onions were offered and, for the most part, declined. We bent our heads and ate, the sudden silence rather like another unexpected guest at the table. Morag—never fond of leaving silent guests or conversational voids to their semi-contented selves—leaned her big belly and pitying eyes toward Harriet. 'How was Padraig when you left him?' she asked. Harriet looked stricken. Victor scoffed and rolled his eyes. Flore thumped the butt end of her knife on the table. (If only it had been a dagger.)

And Ahmie asked, 'Who's Padraig?'

'He's an Irishman, Ahmie, a co-worker of Harriet's, at Woodward's,' Georgina said with a brusque finality. She stood, as though she planned to clear the plates, and sat down again. We weren't finished.

I stared. Was that going to be all that was said? That puny little description of our friend that omitted the brutal fact that his body had, sixteen or so hours earlier, been beaten black and blue? Georgina must have known what my stare meant; she must have known she owed Padraig much more than that.

'We are concerned about him,' Georgina added, 'because someone beat him up last night, in front of Harriet.'

'Beaten up? By who? Why?' Ahmie asked. She clasped Harriet's forearm; there was love—the sweet, protective love of our childhood years—in that grip.

Victor speared a potato off a platter, put it on his plate, and, taking another one on the end of his fork, waved it in the air. 'Potato anyone?'

'He was beaten because of who he loves,' Flore said finally, and I wanted to have been the one to have said it, to have been the courageous one.

Ahmie tsked and frowned. 'Well, who in the world does this Padraig love that would get him beat up?' she asked.

But cowardice reigned; no one spoke. The industrious clinking of knives and forks sharpened.

'Ah,' Ahmie said. 'I shall guess, then. He's a man like your uncle Hugh.'

'Uncle Hugh?' Georgina said. She put down her fork. We all put down our forks.

'My bachelor brother,' our mother said. 'Our eldest. Long dead now. He and his friend Knox lived in Inverness until Hugh died. They were tailors. I have often wondered what became of Knox. I loved him.'

And, suddenly, we had an uncle Hugh. A man we'd never heard of. From out of nowhere, an uncle, like Padraig Gleason.

'Knox?' said Georgina.

Ahmie nodded. She smiled. 'Would you pass the mustard, dear.'

'How wonderful,' Flore said, in a small voice, to her plate.

And then Victor was pushing his chair back and standing. 'I see it runs in the family, then.' He tapped Llewellyn's shoulder. 'Drink?' he said (and I loathed Victor too).

Was that the match that lit the fuse—those words, his poisonous little laugh, the men going off for a private drink, leaving only the women at the table? A quiet rage rose in me as Llewellyn stood, the kind of rage that promises that if you can just remain calm for thirty seconds, things will end well, you will not embarrass yourself or ruin the evening; but if you can't, well, then it will not be held responsible for whatever you say. Georgina's fuse must have been twenty-eight seconds shorter than mine, or her rage more ferocious. The men had scarcely left the room when her rant began: Were we fools? Did we not understand that bachelors and spinsters, grown people living without a husband or wife, were prone to melancholy, madness, and early death? That abstaining from marriage was unnatural? 'Look at Uncle Hugh,' she cried. 'He's dead. Loneliness kills. People die of it.'

Uncle Hugh? Our brand-new uncle Hugh? Dead from loneliness? Georgina ranting was not unheard of; Georgina on an irrational rant was. We stared. Her chin cocked up, an on-my-high-horse sort of gesture, daring us to disagree with her; but she made a wry face, as if she'd be on *our* team if we wanted to dispute what had come out of her mouth.

Harriet, oblivious to Georgina's confusion, or in spite of it, scoffed, 'Loneliness.'

Georgina turned on her. 'Yes. Loneliness! So why,' she said, 'are you not yet married? Find yourself a husband before it's too late.' She threw her napkin on her plate. 'You're wasting your time with—' I watched her press her lips together. Was she stopping herself from saying something she could not take back? Or from crying? I wondered how she could be so angry and look so sad. When she picked up her crumpled napkin and began to carefully fold it, I wanted to comfort her. But who was I to rob Georgina of the power of her fury.

And why was I exempt? I had no husband. Where was my admonishment to find myself a suitable man? I understood, suddenly, that Georgina knew I'd been happy. She'd read it on my face without knowing the cause of it. For months she'd seen it in my walk. Even my bloody shoes had been happy, and Georgina had known it. There was nothing for her to do now but file my happiness under *unmentionable*.

I heard Harriet shouting: 'Why are you so keen on marrying me off if you're so unhappy in your own marriage? Any old trousers and vests will do for you, I guess.'

'A woman needs a man's name in this world, like it or not,' Georgina countered furiously.

Harriet smirked. 'I'll keep my own name, thank you.'

Georgina snorted. 'It's still a man's name, Harriet. It's your father's.'

They were glaring. Breathing hard.

'Well, good luck to you and your fine name, Mrs. Dunn,' Harriet said. If derision were paint stripper, one wouldn't need that much to clean the hull of an ocean liner.

They'd exhausted themselves. The room felt empty. I looked around the parlour and I thought: She is playing house. Georgina has been playing house with her ambitious husband, but it is all wrong. She does not know how to do it. They do not know how to *be* middle class. The heavy oak furniture, the sideboard with the stack of dainty plates waiting beside her plum pudding, the figurines placed here and there, just so. Not wrong in themselves, not at all, but seeming so here. I had dusted the same ornaments on the Westcotts' side tables; theirs did not look as though they were begging for an elbow.

Harriet was not going to die of loneliness. And nor would I, whatever happened, die of it. But Georgina might. Her marriage was killing her. Melancholy, madness, early death. I said her name. She would not look at me. We all were familiar with the look on her face: she'd gone off again to find her ghost. Pain and pleasure; even then, even seven years after Stephen Salter's death, I understood her ache and the sweetness of her longing. I understand it even now. Georgie had loved Stevie. Every bloody one of us had loved Stevie. But bloody Stevie was bloody well dead. I would not have been surprised if Georgina had leapt up and begun smashing plates. Knocking the knick-knacks off the shelves. Decapitating the figurines, violently, one by one. What else was there to do? That, or weep.

Victor was standing in the doorway, leaning against the frame, watching his wife. Llew was behind him, lost as Franklin was, there in his own frozen Northwest Passage. Victor swirled the golden liquid in his little glass and smiled at it. 'What's all the fuss about?'

Was 'the fuss' the shouting or the silence? Which was it that had pulled Victor out of his dark lair? Can I blink him away? I thought. If I close my eyes, can I make him disappear? Can I?

'Nothing,' Georgina said. When she stood this time, she remained standing. She shook her palm impatiently at Morag. 'Pass me your plate, please.'

Victor came and put his arm around Georgina's shoulder. He pulled her head to his mouth and kissed her, ever so gently, on the temple. He had on a striped purple and gold necktie, and it struck me that my sister must have knotted it for him. Every day, I realized, she knotted this man's tie. How did she do it? Lovingly? Resentfully? I might have warned him: Best to keep your wife happy, O one-armed man, lest she tire of tying that handsome four-in-hand knot for you. Georgina pulled her head away, ever so gently as well, and put down the stack of plates she was holding. She smiled at him, like a good tie-knotting wife should. I stood, aware of the tension in that smile.

'I'm not sure why you're bothering to talk to Harriet about marriage,' Victor said. 'No self-respecting man would ever marry a Tommy girl.'

His decree floated into the silence of the dining room, sinister as a wartime zeppelin.

It was Ahmie, not Flore, who punctured that airship with a perfect short, sharp jab: 'Such big words, Victor Dunn,' she said. She grinned at Flore, as if apologizing for the plagiarism, then a noise that I can only describe as a joyful snort burst out of her.

In our lifetime, Ahmie used to say, it is lucky if we meet five people with whom we can laugh uncontrollably. There were three laughers like that in our family: Ahmie, Georgina, and me. When we were girls, Georgina and I would sometimes laugh so hard we had to get out of the bed we shared, afraid we'd pee it. We'd be helpless with it, in stitches over some small thing only she and I would ever have found funny. I'd forgotten how good it felt to give oneself over to that kind of hysteria.

I think that Georgina tried to but couldn't stop herself; she snorted too. And then the three of us were howling. We laughed until we wept, while Georgina's fine-boned figurines looked on. Joyous, too, or judging? Who can know with those pinched little faces. Victor, most definitely, was not amused.

We didn't stay. When the laughter ended, it seemed it was, most definitely, time to go. The plum pudding would wait; it would not go to waste. The mess, the dishes; we were sorry, we said. I remember that someone stepped on Rue's paw and the dog screamed bloody murder, but I don't remember how we retrieved our coats and hats or got Ahmie dressed in such haste. I just remember Georgina's glossy eyes.

'Come with us,' I said, begging.

She shook her head. She would be all right, she said and smiled. I thought of Victor's neckties.

At the door, Flore turned to Georgina. 'Your uncle Hugh had a husband,' Flore said.

Georgina made her wait. But the look they exchanged was one of mutual regard. Then: 'Yes,' she said, 'one might say that was so.'

RUE

Skylarking. Can one describe human hilarity as *skylarking* when the hilarity is the direct result of human discord? I defer to those more acquainted than I with the causes of both mirth and melancholy. I will say, however, that observing Isla, Georgina (a woman normally considerably more circumspect), and Ahmie (ditto) clutch at their bellies and weep with laughter, whatever the cause, was tremendously pleasing. If that was not skylarking, I don't know what is.

Alas, the fun was short-lived; prosaic order was restored after a string of sighs, short snorts, *oh dears*, and the wiping of eyes. We guests then executed a rather premature departure.

Premature, I say, because—and this was the grandest disappointment of the evening—the plum pudding was, unconscionably, left behind. There it would sit, I thought, languishing on the sideboard, no one to take in its mouth-watering smell. Would Mr. Dunn polish it off with the promised hard sauce before he went to bed? Or would Mrs. Dunn slide it into the trash as she cleared the table and washed the dishes (possibly breaking a few in her fury and haste)? O, Plum Pudding. So near. So unobtainable.

I am not proud; I am easily bought. Victor the one-armed had the most considerate habit of slipping me delectable bits of tasty things beneath the table. It had not taken me long to learn of his fondness (and his weakness) for my kind; when Mr. Victor Dunn was dining, the place to be was at his knee. There would be, I had hoped, a generous morsel of pudding to be had.

Could the evening get worse? Oh, indeed, it could.

At Padraig's we were sweetly welcomed by Mrs. Gallagher (his landlady): 'The dog stays here. Remove your wet boots before you tread muck all over my clean floors. And I want you all out by eight.'

Imagine being tethered, alone (but for three pairs of sodden boots), in the cold and ill-lit vestibule of a boarding house, listening to Mrs. Gallagher shouting up the stairs after Isla, Harriet, and Flore (erstwhile friends!) that 'care of the injured was neither included in the price of the room, no siree, Bob, nor in my *re-per-toire* of skills.'

I admit to sulking and to giving Goldilocks and the bruised-one-who-talks-to-herself the cold shoulder when they returned without Harriet. Preoccupied by my vestibule resentments and thoughts of that precious pudding going to waste, I paid little attention to their whispered conversation, until my name was mentioned.

'Maxwell said I would rue the day I broke it off,' I heard Flore say. (My ears pricked up.)

'Will you?' Isla said.

'No. After what happened to Padraig, I—' Flore said and shook her head. 'I know where I belong. In truth, I always did.' (I returned to the contemplation of my own woes.)

Who is to say what scars or traces of scars may be left after nights such as that one, where such unkind words were bandied about. I would have expected a period of détente, or certainly some acknowledgement of the rotten thing in the state of Denmark. But Georgina is too pragmatic a woman for long-term grudge-holding. And Harriet, well, the girl was besotted; the return of Flore was a balm against both the words spoken during the festive eve's donnybrook and the condition of dear Padraig-the-red.

And I need not have lamented so long and so terribly; the Dunns arrived on Christmas morning, plum pudding in hand.

ISLA

Am I the only one, other than Harriet, who remembers New Year's Eve, 1922, as the night she stopped drinking forever?

We were drunk, every one of us but for Morag, who had given up booze for the remainder of her pregnancy and was a little sour as a result; I'm sure we were boring, as most drunks are. Some were drunker than others. Harriet, of course. But even Georgina was tipsier than usual. Happier too. And Saint Pete's was packed with more revellers than I'd ever seen, all crocked well before midnight. Around eleven thirty, someone vomited on the kitchen floor—not an unusual occurrence at Pete's, given the quantity but mostly the quality of the alcohol—and a fight broke out between the one who'd puked and his friend, whose shoes he'd puked on. Just a couple of sloppy drunkards who'd soon meet the wrath of Saint Paul, Pete's bouncer—no guardian of morality, Paul, but a strict hater of vomiters. Georgina, disgusted, herded us out the door and down the stairs. Harriet complained that it wasn't midnight yet, and Georgina replied that we were eight and that eight constituted a party and we would take our party, of eight, elsewhere.

We *were* eight: Harriet and funny Padraig (still walking with a limp), Flore (Maxwell was, to everyone relief but Victor's, no longer in the picture, or even the country as far as Flore knew), Georgina, Fergal Doherty (so preferable to Victor who was probably somewhere in the East End fleecing a flock of young chumps at a card table), Morag, and Llewellyn. Plus me, makes eight. Eight and three-quarters, if you count the babe in Morag's belly, who, given the pained look on my sister's face all night, must have been kicking to beat the band. (Whoever that bloody baby was, Morag said, he or she was sure to be a music lover.)

The sky was hung with stars, a bright beautiful mess of them, beacons of hope for the year to come, I thought. I hoped. But the moon was the queen of the heavens that night, nearly full. It was gloves-and-hats cold, but not miserably so. We stepped over a few drunks who were not going to feel so happy in the morning if they spent a night on the cold sidewalk. Their less-drunk friends would rouse them before they froze, Georgina decreed, and on we went. The lights in the heavens were matched by the lights that twinkled everywhere down on earth—bright windows through which we could see all the other hopeful humans at their parties, lifting glasses of cheer, or not.

'Georgie,' Harriet asked. 'Where's *elsewhere*?'

'You'll see, Little One,' Georgina laughed.

Little One! What demon of holy happiness had taken possession of Georgina? She'd just hauled Ahmie and Pa's nickname for Harriet out of a dust-covered trunk in the attic.

It shocked me, mostly because it came out of the mouth of Georgina, who had, her whole life, resisted the use of 'ridiculous' endearments. But it had made my little sister purr.

'What?' Georgina said. Her grin at me was so arch I laughed. She took my arm.

It was either the alcohol talking or our Georgina was going soft. The Fergal effect, possibly. Thank you, Fergal.

She led, of course, and we followed. Of course. Poor sober Morag waddled behind us on Llew's arm, calling for us to wait up.

'Elsewhere' was Sunset Beach. Georgina wasn't alone in thinking that the beach in front of Old Joe Fortes's cottage would be a good spot to ring in the new year. Old Joe was dead, but he still had a legion of fans who remembered being taught to swim by him—Harriet-Jean, Morag, and me among them. A lot of the cottages on the water side of Beach Avenue had been burned down by then. Beautifying Vancouver, the city officials said. Just another way the 'so-called City Fathers' could prevent the 'so-called riff-raff' from enjoying the beach, Flore said.

Riff-raff we were that night then, under the man in the moon.

Llewellyn, Padraig, and Fergal searched the shore for good skipping stones, prying them with freezing fingers out of the cold sand. Their movements were slowed by the thickness of their winter coats. And Llew seemed to be finding it necessary to hold his hat on his head with one hand. But the three of them were satisfied as schoolboys as the rocks skimmed the moonlit surface of the water four, five, six times and were gone.

Harriet joined them at the water's edge, rivalrous no doubt. She was an expert skipper. But on that last night of 1922, she was too far gone to be even remotely coordinated. Drunk as a skunk. The men hooted as she lost her balance and her stone skipped once then sank into the dark beneath the shimmering water. She guffawed too. Then, going a bit farther down the shore, she picked up a baseball-sized stone. I watched her stumble back toward us with it.

She turned her back on the shore, planning, I suppose, to heave it backwards, over her head, into the water. As she bent her knees and slung the rock, underhand and with both hands, into the air, I could see its trajectory. It was not going to fall in the water. Not going to give us the big splash she was imagining. It was going in the other direction. No one moved to stop her. No one moved at all. The rock soared up. I looked at Llewellyn, his hand still on his hat. At Padraig and Fergal standing a foot apart, eyes heavenward.

At Morag.

The rock plummeted to the ground, landing with a dull thud in the sand, inches behind our pregnant sister.

I knew Harriet would be instantly sober. I was.

Morag made a small sound.

'Morag,' Harriet said. A whimper, and she fell to her knees.

Church bells rang out. It was midnight. The first seconds of 1923 were upon us, the soberest of revellers ever.

1923

MONDAY, JANUARY 1

A few seconds past midnight

Georgina starts forward. Harriet falls to her knees and lowers her forehead onto the salty muck of the shore. Georgina tries to pull her sister up; by God, the girl will face what she has done. Beyond the roar in Georgina's head, someone else is speaking, calmly. Someone is touching her, gently. It's Isla, holding out her hand. Now Georgina falls on her knees as well. She lowers her forehead onto Harriet's back and feels the heave of her little sister's shame. And again, Isla's hands are on her shoulders, pulling her up, pulling her away, leaving Harriet where she is. Isla is whispering: "Let her be. She knows."

Padraig is the first to move. Georgina watches him shake Fergal's hand. "Well, now. Happy New Year," he says, formal as a parson. He leans toward Llewellyn, hand out. "My, my. Nineteen twenty-three already."

"Happy New Year," Llewellyn says. How dull his voice is. Shock. This is shock, Georgina thinks.

Padraig does the rounds. He kisses Morag and Flore who stand, still as posts, still stunned. Then Isla. He comes to Georgina. He cocks his head at her. He smiles. She does not, cannot, consent to a kiss. Then there he is, bending over Harriet. Georgina hears him: "It was an accident, Harriet."

Georgina feels the gentleness of his touch on Harriet's back.

"Get up," Padraig says. And Harriet does.

Morag turns around to look at the stone that nearly killed her. She bends, awkwardly, and puts a finger on it for a second. "Let's take that home with us, shall we?" she says. "That's a rather special keepsake, I think." Then she steps over it and, circling around behind Isla, goes to Harriet.

"Close your eyes," Morag says, and Harriet does, the obedient four-year-old she never was. With her handkerchief, Morag brushes the sand from Harriet's forehead. "I'm fine. We're all fine," Morag says.

"We're all fine," Padraig repeats. "It was an accident."

Georgina hears the shake in his voice. She cannot move. The muck of judgement is in her limbs. She is at sea, tossed on the peaks and troughs of condemnation and forgiveness; seasick. Nineteen twenty-three is spoiled. Ruined. She wants to go home. She wants to be in bed, in a warm nightgown, with a glass of whisky—the fine little glass Victor gave her as a New Year's present—reading her book. Instead, she is on a beach with a gang of careless drunkards, one of whom has just narrowly missed smashing in the brains of the only sober one amongst them. Careless, foolish inebriates. She bends to pick up her hat, which has fallen on the sand, but Fergal gets to it first. She cannot meet his hopeful eyes as he hands it to her. She is going to disappoint him. That is clear to her now. She cannot give him what he wants. She will not.

Morag speaks. The tone of her voice is so bright it hurts. "Ahmie said that if someone tall and dark and preferably handsome wasn't the first to cross her threshold in the wee hours of nineteen twenty-three, she'd tan our hides."

They laugh. All but Harriet. They are all so forgiving. Georgina cannot fathom why, and because she cannot, she loathes herself. Georgina can only see Morag's brains, splattered on the sand, eaten by crabs and gulls, taken by the tide.

"Who should be the first, then?" Flore asks.

"Me. I want to." Padraig's hand is up, schoolboy eager.

Morag laughs. "You clearly don't understand the concept of the Hogmanay tradition, Padraig. The first-footer has to be Scottish, and he has to be dark-haired."

"Well, that's not fair. Pardon my pun."

"I'm with Padraig. And why does it have to be a he?" Flore says.

Georgina makes herself speak. The word comes out like a warning: "Tradition."

"And a redhead is the worst. It actually brings bad luck," Morag says.

"I don't imagine Ahmie's ready for a break with tradition, Padraig. But give her some time. She'll come to love you one day." Llewellyn looks a little smug, sure of his status as beloved son-in-law.

"A red-headed Irishman? Surely you jest."

All eyes turn to Fergal. He is the tallest and the darkest.

"Who, me? I'm Irish too," he protests.

"We won't tell," Llewellyn laughs.

Fergal turns to Georgina. "Oh, God. I have to meet the indomitable Ahmie?"

"What have you been telling him, Georgina," Isla says.

Georgina cannot make herself smile.

"You'll just have to be the first one to cross the sill. We'll be right behind you," Morag says.

"How's your rendition of 'Auld Lang Syne'?"

Now the panic in Fergal's eyes deepens. "I have to sing? Slay me now, O Lord."

"And the gifts. You have to take gifts."

"Salt, shortbread, whisky, and a lump of coal."

"Well, thank God, then. I have none of that." Fergal sounds so relieved.

"I do," Isla says. "I put a box out back. As long as Rue or the chickens haven't gotten into it, we're safe."

"Or the rats," Georgina mutters.

Morag shushes them all as they mount the front steps. Isla says she'll get the box.

"Un-marauded and intact," Isla says, returning from the backyard and handing Fergal a small crate filled with items wrapped in folds of newspaper. "Go ahead. Knock."

Georgina watches from the bottom of the stairs. Flore has taken Harriet's hand and pulled her up the stairs. At the door, Fergal has faltered. Morag bends forward and raps, then steps back behind him. A light comes on within, and the top of Ahmie's head appears in the window, then tilts back, as if she might be able to see who is there and not just the stars in the sky. Fergal touches a finger to the window, and on the other side of the glass, so does Ahmie. The door opens.

"Ahmie," Morag says quickly. "This is Fergal Doherty."

"Happy New Year, Mrs. McKenzie," Fergal says. He holds out the crate of gifts.

Ahmie looks pleased. "First-footer, Fergal Doherty," she says. "Come in."

Ahmie's eyes are on Fergal's feet as he steps over the threshold. She smiles. There. The Hogmanay tradition is done. Llewellyn and Padraig step aside to let Georgina pass. She lets them go in first, an ounce of the bleakness weighing on her shoulders lifted by the pleasure in Ahmie's eyes.

"Did you bring the juniper?" Ahmie asks.

"Of course," Isla says, reaching into the crate and bringing out a small green branch.

"We're not burning that," Georgina says.

"We are," Isla laughs.

Georgina thinks back to the Hogmanay celebrations of their childhood. Their father always insisted they burn the juniper. And Ahmie always insisted they not. It always got burnt, but first there'd be the water blessing. Pa would pretend that he'd collected the water from a river that had been crossed by both the living and the dead. 'Where's this river?' Ahmie would ask, laughing. 'Yeah,' they'd all shout. 'There's no river near here.' And Pa would laugh and say he'd had it brought all the way from the Assiniboine, a gruelling day's ride away in the best weather. A life-threatening one in mid-winter. He'd sprinkle the water around the house—on the beds, the tables and chairs, on Ahmie, on them. Afterwards, they'd burn the juniper, and the house would fill with smoke, and they'd open all the windows and exchange it with the freezing prairie wind.

Georgina watches Harriet, seated on a kitchen chair with Rue on her lap, refuse the glass of whisky Padraig offers her.

She hears Fergal tell Ahmie, who seems smitten by him, that no, he is not married, no, he has no family here. His family's in Seattle. He's leaving for the United States. "Next week," he says. He nods. He smiles so sweetly at her. "A shame, a shame," Ahmie is saying. "You seem like a very nice man. Our Isla is not yet wed."

"Let's play a game," Morag says.

"Charades?" Flore asks. "I love charades."

"I've got something else in mind," Morag says.

Georgina sighs, imagining herself in bed, alone, with that whisky.

RUE

Given that I have already (and perhaps unfairly) maligned the skunk, the beaver, the rat, the weasel, the chicken, and the vole, you may find it difficult to believe that it is never my habit to speak disparagingly of earthly beings. But it must be said, *human* beings are the oddest. And their secrets: Good Lord. Tragic.

In celebration of the New Year, Morag-the-large-bellied explained the rules of the game: the assembled were to sit in a circle and then reveal a secret about themselves. A Truth or Dare scenario with, I suppose, only the former being of any import.

Predictably, the room was split: grumblers to the left, willing partakers to the right. Those willing to indulge Morag made short work of the grumblers, and everyone was found a drink and a seat. (Harriet-Jean, I noticed, seemed in a daze, and not of the kind induced by spirits. Though a platter of shortbread was unveiled, I thought it best to stay on her lap so that she might benefit from stroking my ears.)

An expectant hush fell. (Not really. It is just a phrase of which I have always been fond.) Rather, the assembled humans warily regarded one another. Smiles flickered. I, myself, smelled fear. Time ticked on. Padraig was forced to tell a joke. Georgina poured herself another rye-whisky.

'You go first,' Llewellyn told Morag. To which, 'No, you go first,' Morag replied.

I know now that I was alone in expecting everyone's deepest darkest would shortly be publicly revealed. That souls would be bared. The rotting fish laid on the table, so to speak. A learned truth: amongst humans, secrets are rarely spoken aloud, and rarer still, in the company of others.

When even Morag, whose nonsensical idea the game had been, could not be induced to speak up, Fergal came up with what he must have surmised to be a wonderful plan: They would whisper their secret. 'To the dog,' he said. *To the dog.*

The ignominy: being passed from lap to lap.

And to what aim, should one not have asked, sharing a secret that would therefore remain secret?

And so, I shall enumerate them here.

Wait, you say. You fault me for my indiscretion. I disagree: the ignominiousness of my treatment quite justifiably accords me that right. (Regret? You are correct. I may later regret, and then again, I may not.)

Ahmie proclaimed that she would go first. (A dram too much to drink, perhaps?) She had previously confided her secret to me, twice on the settee, once in the kitchen over a bowl of chicken soup: she would have, if she could have, stopped having children after Roddy (a secret surely best kept from one's subsequent children, regardless of the reasons).

Morag picked me up by my armpits, and there I dangled for nearly a minute, a rag doll, as she pondered who to pass me to next. 'Padraig,' she declared. Never mind, never mind, I thought, for dear Padraig told me that his father had thrown him out of hearth and home when he was but a boy of fifteen. In spite of his da's dire warning—that should he ever again darken their door, he would do him in—Padraig and his mother (at risk to her own life, Padraig implied) were engaged in a clandestine correspondence by post. Was it wrong of me to pray that Padraig's father would meet an untimely death?

Fergal. Ah, Fergal. The poor man believed that Georgina intended to leave her husband—the following week!—and part with him for a life together in Seattle. I learned before he did that his dreams would be dashed, for Georgina was next.

The brilliant Mrs. Dunn revealed to me that she hoped to take classes at the university in the fall. Which university? I might have asked, wondering, as one must, whether these classes would be taken in Seattle. And as though I had, she added, 'In Vancouver.' Victor, I was most unsurprised to learn during her revelation, thought her plan—to study zoology—ludicrous, and yet, had agreed to support her. One can be certain: his compliance involved his not wishing to lose a wife. (A fair exchange? Perhaps. Methinks, in reality, it was far too hefty a price for Mrs. Dunn to pay.)

Would that everyone found life so singly straightforward as the beautiful Morag: 'I can't think of anything,' she laughed. 'Just, I hope that this baby is a girl. Oh, and I was terrified of cats when I was little.' (The latter is perfectly understandable.)

Harriet hesitated longly, I suppose attempting to think of something with enough gravitas, which, indeed, she did finally light upon: 'I love you, Rue,' she said. Dear Harriet.

Isla: 'I've stopped wondering who my baby might have been.'
Llewellyn: 'I can't stop loving Isla.'

Dogs do not weep, but, oh, our hearts can be broken.

SATURDAY, JANUARY 27

Late in the evening

Sublime: Isla's breast. The perfection of the warm handful of it, her nipple against the centre of his palm. Llewellyn lets the image drift in, drift out. Sweet waking dreams. He's good at this. He shifts on the barstool, a satisfying ache spreading down the inside of his thighs. Llewellyn finds this quiet, calm beauty in tangible things too: the gleaming woodgrain of the bar, the bartender who has the long fingers of a piano player, the man's white cloth wiping away imperfect wet rings. Llewellyn thumbs at the condensation on the outside of his glass; he tilts it, observing the colour of the liquor and the silvery ice, nearly melted. *Dreamer* he hears; with a sigh he lets the sudden image of his father—the disdainful expression, the punishment belt, the neatly combed rows of blond-going-grey hair—float away, too, grateful that letting such things pass is possible.

What else? What else is possible? Here is Isla back, and Morag too. This time it is their bare, freckled shoulders he imagines. Is it possible to love two women? The birds do it.

A chorus of groans erupts from the men playing cards in a smoky corner of this secretly resurrected, pre-Prohibition bar. Cops and gamblers, cops and robbers. Another place that won't be here for long. They'll enjoy themselves for a while, then he and his fellow policemen will shut it down.

"Wait, wait. This one's better." It's Webster telling his stupid jokes again. "So, the customer comes into the restaurant and says, 'Do you serve lobsters here?' And the waiter says, 'We serve everyone. Take a seat.'" Blah, blah, blah. Blah, blah, blah. More groans. On he goes until a few of the men rise from the table. They're between games, taking a toilet break, refilling their drinks. Harassing the girl who'll now empty their ashtrays. They're all so predictable and tiresome, thinks Llewellyn, always the same stupid jokes, the same bragging stories. Two young constables—Horrigan and Whyte? Llewellyn thinks he's got it right—are at the table too. They're pretty new to the force to already be introduced to the card tables. Webster must have brought them. Bloody Webster, taking his cut for overlooking the games. For being allowed to join in. And hasn't he, since their drink together before Christmas, decided he's Llewellyn's new best friend, sticking to him like a limpet. Telling him more tales about Chief MacIntyre's past.

Llewellyn places a few coins on the bar—even if he rarely pays for his drinks, the bartender deserves a tip—and stands to leave. He's tired.

But Webster's just behind him now, at the bar, with another man. Blocking his exit. There's a feverish look to the detective;

he has his hand on the shoulder of the man, as if he means to hold him still. "Have you met Bainbridge?" Webster says.

The man, Bainbridge presumably, is standing a little too close to Llewellyn. Not a big man, he's in shirt sleeves, and his jacket hangs over his shoulder, caught on one hooked finger. There's a single curl that has escaped his slicked-back hair, hanging down his forehead. Llewellyn leans back a little and considers the man. He has that sporty privileged look that his father thinks he should emulate. Already Llewellyn doesn't like him. Mostly, he doesn't like being interrupted. And he doesn't like Webster, either, who is doing something strange with his eyebrows behind Bainbridge's back.

"Can't say I have." Llewellyn frowns and doesn't reach out to shake the man's extended hand.

"Bainbridge," the man says, as if Webster hadn't already told him. He drops his hand. "And you're . . ."

His voice is odd. Thin and unpleasantly high. Asshole, Llewellyn thinks, without any justification. He's in a foul mood now. He looks over Bainbridge's shoulder at Webster, who's got his name on the tip of his tongue. It doesn't take much to make Webster's mouth snap shut. A brief narrowing of his eyes; Llewellyn's got the detective trained to never use his name in public. Webster thinks he's paranoid. Llewellyn thinks it better safe than sorry, especially since Webster's a Steller's jay; he'll blather on to anyone about anything—police business, what he had for breakfast, how he doesn't miss his missing wife.

"Leaving," says Llewellyn.

Bainbridge asks for a rye-whisky and indicates with a nod and a tap on the bar that he'll buy one for Llewellyn.

"I'm leaving," Llewellyn says again.

"C'mon, keep me company," Bainbridge says.

"Game's back on. You in, Bainbridge?" Webster calls from halfway to the table.

"Webster, you and the boys have cleaned me out." Bainbridge laughs and pats at his pockets. "I'll just have a drink with your friend here, if he'll buy me one." Bainbridge takes a stool at the bar.

"I thought you were buying. Gin," Llewellyn tells the bartender.

Bainbridge shrugs. "What line of work are you in?"

Llewellyn laughs. It's the only opening salvo men of Bainbridge's type seem capable of. As if he doesn't know what he does for a living, here in a bar filled with plainclothes cops. Llewellyn has his pat answer: "Automobile sales." He's not all that surprised by Bainbridge's smirk. "You?" he asks.

"This and that. Medical business mostly."

"Medical?" Llewellyn's skeptical. "You some kind of doctor?"

"Not exactly. Let's just say that if you get some girl in trouble, I'm the man to call."

Llewellyn looks down at Bainbridge's hands. It can't be as simple as that. Webster couldn't have just delivered the man he's been looking for all these months. He sees those fingers, with their blond knuckle hairs and neatly trimmed nails, touching Isla, bruising her. He draws a breath, exhales. Forces himself to speak calmly: "You make a living doing it?"

"It's lucrative enough," Bainbridge says. He swipes back his blond curl which immediately flops forward again.

Get a fucking bobby pin, Llewellyn thinks. "I might need that kind of service sometime," he says.

"We all do, friend." Bainbridge reaches into his jacket pocket and passes Llewellyn a card. A simple calling card with only a telephone number on it.

"How do you learn to do something like that?" Llewellyn asks.

"Trying to steal my trade secrets?" Bainbridge opens his mouth and laughs; his teeth are like a horse's. He's piss drunk and, consequently, loose-lipped. Stupid.

Llewellyn is staring at the wet circle his glass has left on the bar. His mouth is so dry. "No," he says.

Bainbridge shrugs again.

Llewellyn can hear Webster's drunken voice getting louder in the corner, telling another joke.

"So, the lady says, 'Would you like to take a nice long walk?' And the man says, 'Sure!' And the girl says, 'Well, don't let me detain you, then.'" There are more groans from the men, and someone tells Webster they'll kick him out of the game if he keeps it up. Webster brays his donkey laugh. Bainbridge guffaws too.

Llewellyn stands. "What's your name again?"

"Granville Bainbridge," he says. "I never did catch yours."

"Thanks for the drink," Llewellyn says.

"You bought it," Bainbridge says.

Llewellyn stands and turns his back on Bainbridge, reaching for his hat and coat on the stool next to him.

"Say hello to Chief MacIntyre for me," Bainbridge says.

It seems to Llewellyn that it's a very long way to the door.

SUNDAY, JANUARY 28

In the wee hours

Georgina smooths her hands across the counterpane. Up on her elbows, she holds her breath. She can't decipher what is being said; the voices in the front hall are too muted. Whispering. It must be about the damn dog. They'll have found her. And whoever the Good Samaritan is who believes it is his duty to knock on their door in the middle of the night to give them this happy news should get a tongue-lashing. It has to be Harriet. Only Harriet-Jean would think that she and Victor would want to know that her darling Rue has been found and that this glorious news could not have waited for a reasonable hour. For all Georgina knows, Harriet has brought the willful little beast with her, and she'll be trotting her muddy paws into the bedroom any second now. She can just picture Rue under Harriet's arm, squirming, wanting to be set down on the carpet.

She drops her head back onto the pillow and closes her eyes, anticipating the bed pounce and the animal's eager breath, foul on her face.

Nothing.

The conversation in the front hall rumbles on. She frowns, holds her breath again, cocks one ear as if this might help her hear better. Curiosity is coaxing her limbs to get up and see who it is, but sleep still has its dull hold on her. And it will be cold out there in the hall. Now, there's the sound of the apartment door closing. Finally. She sighs back down. But a lamp is switched on; a crooked triangle of light filters through the partly open bedroom door, across the floor, and onto the end of the bed. Whoever the caller is, they've lit a cigarette; Victor doesn't smoke and neither does Harriet. Who in the world? She is about to call out for Victor when she hears his voice, both shocked and thrilled: "Oh my God. Is he dead?"

Georgina bolts upright.

It's Llewellyn's voice she hears next: "I don't know. If he is, I didn't mean to kill him."

"For Christ's sake, Llew."

"Have you got any ice?"

"Come into the kitchen," says Victor.

Not the kitchen. She won't hear them there. She scrabbles out from under the covers, grabs her robe, and steps quietly to the bedroom door.

She hears Victor say "Sit," and there's the scrape of a kitchen chair being pulled out, then a sudden thwacking sound. Victor must be trying to chip ice off the block in the icebox, God knows what with. If he's using the good knife, she'll kill him with it.

"You'll wake Georgina with all that racket. Just bring the whole block of ice here."

Georgina presumes that it's Llewellyn who slaps the table several times.

"I can't bring the whole damn thing. It's too big. Bring your hand here. Christ. That does not look good. Oh, for God's sake, put the damn cigarette out."

She hears them fussing around in the kitchen. "Shut the door," she whispers, imagining the ice melting and having to call the iceman for a fresh block tomorrow.

"How about cold water?" says Victor.

"Better than nothing," Llewellyn says.

"You should clean that anyway."

The tap is running; Llewellyn hisses in pain. "Have you got a clean towel?"

Georgina hears Victor opening every drawer in the kitchen, rummaging in each of them. He'll have no idea where the tea towels are kept. In the Hoosier, third drawer down, left side. For a second, Georgina cannot resist the urge she has to go to the kitchen and sort them both out. She takes one step into the hallway and catches sight of herself in the mirror. She stops. Her presence in there would change everything. Shut them up. She scowls at her reflection and leans against the wall.

"Here. Wrap it tight around," she hears Victor say. He must have found a tea towel. There's silence for a minute or two. She can just picture the two of them, playing nurse and patient in there.

"Did you just leave him lying there?"

"I ran. I didn't know what else to do. He was out cold on the ground."

"Did anyone witness this . . . this f-f-fight?"

"There were a couple of others around."

"Others? Who? Th-they saw you?"

"A few of the boys. Webster. A couple of new recruits. I have no idea if they saw me. Probably not. They were drunk as lords. They were waiting up the road for him."

Georgina can't tell who started laughing first, Victor or Llewellyn, but they're both laughing now, and it verges on the hysterical.

"Well, well done, Llew!" Victor says.

It must be Victor who is smacking the table now.

"The bastard had it coming," Llewellyn says, and they laugh again.

ooooo

They're laughing. But Llewellyn feels the exhilaration that had lifted him earlier departing, an owl swooping low over the pasture at dusk. He starts to shake. He fumbles with another cigarette and Victor, still excited, is forced to light it for him.

"Here," Victor says. Victor disapproves of smoking.

Llewellyn takes a deep drag. He remembers that his uncle Clyde had one other rum-runner rule of law. It came from the Bible, he said, which was a lie but made everyone laugh: Strike first; don't let them get a punch in; don't hurt your knuckles.

The short constable, Whyte, he'd come out first, followed by Webster. Horrigan was next, so drunk he was stumbling. Webster was three sheets to the wind too. Llewellyn had moved back into the darkness in the alley across the street. The whole place stank of urine. His heart was beating fast; he could feel its mechanical whoosh pulsing in his throat, hear it in his jaw. The idiots were lingering out front. He needed them gone before Granville Bainbridge came out. He watched Horrigan clap Webster on the back and say something. It may or may not have been truly hilarious—drunks can't be relied on to know the difference—but Whyte shrieked with laughter, and the three of them finally stumbled up the street. Llewellyn kept his eye on the door; when he next glanced after them, Webster and the two young cops had stopped. Horrigan was bent over, puking. 'Move on, move on, boneheads,' Llewellyn said quietly. He pulled his coat close and waited, freezing in the drizzle.

Bainbridge came out, finally, hat on but his overcoat undone. 'Wait up,' he called after Webster and the boys, his voice slurred. 'I gotta piss.'

And there Granville Bainbridge was, coming right toward him, entering the alley, turning toward the wall, unbuttoning his fly. So easy. Too easy. But what to do?

Llewellyn hit him from behind. His first punch seemed only to have knocked his hat off. Bainbridge turned around, his fly still open; he looked astonished. 'Fuck,' Llewellyn said. His hand hurt, and his arms and legs felt useless and numb. He faltered. Bainbridge stepped toward him, lifted his fists in a fighter's stance, and Llewellyn's hesitation ended. He flew at Bainbridge and managed to grab him by his hair, that fucking dangling lock of it. Bainbridge was stumbling but still upright. Llewellyn caught him by the ears. Bainbridge shook his head free. Llewellyn imagined slamming Bainbridge's face against his knee, breaking his nose, but instead they were dancing, clutching at each other's coats, trying to stay on their feet. And Bainbridge was squealing like an animal, a fucking animal. Llewellyn pulled himself loose from Bainbridge's grip and hit him, twice. Bainbridge lurched violently at him, tripped on something, and fell. His head struck the wall. He crumpled to his knees and dropped sideways against a pile of bricks.

Llewellyn bent over him, panting, heaving, waiting for him to get up, but the man was still. He touched his boot, ever so gently, to Bainbridge's back. Nothing. Llewellyn picked up his hat and ran. Granville. Jesus Christ. He'd found Granville.

"Christ almighty," says Victor. "How do you feel?"

Llewellyn looks into Victor's glossy eyes and the blunt truth comes to him: it wasn't Bainbridge who had been squealing like an animal. That terrified sound had come from his own mouth.

"Christ almighty," Llewellyn repeats soberly. "Strange. I feel strange." He had never, in his life, hit anyone. Never fought anyone. Never punched anyone. He'd been hit. By his father. Many times. As punishment. To *educate* him. And for no reason at all. He'd wanted to hit back, a thousand times, but Llewellyn had never found the courage. Not once. The penalty would have been too grand.

ooooo

In the hall, Georgina is holding her breath. They're talking like giddy boys who've trapped their quarry and now, though triumphant, are not sure what to do with it. With him. With whoever it is that Llewellyn has implausibly knocked cold. She has not heard his name. There's a warmth to the conversation that plucks a chord of jealousy in Georgina. It's how men talked after the war. That camaraderie of shared experience, the horrific and the mundane. It was like that with Roddy when he came home. He and his friends. Intimate. Private and privileged. Front-porch talk that was not for the women, not for her. They made her lonely, her brother and his friends. They made her miss Stephen.

She smells another cigarette being lit. Hears a couple of drinks being poured. She leans against the wall, imagining Victor's face, full of admiration.

"I hope to hell I haven't killed him," Llewellyn says.

A glass taps down onto the table.

"I hope you have."

"Well, that would be—" Llewellyn starts, then stops.

"I killed a man once." Victor's tone is soft but not confessional.

"I guess you would have killed some of our enemies during the war," Llewellyn says.

Georgina knows Llewellyn's cautious tone well: a man crossing a stream on stepping stones, his foot treading carefully to find and keep his balance. She treads the same slippery path with Victor.

"This was different."

"How?"

"He was one of ours. A boy. Jack Bodine. We sh-shot him."

Georgina slides down the wall, dropping to her knees. "Good God," she hears Llewellyn say. A chair scrapes back. Whose?

"Anyone would have d-d-done what we did," Victor says, defiance rising in his voice now. His stammer worsening. "The g-g-goddamn boy wouldn't have survived. It was a m-m-mercy killing."

In the hallway, Georgina, on her knees, bends and touches her forehead to the floor.

ooooo

A mercy killing, Victor calls it, and shrugs, as if mercy killings are a daily occurrence, ordinary as barn cats or harbour rats.

Llewellyn will not raise his eyes to Victor's, though he knows the man is waiting for him to look up, challenge him, judge him. He keeps his gaze on the tea towel wrapped around his hand. Bright spots of red have soaked through the white cloth, four dots above his knuckles. He fiddles with the towel, pulling it tighter across his throbbing fist.

At first calm and almost indifferent, Victor tells the story. Llewellyn listens. Jack Bodine had lied about his age. The boy was seventeen, only a little more than half Victor's thirty-one years at the time. He was scared to death, infecting everyone with his fear, but sent anyway to sit in the fetid trenches with the rest of them. Crawl into shell-holes. Shit his pants in the mud. "If he'd waited a year," Victor says, "the war would have been over, and the boy would be out there somewhere now, kissing some girl, happy as a lark. Instead, he's . . ." Victor lifts his arm, slowly, and gives a dispassionate wave at what Llewellyn thinks is the ordinariness of the curtained window or the dripping faucet or the stained sink. The icebox door has been left hanging open; Victor suddenly smacks it shut, that indifferent hand turned angry and violent.

Victor taps his middle finger against the kitchen table, the nail making a sharp, repeated staccato. Llewellyn thinks of unexploded ordnance. He sits still, watching Victor's finger, each tap an echo of the back-and-forth rocking of the boy he's describing, crouched in the trench, his head in his hands, slow fast, soft sharp. The tapping stops, the hand lies flat on the table, forced silent by that undetonated thing inside of Victor.

"Shat his pants the first night out and got blown up the fifth," Victor says, then makes a sound that could be laughter, but is not. There was an artillery attack, just as the sun was setting. The soldier next to Bodine was ripped in two. A perfectly intact head and upper torso and a pair of legs. Nothing else. His middle gone. Blood and intestines and shit and chunks of flesh floating in the mud. Llewellyn leans across the table; he wants to hold his bleeding hand across Victor's mouth to silence him. Instead, he touches Victor's hand, just briefly, and is surprised by the tremor in it. Victor pulls his hand away but his face betrays him; he can't hide the tremor in his chin.

Victor sucks air in through clenched teeth and lets it go. "The sky was as beautiful a pink as I had ever seen," he says. "Orange clouds at the horizon. Streaks of yellow and r-r-red above." Jack Bodine had stopped screaming; he'd looked down and seen the ragged stumps of his own thighs. He'd begged Victor and another soldier to kill him, and Victor and the other man did. They shot Jack Bodine with their rifles.

"Oh, God, Llew," Victor says. "The smell . . ."

ooooo

Victor has stopped speaking. They're silent in the kitchen for a while. Georgina lifts her hands from her head, crouches, then stands. Her husband has never spoken to her of this.

"C-c-cowardice. They court-martialed men for cowardice," Victor says.

"Did they?"

"Of course, they did."

"I'm sorry, Victor. I don't know what I would have done. Probably what you did."

"You can't imagine, Llew."

"No, I can't."

"Men were c-c-court-martialed and some were executed. For being afraid."

Llewellyn doesn't reply.

"I thought I was strong."

"Yes," Llewellyn says.

"I have never been more frightened in my life."

Comfort him, Llewellyn, you stupid man. Comfort my stupid lost husband, she thinks. Instead, she hears Llewellyn say, "I should go. Morag will be—"

"Right," says Victor. "I suppose she raises hell if you're too late." He forces a laugh.

"Well, sometimes," says Llewellyn.

"They're a handful, these McKenzie women," says Victor.

Llewellyn's laugh is forced, too, a grunt. "But we need them, don't we?"

"We do, indeed, Llew. God save us, but we do."

Chairs scrape back. Georgina flies back to the bedroom and climbs under the covers. Victor and Llewellyn are in the front hall now.

"You don't think Georgina's thinking of leaving me, do you Llew?"

"What on earth would make you think that?"

Georgina pulls the blanket up to her mouth.

"This Irish fellow she's friends with. I—"

Llewellyn interrupts. "You don't have anything to worry about, Vic. Georgina's your girl."

Liar, Georgina thinks. Such a good liar.

"I need the woman, Llew."

"She's a good wife," Llewellyn says.

"I'm proud of you, getting that b-b-bastard. Not that Isla wasn't stupid to do what she did. But he deserves what he got."

Llewellyn thanks Victor and says goodnight. The door clacks shut. The hall light is extinguished. Victor enters the bedroom. He takes off his robe and lays it quietly across the end of the bed. Through half-shut eyes, Georgina watches him hesitate in the dark; he is taking off his pyjamas. She rolls away from him, turns her back, but it's too late. He's pressing up against her, rucking up her nightie. As his cold hand slides between her thighs, she thinks of the hunter, this one fresh from his vicarious kill. He bends his mouth to her neck, her jaw, her temple.

"He got Granville," he whispers.

A single tear drips warm down her cheek. She licks it from the corner of her mouth, not sure whether it is his or hers.

RUE

I was not lost, as some had maintained. I have walked the streets of this city for years; I most certainly know my way around. That night, I was merely attempting to follow Llewellyn, the sad-eyed one, but in so doing, I temporarily *displaced* my bearings. Temporarily, I say. Was I not home in the arms of my keeper-women by morning-time? Harriet scolded me and, in great detail, recounted her (and Flore's) frantic night of worry. (Flore, serving tea with biscuits, did not appear frantic in the least.) The old one, Ahmie, greeted my triumphant return with bits of stale scone soaked in milk (delectable). Isla was sent to the butcher on Denman Street for chicken gizzards, which were fried up in butter and served to me on a fine old plate along with a raw chicken's egg. 'You're spoiling her,' Harriet-Jean declared with a petulance she reserved solely for her mother. I could scarcely see how she would come to that conclusion; a raw egg atop chicken innards seemed more than just compensation for someone who had spent a disorienting night roving the docklands in the company of rats. As to my circular ramble, I can only blame my sense of smell, which was, at that time, admittedly already diminishing. (Though I refuse to discount the befuddling stink of the dock rats.)

Be it known: these days I rarely wander farther than a block from home; and Harriet is, of course, long forgiven.

The sad-eyed one's pace was not particularly brisk that night and, at first, I kept up. But, some distance along (the territory being, thus, unknown to me), Llewellyn appeared to change his mind about proceeding on foot (the cold weather perhaps) and flagged down a jitney in which he was carried off at a pace not even my sister, the greyhound dog, could hope to maintain for long.

So, there I was, alone and at the mercy of Night's elements. And I had lost my mark.

Is one's destiny immutable? Humans like to think that they have some control over their fortunes. But there are, perhaps, some events that carve what is written into stone.

Surely Ahmie's thesaurus (she still reads to me from that marvellous book) would contain the word for which I am searching, the one that would have concisely described the hullabaloo that erupted in Ahmie's parlour around eleven o'clock that next morning with the arrival of Georgina and Victor. Oh, it is very kind of you to think that the disturbance revolved around my own troubling night, but no. I refer to the event that seemed to have taken place not many hours after Llewellyn boarded his jitney and was lost to me. We were apprised of this news by the Dunns: the fugitive Granville had been found; Llewellyn had fought with him; he'd been 'left for dead' in an alleyway.

Isla's face went whiter than the band of colour across my withers. She made so mournful a sound my hackles rose and a howl of sorrow bowed my mouth too.

'Not Llew,' Georgina said, bending with uncharacteristic solicitousness toward Isla. 'Granville.'

'Granville Bainbridge,' said Georgina's spouse, with perhaps more gladness than the news occasioned.

For some while, multiple opinions were tossed around and agreed with or derided. There was no consensus until 'I do not think,' the old one said, ominous as the crow, 'that this bodes well for him.'

And though she did not clarify the 'him' to which she referred, on this there was consensus.

ISLA

Morag said she had canned peaches for dessert. She'd poured the peach halves and their syrup into a dark-blue bowl that had been our grandmother's. The peaches were an exquisite orange against the blue, their plush skin freckled with patches of darker reddish-orange.

'How come you have Grandma Oonagh's bowl?' I asked.

Morag laughed and I blushed. Neither of us had ever met our mother's mother, but Ahmie had immigrated to Canada with a few of her belongings, and these had come to be reverently known as 'Grandma Oonagh's things.'

'I didn't mean it that way,' I laughed.

'You can have it when I die,' Morag said, still laughing, and she pushed the bowl and a serving spoon toward me.

Morag wasn't nervous in the last days of her pregnancy, but nor did she want to be alone. And no one wanted her waddling out for provisions along the wet, late-winter sidewalks, so we brought her food, treats, company. If Llewellyn was away with Abraham and Virgil, or working (legitimately working), Harriet and Flore or Georgina spent the evenings with her. I worked the late shift at the telephone exchange, so I had lunch with Morag most days. My meals were paltry offerings; I've never been much of a cook. That pretty canned peach day, a couple weeks before their baby was born, I'd given her mashed hard-boiled eggs on buttered toast. At least the peaches made up for the beggarly nature of the meal.

'I should tell you,' Morag said as I helped her put her feet up after lunch, 'that Granville Bainbridge didn't die.'

'Oh?' I said.

I already knew that Granville Bainbridge wasn't dead. Llew had told me that morning. He'd left a note at the house asking me to meet him at Almond's Ice Cream down by the beach in the morning. It's important, the note said.

He showed me his bruised fist, his still raw knuckles, and there was no pride in the gesture, only an uneasiness that he could not hide, not from me. We both knew: another time I would have kissed his hand. As we walked out on the English Bay pier, he told me that he was 'pretty sure' Bainbridge didn't know who his assailant had been. That the official story at the police station was that Bainbridge had been found by Webster, semi-conscious in an alleyway. Some rounder, Webster reported that Bainbridge had said, had hit him from behind and made off with his watch and his wallet.

'You robbed him too?' I said, appalled.

'No! I didn't touch him after he fell,' Llewellyn said. 'Bainbridge is a lying bastard.'

'On top of everything else,' I said.

Webster had let Bainbridge walk away that night, and the man had disappeared. The telephone number on the card he'd given Llew was no longer in service. Granville Bainbridge wasn't just a lying bastard; Granville Bainbridge was a ghost.

'I shouldn't have run,' Llew said.

I'd never have agreed with him about that.

Llew had also told me something else: he'd seen me and Gianluca out together. 'Jealousy doesn't suit you, Llewellyn,' I said, though softly. He'd nodded. I had to look away; I would have drowned in his hurt. The sun was rising behind us. A cold February wind whipped up and tugged at our coats. At the end of the pier, he turned to face the rising sun and leaned up against the railing. He shoved his bare hands in his pockets. 'Do you ever notice how beautiful grey and green are together?' he said. 'You look at the fog or a cloudy sky and you see the green, that dark shade of the cedars or the green of spring, against the grey. It's so beautiful. I can't wait to show the baby that.'

'Such a relief,' Morag said. She patted her huge belly. 'Who'd want a man's death hanging over their head?'

I nodded. 'Who indeed.'

Morag's eyes lit up. 'Oh, here,' she said. 'Put your hand here.'

I crouched beside her, and she pulled my hand beneath her maternity smock, onto her warm belly. She pressed her hand over mine. I looked down at the floor, concentrating, waiting for the movement of the creature swimming inside her, loving the warmth of her skin. Then a small firm foot or elbow or knee was moving against my hand. I looked up at my sister, smiling.

'He loves you, you know.'

'Who?'

'Llew. He'd do anything for you.'

I pulled her smock down, kissed her belly, and stood. 'That is good to know,' I said.

Out at the end of the pier I'd told Llewellyn that I would never meet him again, not alone. He'd held his arms out to me, and I could feel the wind stealing my resolve. Surely you can touch him, let him hold you, one last time, the cold pleaded. A gull screeched above us. We both looked up. I said goodbye. I left him there, my Pocketman.

FRIDAY, FEBRUARY 9

Evening

On the streetcar, Georgina rises to give a dapperly dressed old man her seat.

"Oh no, miss," the old man says. "I'd never take a seat from a lady." He thumps the end of his cane on the floor twice. "But this youngster should mind his manners, shouldn't he?" The boy in the seat across the aisle glances up myopically, seems confused for a moment, then goes scarlet. He jumps up, mumbling apologies and something about his book being *gripping good*, and hurries toward the back. The old man takes his seat.

"Young people these days," he says. "Good for nothing."

Georgina nods once. She'll be polite but not encouraging. She has other things to contemplate, such as why she had imagined that her old friends wouldn't want to see her once she married and stopped working at Leckie's.

Earlier, at five o'clock, standing in front of the so-called Fairview Shacks and watching the university students flow out of the buildings, imagining herself there, Georgina had bumped into Gladdy Horan and Lillian Bostrom. She hadn't been sure at first. Were those her old workmates coming up the street toward her? Then she was certain. It was Gladdy and Lillian. Arm in arm, practically prancing along West 10th, happy as clams. Georgina had turned, pulled her scarf up to her chin, hoping her two old friends from the shoe factory wouldn't notice her. But they had. Because there was Gladdy waving and calling out Georgina's name. 'Georgie Mac!' Gladdy had shouted as she and Lillian hurried toward her.

Why had she been so shy to see her old friends? Georgina looks out into the dark street when the tram comes to an abrupt stop. The woman next to her, who has been slouched, sleeping, jerks upright. Her warm head has left a melted spot on the streetcar's steamed-up window.

"Have you ever heard of the Cariboo Road, miss?" The old man must not care that she is not looking at him, possibly not even listening. "Well, I helped plan it. Eighteen sixty-two. Before this here was even part of the country. Maybe before your father was born. Men risked their lives up along the Fraser Canyon. Toiling with their bare hands."

Georgina glances at him now. He does not look like a man who toiled with his bare hands.

Lillian had thrown her arms around Georgina and reminded Gladdy that it was Georgina Dunn now. 'Where've you been, Georgie? We haven't seen you in ages,' Gladdy said. 'And what are you doing in this part of town?' Lillian had asked. Gladdy was still clasping Georgina's hand. They were smiling at her, a couple of Cheshire Cats. Georgina smiled too. And then her old friends had invited her to join them for a meal. They were celebrating. 'What?' Georgina had asked. 'Lilli's divorce!' Gladdy crowed. 'She's finally free of the old bedswerver.' 'To think that I will never again have to fry onions up the moment I get home from work!' Lillian laughed. 'Onions?' Georgina asked. 'So the smell would make him think supper was on the way,' Lillian and Gladdy said together.

The old man has turned to the older woman next to him. "Wait till they're humbled by life, the young ones. Then they'll understand, won't they?"

Humbled? Seeing the girls had brought back the smell of the factory: leather, oil, sweat. Was their work not humbling? Isla's near death, the attack on Padraig. Stephen's death. Roddy's and Pa's. All her miscarriages, not life? Not humbling?

Georgina reaches into her handbag and retrieves the small bundle she had wrapped up in her handkerchief. She unfolds the edges. The shrew—it's dead; she found it in the grass in front of a house after leaving Lilli and Gladdy—is a soft charcoal grey, its winter colour. Probably a vagrant shrew. She is sure now, looking down at the animal lying so sweetly in her palm: she will go to university; she will study zoology. She doesn't touch the creature, though she peers at its little forelegs and its tiny blind eyes.

Here is humble, she would like to tell the man. Death. Loss. No one is alone in having met humble, sir.

Morag has called her a shrew, more than once. But a shrew is so pretty. She folds up her handkerchief and smiles to herself. In her pocket, she has Gladdy's and Lillian's telephone numbers.

SATURDAY, FEBRUARY 10

Morning, early

Harriet strokes the smooth green velvet of the settee, soft as Flore's skin. What time is it? She can't be bothered to reach for her watch; she is half-awake, cramped and cold on the settee. And now doubly irritated with her mother. Yesterday, while Harriet and Isla were at work, Ahmie took foolish pride in rejecting Victor's offer to have a fresh supply of coal delivered. Now they will have to wait until the start of the week and, in the meantime, freeze. Thank heaven she did not refuse the share of the rent Victor pays each month. Harriet burrows down and pulls the blanket up over her ear. Through the window, the sky is a light grey-pink. An eight-year-old Harriet would have pondered why the city turns this soft colour when it snows. A nine-year-old Harriet would have spent an afternoon quizzing the various authorities in her life—her father, Ahmie, Roddy, Georgina—and been satisfied, or not, by their answers, depending on the degree of conviction in their voice. At the moment, twenty-year-old Harriet doesn't care to know why the sky is pink; she's too tired. The thought passes. A car passes. Its headlamps illuminate the queer patterns the frost has painted on the windowpanes and makes new patterns on the ceiling. She will, she thinks, make an onion and potato pie for Morag today.

She sleeps again. She's woken by the sound of the front door opening; Isla comes in. Now Harriet does pat the side table for her watch. "Where've you been?"

Isla puts her finger to her lips and slips past, into her bedroom.

Last night was Harriet's turn to sleep on the settee in the front room so that if Ahmie cried out in the night, as she has been doing lately, someone would hear her. She shimmies her feet, one against the other, to bring some warmth, too lazy to get up and put on a pair of socks. The sky's colour has changed. It's morning. She's fully awake now. Where does Isla go?

Harriet saw her yesterday—Isla, and Gianluca Padula. Harriet was walking alone in the park, lifting her knees high, so pleased with the way her feet cut perfect prints in the virgin snow and pleased, too, with the sound, that squeak she remembers from the prairie winters. She was thinking that here, where late winter is usually rain, this snow wouldn't last more than a day. Especially in February. She was thinking that the daffodils were ready to come up beneath it, for heaven's sake. And when she looked up there was Isla, fifty yards ahead of her at the edge of the park, with two children, a little boy holding her hand, a girl, slightly ahead, making high-step footprints in the snow, just as Harriet had been doing. Harriet went to call out to Isla—Who were these children? Had she found another job?—but there was a man there too; Gianluca Padula was running along after her, towing the littlest boy on a sleigh. He drew a snowy circle with the sled around Isla and the children, who then chased after him.

Harriet let them move away. She turned and retraced her steps, ruining the perfection of her footprints, stepping in each one to create the trail of a beast with toes at both ends of its feet.

She shivers on the settee remembering the silvery thread of laughter that had reached her over the snow, and the way her sister had looked up into Gianluca's face.

"Isla?"

It's Ahmie. Harriet lies still, hoping that her mother will drift back to sleep. But Isla's bedroom door opens. Harriet pushes up on one arm and groans. "Leave her," she says.

"I'm up anyway. I'll do it," Isla says. She pats at the air as if she actually has her hand on Harriet's arm. "Go back to sleep."

"I wasn't sleeping," Harriet says.

Harriet sinks back on the settee and watches her sister cross the hall. What a wraith. Summer never came to Isla's body this year. Compared to Morag, who is peonies and hydrangeas, pink and so voluptuous now, Isla is winter. She's twigs, crisp and breakable, dried grasses in a winter field. Because Isla works evening shifts at the telephone exchange, they do not see each other as much anymore. Harriet would like to tell someone how glad this makes her, but who would understand? She has grieved her sister once; if she does not love her too much, if she does not care too much, she will never have to suffer the pain of grief again. But this thought makes her sigh; she knows, somewhere, that grief can never be sidestepped.

From the bedroom come the familiar sounds of Isla hushing Ahmie. Harriet stares at the ceiling for a minute longer then sits up, her cold feet now on the cold floor. It'll be a two-person morning, soothing their mother.

They've awakened Rue with their talk. Rue stands, stiff—*dog interrupted*, her baleful eye seems to say—on her bowed legs. Harriet lifts the dog into her lap, bends over her, and sniffs at her soft fur. Oh, the sweet smell of her, like rising bread dough. For a moment, Rue is still, as if patient indulgence is her job, then she squirms off Harriet's lap and settles in the warm spot Harriet has just left. "Say thank you," Harriet says, and Rue raises her snout once and sniffs; *Thanks for finally giving me some bloody room*, she has likely said.

Harriet stands. Isla is reading the soothing words of the thesaurus to their mother: *cunning*, *crafty*, *artful*, *skilful*, *subtle*, *feline*, *cunning as a fox*, *as a serpent*, *wily*, *sly*, *slim*, *deceitful*, *arch*, *pawky*, *shrewd*, *acute*, *sharp as a needle.*

Pawky? "Just give her a dose," Harriet says from the doorway.

Isla looks up. How sad she looks. "She doesn't need one," she says.

Harriet shakes her head. She presses her back against the door frame and stretches out her arms. Finally, she sits on the end of the bed. Harriet has much less patience for the hand-holding, the temple stroking, the murmuring than Isla does. "Look at her. Just give it to her."

Isla relents. "Bring me the bottle then."

Isla measures out the laudanum drops—far fewer than Harriet would give—and Ahmie drinks from the glass, her face tipped up like a child.

After, Ahmie smiles at them. "What are you two doing here?" she says.

Isla pulls the covers up to their mother's shoulders. "Nothing, Ahmie," she says, and she laughs. "Nothing at all."

After breakfast, Isla pulls her chair right next to Harriet's, takes her hand, and leans her head on Harriet's shoulder. Isla is not the skin and bones Harriet has imagined. She is softer.

"Why is Ahmie like this? What happened to her?" Harriet says.

"She wasn't always like this. Don't you remember what she was like before Pa died? She was . . . fun."

"Fun?" Harriet snorts.

"Well," Isla laughs, "she was. I remember when she was happy."

"I think Ahmie died when Pa died."

Isla is silent for a while. "Do you?" She rubs her chin against Harriet's shoulder bone, the way she used to when they were young.

"But she was sad even before Pa died," Harriet says.

"She was sad about Roddy going to war. Is that what you mean?" Isla says.

Roddy's death, the forbidden subject, hangs in the air between them. Harriet says, "It makes me angry, the way she is."

"Angry." Isla lifts tender eyes to Harriet's. "Can you be angry at someone for being sad? Ahmie lost the thing she loved most when Pa died."

Harriet is silent, embarrassed. If she lost Flore again, she would die. "Did you love the father of your . . . Like that?"

Isla doesn't look at her. She runs a finger down Harriet's shoulder and arm all the way to the end of her fingers, then she does it again. "I did," she says.

ISLA

Harriet was making an onion pie to take to Morag's. Onion pie. Hardly an ideal meal for a hugely pregnant woman with bad indigestion and days away from giving birth. But Harriet was cooking. Who was I, the non-cook, to pass judgement. She handed me two big onions to chop and fry while she peeled and sliced potatoes. After the pie went in the oven, she sat and cut small hearts out of the leftover pastry with a sharp little pocketknife that I'm sure had once belonged to our father. She lined the hearts up in a row, from large to small, on the edge of the table, then peeled them up again and stacked them, in the same order.

Harriet had said that Ahmie made her angry. Was it fair to be angry at someone for grieving? Grieving endlessly? I suppose it might be. God knows there were days when my patience with my mother ran so thin I know I made her melancholy worse. Harriet also told me she missed Ahmie. That, I understood.

'Where have you gone, my darling girl?' my mother had asked. I could have asked her the same question. Where had my darling mother gone?

Conventionality might have been found in Ahmie's thesaurus, but it and its synonyms didn't run in her veins. By the time I was in elementary school in our little prairie town, I knew there was not much of the normal in Ahmie. She was not a churchgoer, which would have automatically set the town's tongues to wagging. And she spoke her political mind as a man might. Surely behaviour considered unbecoming in a woman. At home, there were no quiet sewing evenings, the lot of us girls going blind cross-stitching samplers under the pathetic light of oil lamps (though we spent time reading books about women who did just that). If Ahmie picked up a needle, it was to sew something practical—clothing—or to darn or repair it. And there was nothing fancy about what she made. There may have been a simple blanket stitch done in contrasting thread on the hem of a nightie, but that it was done in blue or red or black on white said more about what spool Ahmie had found at hand than any sense of need for adornment. If we wanted something fancy, we had to sew it ourselves. (Morag, not surprisingly, learned to sew quite well and at quite a young age.)

And while in other houses the girls we knew worked indoors and the boys worked out, Ahmie had no such notion for herself or for us. Her world was outside with Angus: the plains, the garden and what they grew in it, the grub-pecking chickens, the fat rabbits in their pens, our goats, the sheep, the cow (Isobel), and Annabelle, our old horse. An oddly shaped potato with a face on it or a pair of entwined carrots that looked like crossed human legs—these made Ahmie laugh. She named our animals, even if we would later be eating them. (Pa and Morag protested the giving of names, on moral and compassionate grounds, they said, though there was no such protest over the eating of them.) Canning and bottling—all the preparing for winter—took place in a shed Ahmie and Angus had built, a summer kitchen of sorts. And when winter came, Ahmie played with us. We built snow forts and sledded and trekked across the fields on rawhide snowshoes made by the Indians. And when it was too bitterly cold to play outside, we read. Ahmie and Pa both read aloud to us until we could read by ourselves. Most of our books had been on the voyage across the sea with them. Occasionally, when we could afford it, new books were ordered, and these arrived by post in exciting brown-paper packages that Ahmie unwrapped, her delight matching ours.

So, what happened to Ahmie? What happened to my once fierce and playful mother?

I used to try to imagine my parents when they were young. I'd lie awake, plotting their life together on a timeline, embellishing their stories, writing my own. Being witness to their lives, I thought, might help me understand the slow evaporation of my mother's spirit.

I drew them: Angus McKenzie and Millie Sutherland, so young and pretty. I made Angus bearded, which I imagine he actually was as a young man, thin but handsome, already deaf in one ear, a blacksmith from the next village over. In my version of the story, Millie (soon to be Ahmie) is wiry and strong, tall (taller than Angus), dark-haired and dark-eyed, like Harriet is now. Millie is twenty-three years old, expected and expecting to be a spinster. Living with her widowed mother, a crofter. The rest of her brothers and sisters are married and gone (or just gone; now we know, one of them, Hugh, is dead). One summer's eve, Millie is leading their Highland pony Mairi home when Angus encounters her for the first time on a path behind the village. (Romantic, no?) Millie has a smile fit to break a heart, and Angus is not the first man to feel his splinter in two; he is instantly besotted by love. He has never met the likes of her. She is smart and that good word—winsome. And he does not even know yet that she makes the best currant buns in all of Scotland. But one thing he knows: he cannot live without her. One day soon he'll tell her, and then and there, she'll agree to be his wife. When this actually happens, he is deliriously happy. When this happens, Millie, our mother to be, is surprised and relieved. In fact, it is the relief that is so besotting. (Besotting? Never mind.) Happiness, for Millie, is an afterthought, but come it does, and very quickly. This man is her match.

Angus calls her his wild girl. He does not intend to tame her. (In my story, his sperm does that.)

As they cross the ocean, I'm sure they're still happy. If they're not, not entirely, I make them so, even though they must leave Baby John behind, dead and buried. There's Ahmie at the prow of the ship, downcast but stoical, and probably seasick. Georgina is kicking to beat the band in her belly, and Roddy, their wee man, now two years old, is sweet in his papa's arms. So . . . Onward, our mother thinks.

Millie has become Ahmie. I presume that there is something that niggles at her spirit when Angus, too, takes to calling her by this baby name given her by Roddy (she who will only ever call our father Angus). On the other side of the ocean, she lets this little annoyance fly out the train's window as they rattle past millions of trees to the tiny prairie town Angus has (mysteriously) chosen as their new home.

It is four years before the turn of the century. There is not much need anymore, even in Carberry, for a blacksmith. And it is unfathomably cold. Then it is unbearably hot. And then it is cold again. On and on, through the seasons, Ahmie works alongside Angus. She milks the goats and shears the sheep, like a farmhand would if they could afford one, and she learns to spin wool and knit (thick and lopsided but very warm) sweaters. She rides the sweet old nag bareback, missing her pony Mairi, missing her mother, missing home. She is still Angus's wild girl, but isn't she just a wee bit smaller in spirit every day. Because wasn't this his dream, not hers?

This part is definitely not speculation: Morag chases me out of Ahmie's womb (we are barely a year apart). And this might or might not be speculation: for four years, after Morag, Ahmie is relieved to be done with childbearing. Every time she has fallen pregnant she has spent the nine months calculating the odds that, one, she will die in childbirth and, two, the child will die from some illness, infectious or otherwise, at birth or soon after. (Aren't there *Baby* gravestones everywhere, in all the graveyards?) Or that the boys she produces will be fodder for war. But Ahmie loves Angus too much to keep him on his side of the bed. And then—well, well!—another little dark-eyed thing shows up—Harriet-Jean. Angus is not dismayed. Ahmie feigns motherly happiness.

My father might be more at ease with babies than Ahmie is; I can't decide. But if that is so, this both gladdens and annoys Ahmie, and occasionally it makes her grey with motherly guilt. It is 1903. And I am five. Ahmie is thirty-five, now considerably less wild. This is the point at which I imagine the gloom might start sweeping in, ferociously, like a spring tide. But Ahmie doesn't know anything about spring tides yet, does she? She hasn't lived on the ocean yet. They have yet to pack up their children (miserably unhappy children who do not want to leave their prairie home, their prairie friends) and make another move, to the far coast of this too vast country.

It is 1910. The month of May. (King Edward VII has just died.) There Ahmie is on the train with her head out the window, breathing in the air of the shocking Rocky Mountains. Here she is, back in her seat in the second-class car, her eyes all glossy (has she been crying), her hair windblown, undone. Angus smiles at her. He takes her hand. Her smile is a little wistful, I think. She does not know, of course, that she will have only seven more years with her beloved husband or she might have—what?—smiled more bravely?

Whatever Angus's west coast dreams, the only work a half-deaf forty-two-year-old ex-blacksmith can find in 1910 is in the woods. Off Angus goes to the logging camps up the coast. He tells his darling Ahmie that he won't be away long. (We, too, are told this.) Weeks and weeks and weeks on end, Ahmie is alone with the five of us. The five of us are alone with Ahmie. Angus writes. Ahmie replies. They miss one another like the heavens in daytime miss their stars. He comes home now and again, filthy and exhausted.

And then, bloody hell, one summer afternoon, he dies. Angus *dies*.

It was an accident, they say, poor Freddy Hay. (Did the choke chain snap, or did young Freddy do something wrong?) At the burial, that's Freddy dropping on his knees in front of Ahmie, the boy in the ill-fitting suit who cannot stop crying.

Freddy's memory of that terrible day may or may not fade over the years, but we don't know Freddy Hay anymore, so his state of mind is not of much concern to us. But Ahmie. Oh, Ahmie.

I told Harriet a variation of my Ahmie and Angus story that potato and onion pie morning. I hoped I would be able to gently skirt the fact that we were two daughters, sitting at the table, missing their mother who was in bed in a room twenty feet away. Two witnesses to the trade she'd made: her family—worse, her life—for an endless drowning grief.

Harriet had listened quietly, then she'd retrieved the chicken scrap pail and swept all of the pastry hearts she'd so carefully stacked up on the table into it. I thought maybe I'd upset her with my rambling thoughts. If I had, she wasn't going to let me know.

'Sugar sandwiches for dessert?' she'd asked, bright as a yellow button, as if I hadn't just been dissecting the impenetrable mind and soul of our mother.

'Sounds perfect,' I said.

I wondered if between us Harriet and I could have come up with the name of one woman who in the past decade had not lost someone. A husband, a brother, a son. War widows abound. Bereaved mothers abound. In fact, isn't the world thick with grieving women still rereading that brutal telegram from 1914 or 1918: *Your son, husband, father is dead*. In capital letters. Capital *K*, *Killed*. And those killed by the flu? We who survived the war and the pandemic, we recovered—emotionally, mentally—despite our dreadful losses, didn't we? We went on. Why not Ahmie?

I thought that morning of Dr. Blakeway, the man who first prescribed laudanum to Ahmie. To calm her nerves, the old man said. Was he dead? I hoped he was. Otherwise I wanted a word with him.

Harriet opened the oven. The pie was done. It smelled delicious.

'I don't want Ahmie to have any more laudanum,' I told her.

Harriet raised her eyebrows at me but said nothing. We were both silent for a while, Harriet in her own Ahmie world, I imagined. Or not. I wasn't thinking only about Ahmie anymore. I was thinking of Llewellyn, hands in his pockets, standing at the end of the pier in the cold that morning a week or so earlier. What was it that brought the tears to my eyes then: the grief that swept me, or the sudden understanding that Ahmie and I shared it? I knew where my darling mother had been. I knew where she'd gone.

'Can Ahmie and I come to Morag's with you today?' I asked. I suppose I had expected Harriet's look of surprise; Ahmie hadn't been coaxed out of the house since our disastrous Christmas Eve, and before that, in ages. Why, I wondered, feeling oddly elated, had we stopped trying?

'Of course,' she said.

I watched her puttering about in her stockinged feet, buttering the bread, sprinkling sugar on it, talking to the dog, smiling at nothing in particular. I knew that smile. I'd seen it in the mirror. A woman in love. I wanted to say something, but how does one acknowledge the love that no one dare talk about?

'Happy?' I asked.

'Mm-hmm,' she said. She put a tin of canned pears in a basket along with the sugar sandwiches, then leaned back against the sink and crossed her arms. 'Maybe Morag's baby will make Ahmie happy,' she said.

'She might,' I said.

That look of surprise again. 'You think it's a girl?'

Did you love the father of your child? Harriet had asked.

'I do,' I said.

MONDAY, FEBRUARY 12

5:30 in the evening

Llewellyn has missed the Interurban to New Westminster on account of Virgil's baby news.

'I won't be coming out with you and Abraham tonight,' Virgil said. 'Yes, Elinor's fine. The baby too. A girl! Ten fingers and toes.' 'Have you named her?' Llewellyn asked. 'Reva,' Virgil told him. 'I wanted Vera, but Elinor wouldn't have it. Too many Vs in the family already, she says,' Virgil laughed. The man was crackling with excitement. 'You should see her, Llew. She's the most beautiful thing in the whole wide world.'

Llewellyn can't imagine big Virgil with a little baby in his arms. He can't imagine a baby in his own arms, either, but the thought of it gives his heart that queer skip again, half trepidation, half awe. He runs down the hill in the dark and turns onto the wharf, smiling. He loves all these stinks: creosote, the dank of the Fraser River, the cold night air.

The *Queensolver*'s engine is running and there's just one man on deck, a boy really, no more than seventeen, hands on his hips, waiting. The boy gestures wordlessly toward the one remaining hitch on shore. Llewellyn loosens the line from around the bollard, tosses it toward the boy's outstretched hands, and steps onto the *Queensolver* as the boat glides away from the wharf. She's sitting high in the water.

"Sorry to be late. Have we met before?" Llewellyn asks, smiling, extending his hand.

"Don't think so."

The boy glances at Llewellyn's outstretched hand and bends to stow the line. He remains crouched, fiddling with something below the gunwale.

Llewellyn drops his arm. It's not unusual to meet this kind of monosyllabic person on a rum-runner's boat. They're either the wisely cautious or the generally unsociable type, neither of which bothers Llewellyn. And Abraham often has some extra crew when needed. When the boy stands again they are already out into the Fraser, the motor powering up slowly, churning up the river's brown water in the dark. Llewellyn follows him into the cabin to see if Abraham has heard the news about Virgil's new daughter.

He's surprised to see the wide back of a stranger behind the wheel. "Where's Abraham?" Llewellyn asks.

"He's sick," the man in Abraham's chair says without looking back.

"Sick?"

"That's what I said."

There's an instant flood of disquiet in Llewellyn's gut. He knows it's wisest to be friendly out here on the water. "Boat's sitting kind of high. You've already loaded up or—"

"Light load tonight."

"Special errand," says the boy. He says this breathlessly.

The boy makes Llewellyn think of a mouse. Squeaky. Or is it a rat he reminds him of? Llewellyn shivers: a cloud has just slid over his happy valley and blocked the sun. "So, what do you need me for?"

Neither the boy nor the man piloting the boat answers, though they glance at one another.

If Abraham and Virgil were on board, Llewellyn would have stayed inside and shared a drink with them; it's that cold. But these two strangers have made it as chilly inside the cabin as out. Llewellyn finds his usual spot outside, beside the starboard gunwale, where he always sits when the weather is fair. His coat is warm but not warm enough; he's glad for the muffler Morag knit him.

He fingers the carving he made months ago in the chipped paint of the gunwale: *ISLA*. This shiver isn't from the cold. He folds his arms across his chest and tucks his gloved hands in his armpits.

They are taking the Annieville Channel on the south side of Annacis Island. It's slow going; the man at the helm is navigating around chunks of ice. The river froze this year for the first time Llewellyn can remember. People skated on it. He knows this part of the Fraser well. He grew up near here. He and his friends Walter, Larry, and Stan used to fish off the jetties that still hang precariously over the rushing water, and toss sticks into the river to see how quickly the current would carry them away.

They're not even twenty minutes out of New Westminster, still abreast of Annacis, when the boat slows and the engine is cut. Llewellyn scans the dark shore. There's no sign of a waiting transport boat. The only lights he can see are reflections of the *Queensolver*'s own running lights, red and white in the pitch-black.

"Problem?" he calls out.

He turns to pull the cabin door open; it's locked. The pilot still has his back turned, both hands rigid on the wheel, but the boy looks at Llewellyn. His eyes are filled with a gleaming terror.

Llewellyn feels his blood rush from his groin to his armpits; his knees, suddenly weak, nearly drop him to the floor. He slams at the door with his fists. Over his shouts, the sound of another vessel reaches his ears and a powerful motor launch glides by, then comes back to roll in a slow circle around the *Queensolver*, rocking the boat in its wake. His first thought is of hijackers. His next is of something more dire than that. He can see the big boat's starboard running lights as it moves to the *Queensolver*'s port side. Llewellyn crouches down, breathing hard.

"Stop in the name of the King," someone shouts.

Christ Jesus, Llewellyn thinks, relieved. It's the police. He stands and waves his arms above his head. Shouts. Then he covers his eyes when a spotlight from the other boat is trained on him, blinding him.

The peal of laughter he hears takes a knife to his relief and slices it in two.

"Llewellyn McFee," a voice calls out. "Do you know how to swim?"

For a second, Llewellyn smiles. Then: One crow. Ten crows. A hundred thousand crows. Dark shadows. Fear.

His answer, so innocent, so quiet: "No." He can't hear the river anymore. No one will hear him. And his question, of no import: "Why?"

In the silence, the voice comes: "Chief MacIntyre says hello." Then, the sharp report of a gun; the searing pain in his left shoulder, the force, like a strong slow hand, pushing him over the gunwale; the dark water, wrapping him in its cold arms; the *Queensolver*'s engine starting, purring, moving away, so far away.

He twines his fingers in Morag's dark hair, kisses her neck, inhales her seaweed scent. Slides his hands over her belly. Feels her whispering to him: Llew, Llew, Llew.

The sky parts. The moon is singing. He closes his eyes. Sweet Morag. Such stillness. Such peace.

Morag.

Isla.

Isla. The yellow-headed blackbird landing on her outstretched hand.

ISLA

Her labour pains came, irregularly at first, still far apart, the late afternoon of February twelfth. Swells, like salty waves, she described them, tightening across her belly, then rolling far out to sea. She held my hand. Told me not to leave her. She seemed to be drifting in and out of sleep. Occasionally she moaned and pressed her flushed cheek against the pillow.

I called Llewellyn; I'd just missed him, I was told.

Georgina and Flore came, and we took turns rubbing Morag's back or just hovering at the foot of the bed. She wouldn't go to the hospital; she hadn't planned to. The hospital was where people went to die, she said. The midwife, Mrs. Chrystal, had been called. She'd assured us that until the contractions were more regular, Morag only needed to be comforted. We were to call her when 'things got serious,' she'd said. 'Things got serious? What,' Georgina asked, 'in God's name, is that?' Ahmie had, rather oddly, given me instructions on the proper technique for boiling water. I heeded her and put a pot on the stove and we kept it replenished all night.

'Waves now crashing on the shore,' Morag said after the first hard contraction came and went. The corners of her mouth curled up in a smile, but she was already somewhere else, the look in her eyes distant as some unknown country. 'Llew, Llew, Llew,' she said quietly after every contraction, until, as the night wore on, her words disappeared, replaced by animal sounds.

Harriet clattered in with her skates and hockey stick, nearly as sweaty and hot as Morag was, around nine o'clock. We sent her—and her wild, frightened eyes—to check on the boiling water. We were all so inexperienced. Not one of us had ever attended a birth before, though Georgina remarked briefly that she remembered listening to Harriet being born; she turned her back before Morag, or Harriet, could see the expression on her face. Things were serious enough, we decided. We called the midwife.

Morag wanted to walk. We paced with her, one of us on either side of her, back and forth in their little bedroom. When she couldn't walk anymore, she knelt on a pillow on the floor at the foot of the bed. Between contractions she shivered as if she was cold and we wrapped sheets or blankets and towels over her shoulders. We held her. When her waves hit, she was hot and threw off the blankets. She roared, a ragged animal sound that caught in her throat. Sometimes, when the pains relented for a moment, she whimpered. Or she huffed with the midwife, loud, breathy pants through her nose, hammering a ha-ha-ha note into the room. Georgina and Flore joined them, making the same noise.

'Goddamn Virgil and Abraham,' Morag screamed once, as a contraction slid away. 'Where have you taken my husband?'

She blindly shoved away the handkerchief Georgina offered her and with a bare hand wiped at the sheen of sweat on her face. 'Do you know what he asked me this morning? He asked, *What if I never see an American bittern?*' and she roared as she was gripped again.

It wasn't until after midnight that the midwife got Morag off the floor and onto her feet. It was time, she said. She urged my sister toward the bed, but Morag stopped halfway, caught in a contraction. She braced herself on the dresser, leaning her arms and forehead on it. The labour pains were ceaseless then, each running into the next. Morag's belly heaved strangely, an alien, mesmerizing thing. Though her legs shook, she wouldn't be moved from her spot in front of the dresser. The patient midwife squatted on the floor behind her. She'd had plenty of experience with stubbornness, Mrs. Chrystal told us, laughing, including her own. Georgina and Flore knelt on either side of Morag, their hands holding and stroking her legs, steadying her.

'I can't. I can't,' she cried. Then, 'Llew, Llew, Llew.' I wept myself at the helpless tears leaking from the corners of her eyes.

Morag and Llewellyn's son was born a few minutes after one. The thirteenth of February. Georgina and the midwife caught him. He cried, lustily, immediately. I swear he was crying even before his shoulders had come out of Morag.

The midwife placed him in the blanket I had ready and then she inched Morag over to the bed, me following closely, as she hadn't clamped or cut the strange blue-white cord that connected this blood-and-guck-covered boy to his mother.

'We'll just wait for the cord to stop pulsating,' the midwife said, as she examined the baby on the bed next to Morag.

'Is he all right?' Morag asked.

'He's the smuggest little lad I've ever seen,' the midwife said, wiping at him gently. 'Look at those cheeks!' she laughed. She showed us his 'stork bites,' the little red marks at the corners of his eyes. 'I prefer to think of them as where the angels have kissed him,' she said. She placed the naked baby on Morag's chest and covered him with a flannel blanket. Then Mrs. Chrystal checked her pocket watch and announced the hour: one eleven a.m. 'Give or take,' she said.

'You're sure he's all right?' Morag said. Her hands touched him so tentatively.

I sat on the edge of the bed, staring at the baby—his pink mouth, the mess of blond hair, blond eyebrows, pale lashes—and fell in love. Madly, hopelessly in love.

'He's perfect,' I said, and my tears flowed.

Morag was weeping too. 'I had a premonition this morning,' she said. 'I thought he would die, or that I would.' She clasped the midwife's arm. 'Am I going to die?'

'Shhh,' Georgina said softly. 'No one is dying.'

'You're right as rain, Morag. Put the lad to your breast, lass,' the midwife said. 'It'll help with expelling the afterbirth.' And she clamped and cut the cord.

Beneath the blanket, one of the baby's feet was exposed. I took it in my hand and nearly sank to my knees; the second and third toes of the little foot were webbed. Just like his father's. I bent and kissed them. I anointed the baby's feet with my tears.

Morag was brought a spoonful of honey and cooled tea; finally, the boiled water came in handy.

'Where'd this blondie come from?' the midwife asked. She was seated on a chair beside the bed enjoying a glass of whisky and a slice of bread and butter slathered in blackberry jam.

'Llewellyn was blond when he was little,' Morag said.

'We thought for a while there that you'd be born a Monday's child, little fella.' The midwife ran her thumb along the baby's spine. 'Monday's child is fair of face, but Tuesday's child is full of grace,' she said.

Morag touched the baby's head. 'Full of grace.' She was exhausted, but the euphoria in the room, hers and ours, was going to take hours to wear off.

'These are your aunties,' Morag said, addressing the boy asleep on her breast. 'Here's Georgina, this is Isla, and Harriet, and that one's Flore. She's an honorary auntie. They are going to love you forever and ever.' She looked at each of us in turn. Her eyes, so filled with love, were also bare and vulnerable. Almost sad.

Had she, I have since wondered, already seen the future?

'What are you going to call him?' Harriet asked.

'Llew chose his name,' Morag said, looking upon her beautiful child. 'He'll be Aloysius,' she said. 'Aloysius Rufus McFee.'

RUE

I remember the night the boy with the impossible name was born because I was there. (Albeit locked out of the bedroom. Did they think I would run off with the placenta?) The noises coming from behind that closed door were Pure Animal. I attempted to remain quiet, for I had been instructed to do so on more than one occasion that evening. A canid, you must understand, cannot resist the call of the wild, especially when that call comes from the mouth of a woman. And the smells! Oh, Lordy. More delightful than the butcher's.

Harriet came out of the bedroom thrice, I suppose to calm me, but each time her hand trembled on my back, and her eyes: terror and bewilderment. Who, then, one must ask, was the calmer and who the calmee?

So, what an enormous relief it was when Morag finally squeezed the squalling thing out and the world, for a while, a very short while, sat right in the heavens.

I am two years older now than I was then. Daily, my body betrays me in new and unfathomable ways. I do not hear well anymore. I have clouds in my eyes that make me think that strange beasts—at which I sometimes bark and thereby embarrass myself—are on the horizon. My hind legs grow more feeble every day. And so, most often, I rest. I sit where it is warm and where I can feel the sun upon my old bones. (Padraig sometimes places me on the forbidden chesterfield, upon which I am able to lengthen my sun-bathing time.) They say I am warty and lumpy. I am persuaded that this is always said with affection, but warty and lumpy I am. (Sigh.)

What a fine day it is today. It is the sort of spring morning when latent scents are revivified by the warmth of the sun. My mistresses, Flore and Harriet, say we are going to the park. I know, now, that by *park* they mean the *cemetery*. Padraig, dear Padraig, earlier declared that he would not come along. He will, he says, be otherwise occupied with his rather lovely friend, Julian. (The *rather* and *lovely* are my own descriptors, note.)

Yes, Reader, she married him. (Oh, do pardon me. Flore has recently read *Jane Eyre* aloud to Harriet and me, and Miss Brontë may be influencing the flavour of my parlance this morning.)

Twist my (wretched) foreleg and I will still never declare which of the three I thought more beautifully attired on their wedding day—Padraig in his elegant grey tailcoat and yellow cravat, Flore in her sleek pale-grey gown, all lace and light flutter, with that burgundy hat, or Harriet-Jean, who was neither elegant nor sleek but satisfaction personified in trousers and a vest. Her shirt was white, and she wore a McKenzie tartan tie that had been her father's. The father Rozema came from San Francisco by train; the mother sent her regrets from

Rotterdam. In the Unitarian Church on the other side of the inlet ('the only appropriate setting for this godless group,' I overheard Victor say to Georgina as they mounted the steps, the snarker), Mr. Rozema gave Flore away and Harriet gave Padraig away. Flore said her father would not stay in Vancouver long, and indeed, he did not. But he threw, in my admittedly limited experience, an exceptional party in the garden of a friend of Flore. Even Ahmie was inveigled out of her greying Victorian garb, and she danced with me on the lawn.

Ah, here they are now. They have come for me, these paragons of simultaneous sorrow and joy. (No, I shall not talk of death or any other category of loss on this cloudless day.) Flore has my collar, Harriet my leash. Adieu! We are off.

ISLA

Twenty-six years, one month, and two days—our Morag.

After she died, after the McFees agreed to let her be buried beside Llewellyn and we had her name carved in stone to make it, finally, believable, I remembered again how Morag had told me that when she was in labour she had seen our ancestors—aunties and great-aunties and grandmothers, women in long dresses, their hair down—walking solemnly around a grave, a child's, overgrown with grasses and wildflowers. The tombstone sat inside a cast-iron fence, and the circle of ground around it was worn by the tread of their bare feet. An auntie took Morag's hand: *We've been waiting for you,* she said.

She made them wait. Almost two years. I hope they were there to greet her.

Morag had another vision the night Aloysius was born. The midwife had gone. We'd turned off the pot of boiling water. Gathered up the mess of bloody linens to be laundered. Swept up the breadcrumbs Mrs. Chrystal had dropped. Georgina, Harriet, and Flore had kissed Morag goodbye, admired her wee son one more time, and quietly closed the door, promising to return early in the morning. I'll stay, I'd told them, until Llew comes home. We lay side by side on the bed, Morag and I, the swaddled babe between us. We'd left the lamps burning—for Llew, Morag insisted—but we must have fallen asleep. I felt her sit up suddenly, and when I opened my eyes she was looking toward the door, smiling. 'Llew,' she sighed. Relieved, I turned to greet him too. There was no one there, of course.

Real men, living men, men without bullets in their bodies, came to the door shortly before nine that morning—the detectives Francis Webster, Andrew Morrison, and a young constable whose name I'd never heard. Morag was wide awake, still in bed, gazing at her newborn. She was dying to show him to Llewellyn, with whom she was justifiably furious, or so we all agreed at that point. 'Who's that come to admire my son?' she called from the bedroom when she heard their knock, the proudest woman on earth.

Ah, if only not opening a door could alter history.

Harriet threw it wide, smiling. And there stood the three-headed hound of Hades.

Webster, breaking down before he'd even uttered a word. A man we did not know, the despair of disbelief set hard in his young eyes. And Morrison, reaching to put his long-fingered hand on Harriet's shoulder.

No need to bend solicitously toward her, Mr. Morrison. No need to recover your emotions, Mr. Webster, so that you might speak the foulest words. No need for any of you to hover in the doorway and say 'I'm afraid we've had some terrible news.'

Abraham Driessen had been found first, on the wharf in New Westminster. Shot to death, a single bullet in the back of his head. Did you put up a fight, Abraham, when they came to take your boat? Or did the bastards catch you unawares? Llewellyn was found by a river worker early in the morning, face down in the freezing water, his body eddying against the stilts of a jetty in the South Arm of the Fraser. His bullet? Through his heart, I'm afraid, Andrew Morrison said.

These details, Mr. Morrison. No thank you. No thank you.

Did you think of us, Llew? Did you think of us?

I hold tight to another, sweeter memory now, one that occurred while Morag still lived: I am alone in the parlour, sitting in my mother's mustard-yellow horsehair chair which has been transported from our old flat on Comox to Harriet and Flore and Pȧdraig's apartment on Vine Street in Kitsilano. I've come for a Sunday visit. Everyone's in the kitchen, preparing supper, even Ahmie, who lives upstairs from them now. Ahmie has been more at peace for a while, there in the little bedsit that is all her own, shared only with her books of poetry, her gramophone, the precious thesaurus, Pa's Inverness tea tin, and Grandma Oonagh's things. And no laudanum. Rue sidles into the parlour with the sideways gait of a drunk. She's old. Her hindquarters have shrunk, her tail droops, her backbone rises under her skin like a Lilliputian mountain range. She searches the room with her cloudy eyes. It seems she finds me, or I think she has, because she gazes in my direction for a moment, her nose lifting two or three times into the air, then she curls onto a cushion on the floor, her back to me, contented, it seems. I love old Rue.

The front door opens and Morag's there, with baby Allo in her arms. It's February, so he's almost a year old, not walking yet, but ready to. Morag strips off his knitted coat and hat and mitts and sits him on the floor. I am quiet, waiting to see what he will do. Aloysius smiles—this wondrous baby always smiles—and he crawls to me. And when he is at my feet he stops and looks down at them. I am wearing Roddy's socks, or maybe it is a pair of Pa's, I don't know which, and it doesn't matter. Ahmie has kept them for wintry days. There's a small hole I've been meaning to darn in the toe of the left sock. Aloysius lifts his chubby little pointer finger and carefully touches my big toe through the hole. He looks up at me and beams, his joy the kind the universe reserves for children alone. How Llew would have loved this beamish boy. His beautiful beamish boy.

Two laws of big families: children in them always have someone else to point the finger at; and the odds are good that one or two of those children will be lost before they're grown. At five, they will step on a rusty nail and the infection will be fatal. At ten, the river will sweep them away on their jerry-built raft. If they survive to twenty, they'll die in childbirth or be sacrificed by the warmongers or snuffed out by the flu. Maybe, one of them, your fifth child, a girl named Morag Elisabeth, will die of tuberculosis. At twenty-six years, one month, and two days.

I don't know why we could have expected to beat the odds when so few others do. But nothing in the world would have prepared us for losing Aloysius. Not this way. Nothing.

We cannot not talk of him, not yet—our beautiful Allo, taken—stolen—by his grandparents, Havelock and Hattie McFee. They would, the McFees told the judge, do a better job of raising that orphaned boy than we could. After all, they said, they'd raised Llewellyn. And look how he turned out.

(You did not weep at your own son's burial, Mr. and Mrs. McFee.)

Two years, one month, and twenty-two days old—our Aloysius. Lost to us.

Angelo is five now. He won't let me snuffle the back of his neck anymore, unless he is very tired. Then he pretends to only tolerate it, but I think he still secretly loves it. Sal—he turns seven next week—is beautiful and studious and bright as a penny. Mariana has eyes so dark she could be mine. At eight, she's feisty and athletic. She reminds me of Harriet at that age. The babe in Flore's belly is due in a few weeks. How different will life be for their child, or for the Veltri children who arrived in the world nearly a generation after my sisters and me? They could live through the twentieth century, and even into the twenty-first if they're lucky. Very lucky.

Aloysius too. One day, when I find him again, I will tell our beautiful boy about the people who loved him. And those of us who always will.

We talk of Llew and Maria. Maria left Gianluca her love of the shore, of music. Her bright mind. And her beautiful children. Llewellyn left me his birds and his trees and flowers. The ocean. I cannot walk outside without thinking of Llew. I *go* outside to think of him. Llew and his elusive American bittern. And the memory of a love that I, even now, even with Gianluca, imagine will never be surpassed. It is the same for Gianluca. We are partners, companions, lovers, husband and wife. And yet, when we hold one another's hand, we are not two, we are four.

Morag would be proud of me; I pilfered some sweet peas from my neighbour's garden before the sun came up this morning. It's a beautiful day. Not a cloud in the sky. The girls—Harriet, Flore, and Rue—will come for lunch later. They're going to the cemetery first. If it was August, I would find fresh peaches to put in Grandma Oonagh's beautiful dark-blue bowl for them. Morag would like that too. Today, tinned peaches will have to do.

NEAR THE END OF MAY 1925

Here are two women. Lying on the grass. Fingers locked. By the gravestone, an old dog. It has dug up the sweet pea seeds that one of them just planted. It rolls on its back, unrepentant. The woman in jeans calls the dog's name—*Rue. Rue*. Off it totters, across the cemetery's uneven lawn, the scent of spring roses in its nose.

The pregnant one says, 'Did you bring the camera?'

'I did.' The other one rolls up on one elbow.

'Take a picture of me, then, for posterity's sake, and I'll take a picture of you.' She smooths her maternity smock over her belly but doesn't rise.

'But I want a picture of us together.'

'Just turn it around then. Hold it up in the air with your arms.'

'Will that work?'

They laugh. The photo is taken. It captures them lopsidedly, honestly: their sadness, their joy, two perfect parts of this cloudless day.

The baby, the one who will be Ada Morag Gleason, kicks. Hard. Chosen, wanted, she is ready to be born.

ACKNOWLEDGEMENTS

Heartfelt gratitude to my brilliant agent, Hilary McMahon at Westwood Creative Artists, and to my big-hearted editor, Michael Holmes at ECW, both of whom saw the beauty of this story and the enduring value of it.

To the Ontario Arts Council and Canada Council for their generous support. To BC historians/researchers/advocates/activists James Johnstone, Aaron Chapman, Tracy Penny Light, and Stuart Smith, for their help in lighting my path to the 1920s. (And please note: any legal, medical, or historical inaccuracies or liberties taken in this fictional story are entirely on me.) To the helpful folks at the High Life Highland Archives, Dingwall School and Community Library, and the Orkney Library and Archive, Kirkwall, both in Scotland, and to the City of Vancouver Archives (where I held an illustrated hardware store catalogue, a policeman's notebook, and a socialite's daily diary—all a hundred years old—in my hands), and the B.C. Archives in Victoria, both founts of information and delightful rabbit holes.

Many thanks to the whole wonderful crew at ECW. To Rachel Ironstone for her outstanding copyedit and David A. Gee for his beautiful cover design.

Thank you to Patti Henderson for baseball facts, Patrick Higdon for bird inspiration, and Ted Smith for boats and tides. And endlessly happy thanks to my readers and/or fairy godparents: my classmates at Banff, and Edyepat Best, Cathy Cappon, Amanda Cliff, Lieve De Nil, Berenice Freedome, Ken Higdon, Peter Higdon, Joss Maclennan, Nina McCreath, Marilyn Nairn, Ben Peachey Higdon, Patrick Peachey Higdon, Jessie Smedley (whose alluring 1922 portrait inspired me every day), Cindy Sutherland, and the wise Wendy Waring. And to Lorin Medley and Tracy Westell who provided the couches, beds, porches, and bathtubs on or in which I wrote parts of this book.

Finally, to every person who has, in any way, raised their hand in support of choice.

PETER HIGDON

CHRISTINE HIGDON is the author of the award-winning novel *The Very Marrow of Our Bones*. Daughter of a Newfoundlander and a British Columbian, she lives part-time in Nova Scotia and the rest of the time near the lake in Mimico, Ontario, where she longs for the ocean.